Bodies of Light
Hot Spell

Anthologies:
Brits in Time: Shortest Night
Treble: Wild About That thing

Seasonal Shorts:
Halloween Heart-throbs: Rendezvous
Christmas Spirits: Tomorrow's Gifts

By Lily Harlem

Candy Canes and Coal Dust
Thief
Escape to the Country
Unhealthy Obsession
The Unwholesome Adventures of Harita

Anthologies:
Treble: Orchestrating Manoeuvres

By Elizabeth Coldwell

The Christmas Box
Abyssinian Heat
Her Dream Lovers
Missing in Milan
Something Within Him
Neil and Obey

Anthologies:
Cougars and Cubs: Something Within Him
Treble: Three Part Harmony
Subspace: Away From It All

By Wendi Zwaduk

Learning How to Bend
Must Be Doing Something Right
My Immortal
You'll Think of Me
Tangled Up
Careless Whisper
Please Remember Me
What Might Have Been
Ever Fallen In Love

Anthologies:
Treble: Savin' Me

By Imari Jade

Something to be Thankful For
Prying Eyes

Anthologies:
Treble: Rhapsody

TREBLE ANTHOLOGY

TROUBLE AT THE TREBLE T
DESIREE HOLT

WILD ABOUT THAT THING
LISABET SARAI

ORCHESTRATING MANOEUVRES
LILY HARLEM

THREE-PART HARMONY
ELIZABETH COLDWELL

SAVIN' ME
WENDI ZWADUK

RHAPSODY
IMARI JADE

Treble Anthology
ISBN # 978-0-85715-749-2
Trouble at the Treble T ©Copyright Desiree Holt 2011
Wild About That Thing ©Copyright Lisabet Sarai 2011
Orchestrating Manoeuvres ©Copyright Lily Harlem 2011
Three-Part Harmony ©Copyright Elizabeth Coldwell 2011
Savin' Me ©Copyright Wendi Zwaduk 2011
Rhapsody ©Copyright Imari Jade 2011
Cover Art by Posh Gosh ©Copyright 2011
Interior text design by Claire Siemaszkiewicz
Total-E-Bound Publishing

Published in 2011 by Total-E-Bound Publishing, Think Tank, Ruston Way, Lincoln, LN6 7FL, United Kingdom.

TROUBLE AT THE TREBLE T

Desiree Holt

Dedication

To every cowboy who rides by my house or waves to me as I cruise past his ranch in my truck. You inspire me.

Chapter One

The jukebox had been playing nonstop in the honky tonk since five o'clock, nothing unusual for a Friday night. People got off work for the weekend, ranch hands started filtering in, the beer began flowing and soon the postage-stamp-sized dance floor was filled with bodies gyrating to old and new country tunes.

Cade Thompson sat with his brothers, Justin and Mark, at a table in the corner of Treble Shooters watching people move to the music — faces flushed, hips wriggling, practically having sex with their clothes on while Travis Tritt and Lady Antebellum echoed off the wooden walls of the honky tonk. They'd spent a hard week with the hands moving cattle from one pasture to the other and culling those for branding. Tonight they'd decided to give themselves a break from the ranch and hang out at the bar they'd bought when the previous owner died. Spring Valley was small enough as it was, with few entertainment options. They didn't want to see the only real place their hands could hang out close down.

Getting a full-time manager on a permanent basis, though, had been harder than they'd expected. Apparently the list of people who wanted to relocate to Spring Valley was a short one. The men had been burning both ends of the candle — running the Treble T ranch during the day and taking turns running the bar at night — when fortune had finally smiled on them.

Now Cade looked over at the bar, watching as Marti Jensen poured three drinks at once without breaking a sweat, and gave silent thanks once more for the day she'd walked in. He admired the way she kept her cool with all the chaos around her — the raised voices, the clicking of pool balls, the heavy thump of a bass and the squeal of the slide guitar, the lone waitress fighting for her attention along with everyone crowded at the bar demanding their drink *now*.

She was tall, maybe five ten.

Just right for three brothers who all top six four.

Stop! What are you thinking?

But he couldn't take his eyes away from her lush body. The way the Treble Shooters T-shirt fell softly against her ripe breasts and the jeans clung lovingly to the finest ass he'd seen in a long time. The way her riot of curly black hair cascaded down her back and framed a face with high cheekbones, violet cat's eyes and full, sensual lips. He'd wanted to fuck her since the day she'd walked in with the San Antonio classified rolled up in her hand and said in her saucy tone of voice, "Someone in here looking for a manager?" And ever since, he'd done his best to try and push the thought out of his mind.

She'd had excellent references and they still wondered why the hell she'd wanted to come to a tiny spot in the road like Spring Valley. But all she'd tell them was it had been time for her to move on. She had moved into the furnished apartment over Treble Shooters and taken over the bar as if she'd been running it forever. Nothing seemed to faze her—not the normal complement of drunks, not the cowboys who came on to her, not the over the top crowds that jammed the place on weekends. She was a godsend, delivered up to them as if by fate.

And he still wanted to strip her naked and fuck her blind.

Damn, damn, damn.

Justin leant close enough to be heard over the high noise level. "Better put your tongue back in your mouth, big brother. That's one body you won't be licking unless you want to go looking for another manager."

One corner of Cade's mouth kicked up in a grin. "Maybe I could make it part of her employment contract."

"Thought of that myself a time or two," Mark chimed in. "But you know the rules about mixing business and pleasure."

"Unless, of course, she indicates she's interested," Cade told him.

"Which she hasn't," Justin reminded him.

But at that moment, Marti looked up from behind the bar, caught his eye and an unexpected jolt of electricity sizzled between them. Cade's cock instantly hardened to steel and a low ache set up in his balls. Was she sending him some kind of signal? He'd sure like to find out.

"You won't get any answers by staring at her," Justin chuckled.

"Maybe I just did," he said, almost to himself.

"Well, she won't be interested on a Friday night, anyway," Justin pointed out. "She's got all she can handle behind that bar and more."

"Maybe so, but we've been too damn busy at the ranch. We've done so long without that my hard-on might not go away for weeks."

Mark laughed and leant across the table. "Then we'd best figure out what to do about that."

At that moment, the fates delivered a bundle into his presence in the form of Shannon Moore. Five seven, curved in all the right places, blonde hair tumbling down her back in lustrous curls. Cade knew every inch of that body, as did his brothers. She'd played their games more than once. When she plopped herself into his lap, he wondered if she was ready to play again.

She looped her arm around his neck and put her mouth right next to his ear, her breath like a warm breeze, and murmured, "Long time no see, cowboy. How's tricks?"

He wrapped an arm around her waist and shifted her so his cock pressed firmly against her bottom. "Feel that? Tell you just how things are?"

Her face flushed red and heat flared in her eyes. "How about a dance?" She looked at Mark and Justin. "One with each of you?"

Justin grinned. "Suits me. But one of these times I want to go first."

She laughed as Cade stood and set her on her feet. "Invite me over again and I think that can be arranged."

There was a brief pause in the noise level before the jukebox clicked over to the next tune and cranked out Thompson Square's slow honky tonk melody, *Are You Gonna Kiss Me Or Not?*

"That's our cue," Cade said, leading Shannon to the dance floor.

He wedged them into a tiny space at a corner of the floor then pulled her body hard against his. She leaned against him, wrapped her arms around his neck, and sighed when his hands lowered to grab the cheeks of her ass tightly. He ground his pelvis against hers as they caught the rhythm of the music.

"Feel that, sugar?" he murmured in her ear, below the noise level. "Feel just how hard I am." His cock was pressing hard into her pussy, her heat blazing into him even through the layers of their clothing.

"Oh, yeah," she breathed.

Cade glanced quickly around and realised half of the people on the dance floor were all but fucking to music with their clothes on. Bodies were glued to bodies, hips swaying, arms wrapped around each other.

Jesus! Cade thought. *At least no one – especially Marti – is paying attention to us.*

He closed his eyes momentarily, inhaling Shannon's familiar essence, the light perfume she always wore that had become so familiar with all their sessions together.

And that's what they are, he reminded himself. Sessions. Hours together, the four of them, to play their erotic games. He knew the sexual desires of the Thompson brothers had become well known in the county. Almost notorious. While they were highly respected as ranchers, they were envied by most men for their sexual activities. And there never seemed to be a shortage of women to accept their invitations.

He opened his eyes and glanced around again. Marti was busy at the bar pouring drinks, not looking up at all. If he kissed Shannon on the dance floor, she would hardly notice.

"Well, sugar? Like the song says, are you gonna kiss me or not?"

In tacit invitation, she tilted her face slightly.

Cade shifted his head so his mouth could find hers. As they swayed to the music, he licked the outer edges of her lips, tasting the lingering flavour of the margarita she must have had earlier before sliding his tongue into her hot, willing mouth. Her own tongue met his, dancing with it, gliding over its surface.

Oh, yeah. Thank you, Shannon, for saying hello tonight. I damn well needed this.

Her breasts, soft mounds of flesh, pressed against his chest and her nipples were so hard he could feel them even through her bra and the soft material of her T-shirt. He moved his tongue over hers in a rhythm that captured the beat of the music, until he felt the heat simmering all the way from his toes to the top of his head. If he wasn't careful, he'd come in his jeans on the dance floor and embarrass himself.

By the time the song ended, Cade was sure he could fuck her in five seconds flat. When the next song kicked in, another Thompson Square favourite, *If It takes All Night,* Cade took that as his cue. He slid his hands caressingly over Shannon's, then put about an inch of space between them and took her hand.

"Come on, sugar. How about a sleepover at the Treble T?"

She winked at him. "I thought you'd never ask."

One good thing about Shannon. She'd done the sleepover thing before and knew the ropes. Not to mention the fact that she was hot as a pistol and game for anything.

"Did you ride over in that funky Jeep of yours?" he asked when they reached the table.

"Uh-huh. You might not like it, but it gets me where I want to go."

"Give Mark your keys," he told her. "You'll ride in the truck with Justin and me."

"Hey!" Mark objected. "How come I have to ride solo?"

"Your turn to draw the short straw, bro."

He pulled some cash out of his pocket and dropped it on the table. The brothers might own the honky tonk and get their drinks for free, but they always tipped the waitress. They knew how hard she worked, especially on a Friday night.

Cade waited until Shannon dug her keys out of her pocket and handed them to Mark. "Take good care of it, big boy."

He laughed. "Anything I could do to that hunk of junk would only be an improvement. Why don't you get yourself something new?"

She grinned at him. "Sentimental value. That old Jeep has seen a lot of things in its time."

"Well, let's get going," Cade urged. "There's a lot *I* want to see."

He guided Shannon towards the door, his brothers behind him. He glanced over towards the bar, planning to let Marti know they were leaving, but her eyes were already on them. And if he didn't know better, he'd think that was jealousy smouldering in them.

Interesting. And intriguing.

Maybe tomorrow he'd find time to swing by here and spend a little time chatting with Miss Marti Jensen. Get the lay of the land.

So to speak.

The difference in noise level when they walked out of Treble Shooters was so noticeable that for a moment Cade wondered if he'd gone deaf.

"I've never figured out why it's necessary to crank the jukebox up so loud," he grumbled, fishing for his keys.

"Cranky, cranky," Justin teased. "First sign of advancing age."

"Yeah, yeah, yeah. Let's just get going."

"I'm right behind you," Mark called, heading for Shannon's ride. "Don't get started without me."

"Wouldn't think of it," she giggled.

Cade climbed into the driver's seat while Justin hoisted Shannon into his lap in the passenger's seat.

"Don't wiggle too much, honey," Justin told her in a low voice, "and we don't need to worry about seat belts."

"What are you doing?" she giggled.

"Just checkin' to see how ready you are to play."

As Cade pulled out on to the highway he glanced sideways and saw Justin's hands against Shannon's tummy, his fingers busy with her zipper. Suddenly an image of Marti slammed into him. Marti sitting on Justin's lap. Marti with her legs draped on either side of his. Marti moaning low in her throat.

Heat blasted into his groin and stabbed his balls.

Shit, shit, shit!

What the hell was he doing, thinking about that? His brothers were right. Marti Jensen had to be off limits.

From the corner of his eye, he saw Shannon move slightly as Justin worked his hands inside her panties.

"Hey, Cade," he said, "she's waxed that sweet little pussy. It's all bare."

"Yeah?" He gripped the steering wheel as lust shot through him. "Tell me about it."

"It's like pure satin," his brother said. "So soft and smooth. And oh, lordy, she's already slick and wet. I can feel that cream on those pussy lips just making my finger slide over her skin."

"She hot inside?" Cade asked, wondering why he was torturing himself and forcing himself not to break the speed limit to get to the ranch. Again, the image of Marti splashed itself on his brain, and he wondered if she trimmed or waxed her cunt. What it would feel like to slide his fingers over it.

Stop it!

"Let's see." Justin's breathing was getting choppy. "Kinda tight quarters here but oh, yeah, I can get two fingers inside her. And damn, that little cunt's just burning up."

"You guys drive me crazy," Shannon groaned, her voice unsteady.

Cade sensed her trying to move against his brother's touch.

"Just hold still, honey," Justin told her.

"Oh, God," she cried. "Oh, oh, oh."

"Tell me what you're doing," Cade demanded, gritting his teeth. They'd all discovered early on that half the fun of sharing a woman was describing what each of them did to her.

"I found that hot little clit and she nearly jumped off my lap. Shannon, baby, if you hold real still I'll get you off. Would you like that?"

"Yesss," she cried. "Please."

"Don't even want to wait until we get to the ranch?" he teased.

"No, no, no."

From the corner of his eye Cade saw her toss her head back and forth.

"Kinda tight quarters here, sweet thing, but I think we can make it work. You just hold on here."

"What are you doing?" Cade asked again, his fingers so tight on the steering wheel he wondered why he didn't leave dents.

"I'm pushing her jeans and panties down enough so I can get at her with both hands. Ah, okay, there we go. Now I've got two fingers inside her again and I'm workin' on that swollen little clit. Like that, Shannon? Like me to finger fuck you and play with your little button here?"

"Yes, yes, yes."

Cade glanced sideways briefly and saw Shannon leaning back against his brother, her arms straight down at her side.

"Eyes straight ahead, bro," Justin reminded him. "I'll give you a blow by blow."

"Well, get on with it."

"Okay, then. I've got three fingers inside her now and the little pussy is still just as tight. I'm rubbing her clit, pinching it and stroking it and she's hot as a pistol. Oh, shit, I can feel more cream inside her. You close, honey? Yeah, I think you are."

"Get her off now," Cade ordered. "And Shannon, you scream your pleasure."

"Here we go," Justin said. "Feel my fingers moving faster, honey? Oh, shit, Cade, I feel those cunt walls quivering now. She's tensing up."

"You still working on her clit?" Cade asked.

"Damn straight."

"Keep rubbing on it."

"Oh, yeah, Oh, yeah. Bet on it." He paused. "Here she goes. Okay, okay, here it comes. Here it comes. Oh, shit, yes. God, she's about to break off my fingers she's clamped down so tight around them. Cade, she's coming like crazy."

And Shannon's scream of satisfaction echoed loudly in the cab as she jerked in Justin's grip, the sound stretching out until it surrounded them. Cade had to move one hand from the steering wheel and clamp it over his cock, which was straining painfully at his fly. He ground his teeth together to hang on to his control. He was eternally grateful the ranch was in sight.

"Lick my fingers, Shannon," he heard Justin murmur in a low voice. "See how good you taste."

And then he was through the gate, down the long drive and pulling up in the gravel parking area. Mark slammed into the spot next to him two seconds later.

"I hope y'all didn't use it up on the way here," he grumbled as he stomped towards them.

"Hell," Cade said, "we're just getting started."

Justin led Shannon into the house, his brothers hot on his heels. He'd refused to allow her to zip up her jeans, only letting her pull them up past her hips so she could walk. When she was standing in the middle of the great room, he knelt to remove her boots, lifting one foot at a time and pressing down on the heel to ease them off her feet. She stood there silent, shaking slightly with need. He could smell her arousal, a musky scent so strong he was sure it permeated the room.

Once the boots were gone, he rose and tugged at her T-shirt.

Although it wasn't really cold, Cade lit the fire that had been laid in the fireplace. He always thought there was something so sensual about having sex by firelight. Mark flipped on the switch for the CD player that always had a stack of disks in it. The mellow sounds of Reba McEntire floated out into the dimly lit room, singing *When's It Gonna Be My Turn?*

Cade came up behind Shannon and put his hands on her shoulders.

"We're all gonna get a turn, right, sweet cheeks?"

"You bet." The sound came out on a choppy breath.

"Then let's get you naked."

He eased her T-shirt over her head. Only a flimsy concoction of satin and lace restrained her full breasts. He flipped the catch open and then the bra was gone and her breasts were resting in his large palms.

He looked at each of his brothers who gave slight nods. It was understood that Cade, as the eldest, would always take the lead. Everyone got his turn. Everyone got to fulfil his special desires. But Cade was the one who set the tone.

"Justin, you got a taste already," he said. "Mark gets to move up in line."

Justin stepped back but not far away, his eyes watching avidly as his brother came to stand in front of Shannon, rest his hands on her hips and bend his head to capture one nipple in his mouth.

"Ohhhh." The soft sound whispered from Shannon's lips.

"Feel good, baby?" Cade nuzzled her neck and licked the spot behind her ear then nibbled at the lobe.

"Real good," she murmured.

Mark took her other nipple in his fingers and tugged and pulled while his mouth sucked until the tip was pebbled and stiff.

"We need to get the rest of her clothes off," Justin reminded them.

"Well, go ahead and finish what you started in the truck," Cade told him.

Justin knelt beside the woman, being careful not to get in Mark's way, and pushed both jeans and panties down until they were around her ankles. Again he lifted first one foot and then the other until he could toss the garments aside.

"Tell us how wet she is," Cade said, kneading Shannon's breasts while Mark worked her nipples.

Glancing down he watched Justin slide one hand up the inside of Shannon's legs until he reached her pussy. When he slipped two fingers inside Cade saws his eyes light up.

"Still wet and ready," Justin said.

"I get the next taste," Mark said, lifting his head from her breasts.

"Let's get to it," Cade growled.

He stooped, lifted Shannon in his arms and carried her to the big, wide couch against one wall. He set her on her feet only long enough to strip off his own clothes before lying down and placing her on top of him, her back to his front. Shannon sighed with anticipation. She'd played with the Thompson brothers before and knew exactly what was coming.

Cade arranged her legs so one was resting along the back of the couch and the other was draped over his, leaving her wide open to his brothers. Mark, now also naked, knelt at the edge of the couch, spread the lips of her cunt with his fingers and took a moment just to look.

"Damn, that's pretty," he murmured.

In the next instant he bent his head and licked a long stroke with his tongue the length of her slit. She shuddered at his touch, her bare buttocks flexing against Cade. His cock jumped in response.

I should have pushed my cock inside her ass first.

No. That's for later. She'll be damn ready by then.

Justin knelt at the foot of the couch, situating himself so he had a good view and wrapping his fingers gently around the ankle of Shannon's leg that was against the couch.

"Man, she's juicy." His voice was harsh with need.

"Tell me what she looks like," Cade ordered, cupping Shannon's breasts and squeezing her nipples.

"Pink and wet," Justin said. "Just like she felt. Those pussy lips are sure swollen. And Mark's just lapping it up."

"How many fingers can she take right now?"

Mark lifted his head. "Let's check and see."

Justin moved her leg across his brother's thigh to open her up more. Against his body, Cade felt Shannon move slightly — wriggling her fine ass against his hungry cock — and he swallowed a groan.

Mark slid two fingers inside Shannon's tight cunt, added a third and then a fourth.

"Four," he said in a hoarse voice. "She's got four inside her."

Cade shifted both himself and Shannon so he could reach down to find the bare lips of her cunt and spread them wide.

"Lick her clit and finger fuck her," he ordered his brother in a tight voice.

Mark bent to his task, Shannon whimpering and trying to move in Cade's tight grasp as Mark's tongue flicked rapidly over her clit and his fingers moved in and out of her. Cade felt her body tense on top of his, her cries increasing. She tried to thrust her hips but Cade was holding her too tightly.

And then he felt it, the convulsive tremors that shook her body as her orgasm swept over her. Mark continued to ply her clit and move his fingers in and out of her grasping pussy even as she tried desperately to squeeze her legs together. Justin gripped her ankle and bent to look over Mark's shoulder so he could get the best view.

At last her body stilled, her breathing sharp and uneven. Little cries still burst from her as Mark lapped at the last of her cream. He slid his fingers from her, the skin shiny with her juices, and painted her breasts and her navel. Then he brought them to his mouth and deliberately licked each one.

"Feelin' good?" Cade breathed in her ear.

"Yes." She was still struggling to even out her breathing but her voice held a note of satisfaction.

Mark sat down on the floor, cross-legged, and Justin lounged at the end of the couch. Both had greedy looks on their faces. The music changed and Kenny Chesney's *Live a Little* floated out into the air.

"That's our theme song, sugar," Cade murmured in her ear. "Live a little, live a lot. You ready to do some livin'?"

"Uh-huh." She let out a long sigh. "But I want to know which one of you's going to fuck me first?"

Cade laughed, a sound rumbling up from deep in his chest. "Why, all of us, sweet thing. You know that."

"Well, get to it."

Yes, Cade thought, she was just what he needed tonight. Even though he wished it was someone else in his arms. Pushing those thoughts away he sat up, taking Shannon with him.

"Get the pillows," he told Mark.

They kept a stack of giant floor pillows by the hearth and now Mark pulled them onto the floor and arranged them so they almost formed a king-sized bed.

"I'm on the bottom tonight," Justin said. "Cade, we agreed. Right?"

"You got it, little brother."

He wanted Shannon's ass, anyway.

Justin down on his back on the pillows, stroking his swollen cock and eyeing Shannon's flushed body. Cade opened the drawer of a large squat table, took out the box inside and removed a condom, which he handed to Justin. He watched while his brother expertly rolled the latex on to his shaft before removing another one and a small tube.

"Come here, baby," Justin coaxed. "I'm ready and waiting for you."

She straddled his body, Cade's hands on her hips steadying her as she lowered herself on to Justin's hard erection.

"Lean forward, Shannon." Cade's voice was rough with lust. "You know how to do it, sugar."

As soon as she had taken Justin completely inside her, she tilted her body enough that Justin could cup her breasts and pull one of her nipples into his mouth. With her ass tilted in the air, Cade knelt behind her, squeezed some of the gel from the tube onto a finger then applied it generously to her tight anus.

"Ooooh," she moaned, as he slid one finger deep inside her.

"Still just as hot," Cade groaned, adding more lube and a second finger. "I can't wait to get my cock inside you again."

After sheathing himself, he spread the cheeks of her ass wide again, positioned the head of his dick at her opening then slowly but steadily thrust inside her. He could feel the thick length of Justin's cock through the thin membrane separating the two channels and the sensation made him even hotter. Harder. His balls ached so badly he didn't think he could stand it much longer.

"Your turn, Mark," he instructed his brother. "Shannon, lift your head."

For some women what came next might have been awkward but Shannon had played their games with them often enough that she knew the drill. Knew just how to accommodate them. As Mark knelt beside her she turned her head and opened her mouth to allow his cock to slide in over her tongue.

"Got you filled up now, sugar," Cade crooned, gripping her hips to steady himself.

The music changed again, this time to a heavy, fast, thumping beat and in perfect coordination the brothers began to move.

In, out. Back, forth.

Justin sucked noisily on Shannon's breasts while Mark and Cade made harsh, sensual sounds.

In, out. Back, forth.

The music pumped its beat into the room and the Thompson brothers pumped their cocks into Shannon. As the music reached a crescendo—a fast drum riff, a squealing guitar, the heavy bass—and exploded in a burst of sound, the three brothers exploded into her body. Cade felt Justin spurting his hot release as his gave up his own, hot liquid against hot liquid. Mark let out a shout as he emptied himself into Shannon's mouth.

As if on cue, the music changed again, the slow, mellow sound of *It's All Over Now* washing over them.

How appropriate, Cade thought as he eased himself from Shannon's tight grasp and stood to dispose of the condom.

The air was thick with the heady aroma of sex and the sweat that covered each of them. Mark collapsed onto a pillow, stroking his now limp shaft. Justin lay back, spent, as Cade helped Shannon ease herself from his brother's body. She tumbled to the side, her entire body flushed with the afterglow of raunchy sex, eyes dilated, full lips open and panting.

Cade lowered himself to another of the cushions, dragging oxygen back into his lungs. Fucking Shannon had given him the physical release he'd needed. Why, then, as he closed his eyes for a moment, did another face swim before his eyes? A face framed in thick, lustrous black hair. A face with violet eyes burning with heat. With sensuous lips partly open as if waiting for his tongue or his cock.

Fuck, fuck, fuck.

He had a feeling he was in deep trouble. And he wasn't sure how to get out of it.

Chapter Two

Marti leaned on the bar and sipped at the cold drink she'd poured for herself from one of the taps. It was Monday morning, the first Monday of the month, and she was doing the inventory for the month. Sundays they were closed, thank the Lord, giving her time to rest up from what was always a wild and noisy weekend. While Treble Shooters and Spring Valley were definitely different than San Antonio had been—or Austin or Dallas or Houston—and the clubs she'd worked there, she'd discovered there was a lot more action around this place than she'd expected.

Not that she was complaining. The harder she worked, the easier it was to forget all the troubles that had chased her here. She swallowed a sigh as she filled out the inventory order. She'd started a small lunch menu a couple of weeks ago. About a month after she'd started, she realised people would peek in during the day who just wanted a quick burger and a beer. The business was small but steady. The Thompson brothers were surprised at the steady clientele, but pleased.

She liked the people who came into the bar, even if it did get rowdy on the weekends. But hell, she was used to ranch hands letting off steam. They weren't nearly as bad as the rodeo riders she'd had to deal with.

The Thompsons had pretty much given her free rein once they realised she knew what she was doing. It made for a great work situation, especially with the free apartment on the second floor. Cade, the oldest one, had explained how and why they'd bought the bar, and how they'd fumbled along with temporary help until she'd answered their ad.

Her references had all checked out, but she'd known they would. She was just glad they hadn't felt it necessary to check into her personal life. Marti sighed when she thought about all the reasons she'd come here to this little town. Her personal relationships had burned her badly—men who said they understood her needs then threw them in her face. When she'd been hired to manage Treble Shooters, she decided maybe she ought to give up a personal life altogether. Less hassle. Finding someone who didn't think she was weird…

Don't go there.

Marti finished writing the inventory. In a minute she'd fax it to the liquor distributor. Yesterday, she'd driven into Kerrville to the grocery to restock her kitchen supplies, so she was all set there. She was startled to hear the back door opening and for a moment she tensed with unpleasant anticipation until she heard Cade Thompson call out.

"Just me, Marti." His boot heels clicked on the floor as he made his way down the short hall and into the main part of the honky tonk.

"Hey, Cade."

She sensed him even before he walked up to the end of the bar. It was hard not to sense Cade Thompson. As tall as his brothers, he had the broad shoulders and lean hips of a stereotypical cowboy...but there was nothing stereotypical about this man. His rugged face shouted masculinity, the square jaw and slash of cheekbones setting the stage for eyes as brown as coffee with thick, dark brown lashes. His faded chambray work shirt hugged his muscular frame and was tucked into worn jeans that clung to his hips like an old friend. He oozed testosterone in an amount that Marti was sure should be illegal.

Of course, *all* the brothers were hot, hot, hot. And Daisy, the waitress who worked at night, was only too happy to share the gossip with her about their high-flying sex lives. Too bad she had sworn off sex. The Thompson brothers might be just what she was looking for.

Nope. Don't go there. You don't fuck the bosses.

But holy hell, when she looked at the man approaching, her breasts ached and cream gushed in her pussy.

They hadn't been in, any of them, since a week ago Friday night, when they'd left with the hot sexy blonde who'd plastered herself all over Cade on the dance floor. Of course, he'd been doing some plastering, too. Marti had bitten back the tiny flare of unexpected jealousy and done her best to banish it from her mind. But that night when she'd gone to bed, she couldn't help remembering everything Daisy had gossiped about. Couldn't help imagining the brothers — especially Cade — doing all those things with the blonde. Her sleep had been anything but restful.

Now, as she looked at him, she wished she'd taken a little more time with her appearance, but she hadn't expected to see anyone. In a hurry to get things squared away in the bar, she'd pulled on an old pair of jeans and a T-shirt and tugged her hair back into a ponytail. Treble Shooters wouldn't open for lunch for another hour. Plenty of time, she'd thought, to change clothes and swipe on some mascara and lip gloss. She hadn't expected Cade Thompson to just drop in.

Trying to be casual about it, she grabbed the work shirt she'd tossed onto the bar and pulled it on in an effort to cover the nipples poking against her T-shirt. Not much she could do about her damp crotch, so she just hoped the scent of her musk wouldn't carry on the air. She grabbed her drink and drained it, wishing it would cool her down, then smoothed back a few strands of hair.

Cade stopped about ten feet from her, his mouth kicking up in that devastating grin.

"Had to run to the feed store and just thought I'd stop by and check on things. We haven't really taken much time to talk to you, my brothers and me, in the past couple of weeks."

"I hear it's branding time out at the Treble T. That must take up all the hours in the day."

"And then some." He grinned. "Besides, you run this place so well, you don't even seem to need us. But I figured as long as I was in town I'd stop in and make sure things were okay for you. See if there was anything you needed."

"I'm doing just great. Thanks for asking." She took a step back. Then another. Getting too close to Cade Thompson was a very bad idea.

"Apartment working out okay?" he asked.

"Perfect. I really appreciate having it."

He shrugged. "No problem. It would just go to waste anyway. So. You've got everything under control here?"

"Absolutely." *Except I wish I could see you naked.*

"Good, good. Glad to hear it."

He was watching her with those coffee-brown eyes, a penetrating gaze that seemed to see right inside her. Marti's stomach clenched and a pulse throbbed deep inside her womb.

"Um, can I get you something, Cade? Coffee? A beer?"

His mouth curved in that heart-stopping grin again. "A little early for beer, but I'll take a cup of coffee if you've got some."

"Sure. Um, I'll get it for you right now." She had to walk past him to get to the coffee pot. "Why don't you, um, take a seat?"

"I'm good." He was still grinning and there was something so sensual about it, she felt her knees weaken.

"O-Okay." What was the matter with her? She couldn't seem to get one sentence out without stammering.

She walked to the end of the bar near to where he was leaning on the long polished wood counter and bent down to take a mug out of the lower cupboard. He was so close she couldn't help brushing against him. The moment their bodies made contact, electricity zinged through her with such force she almost dropped the mug.

"You okay, Marti?" His tone of voice held a tinge of amusement.

"Uh, fine. Yes. Good."

She was trembling slightly when she set the mug on the bar and Cade closed his big warm hand over hers. God, his touch was enough to melt her panties.

Do not screw up this job. Do not. Do not.

"Marti." His voice was low and deep. "Look at me."

She forced herself to raise her eyes to his. He took his Stetson off and set it on the end of the bar. His grin had morphed into a sensual smile.

"Are you afraid of me?" he asked, his hand still holding hers.

"Why, no, Cade." She forced a calmness she definitely did not feel. "Should I be?"

"Definitely not." His hand slid over her wrist and along her arm, his fingers reaching beneath the rolled-up sleeve of her shirt to stroke the skin of her forearm.

Marti was afraid she might actually have a full meltdown right there.

"Your, um, coffee's getting cold," she pointed out. But she didn't move her arm. In fact, she seemed unable to move any part of her body – a body that was suddenly throbbing with such intense need she knew he had to sense it.

Cade stroked her arm once more before lifting his hand to touch a finger to the hollow of her throat.

"Your pulse is beating like a drum," he commented, rubbing his finger back and forth over the tell-tale spot. "If you're not afraid of me then it must be something else. Want me to guess what it is?"

She shook her head mutely, mesmerised by his gaze.

His hand slid up to cup her chin. "See, here's the thing. My brothers and me, we never mix business with pleasure. Unwritten rule. I think you feel the same way."

She nodded, all the while thinking, *For you, I'd break every rule in the book.*

"But every once in a while some rules are made to be broken. Don't you agree?"

Again she just nodded, incapable of speech. She wanted Cade Thompson in her bed more than she wanted her next breath. Along with everything else she knew he had to offer. Because he had no idea that his idea of fun and games and hers were pretty much the same. The problem was, Daisy had also told her that the Thompson brothers simply used women as playthings, never forming any attachments. And the women were so turned on by the sexual adventures they didn't care. Just lined up to take their turn.

But Marti had been down that road already and been burned more than once. She was tired of just being another notch on someone's bedpost because her sexual desires reached outside the lines. She wanted something a little more. But she didn't think she was going to get it at the Treble T, and if she gave into her urges, accepted Cade's unspoken invitation, how would she survive afterwards when she became just another name on their list?

"Marti?"

His voiced jolted her out of her mental wanderings. His face was so close to hers now she could almost count every one of the thick eyelashes.

"Y-Yes?"

When he spoke his breath was a warm breeze fanning her face. "You're probably the best damn manager we could get for this place. You know your stuff, handle the drunks, make everyone happy, run the place in a businesslike manner and we're making money. A manager like that's hard to find."

"Th-Thank you." God, she was still stammering. And she seemed rooted to the spot. His warm fingers were still holding her chin, the contact sending shivers skating over her skin.

"But, see, here's the thing." His mouth hovered so close to hers, their lips were almost touching. "I want to fuck you more than anything in the world. What do you say about that?"

Shock raced through her followed by such intense lust she was sure she'd burn alive.

"Say something, Marti," he coaxed. "Say yes. Or no. Or tell me to go to hell. Do something or I'm going to kiss you."

But she couldn't move, couldn't speak, could only stare into those hypnotic eyes that burned into hers. And in the next second, he closed that tiny space between them. His lips were warm and firm, pressing lightly against hers, then harder. His big hands cradled her face, holding it in place for him as he deepened the kiss. His tongue was like a lick of flame as it traced the closed seam of her mouth. Automatically she opened for him and that devil tongue swept inside, igniting every surface.

At thirty-two, Marti had certainly been kissed plenty of times, but they were all amateurish efforts compared to this. *This* was a kiss. Cade Thompson drank from her mouth, sipped from it, touched every inner surface. Dared her tongue to dance with his. Sucked it into his mouth.

She was sure she stopped breathing. Every nerve in her body was on fire, her skin felt too tight. And with every throb of the pulse deep inside of her, cream soaked her cunt. Right at the point where she was afraid she'd pass out from the pleasure, Cade lifted his mouth from hers.

"So tell me, Miss Marti Jensen. Does this send you running back to San Antonio or any of the other cities you came from? Because I'm taking a big chance here of losing a damn fine manager."

"No," she whispered. "I'm not running."

What she really wanted to do was rip off both her clothes and his and take him down to the floor right there behind the service bar.

He licked her lips with the tip of his tongue. "Good. That's good. One more thing."

"Y-Yes?"

"You know about my brothers and me? I'm sure Daisy Brooks has managed to fill you in on every erotic detail."

She nodded, her gaze still locked with his.

"Still not running?" he asked.

She shook her head. "I-I want this job. I *need* this job."

"Be clear about one thing," he said. "Your job doesn't depend on whether you spend a night at the Treble T. Either before or after."

"Okay," she whispered.

Finally he dropped his hands and took a step back, lifted his hat and set it back on his head. "I'll be back."

"You didn't drink your coffee," she called after his retreating figure.

He laughed, a loud, lusty sound. "That's okay. I'm hot enough."

She heard the back door close after him.

Holy shit!

What had she just done? Probably made the biggest mistake of her life. She'd come here to get away from all that, convinced that her sexual appetites could only get her into trouble. And now look.

She leaned against the service bar for a long moment, willing her racing heart to slow down, forcing herself to even out her breathing. Finally she picked up her inventory list and went back to the tiny office to fax it to the liquor distributor. Maybe Cade Thompson would forget all about this little visit and her life could go back to what had lately passed for normal.

Yeah, right. And maybe I'll win the lottery.

* * * *

Cade cursed himself all the way back to the Treble T. What the fuck had got into him? There were plenty of women all over the county to pick from, including those like Shannon who were used to their games and knew there was no commitment on either side. Safe. Uncomplicated. So what the hell was he doing making a pass at Marti Jensen?

He knew the answer and didn't like it. He'd wanted her from the minute he and his brothers interviewed her. The minute he'd seen her walk up the outside stairs to that apartment with tight jeans covering her fine ass. What he didn't want to admit to himself was the urge to demand more from her.

And exactly how would that work out, asshole? Maybe you're not even anything close to what she wants. For any reason.

But he had a gut feeling about Marti. He just didn't know if he could trust his instincts or not. He'd made his play before he could catch himself. Now he had to figure out what to do next...now that he'd opened up this Pandora's box.

He was still cursing himself when he parked at the ranch then slammed out of the truck. His boot heels made indentations in the gravel as he walked to the barn. No one needed to tell him he was twenty-five kinds of a fool. He'd probably just done the stupidest thing ever, and he had no idea what to do about it.

"Somebody step on your tail?"

He heard Justin's laughing voice and looked up. His brother was astride his favourite buckskin gelding at the edge of the parking area. He was leaning forward casually, arms crossed and resting on the pommel of the saddle, the reins held loosely in one hand.

"My tail's just fine," Cade snapped and kept walking towards the barn.

"Well, let's see." Justin urged the horse forward and followed Cade. "You went to the feed store and I didn't hear any shouting clear from town, so they must have taken care of the order just fine."

"No problem," Cade growled, still walking.

"Shannon's out of town for the week so you couldn't have had a run-in with her."

"Leave it, Justin." Cade stomped into the barn.

Mark looked up from where he was cleaning a saddle. "What's got your dick in a twist?" he asked. "You look like someone just told you either the price of beef dropped to five cents a pound or there's a law forbidding any kind of sexual activity for the next year."

Justin had ridden the gelding into the barn. Now, he swung out of the saddle and began to remove the tack.

"Big brother stepped in some kind of shit," Justin teased. "I'm just tryin' to figure out what it was."

Cade wished they'd just shut up and leave him alone. He didn't want to admit what a stupid thing he'd done. Or think about how he was going to fix it. Problem was, he didn't want to get out of it. He wanted to strip Marti Jensen naked, eat every delicious inch of her and then plunge his aching cock so deep inside her there wasn't even room for a whisper of air.

He started to open the door to the tack room but Justin was suddenly in front of him.

"Uh-oh," he said. "I know that look. What have you done, big brother?"

"None of your damn business," he growled.

"Shit." Mark had come up behind him. "I'll bet fifty I know what he's done." He put his hand on Cade's shoulder and spun him around. "He went by Treble Shooters and put a move on our very valuable manager. Right, Cade?" He was right in Cade's face now. "That's what you did?"

"Shut up." Cade tried to shake him off.

"Wait a minute." Now Justin was standing beside him. "I thought we agreed she was off limits."

"Unless she was willing," Cade pointed out.

His brothers stared at him. Justin frowned. "Are you telling me she is?"

"Does she know about us?" Mark asked.

"Yes and yes." Cade gritted his teeth. "But I'm thinking I need to figure out how to pretend she and I never had our little talk."

Because I have a feeling if I get started with her, it will never be over. And then what do I do?

"I think that horse may already be out of the barn," Justin laughed. "I just hope you haven't cost us a damn fine manager."

Cade held up a hand. "I was very clear with her about that. The choice is hers and no repercussions, no matter what she decides. Or what happens."

"But you still think you need to dial it back," Mark said.

A muscle jumped in Cade's cheek, a sign of his frustration. "It was an impulse, damn it. I thought I'd stop into the bar and see how things were going for her. If she needed anything. But damn it, five seconds next to her and my cock was already talking to me."

Justin stared at him with open curiosity. "So where did you leave it?"

He shrugged. "I guess the next move is up to us. We can just forget about it, and I can figure out some way to grovel and tell her I had a momentary lapse of sanity"

"That oughta be great for her ego," Mark chuckled.

"Or we move forward with this and invite her out to the ranch. Treble Shooters is closed on Sundays."

Mark and Justin looked at each other then back at Cade.

"We could be taking a big chance on losing her here," Mark said at last. "But we did say the other night that if she was willing, we wanted to do it."

Justin clapped Cade on the shoulder. "I think the invite should come from you, big brother, since you're the one that stirred the pot, so to speak. Just make sure she understands what she's walking into."

"Oh, like I said, Daisy's filled her in on all the hot, sexy details, so she knows."

"Then I think you need to try and set things up for next Sunday."

Cade glared at his brother. "I think Marti Jensen might be a little different than the other women we bring here. She may be a bar manager, but she's got more class than Shannon and her friends. And she needs more than five seconds inside the door before we tear off her clothes."

"Hell, we'll even grill prime steaks and break out the best whisky," Mark said. "Let's just make this happen."

* * * *

Marti spent most of the week mentally chewing herself out for the episode with Cade Thompson. She'd been burned so many times before by men who were willing to play her games then walked away afterwards. At least with the Thompson brothers she would be on a level playing field, sexually. She wouldn't have to explain her outrageous tastes.

But Daisy had been very explicit in detailing their escapades and definite about letting her know that women were just casual playthings to them. If she agreed to an 'episode' with them, how would she handle it afterwards? She really, really didn't want to leave Spring Valley. The tiny place was growing on her, as were the people she was getting to know.

She alternately hoped Cade would drop in again and tell her the whole thing was a big mistake, no hard feelings — and waited for him to come by and invite her out to the ranch for fun and games. By Friday night, her nerves were so raw she jumped at every little thing. She even dropped a glass in the kitchen when Daisy came through the swinging door and startled her.

"Sheesh, Marti." Daisy shook her head. "What's with you, anyway? You look like you're about to fly out of your skin."

"Nothing," Marti muttered. "Just...not sleeping too well."

"Honey, you need to get out and get yourself some kind of life. You eat and sleep this place. It's not healthy." She leant closer to Marti. "Spring Valley may be small but there's some damn fine men wandering around here."

Marti shook her head. "Not interested. But thanks, anyway." She dumped the remains of the glass in the trash. "Anyway, I hear the noise level rising out there, so why don't you go on out and see who's thirsty for a drink."

She gave herself a count of ten before emerging into the bar area again. The jukebox, again at full volume, kicked into Lady Antebellum's *Need You Now*. The couples on the floor were dry-humping to the music, and just as it hit the chorus, "And I don't know how I can do without, I just need you now," the front door opened and the Thompson brothers filed in. Cade's eyes homed in on hers and their gazes locked up tight. He gave the barest of nods as the three of them worked their way over to a far corner.

There were no empty tables but that didn't seem to bother them. In fact, they probably loved the fact that the place was packed wall to wall. Justin managed to squeeze into a booth with four other people and Mark wandered back to the pool table area. But Cade just leaned against the wall in a position that gave him a clear line of vision to her.

He's probably forgotten all about what happened. It meant nothing to him. He was just playing with you. Pay attention to work.

Customers sitting at the bar were demanding her attention and Daisy was at the well shooting orders at her, so thankfully for the next hour she was too busy to even think about Cade Thompson. But she could still feel his eyes on her, no matter what she was doing. During a brief lull, she went into the kitchen to get a large bag of nuts to refill the bowls on the bar, then turned...and nearly walked right into the man himself.

"Oh!" She clutched the large plastic bag to her chest like armour.

"Sorry." His mouth curved in its lethal grin. "Didn't mean to startle you."

"N-No problem. Did you want something? Because I really need to get back out there."

"Want something? Oh, yeah." His drawl was low and thick as warm honey. "But I don't think this is the time or the place."

"Cade, I—"

"Shh. It's okay." His fingers caressed her flushed cheek. "I just wanted to ask you if you'd like to come out to the ranch Sunday. Spend the day." He paused. "And the night." And just in case she misread the invitation, he added, "With me. And my brothers."

Marti knew exactly what he was asking. She drew in a breath and let it out slowly.

"What time?"

"Come out around one o'clock. We can all take a swim in the pool while it's warm." He leant down and brushed his mouth over hers. "See you then."

She watched him walk back out into the noise and the crowd.

Well, Marti, you're in for it now.

Chapter Three

Marti spent all of Sunday morning grooming herself for the day ahead. She lounged in a lavender-scented bubble bath, shaving her legs and under her arms and carefully trimming her cunt so there was just a thin line of hair defining each lip. She smoothed lotion into every inch of her skin and changed clothes five times before settling on jeans shorts and a three-quarter sleeve blouse with the tails tied right beneath her breasts. The shorts were low riders, exposing her navel and the tiny jewelled butterfly hanging from it on a thin ring. She wondered what the Thompson brothers would think of that.

Finally, after brushing her hair out three different times, she pulled it back in a gold clip, slipped her feet into thin-strapped sandals and headed out to her SUV.

Fish or cut bait, Marti girl.

All the way to the ranch, she alternated between heated anticipation and tense anxiety. She still wasn't sure she was doing the right thing by actually accepting the invitation — knowing exactly what she'd be walking into, thank you very much, Daisy — but the fantasies spinning around in her mind had her so thoroughly aroused there was no way she could have changed her mind. By the time she reach the Treble T, navigated the long driveway and parked in the gravel area beside the ranch trucks, anticipation had won out.

When she climbed out of the SUV, she heard music, male voices and the sound of water splashing from in back of the house. She hitched the thin strap of her purse over her shoulder and headed in that direction just as Cade came around the corner, smiling.

"Thought I heard your car," he said.

Drops of water clung to his skin but instead of a bathing suit — that she could see anyway — he had a towel slung low and knotted at his hips. He walked up to her and, before she could say anything, he cradled her face in his hands and captured her mouth in a heated kiss. The moment his tongue slipped inside, she got that same weak in the knees feeling as before. Her nipples hardened into taut peaks and moisture soaked her panties. She'd kissed a lot of men but none of them had lit a flame inside her like Cade Thompson.

"Hey! Don't hog the company all to yourself."

Marti's eyes flew open. Over Cade's shoulder, she saw Mark heading towards them, also only wearing a towel. Didn't these men have bathing suits? She thought of the tiny bikini she'd stuffed into her purse and wondered if she'd even have a chance to show it off.

"Welcome to the Treble T." Mark had come to stand behind her, his voice husky in her ear, his hands sliding around to the flat of her stomach between her body and Cade's. "We've been eagerly anticipatin' your arrival."

Cade lifted his mouth from hers and smiled at her — a smile that melted her bones and turned her muscles weak.

"I like my method of welcome better. I plan to show you the very best Thomson hospitality, sugar."

In one fluid movement, he lifted her into his arms and strode around the house, carrying her as if she weighed no more than a feather. She could feel his strength wrapping itself around her like a warm blanket. They reached a fence that looked to be ten feet high made of adobe bricks, encircling what Marti supposed was the pool. Mark ducked in front of them and opened a heavy wooden gate so Cade could carry her through.

"Hey, Marti," Justin called from the pool.

He was submerged in the water to his armpits, leaning on the apron of the pool on his forearms. Through the clear water she could see he was completely naked.

"Oh!" she said as Cade set her on her feet. She wondered if he was going to kiss her again. *Hoped* he'd kiss her again. He had the most magic mouth and tongue, coaxing responses from her she hadn't even known she'd been capable of...

But there was Justin in the pool—laughing, a look of hungry anticipation on his face.

Cade followed the path of her gaze and grinned. "We're not very formal around here. I don't remember the last time any of us wore a bathing suit."

"Then it's a good thing you have such a tall fence," she commented then blushed. "Oh, that's *why* you have the fence."

"See? I knew you were smart." He whipped off his towel and Marti nearly swallowed her tongue as she saw the size and girth of his cock standing at attention. Cade wrapped his fingers around it and stroked it slowly.

"Wow!" popped out of her mouth before she could engage her brain. A rush of pleasure surged through her, heating her blood and ramping up her stuttering pulse beat.

Cade just grinned at her—that slow, fuck-me grin. "We'll let you decide later who has the best one." He lowered his voice. "But I bet I'll win."

Mark had come up behind her again and slid his warm hands around to her midriff, caressing the bare skin. His fingers were hot as a branding iron, scorching her skin every place they touched her.

"I think you have too many clothes on to go swimming." His voice was a low thrum in her ear as his fingers unknotted her blouse then popped open the buttons one by one.

Cade stepped closer to her, his gaze travelling over her body. "Is that a belly button ring I see, Marti?" He reached out a finger and touched it. "A butterfly. Is that you, sugar? A butterfly? Flitting from place to place, never settling down?"

Her throat was so dry she could barely swallow. "That's me. Haven't found a good resting place yet."

His fingertip circled round and round the furled flesh, brushing across the tiny butterfly before returning to her skin. "Maybe we can change your mind." He bent for a moment and placed a hot kiss on her navel before straightening again.

"We're definitely gonna try," Mark added.

He slid her purse from her shoulder and dropped it on the nearby table before easing her blouse down her arms. But instead of removing it, he left it hanging at her wrists then tied it behind her, effectively binding her hands.

"That make you nervous?" he breathed in her ear. "That I've got your hands?"

"No," she whispered, feeling his fingers dance along her ribcage to the front clasp of her bra.

Pop! And it was open, the straps sliding down so the garment dangled behind her.

Cade moved his fingertip up from her navel to brush lightly against the tip of each breast. Electricity zinged right to the centre of her pussy, feeding the strum of desire beating there. Still stroking his cock with a slow movement, he pinched and tugged on each nipple in turn.

Marti sucked in a breath.

"Just look at these nipples." His voice was thick with lust. "Such a pretty pink. So lickable. So suckable. Marti, you just take my breath away."

With her hands restrained behind her back, Marti's breasts protruded like an offering at a banquet. Cade stepped closer and bent his head to capture one nipple with his lips, pulling it into his mouth and circling it with his tongue. Cream gushed into the crotch of her thong and her legs trembled. She hadn't expected them to get into this the minute she'd arrived...but in a way she was glad. It eliminated the possibility of changing her mind and hightailing it out of here while they all did their preliminary sexual dance.

Mark's hands slid down the curve of her tummy to find the snap and zipper of her shorts, sliding the metal down with tantalising slowness while Cade continued to suck at her nipples. One lean finger slid between the silk of her thong and her skin. Mark hummed with pleasure when he touched the twin lines of curls before dipping into the wet folds and finding her clit.

Marti leant back against Mark's hard body for support, feeling the thick ridge of his erection pressing against her ass. Her gaze slid sideways to where Justin still hung at the edge of the pool. His gaze was fixed on the action in front of him and a flush of avid greed suffused his face.

"Hey!" he called. "When do I get to play?"

"Soon," Cade told him. "Just let the water keep you cool."

"She's soaking wet, guy," Mark said, stroking his finger up and down her slit. "Real juicy."

"Is her clit hot?" Justin asked.

"Like a match." He rubbed his finger back and forth over it and Marti whimpered as pleasure streaked through her again. "Oh, yeah, hot. And real responsive." He bit the lobe of her ear. "Marti, you are one little treasure, you know that?"

She couldn't do anything more than nod her head, between Cade tormenting her nipples and Mark manipulating her cunt. Cade was close enough now that the head of his erection bumped her tummy, the little bead of fluid at the top a slick streak on her skin.

"Let's get her shorts off," he growled.

"You'll have to do it," Mark pointed out. "My hands are busy."

Marti had closed her eyes to enhance the feel of arousal rushing through her body, so she felt rather than saw Cade move away from her. Then his large hands were sliding her shorts and thong down her legs to her ankles. He must have stooped down because she felt his hands on her ankles, lifting each foot one at a time to pull her clothing away. His hands stroked up the length of her legs, caressing her thighs with a whisper of touch, until his hands met Mark's at the heat of her pussy.

Two sets of fingers probed at her swollen labia, opening her wide. Marti jumped when she felt the flat glide of a tongue up the length of her slit to swirl at her pulsating clit.

"Easy, honey," Mark said. "We've got you."

Fingers lightly pinched her cunt lips and she knew at once they were his. Just as she knew the tongue tormenting her so cleverly was Cade's. In some remote corner of her mind she wondered just how much longer Justin would be content to be a bystander. But then Cade's teeth closed lightly over her heated nub and she didn't care about anything other than easing the need crawling through her. Quenching the fire racing through her and cooling her heated vaginal channel. She didn't remember the last time she'd been this aroused, this quickly.

Oh, wait! Maybe during the time she'd lived with Chuck and Don. But then they'd turned on her and...

No! Don't go there. Just relax and enjoy.

And so she let herself sink into the erotic fog surrounding her, her body being roused into overdrive by the wicked hands probing her everywhere.

"Open your eyes, Marti." Cade's low voice. "Look down."

She forced her eyelids up and lowered her gaze. Mark was bracing her against his body with his arms while his lean fingers still held the lips of her pussy open. Cade was stroking his cock with his hand, pressing the dark purple head against her sensitive clit. As she watched, another bead of fluid formed—a thick white pearl—and dropped onto the point of her clit. The image was so arousing she almost came just from looking at it.

"How does she feel inside?" Justin called. "She looks damn hot from here."

Marti turned her head at the sound of his voice and saw that he was now standing up in the shallow end of the pool, holding his cock in the same way that Cade was. Stroking it with the same slow glide of his hand. Just as he had earlier watched with heat and hunger from the edge of the pool, now his eyes were fastened on the tableau of the three bodies at the edge of the pool.

Cade shifted to slide two fingers inside her, curving them so he could find *that* spot behind her clit and press on it. Marti jerked again, her legs trembling as fire heated her and the thrum of passion raced through her. If not for Mark holding her, she definitely would have collapsed to the deck of the pool.

"She feels wet and juicy," Cade rumbled. "All liquid silk inside. So soft and smooth I think I could come just from sliding my fingers in and out."

"Well, let's make *her* come," Justin told him. "Let's get the party started. But bring her over here so I've got a better view."

Cade backed off and pulled a heavily padded chaise longue to the edge of the pool. Mark lifted her, arms still bound behind her, and carried her over to the chaise. He sat on the edge—legs together, his cocked pressed firmly into the crease of Marti's ass—and draped her legs on either side of his. She was effectively spread wide open, a sight that Justin took in with avid interest.

"My turn to touch?" he asked.

"Go ahead," Cade told him. He was standing beside the chaise, holding his cock and rubbing it against Marti's breast.

"Watch me, Marti," Justin commanded.

She looked down to see him reach up from the water and rub one finger back and forth over her clit, sending electrified sensations jolting through her. A soft moan whispered from her lips.

"I think she's close to ready."

She was definitely close to ready. Just the thought of three sexy alpha males naked with her, arousing her, talking about her the way they did, was almost enough to make her come without any further urging. This was the kind of sex Marti loved, the kind she had trouble finding with the right people.

Stop! Quit thinking about that. Enjoy this!

So she leant back against Mark's muscular body, cradled in his arms, loving the feel of him, of his fingers teasing her cunt. Of his breath warm against her cheek. His tongue tracing the line of his jaw. With her arms still bound behind her, she had no place to put her hands so she rested them on Mark's cock, feeling its length through the towel.

"Holy shit," he ground out. "Easy, Marti. I'm saving myself for later."

But she just made a little humming sound in her throat and kept her fingers lightly wrapped around him. Anchoring herself on the hot shaft.

"Marti?"

Cade—beside her. She looked first at him, seeing the desire etched clearly on his face as he rubbed his cock against her breast and her nipple. And then at Justin, staring intently at her as he probed her channel with two then three fingers. Was she ready? Oh, yes, definitely.

"I am," she breathed, barely able to get the words out.

"Did you say something, sugar?" Mark murmured in her ear.

"I think she said she's ready," Cade told him. "I fucking know I am." He reached down to cup his balls and squeezed them, increasing the tempo of his other hand on his shaft.

"All right then," Mark answered.

The next few moments were a sensual blur for Marti. Mark's fingers worked her clit furiously, while Justin slid three fingers rapidly in and out of her cunt and Cade increased the glide of his hand on his erection. Justin leant forward, slid his tongue across her tummy and placed a hot kiss on her navel, right where the little ring glinted in the sunlight.

"Oh, oh, oh," she whimpered, as the climax swirled deep inside her and spooled its way through her body.

And then it was there—crashing down on her, lifting and spinning her, her body anchored in place only by Mark's strong arms around her. As the first tremor hit, she felt the splash of hot semen on her breast and heard Cade's deep groans of pleasure. The muscles in her cunt clamped down on Justin's busy fingers, and if not for Mark's grip on her, she would have drawn up into a tight ball to ride out the spasms shaking her.

As the fierce tremors subsided into milder aftershocks, Mark stroked the lips of her cunt and Cade rubbed his spent cock over her nipple again and again. Mark undid the sleeves of her shirt then tossed the wet garment to the side, along with her bra, freeing her hands. Marti lay back in Mark's arms, spent and exhausted, waiting for her thundering heartbeat to ease. She was breathless and sweaty and temporarily satisfied. But the erotic nature of the scene and the anticipation of what was yet to come kept her riding the thin edge of desire.

"I think we could all use a dip in the water." Mark leant forward, moving her with him. "Here, Justin. Catch. And don't miss."

He eased Marti forward and gave her a gentle push. She fell headlong into Justin's arms, catching the laughter in his eyes as he helped her slide into the pool. The water felt good on her slick, heated skin. Justin splashed water on her breasts then eased his hand down to push the cooling liquid against her hot pussy.

"Spread your legs, sugar. Let me make that little sore cunt feel good. We aren't half done with it."

He arranged her so she leaned against the wall of the pool, then nudged her legs apart with his foot. Marti looked down to see his impressive cock bobbing in the water and remembered what Cade had said earlier. She might indeed have trouble deciding whose was the most outstanding. And she hadn't even seen Mark's yet.

But apparently Mark was about to remedy that. He rose from the lounger, whipped off the towel and stood at the edge of the pool. Marti made a small O with her mouth. Was it a genetic thing that had all the Thompson brothers so well hung? Heat flashed through her as she imagined taking all their cocks at once—one in her mouth, one in her pussy and one in her ass. She shivered at the imagery.

Marti was suddenly conscious of all three brothers looking at her intently—Justin, still splashing water between her legs, Cade, in the pool on one side of her, and Mark, who had just slid into the water on the other side.

"So tell me, Marti Jensen," Cade said. "Besides being a hot shot bar manager, where'd you learn to be so sexy? I know Daisy probably gave you an earful about how we like to play, and I'd have sworn our brand of sexual hijinks would have scared you off."

She gave them a sultry smile. "You don't think I'm going to tell you all my secrets, do you?"

Cade slid his fingers into the damp strands of her hair and bent his head so his lips were just a breath away from hers. "Oh, I think we have ways of coaxing it out of you."

His mouth came down on hers, his lips soft but firm, his tongue probing, seeking until she opened and let him in. God, he had the most erotic mouth she'd ever kissed. Sinful, in fact. His tongue probed and licked while Mark, on her other side, caressed her breasts and teased her nipples. And Justin, who'd waited so patiently for his turn, was rubbing his impressive cock against her already sensitive clit.

"Open up, honey," Cade whispered into her mouth. "Let my brother in."

She'd thought they'd at least give her a few minutes to catch her breath, but apparently a few was all she would get. Justin rubbed his shaft lower against the lips of her pussy. And incredibly, as Mark continued to knead her breasts and pinch her nipples and Cade ate at her mouth, desire stirred and came to life. The heat of it fired the nerves in her pussy and warmed the blood in her veins.

"Her nipples are hard as diamonds," Mark said. "She's already hot again."

"It's a good thing," Justin said, his voice taut with need. "'Cause I'm ready to go. Give me a hand here, guys."

"You going first today?" Cade's voice was thick with lust but still held a note of amusement. His lips were now barely touching Marti's.

"I think you need a little recovery time, big brother. So how about it?"

She wasn't sure what to expect until Mark and Cade each lifted one of her legs and supported it with their arms, opening her wide for their brother. Justin slid his fingers inside her again, thoughtfully testing to see if she was slick with something besides the pool water. She saw his eyes flash when he found her rich with cream.

"My turn," he told her. "I get first crack at that sweet little cunt and I can't tell you how I've been looking forward to this."

Marti forced her eyes to stay open so she could watch as he wrapped his fingers around his erection and nudged her opening with the broad head. Like his brothers, he was thick and long and hard as steel. Rocking his hips back and forth, he eased himself into her until she'd taken his full length. His balls slapped against her ass as he pumped into her, slowly at first then faster.

Cade, who still had his other hand threaded through her hair, cradled her head. But this time it was Mark who pressed his mouth to hers and thrust his tongue inside. His lips were harder than Cade's, with more ardour, and his tongue swept everywhere, dancing with hers. As Justin pumped his hips faster, Mark increased the movement of his tongue so that they were fucking her in two places like a well-choreographed ballet.

Mark's tongue was so deep in her throat she could barely breathe, but the slide of it over her skin was intensely exciting. She gave Mark back as good as she got. Justin continued to drive into her, harder and faster, his cock thickening even more. As he neared his release, he gasped out, "Please tell us you're on the pill."

"Mmm," was all she could manage with her mouth consumed by Mark's.

"All…right, then."

He barely got the words out before Marti felt the spurt of his release in her, and that triggered her own climax. Justin grasped her by the waist and pulled her hard against him while her pussy clamped down on him, milking his cock, sucking him deep inside her passage. She clung to his shoulders for dear life as the spasms rocketed through her, shaking her, the water around them swirling with their movements.

Marti closed her eyes as she spiralled out, the tremors finally easing until they subsided. Cade and Mark eased her legs down. Each slid an arm around her, cupped a breast and soothed her until her body relaxed again. Justin leant forward and brushed his mouth over hers. He kissed the belly button ring again then smiled at her, that sexy Thompson smile.

"You're a winner, Marti."

She certainly hoped so, especially for one of the Thompson brothers. Cade. The oldest. The hottest. The one she'd focussed on from the day she'd first met all three of them. Now she had to work hard not to let it show. That wasn't the way they played. It was all of them or none of them, a fact that gave her a tiny stab of regret.

What the hell, Marti? This is the way you like it. You changing direction all of a sudden?

She smiled back at Justin and pushed the errant thoughts from her mind.

* * * *

Mark had taken drinks from the refrigerator in the outdoor kitchen—beer for the men, a wine cooler for Marti—and they relaxed and recovered at the side of the pool, their faces flushed with the heat of sexual activity and anticipation of what was yet to come. Marti laughed and joked with them, obviously comfortable and at ease with the situation. Cade would have given a month's receipts from the ranch to know how she'd got to this point in her life for her to be so at ease with the situation.

On top of that, he was doing his best to control an unfamiliar feeling that he vaguely recognised as jealousy. He couldn't remember ever being jealous of his brothers in his life...except for the time he'd broken his leg and they'd got to go into San Antonio to watch the Spurs play while he had to stay home. The three of them had played their games with a list of women longer than he cared to think about without the green-eyed monster ever creeping in.

Oh sure, they'd all agreed that one of these days— sometime in the distant future—they'd need to think about settling down, getting married. But no one had yet figured out how they'd be able to adjust their sexual appetites to accommodate that. Not to mention the fact that it would take a pretty special woman to agree to their situation.

Maybe it was turning thirty-six last month—seeing forty stare him in the face—and realising he needed some structure to his life. Maybe he was just tired of the same vapid females they brought to the ranch.

Or maybe—shit, he could hardly even think about this—it had something to do with Marti herself. The minute she'd walked into Treble Shooters to meet with the three of them about the job, he'd felt an electrified connection that he'd never had with anyone else. It wasn't just the physical appeal. Truth be told, some of the women they'd played with might have been more beautiful. Maybe. But Marti was the whole package—looks, brains and a vibrant personality. A sense of self he found missing in most women. And an aura of sexual knowledge that very few women had. At least the ones that he knew.

She was a woman a man could hold on to for the long run.

Hold it, Cade. You're letting your mind wander into dangerous territory. That's not even on the table here. Right? Right?

"Cade, you falling asleep on us?"

Mark's teasing voice broke into his abstract wanderings and he mentally shook himself. His eyes strayed to Marti's naked form stretched out face down on one of the loungers. Justin had just commented that she really needed sun block so she wouldn't burn in the hot Texas sun and had picked up the bottle they'd left on the umbrella table.

Marti turned her head and gave Cade a lazy smile. "You going to help here?" she asked. "Or you just planning to watch?"

Was that a signal of some kind she was sending him? Was he reading a message in her eyes that wasn't really there?

Stop this shit. What's gotten into you, asshole?

"Cade?" Mark's voice was impatient.

"On it." He dug out his usual smile and tried to bury all the disturbing thoughts clashing in his brain.

Mark was already sitting at the edge of the wide lounger smoothing the thick lotion into Marti's shoulders and arms. Justin sat at the foot of the chaise working on her ankles and calves. Cade smiled to himself as he knelt on a towel beside her.

I get the best part.

He took the bottle from Mark, squirted some of the liquid into the palm of one hand then began to stroke it over the sweet curve of her ass. Her muscles tensed slightly at his touch then relaxed again. Her head was turned so she could see him and when his hot gaze locked on her sultry one, he swore he saw the same mysterious, knowing look in them as before.

What's going on here?

He kept stroking her buttocks in a smooth circular motion, first one cheek then the other. He grabbed the bottle to squeeze more lotion, dripped it right at the top of her crevice and began to stroke his fingers through that hot, hot crease. He deliberately kept his touch light, especially when his fingertips brushed over her anus, but even that soft touch was enough to bring a tiny moan of pleasure from her.

"I think we need a little more sun block here." Need thickened his voice. "Wouldn't want anything this tender to get sunburned, would we?"

"Need any help with that?" Justin teased.

"I've got it. Thanks."

And I'm going to keep it. Whatever else happens, I'm the only one that's going to have her ass today. Period.

Whoa there. What's going on?

Again he shook off the stray thoughts and pressed a little more firmly on that tiny opening. She moaned again and he pressed hard enough that the tip of his finger popped through the tight ring of muscle.

Justin was working his way up the inside of her legs towards her sweet little pussy. He nudged her thighs apart with his hand and the movement made her ass clench, trapping his finger inside her. Cade's cock sprang to life, throbbing with a sudden wave of need. He pressed deeper with his finger and stroked her hot inner tissues. Justin had reached her pussy by now and when Cade spared him a glance, he saw his brother's fingers stroking the lotion over sweet pink pussy lips. Mark had moved his hand and was applying the liquid to the sides of her breasts.

Marti was whimpering now, delicious little sounds that sent bolts of lust straight to Cade's balls.

Cade moved his head so his mouth was at Marti's ear. "I don't care what else happens," he whispered. "I'm going to have your ass. Just me. You keep that in mind, sugar."

She trembled both at the words and his tone and that same mysterious look flashed in her eyes again.

"We need to turn her over," Mark said. "I think we've covered every inch of her back." He chuckled. "That is, Cade, if we can talk you into taking your finger out of her sweet ass."

Cade just grunted, but he stroked his finger in and out twice more just for good measure before pulling it free and wiping it on the towel. They turned her over and he took his first really good look at the front of her. Firm breasts, not too large and not too small, with dusky rose nipples pointing straight up at him. A stomach just slightly rounded, softening the toned lines of her body. And the most tempting cunt he'd seen in a long time, the hair neatly trimmed to form just two defining lines. He was afraid he'd come just from looking at her.

This time Mark took the bottle of sun block and squeezed a line of the lotion straight down her body, beginning at the hollow of her throat and trailing all the way to her cunt, pooling extra just at the top of her mound.

"Spread your legs, honey," Justin told her in a husky voice.

Mark and Cade each took one breast, kneading the mounds and pinching the nipples while Justin worked his way up her legs from her ankles. They all moved their hands as if in an orchestrated plan towards her pussy, reaching it at the same time. Three pairs of hands worked the lotion into her. Cade went immediately to her clit while Mark and Justin each worked one side of her pussy lips.

Marti was moaning even louder now, fisting her hands to hold her body still as they pulled and rubbed her clit and stroked fingers inside her.

"Just hold still, sugar," Mark murmured. "Let us pleasure you."

But Cade was having a hard time keeping it together. His cock was nearly bursting from its skin with his need to be inside her. The brothers had always prided themselves on their great control but, with Marti Jensen, Cade found his eroding by the moment.

As if by unspoken agreement they all stopped at the same time.

Marti's eyes flew open. "You're stopping? Now?"

"This is the build-up, sugar," Mark said. "The next act has you taming all three of us at once. That turn you on, Marti?"

"Yes," she breathed.

The flush turning her cheeks a beautiful shade of pink showed them exactly how aroused she was. The men looked at each other and grinned.

"I say we all take a swim," Mark suggested. "Then we'll throw the steaks on the grill." He pinched Marti's clit. "Gotta keep up your energy, sweet thing."

Cade could see she wanted to say more. Maybe protest the delay. But she just smiled her usual sexy smile...except when her eyes turned to him. Then her glance was smouldering and...something else.

What the hell?

"I think I'll turn on some music." Anything to distract himself. He rose to his feet and walked to the sliding doors that opened into the great room. Reaching inside to the wall, he flipped the switch for the CD player that he'd loaded earlier, and Carrie Underwood's voice floated out to them with the hard lyrics of *Some Lessons Learned*.

Cade wanted to ask Marti what lessons she'd learned that had brought her to this place and this time, but he knew enough to keep his mouth shut. He was struggling enough with the unfamiliar feelings that had grabbed him and refused to let go. Instead he followed her and his brothers into the pool. He dove beneath the water and came up behind her, sliding his fingers through the crevice of her ass before surfacing.

Mark was already standing in front of her, pulling and tugging on her nipples while his mouth ate at hers. Cade pressed himself to her back, pushing his throbbing cock against the crease of her ass before taking it in his hand and rubbing it up and down that hot slit.

Then he moved away, as did Mark, and the men began their usual water games — dunking and tackling each other while moving Marti back and forth between them, using every opportunity to touch her breasts or her cunt or her ass. They knew what they were doing. To take all three of them at once, she'd need to be at a high state of arousal and they were working her up to it.

After a while, they all pulled themselves out of the pool. Cade settled Marti again on the chaise longue while he and his brothers went about the process of putting the meal together. They ate at the umbrella table, talking as if eating a meal in the nude was the most natural thing in the world.

And then it was time for the main act.

Chapter Four

Once dinner was over and everyone had pitched in to clean up, they moved into the great room and spread all the giant-sized pillows out on the floor. While Marti waited for them, Cade quietly faced down his brothers in the kitchen about who exactly would fuck Marti in the ass. Justin reminded him they always took turns but Cade was resolute and stubborn.

"Jeez, Cade." Mark studied him. "Something going on here we should know about?"

"No." Cade shook his head and looked away. "Nothing."

"Bullshit." This was Justin. "You've got a weird look on your face. If there's a problem, you need to spit it out right now."

"My only problem is I claim her ass and that's that. Deal with it." He stalked from the room, aware that his brothers were staring after him, feeling their eyes boring holes in his back.

There shouldn't have even been a discussion about anything. They rotated who fucked their current playmate where, and technically Marti's ass should belong to Mark today. But today Cade was consumed with the need to be the one who took her there. To possess her.

Possess? What the fuck was up with that? Shit, shit, shit.

He was dealing with feelings he never expected to have and he wasn't sure how to handle them. He only knew her ass was his and he'd fight both his brothers to claim it.

He walked straight to Marti, who was sitting cross-legged on one of the pillows right where they'd left her. She turned her face up to his with a quizzical look in her eyes.

"Is there a problem?" she asked.

"No," he thundered. "There's no damn problem. I wish people would quit asking me that."

Deliberately he placed his hands beneath her elbows, lifted her to her feet then claimed her mouth like a wild animal claiming its prey. He thrust his tongue deep while gripping her head and slanting it to allow his tongue to move deeper. He felt her momentary surprise but then she just clutched his wrists, pressing her own tongue against his. Dancing with it. Duelling with it. He licked the smooth inner skin and the soft yet firm tissue of her gums. Swept the tip of his tongue over her teeth before plunging it deep into her mouth again. They were both oxygen-deprived when he finally lifted his head.

She stared at him. "Care to tell me what that was all about?"

"It was about kissing you," he growled.

But their gazes locked, and in her eyes he saw reflected back at him what they both knew—it had been about a hell of a lot more than that. And neither of them wanted to put it into words.

The CD player changed and another Underwood song drifted out to them. *Crazy Dream*, one of his favourites. Maybe that's what he was having. Crazy dreams.

Then Mark was beside them, running his fingers up and down Marti's arm and blowing gently in her ear. Tugging her away from Cade and lowering her to the cushions. Cade stood there and watched as his brothers arranged her just the way they wanted her, legs spread wide, arms over her head.

Mark knelt between her thighs and gently opened the lips of her cunt, exposing all the slick pink flesh there. Gently he slid one finger inside her.

"Soft and wet." Hunger edged his voice. He added a second finger and a third before leaning down and capturing her clit with his mouth.

Justin knelt to one side, taking a breast in his palm and closing his lips over the nipples. He flicked a glance at Cade, waiting for him to attend to the other breast. Digging deep for control, he knelt at her other side, palmed her breast and grazed his teeth over the hard nipple.

Marti was making those sweet sounds again, a cross between a whimper and a moan. Just the sound was enough to make Cade's balls ache and his cock pulse. He captured her wrists with his free hand and held them in place over her head while he and his brothers worked her body like a fine instrument, rousing her to the point of uncontrollable need.

From the corner of his eye, he could see Mark eating at her, lapping her with his tongue, tugging her clit with his teeth while he slid three fingers in and out of her very wet channel. Only a few minutes went by before Mark looked up and said, "She's ready."

Cade looked down at her. "You ready, sugar? For all of us?"

She nodded, sharp heat dancing in her eyes, her breasts rising and falling with each shallow breath.

They all moved then. Mark lifted Marti so he could lie down in her place. Cade and Justin helped position her so she was straddling Mark and then lowered her slowly onto his rigid cock. Every muscle in Mark's body tightened visibly as she sank down, down, down onto him, taking him deep inside her. He pulled her towards him and kissed her, then slipped a hand between them and began to manipulate her clit.

Justin knelt beside them, his cock in his hand, slowly stroking it from root to tip. He reached out a hand to cup Marti's chin and turn her face towards him.

"Open wide, Marti," he coaxed in a rough voice.

When she did, he rested the dark head of his cock on her bottom lip and rocked his hips, pushing it inside a little at a time.

And now it was Cade's turn. Although they were occupied with what they were doing, his brothers still glanced at him strangely, waiting for him to make his move. The move he'd been so damn stubborn about insisting on.

He picked up the tube of gel lying beside the pillows and knelt behind Marti in the space between her thighs and Mark's. Squeezing a generous amount on one finger, he spread the cheeks of her ass with his other hand and applied the lube to her anus, the tiny welcoming hole he'd had his finger in so recently. After making sure he'd thoroughly coated the opening, he pressed one finger inside, slowly and steadily, until it was in to the bottom knuckle. He slid it back out, added more gel and this time penetrated her with two fingers.

"You doing okay, honey?" Justin asked. There was obvious tension in his voice as he worked hard to maintain control.

"Yes." The word hissed from her mouth around his cock.

"Lean forward to me," Mark told her, cupping her breasts when she did.

When she did, it elevated her ass to just the angle that Cade wanted. Coating his cock generously with the gel, he spread the globes of her buttocks, positioned himself at her opening and thrust himself into her with a slow, steady glide.

"Mmmm," she moaned around the cock in her mouth.

Cade nodded at Mark, gripped Marti's hips for leverage and began to drive in and out of her hot, dark channel. In, out, forward, back, Mark loving her in cadence with him, cocks rubbing against each other through the thin membrane separating them. Some kind of music with a heavy, steady thump of bass surrounded them and he set his rhythm to it.

In, out, forward back. Faster, faster, faster.

This was heaven, pure and simple. Magic he'd never found with anyone else…and it scared the living bejeezus out of him.

Shit, Cade. You've got trouble at the Treble T. In spades.

He pumped steadily into Marti's willing body, doing his best to wait for his brothers but damn, damn, damn. The woman was about to burn him alive.

"I don't think I can hang on to this much longer," he ground out.

"Go," Mark rumbled, thrusting up into Marti's cunt, feverishly working her clit.

"Now," Justin shouted.

Cade drove in one last time then his entire body stiffened as his climax roared up through him and he pumped his release. As he spurted into her dark tissues, he felt Mark's cock pulse and empty into her pussy and heard Justin shout as he came in her mouth. Marti clamped down, crying out as she shuddered between the two men. All four bodies shook with the force of a shared orgasm, male groans mingling with the counterpoint of Marti's very feminine voice.

The spasms seemed to go on, until Cade was sure they would all spontaneously combust from its force.

And then they were spent, falling against each other in limp exhaustion. Marti collapsed on Mark's chest, Justin fell to the side, and Cade pulled slowly from the snug grip of her ass to roll onto his back. He lay there, totally undone, dragging air into his lungs, trying to sort through the sudden maelstrom of feelings assaulting his sex-drained body.

Finally he roused himself enough to lift Marti from Mark's body. He eased her from Mark's cock and lifted her into his arms. Her head nestled against his shoulder and her arms wound around his neck. A fine sheen of perspiration covered her body and her heart still hammered erratically.

"I'm taking her to the shower," Cade said, staring at his brothers as if daring them to argue with him.

But they just stared at him, stunned curiosity written on their faces.

He strode down the hall to his bedroom then into the huge bathroom. Holding Marti against him, he reached into the big shower and turned on the water, a fine mist spraying from multiple showerheads.

"This'll make you feel real good, honey," he crooned, kissing her forehead.

When the water reached the temperature he wanted, he moved them both into the big marble stall and let the water rain down on them, washing away the heavy odour of sex. He held Marti beneath the stream, brushing her hair back from her face and trailing kisses over her forehead and her cheeks, finally finding her mouth.

This kiss wasn't about sex, though. It was about something Cade wasn't even sure he could acknowledge. Still, he couldn't pull himself away. He had to keep tasting her mouth, smoothing his hands over her wet body, holding her against him as if he could make her a part of him.

Eventually he soaped and rinsed them both, dried them off and carried her to his bed. He didn't even turn on the light as he pulled back the covers and slid her underneath, climbing in behind her. Wrapping his arms around her, spooning her into his body, he closed his eyes and fell into the first peaceful sleep he'd had in ages.

* * * *

It was Monday again, the first Monday of the month, and Marti was again at the bar, writing up her order list for the liquor distributor. Periodically she stopped to sip at the cold drink at her elbow. The past month had been one of the worst she'd ever spent. Worse than when Chuck and Dan had told her they were moving on to someone else, that she demanded too much of them. Worse than when her lover before that had told her how turned off he was by her bizarre sexual appetite. Worse than the long weeks when she'd stood in front of a mirror, wondering if somehow her internal wiring was screwed up. It didn't help that the little radio behind her was playing *I'm So Lonesome I Could Cry*.

Why couldn't she have it all? The man of her dreams...who loved her but also wanted variety. With her. When they both chose. So maybe some people might think her outlook was a little strange. But she hadn't thought Cade Thompson would. And for a few moments that one Sunday, she'd thought they connected. That they were on the same wavelength. That there might actually be something real between them. When he'd taken her into the shower, he'd been so tender with her—caressing her, kissing her. And it hadn't been at all about sex.

She'd slept so peacefully in his arms.

But then she woke up and reality had set in and she'd known she was only entertaining foolish dreams. He could have any woman he wanted, *all* the women he wanted, any *time* he wanted. Why would he ever tie himself down to one, even if she did want them to play games now and then?

So she'd slipped from his bed before dawn, snuck out of the house without waking anyone then raced home to lock herself in her apartment. Her cell phone had rung several times but she'd seen Cade's number on the readout and ignored it each time. Late in the afternoon, a Treble T pickup had roared into the parking lot before slamming to a halt. Boot heels thundered on the steps to her apartment, but she'd ignored the hammering on the door. Just as she'd ignored his angry voice.

"Damn it, Marti, I know you're in there. Open the goddamned door."

For what? So he could read her the riot act? Be sure she understood the rules?

Eventually he'd left and she'd spent a miserable night huddled in her bed. What was wrong with her? The Thompson brothers offered the kind of sex she craved yet she only wanted one of them. Well, okay, sometimes it would be fun to share. But only if she really belonged to one of them and he controlled the situation. That's what she'd really been looking for all this time.

The problem was Cade Thompson had no more intention of tying himself to one woman than the state of Texas did of banning handguns. And without him claiming her, she was sure she couldn't handle another visit to the Treble T. How the hell had this happened? She'd had her heart broken once. That was enough. She'd sworn never to let it out of its steel cage again.

Yet here she was, anguished because Cade Thompson was so far beyond her reach.

She'd been all prepared to do battle with him in person, expecting him to show up any day with murder in his eyes, demanding an explanation for her hasty retreat. Making sure she understood that just because they'd all had a really good time didn't mean he owed her more than any other woman he took to the ranch. Or worse yet, firing her and sending her on her way. But not one of them showed up in the bar. Not even for a minute. And every week her pay was still direct-deposited into her bank account.

She was thankful they'd been especially busy because working herself into a stupor every day seemed to be the best thing she could do. The difficult part was avoiding Daisy's curious glances and prying questions, but she managed to make it plain there was nothing she wanted to discuss. She just didn't know how long she could go on like this. One of these nights, they were sure to come into Treble Shooters again and she'd be trapped.

The ranch hands that came often grumbled about how surly Cade had become and how the brothers didn't seem to be having much fun in life anymore. She wrote that off as just smoke in the wind. It was branding time at the

Treble T, plus she knew they were moving the cattle to winter pastures, so being surly made sense. And they probably didn't have time left over for fun.

Sighing, she finished her drink and headed for the tiny office to fax her order to the distributor. As she made her way down the short hallway, the back door opened and Cade Thompson himself stormed in. His faced looked like a thundercloud about to erupt and tension radiated from every muscle in his body. Marti stopped dead in her tracks, her eyes frantically sliding to the door of her office.

"Don't even think of it," he growled, moving so he was barely an inch away from her. "I waited long enough and you're not locking yourself in the office to get away from me."

"W-Waited?" She clutched the sheaf of paper to her chest. "For what?"

"For you to come to your senses."

Her eyes widened and she felt anger simmer low in her belly. "Come to my senses? About what? We all had a great time that Sunday. I knew exactly what was going to happen. I've played those games nearly all my adult life. Then it was back to business as usual."

"You snuck out of my bed and out of my house." His voice was accusing. "Did I do anything to make you feel unwelcome?"

Her tongue kept wanting to stick to the roof of her mouth. "I didn't want you to have to make the whole 'this was fun but now it's back to life as usual' speech. Been there, done that. I thought if I just left, you'd know I didn't want anything from you and we'd be fine." She tried not to sound pleading. "I don't want to lose this job, Cade."

"What if *I* wanted something from *you*? Did you ever think about that?"

She just stared at him as if he'd suddenly sprouted two heads. "Like what? Another Sunday? That's okay by me." But of course it wasn't. Not when she was just another name on a list to this man.

"No. Well, yeah, maybe. But only under certain conditions."

"Conditions? Like what?"

"Like this."

His mouth came down on hers and he kissed her with a bruising intensity. His tongue stabbed into her mouth, sweeping over every surface, while he slid his hands to her ass and pulled her hard against him. The swollen length of his cock pressed against her through their clothing.

"Feel that?" he asked, his lips still touching hers. "I've been like that every day since you walked out on me."

"Walked out on you?" She was trying to catch her breath. "I just made a clean exit." She swallowed hard. "And if you're so damn hard, how come you haven't had your whole list of women out there to satisfy you."

"Because I don't want anyone but you," he shouted.

They stared at each other, the words hanging in the air.

Finally she blinked. "W-What did you say?"

He let out a ragged breath. "You heard me. I just want you." He frowned. "I'm damned if I know how it happened, but there it is. I was so ungodly jealous that Sunday I couldn't see straight. You know why I wanted to fuck your ass so badly?"

She shook her head.

"Because that way I'd be claiming you. Making you mine. How nuts is that?"

Marti shook her head as if to clear her brain. "I don't understand. I thought you guys *liked* the games you played."

"I do. Yes. No. I mean…"

"What do you mean, Cade?"

He was still holding her so tightly against him she had to struggle to draw a full breath.

His mouth was almost touching hers again. "I want to settle down, Marti. I want a woman who belongs to me. Who feels about me the same way I feel about her." He gave her a lopsided grin. "But who still wants to play with my brothers once in a while." The grin faded. "On my terms."

She tried to find the right words but nothing came to her. She wanted to be sure she understood exactly what he was saying.

"You hear me, Marti? We have something between us that's real. I know you feel it, too. I saw it in your eyes that Sunday. If I'm wrong, just tell me."

"You're not." The words came out as a whisper.

"I've talked to Mark and Justin. They know how I feel. I'm going to build a separate house for myself at the ranch, and I want you to live in it with me. To marry me." The grin was back. "My brothers can have the big house to play all they want until either of them gets ready to settle down. And if my brothers are very, very good, we'll invite them over to play on special occasions."

He was so close his breath was a soft breeze on her skin. Her heart was hammering in triple time.

"That is," he went on, "if it's okay with you. Because I'll be in charge, not either of them."

"O-Okay." She hoped she heard him right.

"Okay, what?" he brushed his lips over hers. "You'll live in the house with me? You'll let my brothers come over and play now and then? You'll marry me?"

"Okay to all of it," she breathed, her gaze locked with his.

"Thank God."

She actually felt the tension ease from his body and he kissed her with new heat and added fervour.

Finally he lifted his head. "Just remember one thing, darlin'."

"What's that?"

"Nobody fucks that ass but me."

Marti wanted to laugh. She knew that was Cade's way of asserting his possession of her. Of making her his. And letting his brothers know just how things were.

"I don't think we'll have to worry about that, big guy."

"Tomorrow we're going to meet with an architect and then get bids from contractors." He turned her and guided her to the back door. "In the meantime, I think you should take me upstairs. If I'm not inside you in the next ten minutes, I might not live."

She laughed, a giddy sound. "I think I can handle that."

Minutes later that's exactly what she did, taking him into her body and rocketing them to an explosive release. But the biggest explosion was her heart bursting from happiness as she realised she'd finally have it all.

She reached over and turned on the little bedside radio. Immediately the notes of Kenny Rogers' *We've Got It All* floated into the room.

Cade looked down at her grinning. "We sure do, darlin'."

"You bet, cowboy."

And then he was sliding into her again.

WILD ABOUT THAT THING

Lisabet Sarai

Dedication

To Cole, with thanks

Chapter One

Ruby could feel it in her bones. It was going to be a good night. Only ten thirty, but most of the tables clustered 'round the stage were full. Lori had already lugged two extra cases of Heineken — tonight's beer special — up from the basement, and from the looks of the empties accumulating in front the customers, they were going fast. The bartender caught Ruby's eye and gave her a thumbs up. Everything under control.

Up front, the Night Travellers hit a dark groove, wailing through *Born Under a Bad Sign*. Zeke's fingers flew over the strings, improvising a high riff, while Jojo's bass kept the song grounded. "If it wasn't for bad luck, I'd have no luck at all," Zeke growled, torturing his guitar to match the pain in his voice. Damn, but the man sounded black, despite the mop of straw-coloured hair he kept pushing out of his eyes. Born in Mississippi, he must've soaked up blues in the water and the air. Certainly he could play with the best. Ruby was lucky to have him and his band, given the pittance she could afford to pay them.

As if he sensed her attention, Zeke picked her out of the shadows at the back of the club. She felt the warmth of the smile he beamed to her, a smile totally at odds with the desperate mood of the song. *You know why Zeke plays here,* her inner critic commented. *You're just taking advantage of him.*

He gets what he wants, she argued with the internal voice that sounded so very much like her mother's. *I treat him fine.* Of course, she got as much out of their relationship as he did. Zeke was a strong man with powerful desires. He could set her on fire. It wasn't her fault that he was so sentimental. You wouldn't expect it from a rough and tumble guy like Zeke Chambers—ten years a New York cabbie, a guy who'd seen every horror the city could dish out.

Her phone vibrated in her jeans pocket, interrupting her train of thought.

"Hey, hon. What's up? You should be in bed."

"I'm going, Mama. I just want to finish this chapter…"

"Isaiah Jones, it's nearly eleven and tomorrow's a school night! You shut your light off right now!"

"Okay, okay, Mama! But don't forget about your meeting tomorrow with Ms Rodriguez."

"Oh, right." Ruby sighed. Isaiah's grades were good but he was so small that he tended to get bullied. She needed to put a stop to that, somehow. "Thanks, hon. Three thirty, right?"

"Uh huh."

"I'll be there, don't worry. Then we'll walk back home together. Maybe stop for a banana split."

"Yum!"

"But only if you go to bed right now, you understand? I don't want to have to come upstairs and make you!"

"Of course. Good night, Mama."

"'Night, sweetie. I'll see you tomorrow afternoon." Ruby fought against the wave of guilt that threatened to swamp her. Sure, it would be better if she could awaken with her son, make him breakfast and see him off to school like a "normal" mom. But the club kept her up until three a.m. most nights.

Isaiah understood. She'd tried staying up until after he'd left, but he had seen how wiped out that made her. He insisted she needed her sleep. At thirteen, he didn't have any problem dressing and feeding himself — heck, he'd been doing it for the past two years, ever since she'd opened the Crossroads Blues Bar. He knew the club was her dream — the dream that had kept her alive after his bastard father took off with his leggy hygienist.

And the bar was finally starting to take off. Just last week, *Time Out* had published a feature about Crossroads. "A bit of Chicago or the Delta transplanted to Fourteenth Street," the reviewer had raved. That glowing memory almost balanced the effects of the letter she'd received this afternoon.

The crowd erupted into claps and whistles as the Travellers finished their number. "Thank you kindly, ladies and gentlemen." A decade in New York hadn't erased the softness of the South from Zeke's speech. "Welcome to our first open mic night here at the Crossroads. Hope you brought your axe, your sax or your harp — if you didn't, well, hell, you can borrow ours! Everybody gets the blues sometimes. This is the place to let it all out!"

Fresh applause greeted Zeke's invitation. He stood up there on the platform — his hands jammed into the pockets of his jeans jacket, his axe hanging around his neck—and grinned like the country boy he used to be. At six-foot-one, with the solid build of a halfback, Zeke was an imposing figure. He'd broken up more than one drunken brawl for her over the past two years and he had a temper that could be scary. To Ruby and Isaiah, though, he'd been nothing but kind. Whatever success the Crossroads could claim was largely due to him.

"To kick things off tonight, I want to invite a very special lady to join us here on stage. She's been through some hard times, friends, and she knows the blues. It's in her blood, passed on from her daddy, Jimmy 'The Harp' Jones. When she sings, she spills her soul. Ladies and gentlemen, put your hands together for Ruby Jones, the lovely owner of the Crossroads Blues Bar!"

Applause filled the club. Zeke's invitation hadn't been a surprise. They'd discussed having her warm up the crowd, and of course, she'd been performing since she was a kid. Nevertheless, his effusive introduction made her feel self-conscious. Ruby wished she'd worn something a bit more glamorous than her usual jeans and tailored shirt.

She picked her way between the tables, headed for the stage. Zeke held out a big hand. When she grasped it, he swung her onto the platform, and quite neatly, into his arms. The crowd roared.

Zeke brushed his lips across hers. His distinctive scent engulfed her—clean sweat, Jim Beam and Ivory Soap. It was like turning on a movie—she instantly remembered the last time he'd been inside her. His blond stubble grazed her cheek. She saw him in her mind's eye—body suspended above hers on powerful arms as he buried his cock in her pussy, fucking her with a smooth, steady rhythm while he scanned her face, focussed on her pleasure. She felt again the way he stretched and filled her. The seam of her jeans teased her suddenly swollen clit. She wondered if Zeke could smell her growing dampness. Hell, what about the rest of the band?

"Stop it," she whispered, pushing against his rock-hard chest.

Zeke released her with obvious reluctance. "I love her," he told the audience, eliciting a chorus of hoots and whistles. Aching, hungry and guilt-ridden, Ruby knew he meant every word.

She smoothed the wrinkles from her blouse, noting in passing the tautness of her nipples, and took a deep breath. "Good evening," she said into the microphone. As always, the amplified sound of her low alto startled her with its depth and richness. "I'm so glad to see you all. I hope you have a great time—that's why I'm here, to make that happen if I can. Like Zeke says, the blues is in my blood. I can't get away from it. I just gotta give in and let it out."

She turned to nod at Zeke and the other musicians. They picked up the intro to Bessie Smith's famous lament.

"Once I lived the life of a millionaire,

Spending my money, I didn't care.

I carried my friends out for a good time,

Buyin' them bootleg liquor, champagne and wine..."

The audience was as silent as a few dozen folks crammed into a low-ceilinged bar could be. Ruby dug deep and let the pain flow out into her song.

"Nobody knows you when you down and out

In my pocket not one penny

And my friends I haven't any..."

Zeke and Jojo gave her solid backing, keeping it simple and strong to avoid drawing attention away from her vocals. She didn't need to think—she'd learned this song at ten years old. She could sing it in her sleep.

She wanted to soar, to turn the sorrow in the piece into some kind of revelation, but worry weighed her down. She couldn't get her mind off the letter. It was from some fancy uptown law firm, scorn hiding behind politeness. *We regret to inform you…*

She paused to give Zeke and Jojo their solos, blinking hard in a fight against looming tears. *The new owner of the building at 127 Fourteenth Street has expressed an intention to not renew the lease.* Two years of her sweat and sacrifice, not to mention every penny she owned, down the drain. *Please vacate the premises on or before … The owner will be taking possession…* Why did she have nothing but bad luck? Didn't she deserve some happiness for a change? What was she going to do?

Zeke's chord change signalled the end of their solos. She nearly missed the cue.

"Mmmmm…when you're down and out…"

Ruby could feel Zeke gazing at her. If she lifted her head, she knew she'd see surprise and concern on his face. And he'd see the wet gleam in her eyes.

Down and out. Her voice wobbled, vibrating with emotion, as they brought the number to a close. The audience screamed its approval. Ruby bowed and tried to smile. She'd beaten the blues before. She wondered if she had the strength to do it again.

As the applause died down, Zeke and his boys struck the first chords of *Rock Me Baby*. Ruby launched into the rollicking tune, the driving beat automatically making her feel better.

"Rock me baby. I want you to rock me all night long.
Rock me baby, yeah, rock me all night long.

I want you to rock me baby, like my back ain't got no bone."

Zeke took up the second verse, giving her a chance to catch her breath. His sexy baritone vibrated deep in her stomach. He always managed to make this song sound so deliciously dirty, especially when they sang it together.

They reached the bridge. Zeke's guitar wailed like a cat in heat. Ruby scanned the audience. Thirty or forty people at least, clustered around the tables or leaned against the bar. Practically every seat in the place was taken. Men predominated, but there were plenty of women, too. She saw black and white faces, age-grizzled hair and sleek, modern dos, ragged jeans and designer sweatshirts.

Young and old, black and white, rich and poor — everyone moved with the music. Everywhere she looked, her customers swayed to the beat — nodding their heads, shaking their shoulders or tapping their toes. That's the way it was with the blues. You couldn't help it.

Except for this one guy, who perched on a barstool pretty close to the stage. He had skin the colour of milky coffee, a shaved head, aquiline features, and wire-frame glasses. He wore the top two buttons of his white business shirt open, the sleeves turned halfway up his forearms and the tails outside his trim jeans. His polished leather shoes looked expensive. The thing that drew Ruby's attention, though, was his aura of total concentration. One foot on the rung of the stool, he focussed on the band, drinking in the music. His lips pressed together. His hands, decorated with gold rings, lay still on his taut thighs. He wasn't grooving with the rest of the crowd, but Ruby could tell he was swallowing up every note.

As though he felt the weight of her gaze, the man turned his face towards her. Their eyes connected. His were dark as midnight, deep as a grave.

A bolt of heat flashed through Ruby's body. She thought she'd melt, right there on stage. Her nipples contracted into rigid peaks. Her pussy, already damp from the effects of Zeke's teasing, flooded with new moisture.

The man did not smile. His bottomless eyes burrowed into her soul.

Ruby felt an insane impulse to jump down and kneel at his feet. She teetered on her high-heeled boots, dizzy with desire, almost tumbling into the stranger's lap.

"Everything okay, darlin'?"

Zeke's whisper pulled her back from the brink. She sent him a quick, grateful smile as they joined their voices in the final verse.

"Yeah, rock me pretty baby, baby rock me slow

Want you to rock me baby, till I don't want no more."

When she looked up, after their bows, the stranger was clapping along with everyone else. *What was that all about?* Ruby wondered as she introduced the first guest who'd signed up for the open mic. *Never felt anything like* that *before.* As she left the stage and headed for the ladies', she didn't allow her gaze to stray in the stranger's direction, but that didn't help. She knew his eyes were following her every step of the way.

Chapter Two

Get hold of yourself, girl. You gotta pay attention to your business.

Ruby splashed cold water on her cheeks and brow and ran her fingers through her riotous black curls. For once, she agreed with her inner critic. Her life was complicated enough without the addition of tempting strangers who inspired irresistible lust.

Her heart was still beating a mile a minute, though. She could see the pulse in her throat, making the brown skin twitch. She was hot-blooded — Zeke often told her that, and she knew it was true — but there was a time and place for sex, and this wasn't it.

Her clit throbbed inside her soaked panties. Her nipples were so sensitive that the rubbing of her lace bra felt like burlap. She closed her eyes and tried to centre herself.

Breathe. That's what her papa used to tell her, before she got up to sing. Inhale, then let all the feelings you don't want pour out along with the bad air. The old trick still worked. Gradually, her skin cooled and her heart slowed to a more normal rate.

When she used the toilet, she saw that her bikini briefs were even wetter than she'd expected. Too bad she didn't have time to nip upstairs for a fresh pair, but she'd been in the john too long already. She needed to get back to work.

Ruby struggled to pull the damp, tight jeans over her ample hips. *It's like I'm a teenager again,* she thought with a bit of an inner grin. *Maybe I'm ovulating or something. There's gotta be some explanation.*

After the relative brightness of the rest room, the dimness of the club left her momentarily blind. She blinked, trying to get her eyes to adjust. It was a minute or two before she paid attention to what was happening on stage.

The band was playing *The Sky is Crying*, Zeke bent over his instrument, coaxing out mournful notes that almost sounded like sobs. Meanwhile, at the mic, in the spotlight, stood the stranger who'd made her sweat. He was picking at Jojo's bass and singing the lead.

Ruby caught her breath. The guy was amazing. His solid tenor voice wrung every ounce of emotion from the lyrics. His fingers walked the strings with a confidence born of long experience. He was every bit as good at Zeke, in his own way. The real deal.

Even on stage, though, his lean body hardly moved. He didn't tap his toes, or sway, or roll his hips. Ruby sensed the energy bottled up inside him, barely contained by his focus on the music. He was still but he was not at peace. The blues gnawed at his soul.

The lust she'd just managed to tame slammed back into her. The music coiled in her belly. Her clit pulsed in time with the beat. She rocked her pelvis and squeezed her thighs. She wanted him. She wanted to strip off her clothing and dance naked, shaking her full breasts and her ripe ass in his face. She wanted to break through his wall of control and make him beg for her.

Zeke raised his head from his picking, tossed his hair out of his eyes, and grinned at the crowd. Ruby's lust expanded. Now she wanted Zeke's burly arms around her, his blunt fingers teasing her aching nipples. She didn't know what the stranger's cock might be like, but oh, she could vividly imagine Zeke's fat rod pounding into her, pushing her closer and closer to the sharp edge of release. She needed that, needed it right now. Otherwise, she'd go crazy.

Her body screamed for someone's touch. She thought about easing her zipper down and slipping a hand inside her trousers. Would anyone notice? The bar was dark and all the customers were focused on the stage. It would be easy—she'd just have to keep quiet...

The end of the song released her from her trance of arousal. Ruby rushed towards the front of the bar, desperate to meet the mysterious bassist. The place had become more crowded, though. She had to inch her way forward through the sweating, clapping throng. By the time she arrived at the stage, the stranger was nowhere to be seen, though the audience was still applauding. Jojo's bass lay abandoned at the foot of the mic stand.

"Hey, darlin'!" Zeke greeted her with his typical warmth. "He's really something, isn't he?"

"Sure is. But where'd he go?"

"No idea. He practically ran off the stage. Almost like he was spooked by the crowd."

Ruby pushed past the doorman, out into the chill April night. She peered into the darkness. The sidewalks were empty. There was no sign of the smooth, self-contained stranger whose touch she'd craved so badly.

Just as well, commented the sour voice in her head. *The last thing you need in your life is another lover.*

* * * *

Ruby flipped onto her back and stretched, working the kinks out of her muscles. How delicious she felt—warm, relaxed, fuzzy with sleep and definitely well-fucked. Her pussy was a bit tender. It fluttered around her fingers as she explored the still-slick folds. Echoes of her three climaxes shimmered through her. There was a twinge at her shoulder, where Zeke had bitten her. She didn't mind. She'd marked him, too—her fingernails leaving bloody crescents along his back. They'd remind him of her for the next day or two.

He slept beside her, his breathing deep and even. A complex perfume hung in the air of her small bedroom—sweat and semen, pussy and sandalwood incense.

She didn't want to move, didn't want to think. She just wanted to lie there with her lover within reach and the rest of the world far away. Being with Zeke seemed to be the only thing that brought her this kind of comfort. She loved Isaiah dearly and enjoyed his company, but in her son's presence she could never quite banish her worries.

The thought of her son roused her. She leaned over to peer at the alarm clock. When she saw the time, she sighed and gave Zeke a gentle shake.

"Wake up, baby. You've gotta go."

In one smooth motion, Zeke rolled towards her and gathered her into his arms. Her breasts flattened against his furry chest. "Let me stay, hon," he murmured, nuzzling the sweet spot under her ear. His thickening cock prodded at the sticky juncture of her thighs. "It's still early…"

"Nearly six," Ruby replied, relaxing into his embrace despite herself. "Isaiah will be up soon. You know how I feel."

"You feel wonderful," Zeke replied, kneading her breast with one hand while wriggling the other between their bodies, down to her pussy. Ruby sucked in her breath as his fingers slipped inside her folds to stroke her clit. "And I can make you feel even better..."

"Zeke..." she began. He stopped her objections with a deep kiss. His moustache tickled her upper lip. She tasted the bourbon he drank between sets. She loved his soft, lush mouth—she couldn't pretend otherwise. The leisurely way his tongue played with hers suggested that he'd be happy doing nothing but kissing her forever.

"You don't really want me to go," he continued when they broke for air. "You're soaking wet, and your clit—" Ruby moaned as he flicked the swollen nub with one calloused digit. " —your clit is like a little marble."

"Yes... Oh, God, yes..."

Zeke reared up and settled back onto his heels, his fingers still dancing between her legs. "You couldn't wait to get my clothes off earlier," he commented. It was true. As soon as the club closed, Ruby had practically dragged him up the stairs to her apartment. "But I can tell you haven't had enough yet."

"No—yes—wait—oh!"

Zeke grasped one of her thighs in each meaty hand and pulled her open. Then he bent and swept his tongue along her cleft. Pleasure shuddered through her. She arched up, wanting more. Her lover teased her, flicking back and forth between her swollen lips, but avoiding contact with her clit. She thrashed underneath him, desperate for direct stimulation.

"Please...please, baby..."

Finally he took pity on her. He burrowed his face into her pussy and sucked hard. Lightning shot up her spine. Tension coiled inside her. Sinking her fingers into his hair, she forced his head deeper into her drenched cunt and ground her clit against his nose.

His teeth nipped the aching bud of flesh. The tiny pain cut her free. Pleasure welled up from her depths and spilled over. His strong hands held her fast, splayed and vulnerable, as she jerked against his still-lapping tongue.

Before the last sparkles of sensation faded, his cock was at her entrance. He drove into her still-quivering cunt, hot and hard. Her muscles clenched around his bulk and a new climax seized her, sharper and deeper than the one before.

Zeke didn't let her rest. He pounded into her again and again, just the way she liked, so fierce she thought he'd split her open. As he thrust, a third come gathered, like thunderheads on the distant horizon.

He raised her hips and draped her legs over his shoulders, manipulating her substantial body as though she weighed nothing. The new position let him go deeper. His cock filled her and took her over. His cock was the only thing in Ruby's universe.

Dimly she felt his fingernails digging into her butt cheeks. The sting was pure pleasure. The pang when he grazed her cervix was pleasure, too. Ruby snagged her rigid nipples and squeezed with as much force as she could muster. Pleasure. There was nothing but pleasure in her universe.

Zeke thrust faster, his rhythm becoming irregular. Ruby knew he was losing control. His eyes were screwed tight. His lips were drawn back from his teeth in a grimace of effort. She could feel his need. All she wanted from the world was to satisfy that need.

"Fuck me, baby," she urged. "Fuck me till I can't walk. Fill me with your jizz!"

His eyes snapped open. He groaned. She felt his cock jerk and dance as the cum surged out.

"Oh, God! Ruby!" he gasped. "Ruby…"

He gazed at her in something like adoration. She wondered, briefly, what he saw in her face. Then he reached down, pinched her clit, and once more sent her spiralling into sweet oblivion.

It took a while for them to recover. When Ruby checked the clock again, she nearly pushed Zeke out of bed.

"Time to get out of here," she urged, a bit frantic. "Now!"

"Now is that the way to treat the man who gave you so many orgasms?" Zeke's gentle rebuke just made her feel worse. However, he was already on his feet, pulling on his jeans.   "When will you let me really spend the night with you, Ruby? You know how I feel."

"Isaiah…"

"Isaiah's just an excuse. He's thirteen, for heaven's sake. He knows what's going on between us. He knows I love him, too. Just as I love you."

Zeke enfolded her in his arms. His denim jacket grazed her bare breasts, waking phantom fragments of her past pleasure. She sagged against him, suddenly tired.

"Let me take care of you," he continued in a soft voice. He brushed his lips over her hair. "Marry me, Ruby."

Ruby stiffened. "No, Zeke. I've had it with marriage. You of all people should understand that. You're my friend."

"I'd like to be more than your friend, darlin'. But I don't want to put you under any more pressure. You've got enough on your plate already." Zeke sighed as he pulled on his boots. "See you Tuesday night, then. Call if you need anything."

"I will." Ruby gave him a solid kiss that generated new heat in her pussy. "Thanks, baby. For everything."

She locked the apartment door behind him. She missed him already.

Chapter Three

Ruby didn't bother to go back to bed. She could hear Isaiah moving around in his room, directly above hers. Belting her robe around the waist, she made her way to the kitchen nook and opened the refrigerator. She'd been right—there were still four eggs, plus milk and a crusty lump of parmesan. She'd make them a proper breakfast for a change.

Butter was sizzling in the cast iron skillet by the time Isaiah appeared. "Mama! You're up!" He gave her an enthusiastic hug, almost causing her to drop the spatula. Ruby loved the fact that he still felt comfortable with that kind of physical affection. Most teenage boys would rather die than touch their mothers.

"Got done so late last night, it hardly seemed worthwhile going to sleep. Maybe I'll nap after you're gone."

Her son sniffed. "Cheese omelette? My favourite!" Without being asked, he pulled half a loaf from the bread box and dropped two slices into the toaster.

"I thought pancakes were your favourite," Ruby teased. "And what about biscuits and gravy?"

"Um — gee, I like everything you cook!" He plumped himself down in his usual chair. Ruby set two steaming plates on the table and seated herself across from him. He dived into the food as though he hadn't eaten in a week.

Ruby took a bite of her own omelette. The heavenly taste of fluffy egg spiked with sharp cheese made her realise she was hungry as well. When she wasn't eating with Isaiah, her meals tended to be pretty irregular.

As his plate emptied, her son became more talkative. "How was the open mic?"

"Fabulous! I'd say there were twice as many customers as usual for a Sunday. It was a great idea, hon." Isaiah and some of his friends had a rock band called Spyder City — Isaiah played bass. After some of the girls in his class had begged to join him and his buddies on stage, he'd suggested that maybe Ruby should invite her customers to perform.

Her son nodded sagely. "I knew it. Everybody loves to be in the spotlight."

"Some impressive talent, too." Ruby's thoughts slipped back to the lean stranger who'd triggered such powerful desire.

"Yeah? Maybe you should invite some of them to be regulars. Uncle Zeke's band is awesome, but people like variety."

"Oh really? Since when are you an entertainment mogul?" Ruby grinned and brushed her hand over his close-cropped skull. "No — don't bother with the dishes, hon. I'll take care of them. You go brush your teeth."

"You sure? I've got time, and you must be tired."

"I'm fine. Anyway, it's nearly seven-thirty. You'd better get going!"

Without further argument her son scampered up the stairs. Like many old buildings in New York, the one that housed Crossroads was taller than it was wide. The bar was located on the ground floor. On the second floor, Ruby had set up an office. The third floor held her bedroom, the kitchen and dining area and a tiny living room. Isaiah had the whole top floor to himself. He'd been thrilled when he'd seen the place – a spacious bedroom plus a second room where he could study and practice his bass or his violin.

If the owner evicts you, you'll need to find a new apartment, too. Ruby's good mood evaporated as she remembered the letter. Resolutely, she pushed the thought into the background. She had ninety days, according to the notice. Today she needed to focus on today's problems.

You could marry Zeke and move in with him. The voice just wouldn't give up. True, Zeke had a big, rent-controlled place on Gansevoort Street, not far from the Crossroads. Not that it mattered. If she got kicked out, that would be the end of the bar. She didn't have the resources to start again.

Damn it, she'd find a way. Determined to get past her funk, Ruby dumped her robe on the bed, stepped into the cramped shower stall and turned the faucet on full blast. Stinging needles of water pelted her skin, almost too hot to bear. She worked up a lather between her palms and spread the soap over her ripe breasts and round belly. *No stretch marks.* She surveyed her body with approval, admiring the contrast between the snowy foam and her smooth, espresso-coloured skin. *Mama was right about some things, at least.* After Isaiah's birth, at her mother's insistence, she'd applied cocoa butter twice a day to keep the skin moist and supple and did regular exercises to regain the muscle tone. Now she looked considerably younger than her thirty-four years.

Not that it had mattered, of course. It hadn't stopped Otis from sleeping with every young bitch who crossed his path. He hadn't seemed to notice he already had a foxy wife.

Ruby massaged a handful of suds into her pubic curls, then slid her fingers into her cleft. The touch woke delicious echoes of her coupling with Zeke. *Screw Otis*, she thought. *I'm better off on my own, without the bastard.* She resisted the impulse to stroke her clit. For one thing, the bud was so sensitive that even the barest contact was painful. *I can take care of myself. I can fuck who I please — just enjoy myself. No strings.* An image of the stranger's handsome, intense face swam into her mind. *Even him.* Her thoughts were edged with defiance. *Why not?*

* * * *

On Monday nights the bar was closed. Typically, Ruby spent Mondays in her office — ordering supplies, paying bills and dealing with all the other mundane aspects of running a business. A blues club might seem like a glamorous and exciting endeavour, but for the most part it was no different than a nail salon or a dry cleaning shop.

She was in the middle of entering the past week's receipts into her computer when the bell rang downstairs. Annoyed at being interrupted, she saved her work then flipped over to the security camera screen. Who could it be? She wasn't expecting any deliveries.

The grainy image showed a lanky male figure wearing a leather jacket. At first Ruby didn't recognise him — he was peering into the diamond-shaped glass panel set in the door—but when he looked up at the camera lens, she caught her breath.

It was the bald-headed, bass-playing stranger from last night.

Her cheeks grew hot with embarrassment and confusion. What was he doing here? The bell jangled once more. Could she ignore it? Pretend that the building was empty? He pushed the button yet again, apparently convinced that there was someone to hear it.

Finally, Ruby pushed her chair away from the desk and headed down the stairs to the ground floor. After all, last night she'd chased after this man. She'd felt bitter disappointment when he disappeared. Now here he was, as if her fevered fantasies had made him appear at her doorstep.

When she reached the door, though, she hesitated. Her heart slammed against her ribs. Her mouth was dry, while perspiration pooled under her arms. She had the sense that by opening to this stranger, she was taking some irrevocable step...something that would change her life forever.

Don't be superstitious. Unfastening the bolt, she swung the door open.

Those eyes—like lasers boring into her soul. Her nipples leapt to attention under her turtleneck sweater. Her tailored slacks grew damp in the crotch.

"Ms Jones?" Even when speaking, the man's voice was musical, a deep river tumbling over polished stone.

"Um—yes? Can—can I help you?" Ruby forced herself to hold his gaze, regardless of the effect it was having on her body. When he finally broke the stare to survey his long-fingered, graceful hands, she rejoiced in her small victory.

"I — I'd like to talk with you, if I might. About a business matter." Strange, but he appeared to be as uncomfortable she was. "My name is Remy Saint-Michel. Here's my card."

As she took the snow-white rectangle, his fingertips brushed hers. Electricity shot up her arm and down her spine. She could practically hear it crackle.

Ruby inspected the card, grateful for an excuse not to look at him. The raised lettering on fine, thick parchment spelled out his name, a phone number and the words "Bienville Associates", presumably the name of his company. Not a clue as to what sort of enterprise it might be.

"Come up to my office, Mr Saint-Michel," she said finally. If they remained huddled in the doorway much longer, she was afraid she might jump him. She led the way through the dim, quiet bar then up the stairs, acutely aware of the way her ass moved under her trousers as she climbed. Was he watching? She knew he was, with the same concentration he'd lavished on her when she'd been on-stage. She was glad she had the appointment at Isaiah's school — she was dressed more smartly than usual.

"Please." Ruby indicated the chair opposite hers. "Coffee?"

"No, thank you." Remy Saint-Michel leaned slightly forward in his seat, legs apart. His hands rested on his thighs. His lips pressed together in a tight line. He was as still as he'd been the previous night. His leather jacket hung loose and open on his broad shoulders. The ribbed jersey he wore underneath revealed the contours of his muscular chest and abdomen almost as clearly as if he'd been naked. Meanwhile his tight jeans made it clear that he was as affected by her presence as she was by his.

He did not speak. He seemed to be engaged in some inner struggle. *Maybe he's having the same problem as me,* Ruby thought, feeling giddy. *Trying to keep from tearing my clothes off.*

Finally, she couldn't bear the tension. "Mr Saint-Michel?"

"Call me Remy." Behind his glasses, his eyes were practically black, but flecked with gold.

"You were here last night...Remy. You sang with the band." She paused, inviting him to continue.

"Yes...um..." His response petered out. Meanwhile the non-verbal signs were stronger than ever. His fingers dug into the flesh of his thighs. His nostrils flared as though seeking her scent. And the bulge in his groin told her all the things he didn't seem to be able to say aloud.

"You were amazing. Have you performed before?"

"Not really. Just for friends — and family..." He stopped again. Ruby had a sense of power held in check, and under that...pain. Was he shy? Last night he'd appeared completely at ease, sure of himself. The blues was about opening up and letting the feelings flow. To do that, you needed to be strong. Brave.

"Are you here because you'd like a job, Remy? Do you want to work at the Crossroads?"

"Yes, yes, that's it." Relief was obvious in his face. His lips relaxed into a half-smile, revealing perfect white teeth. "I want to work for you, Ms Jones. I want to sing the blues. No, that's not right. I *need* to sing the blues." He reached for her and her heart leapt into her chest. All he did was grasp her hand, but it was enough to make her melt.

"I understand," she murmured. She thought she did, too, even though this man was a stranger. She didn't know his story, but somehow, she knew his heart.

As if by a pre-arranged signal, they both rose to their feet. Remy took a step forward, bridging the gap between them. He pulled her against his chest while his arms encircled her. Ruby tilted her chin, offering her mouth. He bent to press his lips to hers.

"Ruby," he breathed, drawing her tighter.

Everything about him was smooth—his lips, his tongue, his clean-shaven cheeks, the hands that slipped beneath her sweater to stroke her back. His kiss was like warm silk slithering over her flesh—soft, rich and voluptuous. She floated, allowing him to feast on her mouth while his fingers roamed over her flesh.

He tasted of anise and smelt of some sharp, herbal cologne. His lean body shifted as he groped, working to unfasten her bra. His rock-hard erection grazed her pubis. She moaned into his mouth.

Her own hands were busy inside his jacket, glorying at the lean muscle she found there. She raked a fingernail lightly across his nipple. He went wild, plunging his hands into her pants to grab her ass and grinding his crotch against hers.

"Wait, wait!" Ruby cried, gasping, afraid he'd tear her best slacks. She broke their clinch long enough to unfasten the waistband, draw down the zipper then push the pants down over her hips.

Remy watched, unsmiling, with that same intense focus that had snared her last night. "I want to see you naked," he said at last. His voice was velvet and ice, shivering through her.

There was no question of disobeying. It simply never occurred to her. She kicked off her boots, stepped out of her slacks and hung them over the back of the chair. Next came the sweater. Ruby worked as fast as she could, wanting to give him what he'd asked—what he'd demanded — but it felt as though she was moving in slow motion. She reached behind to unhook her bra and her breasts bounced free, the nipples taut and juicy as ripe raspberries. His gaze never wavered as she hooked her thumbs into her bikinis and pulled them to her ankles.

Her lower lips felt hot and swollen. Her clit throbbed, barely hidden by the damp tangle of black curls between her thighs. Remy stared at her. The heat built and built, until she couldn't bear it.

"Touch yourself," he ordered. Desperate, without shame, Ruby plunged three fingers into her soaked pussy. A fountain of pleasure gushed in her depths. Her knees almost buckled. Remy noticed. He grabbed her hips and lifted her onto the desk, then stepped back again to watch her. "Continue — please."

Ruby spread her thighs wide, wanting to show him everything. She was rewarded by his raised eyebrows. Moisture dribbled out, pooling beneath her on the wooden surface. She pressed the heel of her hand firmly against her pubic fur. Curving her fingers to catch the pad of nerves near the front of her sex, she stroked in and out. Meanwhile her thumb jiggled her clit, flicking it like a switch. Electricity arced through her.

"Pinch your nipple," Remy commanded. She dug her nails into the nugget of flesh. Pleasure tugged at her clit, pulling her closer to the edge. "Harder. Make yourself come."

Raising her knees and bracing her heels against the desk, she drove her fingers into her hungry sex. With her other hand, she squeezed and pulled her nipples, first one and then the other. Tension coiled in her body, drawing tighter by the instant.

She'd never masturbated with an audience before. She would have guessed that being watched would make her self-conscious. Remy's gaze had the opposite effect. She felt wanton, gloriously slutty, her juices spilling out everywhere, her slick, swollen cunt naked and exposed. The dark hunger in Remy's eyes pushed her towards even greater lewdness. Releasing her tortured nipple, she slouched down so that he could see her anus.

Remy licked his lips as he watched her index finger disappear into her rear hole. Ruby didn't know what made her hotter — the pleasure of that slight penetration or his expression of awed lust.

The knot of sensation at her core was ready to unravel. She hovered on the edge of climax. Without thinking, she closed her eyes so she could concentrate.

"No! Watch me!" Remy growled. She forced herself to meet his incendiary gaze.

Up to this point, he'd been motionless, observing her. Now he ripped open his fly. His erect cock leapt out, long and slender, smooth and dark as milk chocolate. He spat on his palm and pumped himself once.

He's going to come all over me, Ruby thought wildly. The sight, the idea or a combination of the two, sent her spinning into her climax. After the long climb, the release was dizzying. She yelled and thrashed on the desk, knocking her coffee mug to the floor and scattering her papers.

She recovered to find him poised between her splayed thighs, his cock sheathed in latex. "Now I'm going to fuck you," he told her, his lips twisted into the first real smile she'd seen on his face. "The way you want me to..."

Ruby lay back on the ravaged desk, her clit pulsing with residual pleasure. "Yes," she murmured. "Please."

All at once her gaze fell on a scrap of paper near the edge of the desk. "Bye, Mama. Don't forget about Ms Rodriguez." The note Isaiah'd left her this morning...

Remy's erection nudged at her slick folds. "Wait!" Ruby cried. "What time is it?" She raised herself onto her elbows and turned to check the clock on her computer screen. "Two fifty! Oh shit!"

She backed away and swung herself off the desk, then started groping for her clothes.

"What's wrong?"

"I'm sorry." Ruby grimaced as she pulled her panties on over her drenched pubic hair. "I've got an appointment at three-thirty with my son's teacher. I've really got to go." She pulled her sweater over her head then ran her fingers through her curls. "You've got to go, too" she added. "Come on!"

With obvious reluctance, Remy tucked his still-erect penis into his jeans and zipped up. "Have dinner with me tonight." He snared her arm and dragged her into a firm embrace. "Please, Ruby."

She started to melt. If only she didn't have this meeting... "I can't. I'm really sorry but Mondays are the only nights when Isaiah and I can have a leisurely dinner together."

"After dinner drinks, then."

"But Isaiah..."

"I'll only keep you for a few hours. I know your time is scarce. How old's your son?"

"Thirteen."

"Old enough to stay home on his own, I should think. And when's his bedtime?"

"Ten p.m. on school nights..."

Ruby shooed him down the stairs. "I'll pick you up at ten-thirty," he called over his shoulder. She grabbed her coat on the way out of the office.

"I don't know…" Ruby locked the front door of the bar behind them. They stood together in under the awning, with its silvery "Crossroads" logo.

Remy ran his thumb along her jaw line. Ruby trembled at his touch.

"Don't disappoint me, Ruby." She heard the pleading behind the steely imperative.

"All right," she said, checking her watch. Three-ten. Damn. "Ten-thirty. Now, I've got to run."

She hustled down the sidewalk in the direction of the school, but stopped at the corner to look back.

Remy was gone.

Chapter Four

Marisol Rodriguez turned out to be a plump, no-nonsense woman a few years Ruby's senior. She listened gravely as Ruby described the incidents Isaiah had shared, taking careful note of which students had harassed the eighth grader. At first, Isaiah hadn't wanted to name names, fearful of being labelled a stool pigeon. Ruby had worked hard to convince her son to open up.

"I'll inform the principal about this, Ms Jones. Don't worry, we have programmes to deal with this sort of issue. The boys involved will receive counselling first. They'll be disciplined if the problem continues. Meanwhile, we have a group of trusted high school students who can accompany Isaiah back and forth to school if you'd like. It might be good for him to have a male role model in any case, given ..."

Ruby bristled slightly at the implications of the unfinished sentence. Sure, she was bringing up Isaiah on her own, but his father wasn't the sort of man she'd want her son to emulate in any case. She swallowed her annoyance. Ms Rodriguez meant well. "Are any of the monitors interested in music?" she asked. "Isaiah's crazy about rock and roll. He'd love a 'big brother' who could show him some licks."

Ms Rodriguez smiled. "I'll see what I can find out."

Isaiah was waiting for Ruby in the school library. He stuffed his textbooks into his backpack and followed her out to the street.

"So, how about some ice cream?" She gave his shoulders an affectionate squeeze and was pleased that he didn't flinch away.

"Nah, I've got too much homework," he replied. "Plus I've gotta practice. We've got a gig next Saturday night."

"A gig? Where?"

"Shelley Feinstein's dad is throwing her a huge birthday party. She wants Spyder City to play. " Isaiah grinned up at her. "And what Shelley wants, Shelley gets."

"Her parents will be there, right?"

"Not just her parents but the maid and the cook, too. Don't worry, Mama. They're paying for the cab both ways *and* giving us each ten bucks for playing. It'll be our first professional gig."

Ruby suppressed a giggle. The boy was dead serious. "Your granddaddy would be proud of you, hon." Isaiah had only met his grandfather a few times, when the travelling bluesman came off the road. He'd died when the boy was six. But Jimmy Jones was the one who'd given Isaiah his first musical instrument—a harmonica that the boy still cherished.

"Okay, scratch the ice cream then. What do you want for dinner?"

"Can we do take-out pizza from Antonio's?"

"You don't want me to cook?"

"You've got enough to do, Mama. Anyway, we haven't had pizza in a month."

"All right. You're the boss on Mondays. But I'll order a salad, too."

"Whatever. I've gotta go study. Call me when you're ready to phone for the pizza!" They'd reached their building. Ruby unlocked the door and Isaiah scampered up the stairs. Ruby took the two steep flights more slowly. Passing the door to the office, she caught a hint of her own musk. Her cheeks burned and her pussy clenched as she remembered how she'd writhed on the desk, naked and wanton. She was glad her son—hopefully—wasn't old enough to recognise the tell-tale scent.

She needed to talk to Isaiah about tonight, make sure he didn't mind staying alone for a few hours. All at once, she was exhausted. *Not surprising when you're up all night screwing*, commented her internal critic. Ruby didn't have the energy to rebut the accusation. In fact, she could barely keep her eyes open. Not bothering to take off anything but her shoes, she threw herself onto her bed and drifted almost immediately into sleep.

* * * *

A gentle knock on her bedroom door roused her from her slumbers. "Ruby, darlin'? You okay in there?"

Zeke. Guilt threatened to drown her. But why should she feel guilty? She was her own woman. She didn't belong to Zeke or anyone else.

"I'm fine. Just taking a nap. Somebody kept me from sleeping last night..."

Zeke poked his head into the room. "Don't blame me, you little fox!" A warm grin lit his amiable features. "You were the one who jumped me, as I recall."

"And you really put up a fight, too," Ruby countered, sitting up as he settled himself on the bed next to her.

"Yeah, well, why would I do that? I'm not crazy!" Before she could stop him, he swept her into one of his energetic kisses. Today he tasted like the Juicy Fruit gum he chewed while driving his cab. Ruby knew she should resist—Isaiah was upstairs and it was probably close to dinner time, too—but Zeke just felt too damn good. He wrapped his burly arms around her while his tongue burrowed into her welcoming mouth and his moustache tickled her nose. Before she knew it, his string-calloused fingers were busy under her sweater.

"Wait! Zeke baby, hold on!" Reluctantly, Zeke loosened his grip on her body. Desire buzzed through her. She tried to ignore it. "Isaiah…"

"I know, I know." Ruby detected an uncharacteristic hint of irritation in her lover's drawl. "The boy. But he's busy doing his homework. He told me so when he answered the door." He leant back a bit, eating her up with his eyes.

Despite her determination not to succumb to Zeke's charm, Ruby's nipples peaked and her pussy moistened. "You know how I feel, baby."

"Yeah, I do. You're just so hard to resist, lady."

He looked pretty good himself. He wore his work clothes—trim navy blue chinos and a striped shirt with a button-down collar. The trousers weren't as tight as the jeans he wore when he was off-duty, but they couldn't hide the bulk of his hard-on. His eyes sparkled like sapphires under his bushy blond brows and a lock of his honey-coloured hair hung down over his forehead. She fought the urge to brush it back into place.

"I thought maybe I could join you two for dinner," he continued. "Then maybe after, we can all watch a video or something."

He didn't say anything more, but she knew what he was thinking. After Isaiah was safe in his bed, maybe Zeke could spend some time in hers.

Ruby remembered her assignation with Remy—remembered the insane lust he'd inspired. It had been intoxicating, but scary too. For a moment, all she wanted was to say yes to Zeke's unspoken question, to trade the risky promise of a stranger for more familiar pleasures. But she'd given her word to Remy. Anyway, what gave Zeke the right to barge in to her life, assuming she'd be available?

"We'd love for you eat with us," she began, trying to be gentle. "But afterward, I've got a date."

Zeke's forehead knitted into a frown. "A date?" His voice was dark as gathering thunderclouds. "Who with?"

Ruby laid her hand on his arm. That was a mistake. The feel of his warm, firm flesh under the fine cotton made her want to take it all back—to swear that she wanted only him, to beg him to fuck her. "I don't think you need to know," she said, her eyes cast downward

She felt like such a traitor. Of course, they'd agreed when they began that their relationship should be non-exclusive. Still, she hadn't been with anyone else, not for two years. Why should she, when she had a strong, sexy, generous man like Ezekiel Chambers?

But Remy...she'd never experienced anything like the magnetic pull she'd felt in his presence. She had to find out what it would be like to fuck him. To get him out of her system.

"Thanks for being honest," Zeke said softly. "That's something at least."

"I'd never lie to you, baby. That's just plain wrong. Otis taught me that. It's just this one time, anyway."

"You do what you need to do, Ruby. It won't change how I feel about you." He blinked once or twice, then stood up. "Guess I should go."

"No, please—stay for dinner. Just pizza and salad, but we'd love to have you. I'm sure that Isaiah will want to tell you the big news about his band."

"You sure?"

"Positive." Ruby gave him a hug, fighting the urge to rub herself against the still-obvious lump in his groin. "Let's go call Antonio's."

"You got someone to stay with the kid while you're out?" Zeke asked, as Ruby retrieved the pizza menu stuck onto the refrigerator door.

"Um—no... He'll be okay. It's just a couple hours." Ruby's doubts resurfaced. Maybe she really should call Remy and cancel. Things were just too complicated...

"I'll hang out here until you get back, then."

"What?" Ruby stared at him, astonished and grateful. "You're gonna babysit, while I go meet another man? What are you, some kind of saint?"

"Nah, I'm just a guy who loves you and wants you to be happy. I know you won't be able to relax if Isaiah's home alone."

Ruby rewarded him with a kiss. What had she done to deserve him? "You know me too well, baby."

"I do, darlin'. You're like Skynard's free bird. Ain't nobody can put you in a cage."

* * * *

Dinner was surprisingly comfortable. Isaiah chattered on about Spyder City and their upcoming gig. Zeke shared stories from the five years he'd spent on the road before he came north, playing in bars and roadhouses. Ruby talked about her father — brilliant, charming, and restless. "By the time he died, he'd visited every state," she told them, "carrying the Chicago blues to the furthest corners of the country. Back then, everybody knew Jimmy Jones." She didn't mention how much she'd missed him, left behind with her mama for six months at a time while he had adventures and sang his heart out.

Every now and again, she'd catch Zeke looking at her with a wistful half-smile. Still, the way he teased her and joked with her son suggested that he wasn't too distressed by her evening plans.

As it grew later, however, Ruby became increasingly nervous. While Zeke and Isaiah watched TV, she washed the dishes, then disappeared into her room to shower and change. She'd explained that she had an evening appointment, letting her son believe that it was business relating to the bar. This twist of the truth bothered her, but she could hardly tell the boy that she was meeting a man, could she? And she *had* met Remy in the club. He'd even talked about performing.

She deliberately avoided provocative clothing, choosing a batik skirt that flowed to her ankles, a long-sleeved Indian blouse, and a bright scarf to tie back her hair. Nevertheless, when she emerged from her room, Zeke gave an appreciative whistle.

"Stop it!" Ruby scolded, although she was secretly pleased by his reaction.

"Can't help myself. You look gorgeous."

"You always think I look gorgeous."

"You do. It's not my fault." Zeke turned to the boy beside him. "Aren't I right? Isn't your mama beautiful?"

Isaiah agreed a vigorous nod. "Sure is!"

Ruby checked her watch. It was already ten-fifteen. Her stomach did somersaults. "Flattery will get you nowhere, young man. You should have been in bed a quarter of an hour ago!"

"Sorry, Mama. Uncle Zeke and I were having such a good time…"

"I know, it's great to have him here, but I don't want you falling asleep in class tomorrow."

"I'll make sure he gets to bed," Zeke interrupted. "You go ahead." She thought for a moment that he'd embrace her, but he just brushed his lips across her cheek. "Have a good time."

* * * *

Ruby had never been so confused in her life. She stood on the footpath in front of Crossroads, the April wind whipping her hair into her face, scanning the traffic creeping along Fourteenth Street. *What am I doing here, when my lover is waiting upstairs?* At the same time, her stiff nipples tented the cotton of her blouse and her clit beat a steady pulse between her thighs. *How do I know Remy won't hurt me?* When she remembered his uncertainty and his need, though, she was somehow certain she could trust him.

Ten-thirty-five and still no sign of him. Ruby was ready to flee back to the safety of Zeke's arms when a black stretch limo glided up to the kerb. The rear door popped open.

"Ruby." The lush warmth of Remy's voice melted her. "Get in."

She seemed to flow into the dim, leather-scented interior, her bones like jelly, her flesh malleable as soft wax. The door had scarcely closed when he gathered her to his body, taking her over. His smooth lips demanded a surrender she gave gladly. He sucked the breath from her lungs than returned it, perfumed with anise. His kiss was all-consuming, driving out the last shreds of rational thought.

"Ruby," he murmured into her hair, tearing open the buttons of her blouse, scooping her breasts out of her bra and cradling them in his palms. "I haven't been able to think about anything but you." He rolled her straining nipples between his fingers.

His touch opened the flood gates in her sex. In an instant, she had returned to the place he'd left her hours ago—soaked, wide open and desperate for his cock. She broke their embrace and hauled her voluminous skirt to her waist, exposing her drenched panties. Her moist ocean scent filled the vehicle. His nostrils flared and his lips curled into a smile.

Leaning towards her, he drew a fingertip across the wet fabric hiding her pussy. Her inner muscles tightened as sensation spiralled through her. He circled her engorged clit with the pad of his thumb. "Oh...!" Her breath came quick and shallow. Pleasure twined through her, coiling into an aching knot on the verge of unravelling.

Impatient with Remy's teasing, Ruby yanked her bikini down her legs. Her companion buried his fingers in her pubic fur, seeking her centre. "Yes...!" she hissed as he flicked at the swollen bead of flesh. "Ah..." She arched up, lightning coursing along her spine. Still kneading her clit, he sank two fingers into her slick folds. She struggled to open wider, to take him deeper. The elastic waistband of her underwear bit into her thighs.

"Be still," Remy ordered. "Don't move." A flash in the shadowed space of the car, a brush of cold steel against her skin, and the inconvenient garment fell away, leaving her naked and empty.

But not for long. Remy tugged at his zipper and his cock sprang free, urgent and proud. It glistened with pre-cum in the intermittent flashes of light coming through the tinted windows. Saliva pooled on Ruby's tongue. She wanted to taste him, to swallow him whole. More than that, though, she wanted his hard dick inside her, stretching her, filling the aching chasm between her legs.

His eyes met hers, burning with lust in the half-darkness. It took no more than five seconds for him to roll a condom down over his rigid organ. Then he was looming over her, one knee on the seat, the other leg braced on the floor. He seized her thighs, holding them apart, and drove his cock into her hungry cunt.

Yes! Ruby felt instant relief as his silky hardness slid over her heated tissues and settled in her depths. With his cock buried to the hilt, he ground his pubis against hers, triggering frantic spasms in her clit. She was close to coming already. He pulled back. The sucking sound of her clinging pussy-flesh filled the small space. Before she could process her new emptiness, he rammed back into her, taking her over once more.

"Remy..." she moaned as he pierced her again, and yet again. She tried to wrap her legs around his waist. With a growl, he forced her thighs back open. She understood what he wanted, without him saying a word. Stillness...and surrender. She lay motionless beneath him and simply let him fuck her.

It was glorious. He plunged his rod into her pussy, again and again, seeming to increase the force with every entry. Ruby's fingernails scored the upholstery as she hung on for dear life. Each stroke sent currents of pleasure sizzling through her. Her clit beat in time with her lover's thrusts. Taut and trembling, she teetered on the edge of release.

She searched the face hovering above her. Remy's usual composure had vanished, to be replaced by a fierce glee. His brows knotted with effort. His lips drew back in a tense grin, exposing gleaming white teeth. He wielded his cock like a sword, slashing into her, possessing her. She yielded without a struggle.

Their eyes met. *Take me*, she thought—or maybe whispered—letting her last barriers fall. Faint tremors of climax stirred in her depths, slowly bubbling to the surface.

All at once, he was open, too. She sensed pride, gratitude, triumph. Underneath ran a thread of despair. She read it all in his face. For all his power, this man was fragile, wounded, broken.

A shock of connection—he saw her comprehension and mirrored it back. "Ruby..." he groaned, driving deeper than ever, to her very core. She felt the swell and pulse of his flesh as he erupted inside her, then came herself—a rich, full, rolling come, like voices lifted in song. A million strands of pleasure wove into a perfect harmony, a crescendo that left her in a state of limp bliss.

Chapter Five

A cessation of motion brought Ruby back to her senses. In her frenzied lust, she had completely forgotten where they were—driving through the streets of New York in a fancy limousine—but now the vehicle appeared to have stopped. *The driver probably saw everything,* her inner critic commented dryly. *You put on quite a show.*

She brushed the thought away. She had more important concerns.

"How about that drink I promised you?" Remy looked worried and a bit sheepish. "Come upstairs. You can clean up, and I'll find some safety pins for your blouse…"

Ruby surveyed the wreckage of her clothes and shook her head. "No. Take me home, please." She didn't know how she was going to explain her disarray to Zeke, but she had to get out of Remy's presence. He had tucked his cock back into his trousers. However, she remembered it all too well—its smooth, tawny curve, its delightful hardness… A whiff of his herbal scent tickled her nose and her battered pussy ached anew. Their crazy fucking hadn't dampened her desire in the least.

If anything, she wanted Remy more than ever. She'd seen behind his mask of self-control. She understood now that he harboured some secret sorrow. Motherly sympathy mingled with irresistible lust. It was so tempting to believe that her love could heal him.

"I'm sorry, Ruby." He took her hands, running his thumb across the back of her wrist and sending sparks straight to her sex. "Honestly, I didn't intend to overwhelm you. I thought we'd have a nice, civilised cocktail, get to know each other a bit…"

"Never mind. It was what I wanted. I'm sure you know that…" She forced herself to smile, battling a growing panic. She couldn't afford this. Her life was too complicated already. "But I've got to get back to my son. Tell your driver, Remy. Now."

With a sigh and a shrug, he followed her instructions. The limo started to move once more.

"When can I see you again? Tomorrow?"

"I've got to take care of the club. We're open every day except Monday."

"But after closing…?"

"I don't think it would be a good idea." She clutched the edges of her torn blouse, trying to hold it shut and hide her erect nipples. Her body screamed for contact with his. She shifted, putting more space between them. The leather was sticky under her bare thighs.

Remy frowned. "I thought you enjoyed yourself as much as I did…"

"I did—too much. Forgive me, but I really can't handle you right now. I'm terribly sorry. This was a huge mistake. We can't see each other again."

His voice was almost too soft for her to hear his reply. Still, it echoed in her mind as she stood on the kerb, watching the car slide away into the night. "But I need you, Ruby. More than I've ever needed anyone."

* * * *

Ruby poured herself another shot of Johnny Walker and downed it in a single gulp. Alcohol was never a solution — she knew that — but right now she craved oblivion. She didn't want to think.

Upstairs, her son slept — hopefully soundly — and Zeke awaited her return. How could she face him, with her clothes in shreds and another man's cum drying on her skin? *You're a filthy, cheating slut.* A third of a bottle hadn't been enough to drown out the scornful voice. If anything it was clearer than ever. *Just like your miserable daddy.*

No! Her father had loved them, even his sharp-tongued, demanding wife. Ruby remembered the way her parents would disappear into the bedroom together when he first came home, and her mother's satisfied smile afterward. Hot blood. It was her father's legacy, as much as the music was.

She'd always been proud of her sensual nature. Now, though, it seemed to have landed her in an impossible situation. Two lovers…and she wanted them both.

Sure, she'd told Remy to stay away, but would he follow her instructions? He knew where to find her. And if he showed up again, would she really have the strength to resist him? If lust didn't betray her, compassion would.

She swallowed another shot and shook her head. Then there was Zeke. His offer to care for Isaiah tonight was just the most recent evidence of his devotion. A good, decent man, a brilliant musician and a skilful lover who valued her pleasure at least as highly as his own. Ruby grew warm as she summoned memories of his kisses and his cock. She was lucky he hadn't given up on her.

Damn! She loved Zeke. She could admit it to herself, if not to him. And strange as it seemed after such a brief time, she felt close to loving Remy, too. Meanwhile, competing for her time and concern, there was Isaiah and the bullies—the bar—the eviction notice—the bills... It was just too much. For the first time since Otis left, she felt like giving up.

Ruby gulped down another whisky. Finally she was beginning to feel the buzz. A couple more shots and maybe she'd pass out.

But then Zeke would worry, wouldn't he? And what if Isaiah came downstairs tomorrow morning and found her, stinking drunk and barely dressed?

With a sigh, Ruby heaved herself off the stool and headed for the stairs. She might as well face the music. It wasn't like she had a choice.

The room whirled around her. She stumbled, her arms flailing in an attempt to keep her balance. Somehow she managed to sweep the scotch bottle off the bar and onto the floor, where it exploded, raining glass.

"No more booze for you," she giggled, staggering against a stool and knocking it over. The wooden clatter made her ears ring. "You've definitely had enough." Walking was clearly impossible now that her legs had turned to jelly. Ruby crumpled into a heap at the foot of the stairs.

"Nobody knows you when you're down and out," she sang to herself. "Mmmm—nobody..." Her head had filled up with cotton wool. Dizziness seized her when she opened her eyes, so she kept them closed. It wasn't so bad, down there on the floor. Smelt a bit like old beer, but that was okay...

"Who's there?" A harsh voice tore into her half-conscious dreaming. Bright light flooded the formerly dark bar. Pain stabbed behind Ruby's forehead.

"Turn it off," she moaned. "Hurts."

"Ruby? Jeez, Ruby, what's wrong?" Zeke's broad, even-featured face swam into focus.

"I'm drunk. Very drunk." Her laugh turned into a hiccough.

"So I see." He pulled her to a wobbly stand then hoisted her onto his shoulder as though she weighed nothing. "Well, let's get you upstairs." *He's so strong*, Ruby thought, contentment cradling her despite her dizziness. The muscles of his back flexed under her cheek as he climbed the two flights to her apartment. She rubbed her face against the smooth cotton of Zeke's shirt, breathing in his distinctive, familiar scent. *I really am lucky. Any other man would have kicked my ass and then walked out.*

* * * *

"You want to tell me about it, darlin'?" Zeke was stretched out naked on Ruby's bed. Ruby cuddled against his side, her head on his shoulder. The curly hair on his chest tickled her chin. His warmth, his strength — it was bliss. She didn't want to spoil it.

"Was it your date?" her companion persisted. "Did the guy hurt you or something?"

She cringed. Obviously Zeke had noticed her torn blouse. He'd undressed her and then held her under a cold shower, hand over her mouth to stifle her shrieks so she wouldn't wake Isaiah. Then he'd forced her to take an Alka-Seltzer and drink two glasses of water. Now she was feeling almost normal, aside from a profound sense of exhaustion.

"No—nothing like that."

"Did you have a good time, then?"

A good time? What a bizarre way to describe one of the most intense fucks of her life! Ruby just nodded. Zeke might be an angel, but she doubted he wanted to hear all the gory details of her encounter with Remy.

"So why the booze, then? I've never seen you drunk before, in the three years I've known you."

She hiked herself up on her elbow and gazed into his eyes. "Sometimes—well, sometimes it's just too much. Dealing with the bar, raising Isaiah…everything. It's a lot for me to handle."

"You don't have to deal with it by yourself, hon." He drew lazy circles around her nipple with one blunt forefinger. Ruby shivered, the delicate touch evoking shimmers of pleasure. "I'm here to help."

"You're part of the problem, baby." His wounded look unleashed a flood of guilt. "What I mean is, it would just be so easy to depend on you. It's really tempting. But I need to stand on my own two feet. You know that."

Zeke eased her onto her back. "Yeah, I understand, with my head." He trailed kisses from her earlobe down her neck to the hollow of her throat, then tasted the ripe flesh of her breast. His hair was a tangle of gold against her mahogany skin. When he looked up again, she was well on her way to melting, her pussy soaked and her clit swollen. "My heart—well, that's another story. I want to take care of you, and I can't help but feel hurt when you won't let me."

Ruby reached for his sturdy erection, running her thumb over the slippery cap. "There's at least one way you can take care of me, baby."

Zeke settled on top of her. His cock slipped into her moist cleft with no effort at all. "All you have to do is ask," he murmured, setting up an easy rhythm. She hooked her heels behind his back and they moved together, rising and falling like a ship on the waves.

He felt so very good inside her—a perfect fit, stretching and filling every hungry inch of her pussy. She fluttered her cunt muscles around his bulk the way he loved. His mouth captured hers and they shared their breath, joined above and below.

There was no urgency, no strain. They climbed together, pleasure building upon pleasure, the journey as satisfying as the goal. Ruby scraped her fingernails along Zeke's back. As she expected, he bucked his hips and skewered her more roughly. Zeke reached between his legs to press his thumb against her clit, making her moan and squirm beneath him as she always did.

Now he pounded her ferociously, as though he'd split her apart. She gripped her knees to her chest, opening herself to his delicious assault. He bent to catch one of her nipples between his teeth. The slight pain morphed into fierce delight by the time it reached her clit. He fucked her hard, ravaging her body, giving her what she craved. Still, their wild gyrations didn't touch the core of peace, the quiet connection with this man she knew so well.

A pulsing in her depths, a shift in his breathing, some clue told her when he was about to come. Her climax welled up to meet his, sweeping through her with the force of a tidal wave. The last shreds of her worry and guilt washed away, drowned in irresistible pleasure.

"I love you," she whispered, amid the fading echoes of their ecstatic release. She didn't know whether he heard her, but she had to admit truth...and damn the consequences. Zeke deserved at least that much.

* * * *

Ruby woke to find the mellow sunshine of afternoon streaming in her window. She rolled over to check her alarm clock. Well past four! She swore under her breath and tried to rise. Her muscles ached as though she'd run a marathon, her tongue was furry enough to need a shave, and someone was pounding an anvil in her head. *What do you expect when you drink half a bottle of scotch and screw every guy who comes on to you?*

She didn't have time to argue with her mother's proxy. She needed to pull herself together and get downstairs. Happy hour began at five. Zeke and Lori both had keys to the club, but Ruby always liked to be there when the doors opened to customers.

A hot shower soothed some of the soreness away, although she winced when she pointed the sprayer towards her battered pussy. *I've had enough sex in the last twenty-four hours to last me for a week. I've got to give it a rest,* she resolved. Still, the sting of the water on her clit woke memories, and the memories kindled new desire.

She found that she couldn't wear her usual jeans. The friction in her crotch was unbearable, simultaneously painful and arousing. Shaking her head, she donned a calf-length denim skirt and purple knit top.

Three-quarters of an hour later, after mouthwash, coffee and two aspirin, Ruby felt almost human. She checked in with Isaiah, who was busy with homework, then made her way down to the first floor.

The sight that met her almost sent her scurrying back upstairs.

Fading light from the street filtered in through gaps in the curtains. Aside from a pool of brightness at the bar, where Lori was setting up, the club was dim, but there was movement up on the stage, and then, music…

"You said you was hurting,
Almost lost your mind,
And the man you love,
He hurts you all the time,
When things go wrong,
Go wrong with you,
It hurts me too."

Zeke sang the first four lines solo, but a second voice joined in on the refrain, a familiar tenor that made Ruby's heart sink and her nipples tighten. She stumbled, knocking a stool against the wall and drawing the attention of the men at the front of the club.

"Ruby! Look who showed up!" Zeke switched on the spot above the stage. Perched on the chair next to him, cradling an American Deluxe Strat, was Remy. "He says you invited him to play."

"Good evening, Ms Jones." Remy skewered her with that intense gaze, peering across the room as though he'd read her mind. At the same time, his smile looked almost apologetic. "You didn't say when I could start. I figured today was as good a day as any."

Ruby wanted to drop through the earth. Zeke was watching, though, a broad grin curving under his moustache. She swallowed her panic and strode forward, offering her hand. Grace under fire, her papa had told her. That was what counted, when things got tough.

"Mr Saint-Michel." Her skin tingled when their palms locked. He did not prolong the gesture, but she felt the ghost of his touch when he released her. "Welcome to Crossroads."

"Call me Remy."

Ruby nodded, not trusting herself to speak. Zeke stepped into the gap.

"We've been goin' over some arrangements. Remy's gonna play with the Travellers for a while, to get the feel of things. I think you should give him solo billing soon, though. He's a natural."

"You told me you hadn't performed before," Ruby said out loud. *What are you doing here?* she asked silently. *I told you to stay away.*

"Not professionally. I had a restaurant, though, back in New Orleans. I used to entertain my customers." *I couldn't,* his eyes answered. *I need you.*

"I can't afford to pay you anything."

"I understand. I don't need the cash." She struggled to retain her composure as she recalled his luxurious vehicle—and the scene that had unfolded inside. "I sing for the love of it. The blues seems to be the only thing that makes me whole."

"I know what you mean, man." Zeke clapped Remy on the back, clearly charmed by the newcomer. "When everything goes to shit, you've still got blues to lift you up. It's a strange kind of magic, how singin' about trouble and sorrow can bring you so much joy."

Ruby tried to summon some anger at Remy for intruding into her life. The only emotion she felt, though, was desire. She looked from one of her lovers to the other, as they chattered on about chords, tempo, New Orleans versus Delta styles. So different, but both so appealing... She wanted them both. But she'd sworn to herself that she'd quit sex for a while. She planned to keep that vow, no matter how difficult that turned out to be. She just hadn't expected to be tempted so quickly.

"I'll leave you two to work. Let's start the first set at eight, okay?" Ruby had to get out of their presence before the pussy juice started running down her thighs. "I'm going to open up, then grab a bite before the rush."

After unlocking the door to the club, she dragged the "Happy Hour" sign out to the sidewalk. A crisp breeze stirred her curls, but the air she drew into her lungs hinted at the softness of spring.

The impending twilight held a strange peace. She could hear blaring horns and rumbling trucks over on Eighth Avenue, but they seemed a million miles away. Most of the traffic on Fourteenth was on foot. A passer-by bid her good evening. She returned the greeting with a smile. Gradually her heart slowed and the blaze in her sex subsided to a background glow.

She could do this. She could keep control. The club was more important than her personal satisfaction.

Chapter Six

The rest of the night sorely tested her resolve. She tried to stay in the background, giving Lori a hand, letting Zeke and Remy wow the crowd. She couldn't keep her eyes off them. The added voice and guitar gave Zeke's band a richer, more complex sound. The two men alternated on solos — Zeke's raw and energetic, Remy's slower and more mournful, both spectacular. You couldn't tell that Remy was new. He and Zeke read each other's cues, picked up each other's riffs, as though they'd been playing together for years.

At one point, she headed down to the basement to bring up some more beer. She sat on a pile of cartons, her eyes shut, savouring the quiet and the solitude. The scuff of a sole on the stairs interrupted her meditation.

"Ruby?" Remy cupped her chin and raised her eyes to his. The banked embers of her lust burst into flame.

"What are you doing here?" She twisted away from him, into a corner, fighting the attraction. "You're supposed to be upstairs playing."

"We're on break. I was looking for you." Before she could stop him, he pulled her into a fierce embrace, taking possession of her mouth. His tart scent filled her nostrils. Blood rushed to her clit. As though he knew, he pressed his lean thigh into the gap between hers, kindling a blaze of pleasure. Meanwhile, his hands slipped under her jersey and roamed across her bare back, seeking the clasp to her bra.

She rocked against him, the sweet hardness of his thigh making her pussy swell and weep. More hardness lodged against her belly. She let her hand fall from his shoulders to trace the curve of his erection. She burned to feel him inside her once more. One thumb grazed the side of her breast, that delicate spot under her arm. With his other hand, he raised her skirt and groped for the elastic of her panties.

The first exquisite brush of his fingers across her damp bush reminded her of her vow.

"No, Remy!" Pushing him away might have been the most difficult thing she'd ever done. She steeled herself to ignore the hurt in his eyes.

"But...you want me. You're soaked. There's plenty of time. We don't go back on for another fifteen minutes..."

"No." Ruby reached behind her back to refasten her bra. "Please, no. No more sex, not now at least."

"Then when? Just tell me, *chere*, and I'll be there."

"I don't know." She smoothed down her skirt. Deliberately turning her back on him, she lifted a case of beer from stacks against the wall. "Here. Make yourself useful."

"What's wrong, Ruby?" Remy's eyes narrowed. "Is it Zeke? He's your lover, right?"

"No—yes... I mean, we're lovers, have been for years, but that's not the reason I can't make love to you. Zeke and I haven't made any promises. But I need time to figure out what's best for me, what I really need. Not just what I want. I have responsibilities, Remy. I have a dream..."

"I'll help make your dreams come true..." He stood before her, misery etched in every line of his face. She knew he would have grabbed her again if he had not been holding the beer. Ruby's chest ached.

"I'm sorry, baby. You can help by not trying to tempt me. Just be patient. I have to do things my own way."

Remy didn't approach her again. He disappeared after the last set without saying goodbye. Zeke, however, came up behind her as she was locking the liquor cabinets for the night, capturing her in his burly arms.

"Ready for bed, darlin'?" He nuzzled her neck, warm and wet, familiar and soothing. Ruby leant back, letting herself relax into his strength. Encouraged, he hefted her breasts and flicked his thumbs across her nipples, sending sparks skittering through her. "I'm feelin' really good tonight, but I know you can make me feel even better."

His hands moulded her form, across her ribs and down her belly, kneading her ample hips and ass before reaching around again to cup her pubis through her skirt. Meanwhile he rubbed his rigid cock back and forth in the cleft between her rear cheeks. "Feel what I've got for you? I've been craving you all evenin'."

She forced herself to turn away from that delicious pressure to face him. "Not tonight, Zeke. I'm exhausted." She kissed his cheek. "I don't think my body can handle any more sex right now."

"We can just cuddle, if you like. You don't need to worry about Isaiah—he saw me upstairs this morning and didn't bat an eyelash." Ruby shook her head, handing him his jacket. He looked stricken. "Please, darlin'…"

"It's not Isaiah. It's me. I need some time by myself, Zeke. If you love me like you say, you'll let me be."

Anger clouded Zeke's sky-blue eyes. "This is about the other guy, isn't it? Your 'date'. You're fucking him, so you don't want me anymore."

"No, no, baby, that's not it. I swear I do want you. You don't know how much. I'd like nothing more than to invite you upstairs and tumble into bed with you."

"Then why don't you do it?" Confusion replaced irritation. "I don't get it."

"It's hard to explain, but please, Zeke, give me a bit of space. You're my friend as well as my lover. Help me."

"All right. You know I'd do anything for you. But if you change your mind…"

Ruby laughed and gave him a closed-mouth kiss before hustling him out the door. "You'll be the first to know, baby."

Ruby locked the club and trudged up to her apartment. *I did it*, she thought. *I did the right thing.* She should have been proud. Instead, she felt lost, alone and desperately horny.

* * * *

The week rolled on. Word got out about the Traveller's new line up, and the club was packed every night. On Thursday, Remy did a solo set. The crowd went wild. Ruby started thinking about hiring a waitress to relieve some of Lori's load.

Both Remy and Zeke honoured her request and kept their distance. Sometimes she'd catch Zeke eyeing her hungrily or feel Remy's razor-sharp stare stripping her naked, but neither tried to seduce her. As she lay in her empty bed, the evening's music ringing in her ears, she almost wished otherwise. Her body screamed for a touch other than her own.

Friday morning Ruby awoke with the dawn, energised and optimistic. She fixed biscuits and gravy for breakfast, smiling as Isaiah wolfed his down and asked for a second serving.

"Mama—can I stay over at Skip's tonight? We're going to be rehearsing from after school till late." Isaiah was still bubbling with excitement over his Saturday gig.

"I don't want you up till all hours..."

"We'll be in bed by eleven. I promise... Please? Pretty please?"

"Okay, okay! Just leave your phone on in case I need to reach you."

"Sure. You're the best mom in the world."

Hardly the best, when you manage to have breakfast with your son only once or twice a week.

Oh shut up, she told the nagging voice as she cleared the table. Still in her robe, she descended to her office. She extracted the eviction notice from her to-do pile. Today seemed like as good a day as any to tackle the issue. She dialled the number on the letterhead and made an eleven o'clock appointment with Henry Fletcher, Esquire. Mama had always told her to confront problems head-on. Her spirits soaring, she went upstairs to don her best suit, stockings and heels.

* * * *

"I'm very sorry, Ms Jones, but as I indicated previously, my client wishes to remain anonymous. He gave us very clear instructions."

Ruby shifted in the uncomfortable wooden chair. Henry Fletcher's pale, narrow face wore a polite mask, but she heard the hint of scorn in his words. She glanced around the office at the Ivy League diplomas on the dark panelled walls, ranks of ponderous legal tomes, Fletcher's massive desk—all designed to intimidate. She refused to be cowed. "How can I negotiate with my new landlord," she said, keeping every trace of her frustration out of her voice, "if I don't know who he is?"

"The new owner of the premises does not wish to negotiate."

"Then what can I do?" *Don't let him hear how desperate you are.*

Fletcher's nostrils flared, as though he'd caught a whiff of some disagreeable odour. "Simply vacate the premises as requested, Ms Jones. That will be the simplest thing for everyone."

Not for me, she wanted to shout. She pressed her lips together to stop herself as Fletcher's perfectly coifed blonde secretary led her to the door.

She took a cab home. Her earlier energy had fled. She couldn't face the notion of dealing with the subway. The traffic on Fifth Avenue was hellish. It was past one by the time she stepped into the cool, beer-scented dimness of the Crossroads.

Ruby sat at the bar for a moment, gazing at the stage. She could picture them up there, singing their hearts out. Remy and Zeke. Had she made a mistake, pushing them away? But she couldn't handle them both. It was just too complicated. And how could she give one of them up?

Would they still be part of her world if she had to give up the club? What would happen to them all?

Tears gathered in her eyes as she started up the stairs. She noticed in passing that the door to her office was ajar. She pushed it open and took a step inside.

"Why didn't you tell me?" Zeke sat at her desk. He waved a sheet of paper in her face. She recognised the fancy stationery. "Damn it, Ruby, I'm your friend. When you're in trouble, I wanna know!" His normally fair complexion flushed beet red. His brows drew together in a furious scowl and his eyes were blue steel.

"I—I didn't want to bother you," Ruby stammered. "It—um. Well, it's my problem. I figured I'd deal with it."

"Your problems are my problems." He rose to tower over her. "When are you going to understand?" For a moment she thought he was going to take her in his arms. She held her breath, watching the struggle on his face. *Please,* she begged silently. She desperately needed the comfort she knew he could provide.

But he turned away, sinking back into her chair, burying his face in his hands. After a moment, he looked up. His anger had fled. In its place she saw pain and resignation.

"This isn't working, Ruby. I think it's time for me to get out of here. I can't get through to you. Sure, you'll give me your body—though lately not even that—but you won't allow me into your heart. I'm heading back to Mississippi. New York's just too cold for me."

"Zeke—no—please..." Ruby grabbed his arm. Life without Zeke... The idea was too bleak to consider. She'd tried not to depend on him, but now she couldn't imagine what she'd do without him.

"Don't go! Please! I'm sorry I'm so prickly. It's just that—after Otis... Well, I swore that I'd make it on my own, without any man to prop me up. After taking care of myself for so long, it's hard for me to let go. But I love you, baby, honestly I do. And if you stay, I promise to show you."

She pulled Zeke out of the chair and into her arms, holding on for dear life. At first he held back, but after a moment he returned the hug. His warm, masculine scent surrounded her, flooding her with carnal memories. Her nipples sprang to life. Heat flooded her cunt.

He nibbled her ear and palmed her breasts through her best silk blouse. "God, I've missed you, darlin'. I've rubbed myself raw, thinkin' of you…"

"Let's go upstairs." Ruby reached down to stroke his growing erection. "We've got the place to ourselves…"

As though to contradict her, someone rang the bell on the street level. "What the hell?"

Zeke rumbled, licking his way down her throat. "Just ignore it."

"Ah—um… It could be Isaiah. He's supposed to be at a friend's this afternoon but…he might have forgotten his keys…" Reluctantly, Zeke released her so she could check the security camera.

Ruby gasped. The lean, leather-clad figure outside rang again.

"What's he doing here?" It was impossible to miss the suspicion in Zeke's voice.

"I don't know…" She pressed the button to release the lock. Remy bounded up the stairs and burst into the office.

"I've got to talk to you, Ruby!" He seized her hand. As usual, his touch made her burn. "There's something you need to understand. I'm so sorry, I should have told you…" He stopped, sniffed, and sucked air into his lungs, as if inhaling her essence. "Oh, *chere*, I've missed you so these last few days…" Before she could protest, Remy engulfed her, his mouth cemented to hers in a kiss that left her weak and breathless.

"Uh – hum." Zeke's voice shattered the lascivious trance induced by Remy's presence. "So I was right after all." He stood up, favouring them with a half-smile. "If you'll just let me past, I'll excuse myself so you two can be alone."

Ruby released her hold on Remy so she could block Zeke's path. "Wait! Zeke, please! I don't want you to leave, baby. I love you."

Remy whirled her around to face him. "What about me, *chere*? Should I go, then? I was under the impression that you wanted me, but perhaps I was wrong." Fury blazed in his dark eyes, but Ruby saw that was only a mask. Underneath lurked an ocean of sorrow, threatening to drown him.

"No, no – I do want you. Oh God, Remy! I think I love you, too."

"You can't love both of us, darlin'. Be reasonable. You've got to choose." Zeke shrugged. "He's younger than I am, handsomer, a lot richer. Hell, he's even a better musician. Take him. I'll understand."

"Don't be silly. You're the one who's loved and supported her, who's helped her build her dream. I'm basically a stranger. Ruby, *chere*, I don't know if I can live without you, but Zeke's your true love. It'll break my heart, but I'll go. Choose him. It's only right."

Ruby looked from one of her lovers to the other, as each pleaded the other's case. They were both so dear...

All at once the solution was crystal clear. "Who are you, telling me to choose? Why do I have to choose? Why can't I have you both? That is, if you're game..."

"You can't mean..." A blush painted Zeke's cheeks.

"I do."

"Are you sure?" Remy licked his lips.

"I've never been so sure of anything in my life."

A long, eloquent look passed between the two men. Zeke brushed his hair out of his eyes. Remy nodded. Each of them took one of her hands. Electricity sizzled through her.

They led her up the stairs.

Chapter Seven

Ruby sank down onto the bed, suddenly unsure. Without a word, Zeke began to undress. She swallowed hard, her pantyhose growing more sodden by the instant as he revealed his blond-furred torso and muscled thighs. He stepped out of his briefs, setting his erect cock free. It reared up from the red-gold tangle at his groin, swaying a bit, like a tree branch in the wind. Sporting a wicked grin, he stroked it once or twice to coax a bead of moisture from the fat bulb. Ruby clutched the bedspread, her heart slamming against her ribs. Was this really happening?

No sooner was Zeke naked than Remy began to disrobe. He kicked off his boots, then dragged his shirt over his head and tossed it into a corner, to be followed by his jeans. Gone was the composure that had first drawn her attention... Was it really less than a week ago? Urgency and impatience vibrated in his every gesture. His swollen penis arced towards the ceiling in a graceful curve, bobbing with his pulse. He struggled for control, his hands clenched into fists by his sides. His skin gleamed like polished oak, smoothed over the sculpted curves of his hairless chest and lean flanks. Revealed to Ruby for the first time, his naked body was every bit as compelling as his face. She fought the urge to literally throw herself at his feet.

Her suit jacket felt hot and constraining. She shrugged it off her shoulders. The silk of her blouse revealed her taut nipples, straining through the lace of her brassiere. Her musk escaped the confines of her panties and hose. She was dying for them to touch her, but neither man moved. She was the one in charge.

"Please," she managed to choke out, holding out her arms. "Don't make me wait any longer!"

In an instant, they were both by the bed. Remy crouched down to remove her shoes. He kneaded her insteps and arches. She tingled all over. He worked his way up her legs—massaging her calves, working his thumbs into the pressure points above her knees, stroking the insides of her thighs with light touch that shot straight to her pussy. As he worked, he pushed her skirt up into a crumpled mess in her lap. She didn't care. She leant back to give him access to the elastic circling her waist. In one swoop, he relieved her of her underwear and stockings.

Meanwhile, Zeke knelt behind her on the bed, his thighs flanking her hips, his chest against her back, and his erection flattened against her spine. He reached around to unfasten her buttons, his blunt fingers brushing against the heated skin below her bra. The transient contact made her yearn for more. He removed her blouse, taking care not to damage the delicate garment, then addressed himself to the hooks of her bra. By the time she released the breath she was holding, he had bared her breasts. Her plentiful flesh spilled out of his palms. Zeke thumbed the swollen tips and lightning streaked down to her clit.

"God, you've got gorgeous tits, darlin'! Juicy and firm as Georgia peaches!" Zeke gave the aching nubs a pinch, making her squirm. At the same time, Remy's slender fingers parted her labia and warm breath stirred her moist folds.

"Oh..." She hardly had time to moan before Remy's mouth fastened on her pussy. "Oh—oh, my God..." He burrowed into her, sucking her flesh into his mouth while swiping the flat of his tongue across her clit. Sensitised by days of self-imposed celibacy, her hungry cunt spasmed with pleasure under his expert attention. She tilted her pelvis and parted her thighs, trying for more contact. Remy probed her crevice, making her crave deeper penetration, before returning his attention to her clit.

Her whole being concentrated on the tongue dancing in her pussy. A climax curled in her belly. Remy's mouth coaxed it closer to the surface.

All at once there was heat and wetness from a new source. Zeke's ripe lips surrounded one nipple. He swirled his tongue around the engorged bead of flesh, then applied delicious suction. His moustache brushed her bare skin, soft and sensual. Just when she thought she'd burst from the pleasure, he transferred his mouth to the other breast, leaving the first soaked with saliva, chilled and tingling. He used his teeth but Ruby felt no pain, only a brilliant stab of delight.

Remy reacted as her body tensed. He drove his face into her sex, plunging his tongue into her hole, mashing her clit against his nose. The duelling sensations, above and below, drove her into a frenzy. Her lovers worked together to brink her to the peak. That realisation—that the two men were collaborating in her pleasure — was what finally pushed her over the edge.

She came like a thunderstorm sweeping off the plains, spilling out in a flood, ripped by blinding bolts. They held her as she yelled and thrashed, taut and shuddering with near-unbearable bliss. When the last echoes finally rolled away, she opened her eyes to find them on either side of her, smiles of satisfaction on their faces.

"Oh, my God," she murmured. She stroked Remy's cheek with one hand, brushed Zeke's tangled locks off his brow with the other. "Thank you...thank you both... That was amazing..."

"That's just the beginning, *chere.*" Remy eased her onto her back and curled up beside her, trailing his fingers over her breasts. His cock painted her thigh with pre-cum. "You first, man," he told Zeke.

"You sure?" On his knees near her feet, Zeke loomed up, clutching his swollen penis. Fat and veined, crowned by the plump purple head, his organ looked like it might explode at any moment.

"Definitely. You knew her before I did. Here." Remy flipped a condom in Zeke's direction. "You deserve it."

"Well, if you really don't mind..." Zeke dithered, but he was already tearing open the package.

"Damn it, if one of you doesn't fuck me this instant, I'm going to scream!" Ruby raised her knees and spread her thighs. She reached for the sturdy figure of her long-time friend. "Come on! I'm dying to have you inside me!"

"Anything to oblige a lady," Positioning himself between her splayed legs, Zeke slid his cock into her soaked pussy.

"Oh, God!" they moaned in unison. Remy chuckled. Ruby thought that she'd never felt anything so perfect as Zeke's cock buried inside her.

"You're so wet, darlin'." Zeke began to thrust, gently at first, but deep, letting her enjoy every inch of his glorious rod.

"You've only got yourself to blame," she gasped as he picked up speed. "Oh, yeah—that's good, baby... Ah...yeah..."

"Fuck her harder," Remy panted. "That's right..." Turning her head in his direction, Ruby saw that her other lover was fondling his penis, smearing fluid up and down its smooth length. Their eyes met. Once more she had the sense that he could read her thoughts.

Harder, yes. Faster, rougher, raunchier. Wild and deep and dirty, that's what she wanted, and Remy knew it.

"My mouth," she moaned, while Zeke rammed into her as though he'd tear her in two. "Give me your cock..."

The slender black man straddled her chest. His erection grazed her lips. She licked the cap, swirling her tongue over the stretched skin. He tasted salty with a hint of musk. She opened wide and Remy plunged his erection into the offered cavity.

He held still at first, letting her explore. She traced the smooth shaft and flicked at the sensitive underside, then turned on the suction. That got to him. He drove into her mouth, slamming against her palate, pulled back and thrust again. Before long, he had fallen into Zeke's rhythm, ramming into her mouth whenever Zeke skewered her pussy. Arms stretched forward, he braced himself against the wall, filling her throat again and again with his slick, solid flesh.

Ruby relaxed and let them both ravage her. The physical sensations were so intense and complicated that Ruby couldn't sort them out. All she knew was that she loved it. She loved being the willing receptacle of two men's lust.

The harder they fucked her, the more cherished she felt. They were giving her a gift, by loving and sharing her.

All at once, Zeke bellowed. He dug his fingernails into her thighs and ground his cock against her sex. The friction cut her loose, flinging her into orgasm. Convulsing around Zeke's spurting cock, she felt Remy's organ swell against her tongue. She climaxed again in anticipation of tasting him for the first time.

Remy didn't come, though. "Your mouth is sweet," he told her, as Zeke pulled out and stretched out beside them. "But I want your pussy. Over here, *chere*."

Zeke's cock might be flaccid, but his eyes glittered with lust as he watched Remy manoeuvre Ruby onto her hands and knees. She would have sworn that she couldn't have been more turned on. When Remy knelt behind her and rubbed his dick back and forth along her cleft, though, she thought she'd faint with lust.

"You've got such a beautiful ass." He dug his fingers into her cheeks, holding her open. "The first time I saw you, all those curves stuffed into those tight jeans..." He jerked his pelvis, impaling her. "I knew you were a sweet, hot bitch..." He pulled back then nailed her again. "I had to have you" — slam! — "had to do it doggy style." Slam! Slam! "You're so tight, *chere*, and so very, very wet..."

Ruby arched her back, raising her haunches so he could penetrate more deeply. Despite that fact that she'd already had three orgasms — even though her position offered little stimulation for her clit — she trembled, only a breath away from another come.

Remy's cock took her over. She shuddered with pleasure every time he pierced her. Her breasts swung back and forth beneath her, jiggling in time to his thrusts. Sweat dripped from her forehead. She closed her eyes, overwhelmed by the sensations assaulting her.

A low growl broke through her reverie. Zeke sat, propped up against the wall, fisting his cock with both hands. Their eyes met.

"Baby—are you okay?" she murmured, in between strokes. A twinge of guilt tarnished her pleasure. It couldn't be easy for him to watch her being fucked by another man.

"I'm great, darlin'. Really. I've never in my life seen anything as sexy as you two..." He grinned and showed her his fully erect penis. "See?"

"Oh...Zeke..." Her pussy clenched, a tiny climax shimmering through her. "Oh, please—Remy!" She peered over her shoulder. "Baby, I want you both. Now."

The man behind her paused, buried to the hilt. "You sure you can take it, *chere*?"

"Oh, yeah! I can take anything you two dish out, baby."

"I hope you're right," Remy commented, pulling out to leave her cunt aching and hungry. "Zeke?"

The burly bluesman had already settled on his back. His massive cock pointed straight up. She straddled his hips and sank down, embedding him in her pussy. A wave of delight swept over her. He was bigger than Remy and stretched her more. In addition, the position generated delicious pressure on her clit.

Falling forward onto her hands, she gave Zeke a long, deep kiss. "I love you, baby," she whispered. Then she glanced back at Remy. "Baby, I'm ready."

His fingers dabbled in her cunt, gathering moisture. Zeke tensed as Remy's hand grazed his shaft, then thrust up, making Ruby moan. She felt slender fingers padding at her rear entrance, smearing her juices. "Oh..." she gasped as the tight knot of muscle was breached by a fingertip. "Ah—oh, my God." A second finger joined the first, probing, wriggling, working to loosen and open her most private passage.

Otis had fucked her ass once, when he was drunk. She remembered it as embarrassing and painful. Zeke had always been afraid that he'd be too large and hurt too much. Now, as Remy's sheathed cock drilled into her anus, she knew that wouldn't be true. Yes, there was an edge of pain at first, but when she relaxed and let Remy enter, it vanished, to be replaced by pleasure so acute that it was difficult to bear. It suffused her whole pelvis, a sort of glittering ache that grew stronger as he pushed deeper.

"Breathe, *chere*," he whispered in her ear. He was in to the hilt now. There was a moment of stillness. They hung there, the three of them — entwined, connected. She could feel every tiny movement her lovers made, and she knew that they could feel each other. Peace and gratitude welled up inside her. There was no danger here, only bliss. Why had she been so eager to push love away?

Remy shifted slightly. Zeke pulsed and swelled in answer. Together, in perfect synchrony, the two began to fuck her. It was wild, filthy and delicious — beyond anything she'd ever dreamed, let alone experienced.

She opened her heart and her body and let her two lovers in. All the way.

Chapter Eight

It was standing room only at the Crossroads Blues Bar. Apparently someone had talked the place up on the Internet. Now Ruby was turning people away. The new five dollar cover charge hadn't discouraged anyone. There was a line running down the sidewalk, people waving tens and twenties in the hope that they'd be given priority.

It'll die down, she thought. Success was just a tiny bit scary.

She'd been making plans, though, to bring in some other acts. The Night Travellers were sensational, but Isaiah was right. People liked variety.

Variety, indeed. Leaning against the bar, she peered over the heads of the audience. Zeke and Remy were on stage, belting out a decidedly suggestive version of *I'm Your Hoochie Coochie Man*. Zeke had his axe swung low over his groin. He rocked his pelvis as he played, like he was making love to the instrument. Remy was nearly as bad, swivelling his hips like some modern-day Elvis.

Or maybe it was just her imagination. The whole world had been drenched in sensuality since that fateful night when she'd invited them into her bed. It was hard to believe it had been just a week.

She hadn't slept alone since. She'd walked through her days in some sort of voluptuous trance. She never knew when one or the other of them—or both—would pull her into a dark corner and ravish her. She'd pretty much given up on jeans—they were just too darned inconvenient. These days she wore mostly skirts—often without any underwear.

Yes, you've turned into some slut. Fine mother you are, too.

She dismissed the self-criticism. Isaiah had adjusted perfectly well to having two men at the breakfast table. Remy was teaching him slide guitar. Zeke had promised him tickets to see Eric Clapton if his grades were good.

True, she'd been spending less time in the club, but it seemed to be doing fine without her.

Thunderous applause broke her reverie. The spot swung over the crowd to pick her up in the back. "Ruby Jones, ladies and gentlemen, the woman responsible for Crossroads." The warmth in Zeke's voice made her pussy even wetter...and it had already been moist from watching their antics on stage. "Come on up, Ruby!"

She hadn't planned on performing tonight, but what the hell. Remy extended a hand to help her up onto the stage. The haunted look in his eyes was mostly gone. His nostrils flared as he caught the scent of her arousal. Zeke gave her a quick hug, surreptitiously tweaking her nipple.

"Behave yourself!" she whispered, trying to ignore her simmering lust. "What are we doing?"

Zeke ignored her, addressing the audience instead. "Ruby's going to give us a classic—Bessie Smith's *I'm Wild About That Thing*."

"Oh, no..." she said, half-laughing despite herself. "I can't..." Zeke and the Travellers were already into the intro, though. There was nothing she could do. She swallowed her embarrassment and launched into the song.

"Honey baby, won't you cuddle near.
Let sweet mama whisper in your ear.
I'm wild about that thing!
It makes me laugh and sing.
Give it to me, papa,
I'm wild about that thing."

The crowd clapped and whistled. Ruby shot a desperate look at Zeke, who just smiled sweetly. Damn, but that man was sexy.

Remy's guitar took the lead as she started the second verse. He gave her the old laser stare. She felt naked, which fitted very well with the lyrics.

"Do it easy, honey, don't get rough.
From you, papa, I can't get enough.
I'm wild about that thing.
Sweet joy it always bring.
Everybody knows it.
I'm wild about that thing."

By the time the song was finished, she was a puddle of lust. Zeke grabbed her and gave her a kiss — quick but with plenty of tongue. The audience roared. Then Remy followed suit. Her cheeks burned, but she couldn't pretend she wasn't turned on.

"You guys are impossible," she whispered to Zeke.

"And you, darlin', are irresistible." He turned to the audience. "Thank you, people. Maybe we can coax her back later. Meanwhile, we're goin' to change the mood a bit, with that old favourite, *Trouble in Mind*."

Sweaty and flustered, Ruby retreated to her office upstairs. Maybe if her lovers weren't right there in front of her, she'd be able to get control of herself.

She sat quietly, willing her breath to slow. To distract herself, she leafed through the pile of mail on her desk. The top envelope bore the logo of Atkinson, Fletcher and Graham, LLC—her landlord's lawyers. She tore it open. Her preoccupation with her lovers had actually driven the problem from her mind.

She broke into a smile at first reading. Everything was working out so well. Then she reread the letter. Her smile evaporated.

* * * *

Two sets of footsteps sounded on the stairs. Ruby raised her head from her crossed arms.

"Ruby—are you all right?" Remy's hand on her shoulder did not trigger the usual frisson of arousal.

"When were you going to tell me?" Her voice was icy. She held out the letter. "Bienville Associates. That's your company, isn't it?"

Remy actually seemed to grow pale. "Yes, yes—I tried to tell you. That first day, when I came to your office, it was to talk about the lease. And then last Friday, after you visited the lawyers—they called me and I rushed over, to explain…"

"Explain what?" Zeke asked. "What's going on?"

"Remy owns this building. He was going to evict us. Now this letter says that he'll graciously allow us to stay. How generous of you, Mr Saint-Michel."

"Ruby, please. I didn't find out that you were the tenant until that first night at the bar. Meanwhile, my reaction to you... I didn't know what to do. Honestly, the last thing I wanted was to hurt you.

"I bought the building because I wanted to open a restaurant. I had one in the French Quarter, years ago..." The ghosts were back in his eyes. "After Hurricane Katrina, the place was demolished...and my wife, my daughter... I came to New York to try and forget, to start a new life. This place seemed perfect."

"Except for the tiny detail that it was occupied..."

"After that first night, you had me totally confused, Ruby. I hadn't been with a woman since my family was killed. I thought I'd never love anyone again. Then you... I wanted you so badly. I was terrified that I might lose you."

Remy stood there, twisting his hands together, his eyes pleading. Ruby fought down a surge of sympathy. "A lot of concern for yourself, it seems, and not much for me."

"Please forgive me. I love you, *chere*. I've been stupid, but love sometimes is."

Ruby leant back, feeling weary and broken. "If I can't trust a lover to be honest..."

"Give him a break, Ruby." Zeke, who'd been hovering in the doorway, took a step towards her. "He made a mistake. Everyone does, occasionally. You should have told me about the eviction notice, but you didn't."

"That was different..."

"Not really. Love means being open and honest, but for some of us—including you, darlin'—it takes a while to learn how to do that."

Remy sank to his knees before her, his head bowed. The masterful, self-assured man who had swept her off her feet had disappeared. "I'll do anything to make it up to you, Ruby. Please..."

"Look at me," she told him. In his gaze she saw raw devotion and behind that, the shadows of his grief. Her anger melted.

"You can stay here rent-free if you like," he said. "I'll even deed the building over to you."

Taking his hands, Ruby raised him to his feet. "Thanks, baby, but that wouldn't be right."

"Why not?" Zeke asked. "If that's what he wants to do..."

"It would be too easy."

"Does it always have to be hard, darlin'?" Zeke pulled her out of her chair and into his arms. "Haven't you paid your dues? Why not take what fortune's offered?"

"I'd feel like I was selling myself—my love in exchange for the Crossroads."

Remy pressed himself against her back, sandwiching her between them. "Suppose we go into business together," he murmured in her ear. "I'll open my restaurant on the ground floor. You can move the club to the second and third floors."

"Then where will Isaiah and I live?" Ruby began to melt in the heat of their bodies. Remy stroked her hair. Zeke nuzzled her neck.

"With me," Remy said. "I've got a huge place on Central Park West..." His growing erection pressed into the small of her back.

"Or with me." Zeke swept his hands over her hips. "You know I've got room..."

"Or the three of us could find a place together," offered Remy.

"Wait just a minute!" Ruby laughed. "I'm not ready for that. You know I want to keep my independence..."

"And that you're stubborn as a mule, darlin'!" Zeke's tongue tickled her ear. Sparks skittered down her spine to her pussy. "But you don't have to decide right now."

"Yes," Remy agreed, reaching between her body and Zeke's to thumb her nipple. "Just think about it."

Ruby wondered whether she could come just from teasing, fully clothed.

"I will," she agreed. "I promise." Reluctantly she extricated herself from their dual embrace. "But right now I've got a bar full of customers who came here to hear the blues." She took their hands. "So let's go downstairs. And sing."

ORCHESTRATING MANOEUVRES

Lily Harlem

Dedication

To lovely Jo, a most excellent keeper of secrets, I adore you.

Chapter One

I flopped back on my mountain of pillows, gasping, writhing and shoving Enrique—my new thick, black Rampant Rocker vibrator—into my pussy higher and harder. He was great—long, wide and lined with vein-shaped ridges. And because he was so new to my collection, he seemed to have extra energy, extra enthusiasm for pleasing me. It was as if he was competing for a favoured position in my top drawer.

"Oh, yes, yes," I called out, upping the speed and finally letting his wicked forked attachment buzz around my clit. "Oh, yes, Enrique!" I twanged forward, sweat forming in my cleavage and my heart pounding. Flattening my palm over my pussy, I held him against my deliciously tormented clitoris. Electric sensations surged through my nerves. My internal muscles clamped and moisture seeped over his shaft, easing his way as I pumped his impressive girth in and out, in and out.

I squeezed my eyelids shut and instantly Dale's face appeared before me, a hot sheen on his brow and his mouth parted as he gave in to a fierce climax. Tearing open my eyes to shake the painful, memory-laden image, I stared at the huge framed poster of my own face gracing the cover of *Vogue* last month and came—sharp, intense and breath-taking. *God, Enrique is good, worth every penny.*

Panting, I pulled Enrique out and tossed him to the bottom of the bed. He'd served his purpose. Started my day with an orgasm. That was why I'd bought him. Carlo just wasn't doing it for me anymore, his pink, plastic shaft pale and insipid, his rotating glans no longer a novelty and he just didn't hit the spot with his thin little ears.

I glanced at the clock and sighed. Ten forty-five. I supposed I should get out of bed. Perhaps I could go and get a pedicure—I was already fed up with the Baby Bunting-coloured nail varnish I'd had applied three days ago at The Spa. Or maybe Naomi would be up for champagne and caviar at Jenson's. I frowned and tried to remember if she was eating at the moment. I couldn't be sure, but it was worth a try. I rolled onto my stomach and reached for my cell. There were two missed calls, one from my agent and one from my mother. I would sort them out tomorrow.

"Naomi, darling," I said when she answered on the first ring. "What are you doing today? Fancy some bubbles?" I flipped onto my back and stretched my legs up towards the ceiling, a combined inside leg of an impressive sixty-six inches.

"Tiffany, babe, I thought you would be here. It's the Tiara event."

I sat upright and folded my legs. "What...today?"

"Yes, didn't you speak to Rachel?"

I groaned. "No, I've been avoiding her. She's crazy at the moment, too many hormones." My agent of four years was in the first few months of pregnancy and driving me nuts with her talk of babies. As if I would be interested in babies — if I didn't have a perfectly flat stomach I would be out of a job.

"Well you ought to give her a call."

"Yeah, I guess I'll brace myself."

"Come on, snap out of it. Where's your spark gone? Enough moping already, get back out working, if not for the money then for your sanity."

I could always rely on Naomi to say it how it was. Since Dale had left me three months ago, I'd struggled to get my usual enthusiasm for the world of modelling that I loved so much. Some people had their hearts broken and threw themselves into work — not me. I just wanted to lounge around, play with my toys then head out for something bubbly to drown my sorrows in.

"It will do you good, Tiff," Naomi was saying, "to get some gigs in the diary and meet some new people. Don't let him win like this, babe. Show him what he's missing and he'll come crawling back."

Sliding to the side of the bed, I had a sudden rush of determination. She was right. I would snap out of my wallowing. Okay, so Dale had wanted a 'break' from dating one of the UK's highest paid models but still, surely I could find a way with all my connections and attributes to make him wake up to his foolishness. Let him see that I was more than just a face and a body.

I'd made him happy, he needed me in his life, our love was meant to be. I knew all that, so why didn't he?

I stood and squared my shoulders, pulling in a deep breath. Yes, I'd hit him with a media slap so hard he'd crawl back, begging, on hands and knees. I would teach him that asking for a 'break' then not calling all this time to make up was the biggest mistake he'd ever made.

But was it?

Sighing, I walked naked to the bathroom, wondering why my self-confidence felt so low despite being in demand worldwide for catwalks and cover-shots. Naomi was still chattering in my ear, telling me about a concert she'd been to. Two male pianists — Italians — gorgeous and taking the music industry by storm with racy videos and saucy stunts. Shocking the hell out of toffs who thought they knew more than anyone else about classical music and didn't believe it should be played by anyone not wearing a tuxedo or a ball gown.

Finally I heard Naomi bark at a makeup artist, her thin temper slipping as apparently one eyebrow hair was plucked without her consent. "I'll catch you later, Tiff — they're a bunch of morons here — but remember what I said. Get out there before everyone forgets who you are or you get a fucking wrinkle."

I snapped shut my cell phone then reached for my toothbrush and began to scrub by teeth as I called Rachel. "Hewwo, Rach, it mhwee," I said through foamy mint.

"Tiffany, darling, thank goodness you called. I've got the most fabulous opportunity for you today but we don't have a minute to waste. You need to get over to Notting Hill, darling, fast...like, you should have been there an hour ago."

I spat in the sink and stared into the mirror, checking no wrinkles had sneaked up on me overnight. *They wouldn't dare.* "Why what's going on in Notting Hill?"

She sucked in a breath, held the tension for a long, dramatic second then said, "Well." She finally breathed out. "*Ingresso Livello* are filming a new video today and they want *you*!"

"Who?" I asked, pouting at my reflection and tilting my chin. I had a little flush of colour on my cheekbones from Enrique's skilful vibrating. It suited me.

"You, darling, they want you."

"Yes, I gathered that, but *who* wants me?"

She sighed. "*Ingresso Livello*...you know, the pianists that played at The Royal Albert Hall last weekend. Everyone who's anyone went. They had pole dancers alongside their grand pianos and served champagne in glasses shaped like women's torsos at the after party."

"I didn't go."

Rachel put on her sternest voice. "I sent you a ticket and called you about it twice, Tiff, but if you don't open your mail or answer your phone, you're going to miss things."

I tutted, but silently agreed that I really must sort through the ever-growing pile of envelopes by my front door and stop hitting silence whenever my cell rang and it didn't flash the name Dale.

Cogs turned in my brain, sliding and slipping into place as I flicked on the shower. Naomi's conversation came flooding back to me — Italian pianists causing a storm with their sexy videos, hot studs with talented fingers and shameless images alongside beautiful classical music. *Ingresso Livello*, yes, now the foreign name was familiar. I'd heard people talking about them when I'd been out and about in the clubs.

"Okay," I said to Rachel. "Text me the address, call them and let them know I'll be there within the hour...say I had a family emergency or something."

"Great!" Rachel said. "You won't regret this, Tiff. Not only are Ricardo and Nari drop-dead gorgeous, but this video could catapult you into acting. So smile for the camera and do your best not to look so damn depressed."

I huffed and clicked off my cell. Stepped into the shower and let the piping hot water rain down on my body. I was *not* acting depressed, just having some 'me time' while I fixed my broken heart. Surely I was entitled to that. Dale and I had been together for over two years. It was taking a lot of adjusting to not having him there.

I reached for an exorbitantly expensive shower gel and covered my body in vanilla and frangipani suds. Of course I knew Rachel and Naomi were right. When you're a well-known model, there's always someone younger and prettier coming up behind you, happy to take your crown *and* your work. Making the most of this opportunity was the sensible thing to do. I knew that really. Plus it would give me something to do for the day.

* * * *

The address in Notting Hill led me to a grand private home, with black wrought iron gates and a high cream-coloured wall covered in ivy. After paying the taxi fare, I pressed the intercom with my long, French manicured nail.

"Who is it?" an American female voice asked after I'd been forced to press the button twice.

"Tiffany O'Dell," I said, folding my arms and tapping my gold sandal on the pavement. I didn't like waiting.

"Finally! Great, come on in."

There was a buzzing noise then a small gate within the large gate clicked open. I stepped through it, ducking my head slightly then secured it shut behind me. I found myself in a courtyard packed full of terracotta flower pots spilling their pretty contents. I sashayed up to the main door. Just as I reached it, a short lady in a brown and orange checked dress and wearing black, round glasses pulled it open.

"Tiffany," she said with a broad smile and stepped frumpy flat pumps over the threshold. "So pleased to meet you. I'm Nancy, I'm directing the shoot today."

I raised my brows. *Not what I was expecting.* Holding out my hand I shook hers. "Lovely to meet you. So sorry about, er...being late. Bit of a crisis at home, if you know what I mean." I shrugged.

"You're here now, that's what's important. But we must hurry...time is money and all that." She turned and led the way into the high ceilinged hallway. "Nari and Ricardo are keen to meet you. Apparently they are big fans and couldn't believe their luck last week when you agreed to be the guest star of *Il Piacere de Tre.*"

"Mmm, yes, good." I really should have picked up that call from Rachel, and I really must speak to her about booking me in for stuff without telling me. Still, if she hadn't, I supposed I wouldn't be here. "What does it mean, *il piacere de tre?*"

Nancy stopped and turned to me. Behind her glasses her blue eyes sparkled and she rubbed her hands together like a conspirator. "'The pleasure of three', Tiffany, *il piacere de tre* means 'the pleasure of three'."

A sudden knot of apprehension tightened in my stomach. *The pleasure of three.* That was the title of their new piece of music. Naomi's words came tumbling back to me as I followed Nancy up a wide, carpeted stairs. Sexy videos, saucy images, hot studs with talented fingers. *Oh, boy, what have I got myself into?*

Nancy ushered me into a bedroom where a young makeup artist sat reading *Cosmo*, her palettes, pots and brushes spread out on a dressing table. "Sarah will sort you out. She's got your underwear too."

Treble

"Underwear?"

"Yes, that's what you will be wearing for the shoot." Nancy suddenly clapped her hands and her face went stern. "Now step to it, I want this thing ready to go in ten."

The door clicked shut and I dropped my huge Gucci handbag on a chair. "Hey," I said to Sarah.

"It's so great to meet you, Miss O'Dell. I'm really excited to be making you up. It's an honour...a dream, actually."

I nodded. "Thanks, what am I wearing?"

She reached towards a rail, plucked off a scarlet bra and thong set, and held it out for me. "New season La Perla."

I studied it with a critical eye. The lacy bra was balcony style, which would shove up my small breasts and make them appear fuller. The thong had matching lace detail at the hips and was miniscule, but size didn't matter. I had not a single pubic hair to worry about—I regularly had everything from my neck downwards waxed—and my bum was pert, tight, and perfectly smooth after a full body conditioning treatment on Sunday.

I quickly stripped naked. I'd long since lost any kind of embarrassment with taking off my clothes in front of wardrobe and makeup staff. Sarah folded my jeans and T-shirt as I slipped on the beautifully crafted underwear. It made me feel instantly sexy and I couldn't help but wish I'd used Enrique twice that morning to take the edge off my insatiable libido. *God, I miss having a hot, hard man in my bed.*

"It looks wonderful," Sarah said. "The guys will love it."

"You know them?" I asked as I sat on a high stool.

"Well, I only just met them this morning." She gave a shy smile. "But what they say is true."

"What do they say?" I tilted my chin and shut my eyes as she rubbed a light foundation over my chin, nose and forehead.

"That they're gorgeous and charming and no woman stands a chance of a sane thought when they're around."

I opened my eyes. "That's really what people say?" I was becoming more and more intrigued by the mysterious Ricardo and Nari.

"Yes, didn't you see their video to go with '*Schiava del Sesso in Catene*'? It was about as raunchy as MTV would allow. In fact, some countries *did* ban it."

"Dare I ask what *schiava del sesso in catene* translates to?"

She giggled as she swept a huge fluffy brush heavy with powder over my cheekbones. "Sex slave in chains. They had Tanya Berry —"

"*The* Tanya Berry?"

"Yes, *the* Tanya Berry…tied up in a dungeon. She was wrapped in chains, blindfolded and they teased her with a whip while they strutted around practically naked themselves."

I frowned. "And they're classical musicians, right?" I was struggling to get my head around the new concept that had gripped everyone's imagination.

"Oh, yes. There's no lyrics, just sexy music, suggestive titles and raunchy images to go with their performances. Some people are saying they're introducing classical to the younger generations…and some say they are creating smut and using their good looks to demean fine concertos."

"What do you think?"

"I think they're great. I'd listen to their music all day, and after they've put those images in your head, that's all you can think about when you next hear them play. It gets me all hot and bothered wherever I am."

I pouted whilst Sarah applied ruby red lipstick that matched my underwear. When she'd finished, she stepped back and surveyed my face with a critical eye. "That's you done," she said. "Now, go enjoy. I know I would if I were you."

Gulping down a bolt of apprehension, I quickly pulled a brush through my poker-straight, strawberry-blonde hair then followed her to the door. She pulled it open and we walked down a wood-panelled corridor. I was grateful for the warm spring day — too many times I'd had to do underwear shoots in cold conditions and it was impossible to control goosebumps.

"Ah, here you are," Nancy said as we stepped into a large bedroom. It was painted entirely in white. Two floor-to-ceiling windows were lined with sun-dappled white tulle, which fluttered in the spring breeze. The white four-poster bed had matching snow-white drapes looped around its posts and also had white covers and pillows.

"Meet Nari and Ricardo." Nancy nodded over my shoulder.

I turned…and looked up. I was tall, flirting with six feet, but Ricardo and Nari, were taller — considerably taller.

"Tiffany, enchanted to have you here today. I'm Nari." The beautiful olive-skinned man before me held out his hand. I noticed that they were both barefooted and wore nothing but softly worn jeans, their broad chests bare apart from a sprinkling of black chest hair.

Taking Nari's hand, I felt long, fine-boned fingers wrap around mine.

"You are every bit as beautiful in real life as in photographs," he said, his Italian accent subtle and sexy.

I watched as he brought my knuckles to his mouth and pressed soft lips to my skin. He had carefully groomed stubble over his top lip and chin and it scratched my flesh, creating a tingle of sensation that zinged up my arm.

"Thank you." I stared into his chocolate brown eyes. They were heart-stoppingly striking and burnt with sin — great big vats of deliciously bad sin. This man was sexy with a capital S. How had I not taken any notice of *Ingresso Livello*?

"This is Ricardo," he said, releasing my hand.

I turned to Ricardo, who offered me a similar devastating smile with neat white teeth and wide, sensual lips. Super sexy offered up in yet another wonderful specimen of a man.

"Hi," I said, a sudden feeling of shyness coming over me. It wasn't often I was bothered by being studied so closely or by meeting beautiful people. That was the world I lived in. But there was something about these two musicians that had my heart tripping and my female hormones jumping to attention.

Ricardo took my hand, turned it over and lifted it to his face. He pressed a kiss to my palm, slowly and succulently, his black eyes, lined with heavy lashes, not leaving mine for a second. "Exquisite," he murmured, his hot breath fanning over the delicate underside of my wrist. "And absolutely perfect for '*Il Piacere de Tre*', don't you think, Nari?"

"Oh, yes," Nari said, his eyes dropping down my body. "More than perfect."

My nipples tightened within the cups of my bra. The pianists' double gaze was like a heated caress, lingering and hot, live flames licking over my skin.

"So I was thinking," Nancy said, stepping up to the three of us. "That we would start with you guys staring out of the windows, one in each, the translucent tulle gently wafting around your silhouetted bodies. A dreamy, floaty, overexposed image."

"Sounds good," Ricardo said, pushing his hand through floppy jet-black hair. His was longer than Nari's and looked softer. Nari's was in a shorter, neater style, but the same shiny, coal-black.

"Then we'll have Tiffany walk into the shot—best catwalk strut you can do, my dear. Walk right up to them, stop, then place a hand on each of their shoulders as if getting their attention. Make it slow, make it sexy… In fact, let's get the song playing so you can time your walk to the intro." She turned briefly to click her fingers at a young man with greasy hair scraped back into a ponytail. "And I want you to all just go with what feels right to start with, see where it takes us for the first few minutes." She paused. "I'm sure you guys have some ideas."

"Oh, yes," Nari said, sweeping his tongue over his bottom lip and leaving a delicate sheen. "We have plenty of sexy ideas which I'm sure will suit the three of us quite well."

I gulped. *What on earth have I let myself in for?* Of course I could launch into a supermodel tantrum and walk out. Throw my toys out of the pram, so to speak. But I didn't want to. I was as captivated by these two devastatingly gorgeous Italians as they appeared to be with me. My heart was thudding and a quivering knot of desire was growing in the pit of my stomach, sending hot darts to my pussy. I wanted to stay and find out just what sexy ideas they had that would suit the three of us.

Nari and Ricardo moved over to the windows, the deeply tanned skin of their naked backs all the more startling in the white of the room. As they stepped into the piercing shards of sunlight, long shadows stretched out behind them. I watched them move. Both had a similar air of grace and control as they walked. Ricardo's shoulders were slightly broader than Nari's, the denim on Nari's jeans hugged his cute butt just a little tighter than Ricardo's. *Mmm, it would be absolutely impossible to choose between them if one was forced to.*

Nancy directed two cameras into position as the first tinkling, rising notes of *Il Piacere de Tre* filled the air. She turned to me. Pointed at Ricardo and Nari. "Walk," she said. "Like you're intent on taking what your body demands. These men are your lovers, your world, the only thing that can satisfy you."

Should be easy enough to act, since my body was attracted to Nari and Ricardo the way giant magnets pull together. I stepped forward on the deeply piled white carpet, set back my shoulders and became aware of a camera close to my behind. I rolled my hips and swung my arms, the same way I did if thousands of people were watching. I was Tiffany O'Dell—if there was one thing I could do it was strut. My butt wiggled, the thong had settled deep in my cleft but I knew the pretty laced edge would be sitting just below the two perfect dimples in my lower back. I enjoyed showing off my butt and my back— they were great features.

I stepped into the spilling sunshine and came to a halt between the two sexy pianists. Lifting my hands, I then rested them down on the warm skin and hard muscles of their shoulders. Simultaneously they turned to me— slowly, deliberately. I looked between the two and couldn't ignore the lust in their eyes. It didn't look fake or put on for the camera. It looked real and dark and, quite honestly, downright dangerous.

The music picked up a notch, the notes became a little higher and a little faster. Nari took my chin in the cup of his palm and turned me to face him directly. Ricardo stepped in behind me, close — really close. Scratchy chest hairs prickled my shoulder blades, the heat of his skin burnt like a furnace.

There was a camera only a few feet from us and the breeze blew the curtain behind Nari like a gently ebbing wave.

Nari slid his fingertip across first my left cheekbone and then my right, all the while his eyes stared down at me with heated intensity. Ricardo pressed in more tightly behind me and his lips touched my bare shoulder. A shiver of awareness travelled through my body. His soft lips seemed to contain an electric current that was hotwired to my breasts and my pussy.

The curtain blew a little more, the breeze cooling my hot skin. Nari lowered his head, his lips brushing mine in the softest, most delicate of kisses. I fluttered closed my eyes and concentrated on his smell and his flavour — mulled wine floating with cinnamon sticks, rich chocolate praline dissolving on the tongue. The most delicious, intriguing flavour I'd tasted in months.

He pulled back and gazed down at me, but only for a second, because then Ricardo applied pressure to my shoulders and turned me to face him. I reached up and curled my hands around his wide biceps, absorbing the heat and texture of his perfectly smooth flesh. One side of his mouth tilted into a wicked smile as his chest touched my breasts.

I sucked in a sharp breath, my nipples instantly becoming hard, pinched points of desire. Ricardo smelt and felt just as good as Nari, maybe with an added hit of sandalwood in his scent. Sumptuous.

Nari's nimble hands were in my hair, scooping it up then sliding the long silken strands through his fingers. Each tiny tug on the roots of my scalp heightened my awareness of the lean testosterone-saturated muscle surrounding me.

He pulled on my hair, causing my head to tilt to the ceiling. As it did, Ricardo stooped, his teeth grazing the cords of my neck. He nipped slightly then kissed the sore spot. I parted my mouth in a gasp. *This acting business was a doddle when it felt this good.*

"Excellent, excellent," Nancy voice invaded my thoughts. "Perfect lighting in here, and great first take."

Nari dropped my hair and stepped away from me. Instantly, I felt the loss of his body heat on my back and my butt. Ricardo, however, stayed close, allowing me to continue to cling to his arms, his chest still pressed to mine.

"Your skin reminds me of the sweetest summer's day in Tuscany," he whispered, his deep voice quiet and smooth, like silk through water. "And your eyes are the exact colour of the sky above my grandmother's home in the mountains. I used to lie on my back as a child in the vineyard, look up at the endless, seamless blue and know I would see that perfect colour again one day." He pressed his palms to my cheeks, held me still, and looked deep into my eyes. "And today I have finally found it."

As if hypnotised by his smell, his heat and his voice, I gazed up at him. I had never seen eyes as black and deep and as intense as his...well, not since I'd last gazed into Dale's, anyway. Quickly, I beat down a wave of regret for what could have been between me and Dale. His treacle-rich eyes were no longer there for me to gaze into first thing in the morning and last thing at night. That was the past and I had to accept it...or at least learn to live with the painful squeezing of my heart whenever I thought of a lifetime without him.

"People, get with it," Nancy snapped impatiently. "Next shot. Nari, you had an idea about hands?"

"Yes," Nari said, resting his large palm in the small of my back. "I think a shot of all four of our hands on Tiffany's back and—" He slid his fingers on to the top rise of my butt. "—fingering her... What do you call it?"

"Thong," I said.

"Er...yes, thong. That is it, thong."

"Fabulous," Nancy said. "Roll with it, action."

Suddenly both Nari's hands were on me, sliding down my back, once again scooping my hair out of the way. Ricardo squeezed even closer, also exploring the dips and clefts of my long spine with his flattened hands and elegant fingers.

The camera was near again, down at my hip, catching the action that was sure to be highlighted by the dazzling sunshine on the opposite side. My heart rate picked up as someone's naughty finger dipped into the elastic and tugged slightly. *Surely they don't expect me to take them off. Rachel would never have agreed to that.* I tightened my grip on Ricardo's biceps.

"Shh," Ricardo soothed, his warm breath washing over my cheek. "We want to touch you all over. You feel like heaven to us."

Oh God, I do want them to touch me all over, but not with a camera rolling.

"Heaven, paradise and nirvana—all wrapped up in one sweet package," Nari breathed into my ear. "Listen to the music, Tiffany. Feel our hands worshiping you, allow yourself to sway a little, move to the tune. Our tune of adoration."

Squirming slightly under their light fingertip traces and delicate caresses, I soon found myself absorbing their lulling music into my skin. It became part of the touch, part of our embrace, filtering into my ears and settling in my chest and my pelvis. I was getting so turned on—so horny, so hot and feverish—an orgasm was all I could think about. But it was the last thing that could happen here and now.

Vaguely aware of the cameras around us, I tilted my head and allowed Ricardo to kiss down to the hollow of my throat and on to my sternum. I reached up and ran my fingers into his lustrously thick hair—held him a little closer, encouraging him on his way down my body. His barely audible groan filtered up and mixed with a high tinkling section of their composition. The approving groan—evidence that he was enjoying this too, it wasn't just me—served only to further weaken my already pathetically wobbly legs.

Meanwhile, Nari was exploring the centre of my back with his mouth and tongue. I twisted and saw he was kneeling behind me, dipping down to the same level as Ricardo.

The curtain blew over Ricardo's body, though this time the breeze did nothing to cool my feverish flesh as they both headed lower still. Nari, I felt sure, was tugging at my thong with his teeth and Ricardo poked his tongue into my navel before slowly running it around the shallow indentation.

"Perfect, perfect," Nancy cooed. "That's the shot we want. Now, onto the bed."

In a sudden flourish, I was swung into the air by Nari.

"Hey," I said, scrabbling for purchase around his shoulders. "What are you doing?" I glanced at the camera crew and Nancy and Sarah, and it all flooded back to me where I was and what I was doing.

Treble

Nari grinned. "I don't want to spoil the moment." He dipped his head to my ear. "It seems we are orchestrating our manoeuvres perfectly."

"I can walk," I said, wriggling. "I'm just doing my job." Who was I kidding? This was the best fun I'd had for three months. It was even better than the Westwood catwalk last week when Adele Bentley had fallen off the platform and bruised her cheek.

Nari laid me on the bed then sat at the end. "Nancy." He looked over his shoulder. "Remember I told you about the foot thing."

"Ahh, yes," Nancy said and signalled for the camera to come to the base of the bed. "Pan around," she instructed the operator. "A shot of Tiffany lying down first." She frowned at me. "Arms up, dear. Look wanton and satisfied…you're in heaven being adored by these two magnificent beasts."

I quickly did as she asked, stretched my arms above my head and curled my fingers into the slats of the headboard. I twisted my torso, elongating my narrow waist and showing off my slender hips. Sarah rushed over, quickly added a touch of powder to my nose, then stepped away.

"Mmm, very nice," Ricardo said, sitting at the end of the bed opposite Nari and surveying my extended body.

"Ricardo, like this," Nari instructed, scooping my heel into the cup of his palm.

Ricardo followed suit, the cameras swung around and the music picked up tempo, sailing through high notes and crashing to a low, bass tone every few scales.

Both my legs were lifted as my two Italian co-stars began to kiss and lick the top of my feet and rub the arch with dexterous movements. Each touch hotwired exquisite sensations to my pussy. I closed my eyes, sighed and writhed. It felt good, so good, but nobody knew that. For all they knew, I was acting—performing for the camera the same way Nari and Ricardo were.

Their mouths explored higher, kissing and licking their way to my knees, my thighs, my hip bones. I became aware of their weight settling beside me on the bed, their hands exploring my body—stroking, smoothing over my flat belly and just skimming the underneath of my breasts through the bra.

"This is lovely," Nancy cooed. I opened my eyes and spotted her standing at the end of the bed in her fuddy-duddy dress. "But now we want some real action, something suggestive of a full-on threesome. Time to lose the jeans, guys."

There was a great deal of shifting on the bed as Nari and Ricardo shucked off their denims. Both wore tight black Armani boxers...and both had impressive packages outlined by the material.

"Can we go back a few minutes on the composition?" Ricardo asked as he settled back down next to me.

The music flicked around then started again at a slow, sedate, almost trance-like pace.

"*Perfetto*," Nari said, wrapping me in his arms and scooping me on top of him. "Absolutely *perfetto*."

I caught my breath as my chest pressed to his as did my thighs and my stomach... Whew, my stomach hit something long and dense and growing in hardness.

"You will have to forgive me," he murmured softly. "It is not every day I have a practically naked supermodel on top of me. I pride myself in control, but I am, after all, still a mortal man."

Flustered and turned on, both embarrassed and pleased by his reaction to me, I settled a little more comfortably against him, sliding my hands over his marble hard pecs and dropping my head into his neck.

"Yes, that is it," Ricardo said nudging apart my legs and flattening his chest over my back. "But a little higher, *mio angelo*." Wrapping his fingers around my hip bones, he urged me up Nari's body.

I gasped as my mound came into contact with Nari's swollen shaft. And through the soft material of his boxers and the silky gusset of my thong, the first section of my pussy lips parted—just enough for my swollen clit to press against concrete flesh.

Nari tensed. It was as though every muscle in his body froze. I lifted my head and looked down into his desire-heavy eyes. Lust raged in their depths, and his lips were fastened into a tight line.

I opened my mouth to speak, but no words came out. What could I say? That I wanted everyone else in the room gone? Well, except for Ricardo, who had settled between my legs and was licking between my shoulder blades.

"Kiss me," Nari said in a low, scraping voice. "Just kiss me, Tiffany."

Pressing my lips to his, I muffled my moan of lust against his mouth. The concerto had picked up again, building to its high, excitable crescendo.

"Some movement would be good," Nancy shouted over the piano music filling the room. "I'm not a photographer, I'm a film director. Listen to the music. You want it to be raunchy, sexy, the talk of the town—hell, the talk of the world—then grasp the beat, pull the music into your hearts and souls. Move, people. Make love, *show* the pleasure of three."

Ricardo began to suggestively pump his hips against my butt. What had been only a semi-hard bulge against the cleft of my arse was rapidly turning to granite. My heart pounded, every nerve in my body honed in on the musical geniuses surrounding me, holding me, arousing me. I kept on kissing Nari. His breaths were hard and sharp, his facial hair rasped at my chin and his chest heaved against mine.

"Ahh, angel, you are driving me crazy," Ricardo murmured by my ear. "Mother of Mary, give me strength."

My clit was humming, the pressure building, an orgasm teasing me, tripping my heart and claiming my breath. Still Ricardo continued to rock against me, sliding me against Nari's cock. His thrusting movements, breathy groans and sinful kisses were all designed to titillate viewers…and they were about to tip me over the edge.

I couldn't come in front of a room full of people, in front of a rolling camera! *Oh my God, I was going to!*

"Nari," I gasped, breaking our kiss.

"Take it," he whispered, threading his fingers into the hair at my temples. "Take what you want."

My clit was throbbing, bulging against his straining cock. My pulse raged through my ears. The point of no return was rapidly approaching. The music swirled me upwards, harnessing my desire, erasing reality. I bit down on my bottom lip and stared into Nari's beautiful eyes, desperate to keep quiet and controlled even through the moment of no control that had just become inevitable.

Sucking in a breath, I teetered on the edge of bliss and balled my hands into fists on Nari's pecs. Ricardo swirled his tongue into the shell of my ear.

I came.

Hard, fast, exquisitely.

"Ah, ah, ah," I panted, vaguely aware of my eyes rolling before fluttering shut. My mouth hung slack, my heart knocking against my ribcage. Sliding my hands to the sheets, I grabbed them tight as my pussy convulsed around nothing and my clit bobbed against Nari's shaft.

Oh shit! What had I done?

Chapter Two

"Will you come to lunch with us?" Ricardo asked as we walked down the stairs.

Nancy had told us it was a wrap five minutes after my climax, which I vehemently hoped that she hadn't suspected was the real thing. And it was just as well we'd finished—Nari had looked to be in real physical pain as I'd continued to writhe on top of him, finishing the scene.

I glanced at Ricardo's handsome face—at his smooth, golden skin stretched over high, perfect cheekbones and his wide, fleshy mouth. If he hadn't had a career as a brilliant musician, he could have easily stepped into my world. He would be in great demand.

"Oh, I'm sorry, perhaps you are on some special diet," he said, his brow creasing at my hesitation.

"No," I said, waiting as Nari opened the front door. "No special diet, and yes, I would love to do lunch."

"Great," Nari said, slotting a hand against the small of my back and urging me outside. "We're staying at The Savoy, and I hear the food there is very good."

"Yes, it is." Last time I'd been to The Savoy, Dale had been with me. It had been his birthday and we'd celebrated with a romantic candlelit dinner. I'd bought him a Rolex and a ticket to accompany me to Barcelona on work. It had been the most fun I'd ever had on an Estrella Archs shoot, not that we'd seen much of the sun-soaked city, since the Hotel Arts was very comfortable and suited our needs perfectly.

It was warm in London today and as I walked through the courtyard, the heavy, powdery scent of the flowers wafted up to my nostrils. The blooms' colours seemed more vibrant than when I'd stepped into the house earlier—cotton candy pinks, azure blues and citrus orange. My senses were heightened, adrenaline and anticipation pumping through my veins, my body alive with a hunger that was for more than food.

A sleek white limousine with tinted privacy windows hummed outside the gates. A chauffer in a flat black cap held open the door for us to climb in.

I sat in the middle, my two exotic dates close on either side of me. My panties were damp against my pussy as I sat down, and I was relieved to be wearing my dark denim jeans that wouldn't show a wet patch.

As the car pulled into the traffic, Nari took my hand and traced a circle with his long, elegant, almost ethereal fingers. Just that simple act had my nipples spiking again at the thin material of my T-shirt, pushing and straining at the silk of my bra.

Ricardo settled a palm on my right thigh and delicately stroked down to my knee then up to my hip. His hands were every bit as beautiful as Nari's, though the backs of his were hazed with just a little more dark hair. "You were so *molto squisiti* today," he murmured.

"What does that mean?" I asked, feeling small and dainty between them.

"You were 'very exquisite', Tiffany," Nari said, "perfect for *Il Piacere de Tre*. I think both the composition and the images will be a worldwide hit, though again our critics will be turning themselves in twists."

"Which is just what we want." Ricardo murmured, leaning towards my ear and letting his hot, breath wash down my neck. "How can we ever thank you enough?"

Inside I was shaking with desire but I willed myself to appear calm on the outside. "Well, it was my pleasure to help out," I managed, swallowing tightly.

Nari smiled, his mouth stretching wide and small creases darting from his eyes to his temples. "I think it really *was* your pleasure, wasn't it? In every sense of the word."

Tugging at my bottom lip with my teeth, I studied his dark eyes. There was no denying it. He'd looked into my face as I came. He'd seen it, he'd felt it...and he knew exactly what had happened when Ricardo had rocked me against his hard shaft and built me up to a sweet, barely disguised climax.

Suddenly his smile fell. His brow furrowed into three neat creases and his voice dropped to a sexy low tenor. "We really do want to thank you properly, Tiffany, if you could tell us what we can do to repay your kindness."

Oh my God! Heaven offered up on a golden plate.

But could I?

Did I dare?

Lust coiled like a snake in my belly. I wanted them both. I wanted us all naked in a room with no camera, no clothes, nothing—just us and our primitive desires and hours and hours to play and satisfy one another. I'd never had a threesome—Dale had always been more than enough—but the thought of this twin feast of manhood was so deliciously exciting I could barely breathe. And what was to stop me? I was a free agent. No boyfriend to think about. Not anymore…

"Tell us what you want?" Ricardo whispered, hooking my chin with the crook of his index finger and turning me to face him. "Sweet little angel, tell us what you need from us."

I'm having another of my dirty dreams, surely I'll wake up soon.

Nari turned my hand in his, stretched out my fingers and laid my palm over his crotch. His cock strained against the button fly of his jeans, long and thick and solid. "*We* know how we want to thank you, Tiffany," he whispered as Ricardo pressed a kiss to my lips, "though it will mean joining us in bed."

"Yes," Ricardo murmured. "We want to make you fly high, soar like a bird, float on clouds, with pleasure the only emotion you can think of. The only part of your world that exists."

My panties were soaking now and my pussy trembling. My nipples were actually starting to feel painful, they were so tightly twisted.

"Shall we skip lunch?" Nari asked, pressing my hand more firmly over his erection and shifting it gently over the fly. "How about we head for our suite and call for room service later?" His tongue traced the top, uppermost curve of my ear, then he went on in his sexy voice, "I have a feeling our appetites for fine cuisine are of a more primitive variety than silver service."

Dreamily, I nodded. My clit was distended and engorged, hungering for attention. Nari was right—lunch would only get in the way of what we all really needed.

* * * *

The suite I stepped into was like time travelling to a home belonging to Edwardian gentry. Huge windows were dressed with cream and burgundy striped curtains and a decadent Murano chandelier dominated the centre of the room over a mahogany coffee table. A marble fireplace sat waiting to be lit and had a heavily patterned rug on the floor before it.

Nari walked to a drinks trolley and splashed amber liquid from a crystal decanter into two glasses.

"Tiffany?" He held the decanter my way.

"Champagne, if you have any."

Ricardo pulled open a discreet mini bar and plucked out a bottle of Bollinger. "Is this all right?" he asked.

"Perfect."

He popped the cork and white froth gushed out. Quickly, he reached for a flute and filled it with the beautiful fizzing liquid.

"Here," he said, handing it to me with a smile.

I took it and drank deep then stepped up to the window and looked out over London. The heat of the afternoon had made the skyline a little hazy, but the majestic London Eye stood on the other side of the Thames, and in the distance The Houses of Parliament rose from the hustle and bustle of the streets.

"We adore spending time in London," Nari said, coming close beside me and taking a sip of his drink. "Have you ever been to Rome?"

"Yes, plenty of times." I turned from the view.

He bobbed his head as if in apology. "Of course you have, how foolish of me."

"Next time you visit, call on us." Ricardo said from where he was sitting on an over-stuffed sofa, tugging off his leather shoes.

"Thanks, I might." I took another slug of champagne, hoping the alcohol would soon calm my nerves. The room was quiet...too quiet. I felt sure both men would be able to hear the thudding of my heart. Suddenly I had an idea. "Do you have your music available to listen to?"

Nari raised his brows. "You've been listening to it all day. Have you not had enough?"

I shrugged. "It's very good."

His mouth tilted into a wickedly sexy smile. "Well, in that case we have, but you must come this way."

He stepped to a large, white panelled door. I followed, pausing only for a second to allow Ricardo to fill my empty champagne glass.

The bedroom that greeted me was magnificent. I had stayed in many fabulous hotels around the world, so it took a lot to impress me. Perhaps it was perfect because of what I had in mind for the afternoon, or maybe it was because finally, after hours of wishing, here was a bed.

And more importantly, here was privacy.

The walls were graced with delicate, moss-green silk paper dotted with silver fleurs-de-lis. Bespoke dressers and chairs, formal and plush, lined the walls and the bay of the window. The bed was huge, and the same jewel-coloured material that adorned the window lined the wall behind the headboard, giving the impression of richly draped curtains.

Ricardo walked into the bedroom and closed the door. I turned to him just as music filled the air from an iPod docking station — rich, seductive notes that flowed like fine wine, two pianos playing together seamlessly, as one.

"Are you familiar with our last CD?" Ricardo asked, knocking back his drink in one go then placing his glass on the dresser.

I shook my head, glugged on my twinkling flute and caught sight of myself in the mirror. My cheeks were flushed, my eyes wide and my nipples poked against my top, making it impossible to hide my desire for the two men about to thank me for my *acting* efforts.

Nari walked over, took my glass and set it aside. "After today, I think we can safely say you will be very familiar with these particular compositions we wrote."

"And play," Ricardo added, walking to the end of the bed and running his fingers over the brocade like it was a long keyboard. "Come to me, Tiffany. Feel this linen, it truly is delightful." He sat at the base of the mattress.

I stepped towards him, out of habit crossing my sandals over one another to accentuate the roll of my hips as I walked. Though, today I felt as though I was floating.

As I reached Ricardo, I was aware of Nari pressing in close behind me. The rich, earthy scent of whisky hung in the air. I allowed Ricardo to draw me down beside him and watched as Nari slipped my shoes from my feet.

"We will need these off too, *mio angelo*." Ricardo popped the top button on my jeans.

I lifted my hips and shifted backwards on the bed to allow him to wriggle them and my panties down my legs. I knew how wet my panties were and felt embarrassed by the damp stain and wished we could turn down the lights and shut the curtains.

That was not going to happen.

Nari stood and removed his jeans, and I saw the straining erection beneath his tight boxers. He watched, fists clenched, as Ricardo tugged my jeans and panties from my ankles. I was not the only one hopelessly turned on.

Ricardo discarded my clothes to one side and peeled off his jeans and designer shirt. His broad chest, small coffee-brown nipples and the cock tenting his boxers were all hugely distracting to my train of thought.

"This too," Nari said, touching the strap of my vest top.

After pulling it over my head, I dropped it on the floor with a flourish. Nari smiled. Ricardo climbed onto the bed behind me and reached for the back of my bra. He released the catch, freeing my small, high breasts, then slipped the straps down my arms.

"And now," Nari said in a serious tone, running the back of his thumb over first my right nipple then the left. "Now, the fun really begins." His black eyes were burning as he bent and suckled my nipple into his mouth. He rolled his tongue around it then gave it a sharp suck. Excitement curled in my veins and surged through my body. I reached for his shoulders but Ricardo wrapped his arms around my waist. With a simple, effortless twist, I was on my hands and knees, looking down at the neatly starched sheet folded back from the pillows.

I gasped and glanced back over my shoulder. Both men were kneeling by my rump. Nari shucked off his shirt and ran a hand through his short hair.

"*Perfetto culo,*" Ricardo said, smoothing his big hands over the globes of my butt. "The *perfetto culo.*"

I whimpered and dropped my head down. His touch was teasing and light, a delicate massage. *I need so much more.* The flesh of my pussy was aching—aching for a male touch. I had been so long with artificial cock that the need for real, hot, hard flesh was maddening.

Still Ricardo caressed me gently. "Please," I begged, shifting my hips and tossing my head to face the window. "Please."

The music lifted to a dramatic flurry of high notes. "Ah, angel, we are here," Nari said, as a finger slid down the seam of my buttocks, over the tight hole of my anus and on to my entrance. "Is this where you want us?"

"Yes, oh, yes." I was edgy with need, feverish for penetration.

Suddenly two long fingers sank into my pussy. I groaned and writhed and clamped around them. Bucking backwards, I searched for more—needing the filling, stretching sensation the way I needed to breathe.

"I'm going to fuck you first," Nari said as they spread my ankles and knees apart, opening me wider for their investigations and their eyes. "I figure I'm owed first go."

"Yes, yes, please." I heard the rip of a condom wrapper as more fingers explored my intimate folds of wet flesh. Ricardo, too, was touching me. It was as if they wouldn't be content until every part of my pussy was investigated.

The pad of a finger brushed my clit. I gasped and arched my back, wanting to give in to the drug-like feelings they were generating in me. Surrender, control, possession…it was all so divine. "Please," I said again weakly, almost dancing on the fingers invading me, touching me.

"I think she's ready," Nari's voice.

The sensations stopped then the head of a seriously wide, sheathed cock nudged at my entrance. "Oh, God," I mumbled into the bedding.

In one firm push, Nari forged into my body.

"Oh, ow, ow," I cried, pain and pleasure a confusing soup of emotions. His cock was thick and meaty, much bigger than Enrique…and it had been so long since Dale.

He stilled and let me adjust to his size. "Ah, *si, si,*" he hissed. He pulled out nearly all the way then surged back in, more powerfully than before. If he hadn't been holding my hips, I would have shot to the top of the bed. "Ah, sweet heaven, she is so *bella*, Ricardo, so *stretto.*"

He began to jerk in and out, his balls crashing against my vulva. I fumbled for my humming, desperate clit, but just as I found it so did his fingers.

"Allow me," he said in a strained voice.

He flicked across the swollen bud, teasing it from its hood and I cried out at the sensitivity of the nerves he fretted against.

"Easy, angel," Ricardo said. He'd moved to my head and was gripping my upper arms. "Nari's not going to let you come for a while so you have time to do this."

I braced my arms beneath myself and opened my eyes. Inches from my face was Ricardo's impressive cock rising from the black silky hair of his groin. He wrapped his hand around the base of his deep rose-coloured shaft, slid upwards and smoothed over the wide, glassy head then slipped back down to grip the root again.

"I want you to suck my dick while Nari fucks you, Tiffany."

"Yes, yes." My mouth was watering to taste him, saliva pooling on my tongue.

He reached out and tangled his other hand in my hair. But he didn't forge forward. Holding his cock, he allowed me to lick his glans and poke the tip of my tongue into his slit. It was difficult because of the jerking of my body under Nari's thrusts. But I teased at his frenulum and took just his glans in, generating a gentle suction.

"Ah, fuck, yes," he groaned. "Get ready for it, Tiffany, get ready." He let go of the base of his cock, tightened both hands in my hair so my head tipped back slightly, then thrust deep into my mouth, his hips arching and his pubic hair tickling my nose.

Opening wide, I tasted the sweet salt of pre-cum and sucked greedily for more.

"Oh, *si*, that's it," he groaned. He began to slide rapidly back and forth, teasing my throat with each inward push, his timing in perfect synchrony with Nari's—both men hitting full depth at the same time, one in my pussy, one in my mouth.

I matched his groans with breathless moans of my own. The feelings they were creating in me were edgy and spiralling upwards, my clit building to a spectacular climax. I was vaguely aware of the music, which had grown to a crashing crescendo, mixing with the slapping of flesh on flesh, grunting and groaning. The swirling, combining sounds were so erotic to my ears I would never forget them, not for as long as I lived.

Nari's fingers dug harder into my hips as Ricardo continued to fuck my mouth. Somewhere in the recesses of my mind I knew I should be concerned about bruising, but the thought was as fleeting as a wisp of smoke from an extinguished match. I felt so desirable, so wanted, even more so than when I was on a catwalk or at a shoot. I hadn't felt like this since Dale had been in my life— holding me, touching me...

"*Merda*, I'm coming," Nari shouted, reaching up and gripping my shoulder, pulling me back harder on to him. "Come with me. Both of you. Now."

His stern command and the increased pace of his wicked fingers rotating my clit sent me into a freefall of pleasure. I was dizzy and high as ecstasy burnt over my nerves. Black spots filled my vision as pleasure swamped me and my pussy exploded in a series of powerful contractions.

I tried to cry out but couldn't. Ricardo had sent his cock even deeper into my mouth. Behind me Nari was riding through his orgasm, a string of strained Italian words spilling from his lips and his harshly expelled breaths a harsh wind on my back.

I sucked Ricardo's cock with all the intensity of my own climax, as if my life depended on it, as if I would never get enough.

"*Si, si cazzo,*" Ricardo groaned, his fingers tight in my hair, his hips powering into my face.

His cock thickened, hardening over my tongue and palate. I relaxed my jaw and as he butted the back of my throat, I swallowed, taking the smooth crown of his cock even deeper. With my lips stretched around the base to accommodate his size, he stilled.

The first spurt hit my throat and trickled straight down my gullet. I curled my tongue around his shaft like a deep duvet, drew in a thin ribbon of air from around his musky pubic hair and sucked.

"Ah, *si*, swallow it all," he cried out above me. "Swallow me."

He pulled out an inch then pumped deep again, his cock pulsating and pouring salty, viscous fluid into my mouth. This time he stayed lodged there as I sucked every last drop from him.

Nari was bent over me, kissing my shoulders, his cock twitching in my pussy, which was being ravaged by the aftershocks of my orgasm. He'd moved his fingers from my clit, allowing it to retract and throb without being hyper-stimulated.

Eventually Ricardo pulled from my mouth, tugged his fingers from my tangled hair and flopped down on the bed.

I wriggled forward, panting for breath.

"Wait," Nari said, holding my hips. "Let me hold the condom."

His fingers moved down my butt then he slipped his cock from my pussy. As soon as he was out, I allowed my arms and legs to collapse from their kneeling position. My head landed on the plump pillow next to Ricardo.

"You are very giving," Ricardo said breathlessly and reached out to stroke my cheek with the back of his long index finger.

"So are you," I said with a smile.

Nari left the bed. I heard a toilet flush and the sound of running water. "Shall we eat now?" he asked, walking back into the room. There was a rise of colour on his cheek bones, but other than that he seemed to have completely recovered from our strenuous joining.

"Good idea," I said, suddenly remembering I'd forgotten to have breakfast. Dale was always telling me off for that.

Still gloriously naked, Nari reached for the phone on the bedside table. "What would you like, Tiffany?"

I lifted my arms above my head, stretched out my legs and pointed my toes. Dragged in a long, deep breath. "I don't know, maybe some blinis and smoked salmon, or caviar, but only Beluga, and with those little wheat-free cracker breads. Oh, and more Bollinger, ice cold."

Nari placed my order precisely and added two orders of steak and chips to the menu.

Ricardo left the bed and replenished everyone's drinks. As I was taking a refreshing sip of my champagne, a tinny rap song invaded Nari and Ricardo's now lulling music still playing from the iPod.

"What is that?" Nari asked, sipping his whisky and frowning.

"My cell, excuse me." I slipped from the bed and walked into the living area to retrieve my handbag. The song instantly made me think of Dale – it was his favourite and he'd programmed it into my phone one evening for fun. I really should change it since every time it rang I thought of him, something I wasn't supposed to be doing.

I hadn't reached the call in time so I retrieved the voicemail. It was Rachel. She'd scheduled me to go to Paris at the end of the week for the Nicole Farhi show. Tickets at the BA first class desk, reservation at The Ritz. Her voice was stern, commanding – there was no room for argument or negotiation. It was what I'd be doing. End of story.

I shrugged, flicked the phone shut and tossed it back into my bag. At one time I would have been cross with Rachel for leaving me instructions and making reservations without my consent, but it didn't seem to matter anymore. And like Naomi had said, work was the best thing for me. And hey, it was *working* out pretty well for me today. I'd only thought of Dale once since I'd met Nari and Ricardo...or maybe twice, I couldn't be sure. *Well, three times max...*

Slipping into the bathroom, I freshened up. The food arrived and I stayed out of sight until the butler had left. No point risking unnecessary sightings of me in *Ingresso Livello's* room, which would be massive fodder for the press. The hotel was discreet, yes – incredibly so – but still, even a Savoy butler could be tempted with a cheque the size of a couple of years' salary for one juicy story. And me and Nari and Ricardo – *Mmm, that is juicy to the extreme!*

"This looks good," I said, wandering in naked from the bathroom and thoroughly enjoying the hungry looks the men gave to me rather than the food.

"Not as good as you," Nari said, licking his lips and trailing his gaze down the length of my body.

Ricardo frowned. "You don't have to go somewhere, do you?"

I shook my head then nibbled on a blini topped with a thin sliver of smoked salmon and took a swig of champagne. "Nope, nothing doing for the rest of today."

Ricardo grinned and slid his knife into a steak that looked as soft as butter. "Excellent. Now eat up, you'll need your strength. We haven't finished with you yet."

Chapter Three

With my meal finished and my third glass of champagne making my head wonderfully floaty, I spun a naked pirouette by the window, arms up like a ballerina and my small breasts jiggling.

Nari laughed as I misjudged my landing and sat heavily on the cream and gold striped chair to my right.

I pouted and stood again but, as soon as I did, an unclothed Ricardo was there, pulling me into his arms.

"Ah, sweet angel, no more champagne for you."

I locked my hands at the nape of his neck, his hard tendons and muscles pressed to my slender forearms and his wide chest butted up against my breasts. "Oh, I'm fine. If there is one thing I can do, it's drink champagne."

Ricardo stared down at me with his intense black eyes. "I think we can safely say there are many other things you can do."

I giggled and pressed a kiss to his lips. "I'm glad you think so." His cock was growing hard between our bodies, and his chest hair raked at my nipples.

"Mmm," he said, pulling back and licking his lips. "You taste so sweet."

"And you taste of...meat and chips and whisky." I pressed harder against him and his cock bobbed and strained against me. "You taste Neanderthal," I whispered. "Genius pianist turned caveman. I can just see your next video—you both carrying girls over your shoulder to your cave and thumping your chests like Tarzan."

He raised his brows. "Now there is an idea, what do you think, Nari?"

Nari was at our side, also naked. But there was no humour in his expression...just desire—serious, determined, dark desire. "I think time for talking is over." He sucked his index finger into his mouth, withdrew it, wet and shiny, and rested his hand in the small of my back.

Ricardo smile dropped, too. He twitched his brows, his nostrils flared and his hands smoothed down my back until he was cupping my butt in a firm, possessive hold.

Shivers of renewed desire snaked up my spine and stole my breath. The look of carnal need in Ricardo's eyes was turning darker and more sinful by the second, rapidly coming to match Nari's.

"Ricardo," Nari murmured, "are *you* going to show Tiffany just how grateful you are for her involvement at the shoot?"

"Oh, yes," Ricardo whispered onto my lips. He tugged at the small round curves of my butt, separating the cheeks, exposing the cleft right down to my pussy. "I'm going to show her just how much I appreciate her involvement."

Nari's wet finger was in the cleft, trailing down towards my anus. When he reached it, he pressed, just a little, at my tightest hole.

I gasped and tilted away, squashing up harder against Ricardo.

"Tiffany," Ricardo murmured, his lips brushing mine. "I want to show you my gratitude in your most sacred place. Will you let me?"

As he spoke Nari's finger continued to press…and press. My anus clenched, tightened, but still he exerted pressure. I was not new to anal sex, but it had only ever been Dale. Birthdays, holidays, special occasions—it was our thing. The thought of letting Ricardo penetrate me where it required so much trust was both exciting and dangerous and sent hot needles of shameful delight to my breasts, my clit and my back passage.

Before I could say another word, Nari's finger was inside me—probing in smoothly right up to his knuckle.

"Oh," I gasped, clinging to Ricardo.

"Have you been touched here before?" Nari asked, kissing the slight ball of my shoulder.

I nodded.

Ricardo smiled and his eyelids dropped slightly. "Good, then we all know what we are doing."

My champagne glow faded and I was right back in the hotel room, sober as a judge. My yearning for more double action with Nari and Ricardo was the overwhelming emotion, the undeniable want in my system.

But could I?

Of course I could, I'd done it before. Surely it was like riding a bike. Desperately turned on, I tugged at Ricardo's nape and he obligingly lowered his head for my kiss.

Nari spoke in his language — soft, murmuring words that were incomprehensible to me. He added another finger into my back passage and the stretching, invaded feeling I recognised was like a signal for my clit to cry out for stimulation and for my pussy to begin to weep.

"Yes," I breathed, "Yes, I want this, I need this."

As if something unspoken passed between the two men, Nari slipped from me and I was manoeuvred so Ricardo was behind me.

Nari ducked and kissed me, hotly, hungrily. He scooped my small breasts into both his palms, squeezed, massaged and pulled my nipples to tight little points.

I moaned as every nerve in my body went on high alert for more stimulation, more sensation, then grabbed for Nari's shoulders and gripped him hard. Ricardo had sat on the chair behind me, leaning forward, his lips and tongue tracing the dimples in the small of my back, the rise of my buttocks, the seam to my ass...

"Lube," he murmured.

"Table next to you, beside the condoms," Nari answered between kisses. "Bend forward, Tiffany." He released my breasts, took a step back and held out his hands. I grasped them as I tipped to a right angle, my knees weak and my skin feverish with anticipation.

My butt and pussy were on full view to Ricardo. I was open and vulnerable to his fingers, mouth...anything he wanted to insert into me. The feeling of handing over trust and believing in his ability to pleasure me was wonderful and liberating. I couldn't wait for him to get on with it.

Suddenly cool, slippery lube touched against my cleft as Ricardo traced one finger around my asshole.

"Oh, God," I muttered, staring down at the deep pile of the burgundy carpet. Dale had always been so gentle, so reverent with me, and I missed the absolute certainty that I would be handled carefully and only feel pleasure.

"Such a sweet ass," Ricardo said, circling the taut wrinkles of skin of my anus. "You look tight though, angel. You will have to relax for my cock."

I nodded down at the carpet—I could do this, I *would* do this even if Dale wasn't here anymore. I shifted my butt from left to right, almost impatiently.

Ricardo let out a huff of amusement and sank what felt like two fingers into my ass. I bit against my lip as the sensation of dirty delightfulness made my head spin and my body instantly cry out for more. My ass wanted to pull him in, suck him higher.

Ricardo let out a murmur of approval then began to scissor his fingers.

"Ah, ah, ah," I said, jerking at the bite of pain his actions produced.

"Easy, baby," Nari said from above me, "just let him lube you up, it will ease his way."

Repeatedly, Ricardo stretched his fingers into 'v' shapes, easing the tightness from my anus. I shut my eyes and allowed the copious amounts of lube he was applying to soothe and cool the sting.

"That's it. You're ready," Ricardo finally said.

Nari urged me to stand upright. I looked at him. His cock was fully erect, bobbing from his dark coils of pubic hair. His eyes were on fire with lust.

"Don't look so worried," he said, his mouth twitching into a devilish smile. "We are only going to give you pleasure. Extreme pleasure."

He eased me backwards so I was standing between Ricardo's spread knees.

I glanced over my shoulder. Ricardo's big, sheathed cock stuck straight up and his chest was rising and falling as rapidly as mine. He curled his fingers around my hipbones and tugged me slightly, as if urging me to sit on his lap.

"What do you want me to do, just sit down on you?" I asked, incredulously.

"It will be better…this way, you are in control," he said.

Despite my anxiety I was intrigued at the suggestion. The thought of just dropping down and impaling myself on his cock was so naughty, so shocking that my pussy clamped shamelessly at the idea.

"I will help you," Nari said, hooking his suntanned arms beneath my armpits as though giving me a harness.

Ricardo was touching my ass again, smoothing the globes of my cheeks, separating them. I stared into Nari's eyes and sank a little. Ricardo's cock brushed my bottom.

"That's it," Ricardo said. "A little more so I can get into position."

I dropped lower and the wide, smooth crown of his cock butted against my asshole.

"Hold yourself open," Ricardo instructed. "Offer yourself to me."

Suspended over Ricardo by Nari's sturdy arms, I reached down, gripped my cheeks and tugged them apart, separating myself for Ricardo. The gesture seemed so rude and crude, demeaning and exhilarating… I sank a fraction farther, wanting more. Instantly I was aware of a pressure on my anus — hard, unmoving, impossibly wide pressure.

"Relax, angel, relax," Nari said, his lips moving over my cheek to nibble at my ear.

It was hard to relax when I had a maelstrom of sensations besieging me…a lot of desire, a little fear, a whole pile of longing.

"Just sink down and I will be inside you," Ricardo said, his voice strained, his fingertips tightening on my hips.

I did as he asked.

The moment of his penetration was exquisite. Sharply erotic, it generated a furious whack of desire through my entire pelvis.

"Oh, yes, ah, ah," I moaned softly into Nari's neck. "Is he in?"

"Yes," Nari murmured. "You're doing great."

I dropped a little more, allowing myself to adjust to the stretching, burning sensation as I took his thick cock deeper.

"*Si, si*, so good," Ricardo gasped, his fingers rubbing more cool lube into the sore, taut skin of my sphincter. "Sit all the way, take me, take me into your body."

I trembled in Nari's grip and impaled myself some more. A guttural moan rumbled up from deep in my chest. Pleasure was overriding my senses. Pleasure...and the need to come.

"Oh, God," I said, finally releasing my buttocks to try and reach my clit. "I need...I need...here, too." I couldn't manoeuvre enough to touch myself.

"I'll help you," Nari said, sliding one of his hands from under me but keeping firm support there with the other. "You just need to sit all the way and then I can help you."

Ricardo's pubic hair was tickling my butt so I knew I wasn't far from being completely invaded by him. I felt so full, so impacted with cock, I didn't know if I could take any more. But I wanted to.

"*Si, si*, more, baby," Ricardo panted. He was perfectly still beneath me. Somewhere in my befuddled state, I admired his fierce self-control. The need to thrust into me must be agonising for him.

I placed my hands on the arms of the chair, braced myself and sat completely down on Ricardo's cock until my butt was touching his lower belly. I cried out. At the same time my back fell on to Ricardo's chest. It had been so long since I'd felt such exquisite fullness. Having a man in my bottom was so primal and made me feel so violated. But Ricardo, like Dale, also made me feel adored and respected, with pleasure the only goal.

Ricardo curled his arms around me and reached for my breasts. He began to knead them in a slow, firm rhythm.

I death-gripped the arms of the chair. "My clit," I gasped looking pleadingly at Nari. I needed more. I needed my greedy knot of nerves stimulated to turn the stressed discomfort at my anus into erotic pleasure. I was so expanded, so taut, and the very back section of my portal was on fire.

"I'm here," Nari said, dropping to his knees in front of me. "Open up."

I spread my legs as best I could within the confines of my position. Instantly his hands were on my pussy, stroking the soft folds and searching out my clit.

Dropping my head against Ricardo's cheek, I shut my eyes and became lost in the heady world the two beautiful pianists had taken me to. Only sensation existed – touches and caresses and all the time, their music rang through my ears.

Nari lifted my legs to place my knees over Ricardo's thighs, opening me farther for his eyes and his touch. "You look so beautiful like this," he crooned, the pads of his fingers circling my clit. "Ricardo's dick has stretched your tiny body so much...so, so much." His fingertips brushed over the smooth skin between my entrance and my anus. "You are all quivering and thin around him. You couldn't take any bigger, angel."

When I opened my eyes and looked down, I saw his face dipping between my legs, his tongue poked out to take over where his fingers had left off. I groaned as he made contact with my clitoris and jerked my hips slightly, which elicited a gasp from Ricardo.

"Oh, oh yes, yes, yes," I said, releasing one of the arms of the chair and clutching at Nari's short hair. "Please, make me come, please."

Nari's licks grew determined, flicking over my clit, suckling and rotating...building me up. He added his fingers to his ministrations, shoving two, maybe three, deep into my soaking pussy.

I called out in bliss and tugged at his shiny hair. His fingers stabbed in and out, fucking me harder.

My orgasm claimed me with ferocious speed, shunting the air from my lungs as my whole pelvis convulsed and went into spasm. Floating on a cloud of ecstasy, I became aware of Ricardo's cock pumping within me. I wasn't the only one climaxing.

"Ah, Mother of Mary," he groaned, his fingers clamping like pincers on my breasts. "Sweet heaven above and all the angels."

My entire body was shaking, quaking and trembling, my breaths tortured and fast. Nari slowed his fingers, reduced the use of his tongue to a gentle lapping, and carefully and considerately brought me down from my high.

My body sagged against Ricardo, seeming to melt against him. His cock softened slightly but I could still feel him deep in my rectum. I shut my eyes and was greeted with blackness, a deep, dark well of carnal satisfaction.

My God, these men are talented.

Chapter Four

Nari eased me from Ricardo then held my weak body in his arms.

"Did that feel good," he asked, kissing me softly and sweetly with spiced lips that tasted of me.

"Yes," I said, "More than good, it was amazing."

"You are very special," Ricardo said, standing behind me and dropping a kiss into my hair. "The perfect woman to share the pleasure of three with."

"Mmm," I managed, feeling utterly sated. "Pleasure of three, perfect."

Nari laughed. "I think we have fucked her into a trance, Ricardo."

I fluttered my eyes closed...all I could think of was sleep. My bottom felt empty but scorched, my pussy a swollen mass of satisfaction. The music still playing was dreamy and floaty like a lullaby.

"Let's lay her on the bed," Ricardo said, swinging me up into his arms. "We could probably all do with a siesta."

* * * *

I awoke to find dusk filling the room with pink and purple light. My first thought was to use the toilet. After easing up from between the sleeping bodies of Nari and Ricardo, I tiptoed into the bathroom and shut the door. Even in the bathroom, the gentle piano music from Nari's iPod still played through the speakers.

After relieving myself, I washed up and stared in the mirror. I looked like a completely wanton supermodel. My hair was bed-tousled and my makeup smudged. My lips and breasts appeared a little swollen and bruised.

I ran my hands down my body. My hips were tender from being gripped but there was no sign of any marks...yet!

Spotting a still-wrapped complimentary toothbrush, I took advantage and quickly scrubbed at my teeth. The hotel body lotion smelt nicely of almond and ginger. Slopping a generous dollop into my palm, I set about slathering my body in it. Mmm, the scent made me hungry again.

Eventually I headed out of the bathroom, intent upon finding caviar and champagne.

I stopped in my tracks.

My jaw slackened and my breath hitched.

Nari and Ricardo were awake.

Nari and Ricardo were on the bed, kissing—passionately. An animalistic mating of mouths, as if they were having a battle for control. Their limbs were wound together, tangled and twisting. Big, long hands smoothed and explored hard, tense bodies.

I went to speak but couldn't. Went to move but was glued to the floor. The need to watch them was irresistible, compelling.

But why was I so surprised? Two talented musicians who composed and played together like a single person and who travelled the world performing and being adored were bound to have a very special connection.

Of course they are lovers.

My brain whirred. It wasn't like they were homosexual. They were bi. They'd proven that much to me this afternoon...but what about their videos? The sexy, sultry images that had the world talking about *Ingresso Livello*. No one would ever guess that they were into both, that they swung both ways. They were so fiercely masculine, so saturated in testosterone...but now, of course, it was that very fact that made them all the more erotic for me to watch.

Legs slightly weak, I walked to the chair and sat down, tilting my head and continuing to observe their fierce kissing and writhing bodies.

Suddenly Ricardo pushed at Nari, sending him over onto his stomach. Between one breath and the next, Ricardo had dragged Nari to the end of the bed and bent him over—Nari's rump stuck in the air, his arms were locked beneath him and his head hung low.

Ricardo looked over at me and stared for a moment with an expression of mild confusion.

Then he grinned and slapped Nari on the butt, hard and stinging. The sound sliced through the room, and I knew the slap would have hurt like hell.

Nari jerked forward but didn't cry out.

Ricardo soothed the already burning red mark with his palm, but only for a second, because then he rained down a blow on Nari's other cheek.

This time Nari yelped as the air was forced from his lungs with the strength of the blow. He jerked his head upwards.

My butt tingled and I winced for him.

"Shh," Ricardo said, again soothing the mark.

I realised that there had been a shift in power between them. When I had first met Nari and Ricardo at the shoot, Nari had seemed to be the forceful one, the one with the ideas and opinions. It was he who instructed Ricardo and expected to be obeyed. But it appeared that in the bedroom the power control switched to Ricardo. Nari was submissive, bent before him with his long, muscular body trembling, quivering — offered up for Ricardo's pleasure.

Ricardo smoothed his hand down the cleft in Nari's ass the way he had mine, his fingers shiny with lube, which must have been within reach on the bed.

I trembled a little as he shoved two of his thick fingers into Nari's anus. Nari groaned and dropped his head down again. I studied his cock, erect and bobbing, the slit shiny with pre-cum. Despite his yelps and groans, he was thoroughly enjoying having Ricardo dominate and invade him.

"I'm going to fuck you hard today…really hard," Ricardo said through gritted teeth. "You think you can take it?"

"*Si*, oh God, *si*," Nari moaned, arching his back, offering his puckered hole higher.

Ricardo pulled his fingers from Nari's ass and fisted his own massively swollen erection. He positioned the head of his cock at Nari's entrance, wiggling it slightly to make sure he had purchase at the very centre of the clenched sphincter. Then in a sudden, fast penetration, he slammed into Nari's ass.

Nari yelled out. His neck snapped up.

"Take it," Ricardo snarled. "Take it all."

I hardly recognised the sweet, calm, controlled lover who had taken me in the ass so carefully and reverently. Now he was wild, animalistic, pleasure his only destination whatever the means of getting there.

"Oh, God, harder, faster," Nari shouted out, fisting the bedsheets. "Give me everything you've got. I can take it."

Ricardo grunted, gripped Nari's shoulders and dragged him back onto his impalement with a violent thrust. His teeth were bared and as he pumped wildly I could see the dimple in his right buttock dipping and filling, dipping and filling. Both men's bodies were glistening with sweat, their acres of perfect golden skin rippling beneath the surface with the effort of their joining.

Nari reached down and fisted his cock, began to pump it, masturbating as Ricardo fucked him.

A naughty idea sprang into my head. I wanted to be part of their mating, part of their ecstasy.

Rising, I licked my lips, stepped to the end of the bed and caught Ricardo's eye.

His gaze was misted, possessed.

"Can I suck his cock?" I asked.

Without a pause in his thrusting, Ricardo nodded. Then he tipped back his head and shut his eyes.

I sank to my knees, just managing to fit between the bed and Nari's body.

Wrapping my hands around his turgid erection, I bumped against his moving fist.

He looked down at me, his expression one of pain and ecstasy. "Ah, *bella*, Tiffany, angel, yes, *si*, *si*."

I smiled and licked my lips. He stilled his hand, gripping the root of his cock. Excitement coursed through my veins as I tipped forward and took the head into my mouth. He hissed above me, cupped my nape and held me firm.

With my head held prisoner, Ricardo's thrusting sent Nari rushing in. Quickly relaxing my jaw and throat, I clung to his thighs. His cock was so thick and long, and tasted musky and masculine on my palate.

"Suck it hard, Tiffany, no mercy," Ricardo ordered. "It's how he likes it, hard and rough. Use your teeth."

Nari groaned and his legs muscles trembled beneath my palms. I let my teeth graze his shaft as he pumped in and out, increasing the tension as he moaned in tortured bliss. I was entrenched in their joining, invested in giving back to them the exquisiteness of my earlier climax — returning the giddily euphoric favour.

The already wild pace picked up and I was almost knocked over. If Nari hadn't been holding me, I would have been a heap on the floor, but his hand on my neck kept me attached to him. There was nothing gentle or romantic about their fucking — it was violent and feral, as if they were angrily seeking a pleasure that they were frustrated they even needed.

Salty fluid began to seep from Nari's cock. He hardened further, his slit widening.

"*Cazzo, cazzo*, now!" Ricardo shouted.

Nari yelled out, his fingers dug into my scalp and he poured his seed into my mouth. I gulped and swallowed, breathing impossible. More and more came, his cock pulsating and sliding deeper and deeper. My head began to spin, my eyes blurred.

Ricardo grunted, stilled and then he was shouting in his own language, loud and uninhibited. I pulled back and Nari released me, allowing me to drag in a lungful of air. Gasping, I stared up into his face as his lover filled him with his desire. Nari's expression was one of pure bliss, beads of sweat had formed in his stubble, his eyes were tight shut and his mouth hung slackly open.

As suddenly as the whole thing had started, it was over. Ricardo must have pulled his cock from Nari, because he stepped away, leaving me kneeling in front of Nari, who appeared frozen.

I slid to the side, stood and touched Nari's shoulder. "Are you all right?"

He straightened, opened his eyes and turned to me, his mouth tilted into a smile. "Never better."

Ricardo appeared on his other side and stroked his finger down Nari's cheek. "I'm sorry if we surprised you," he said, looking at me.

I shrugged. "Not much surprises me anymore. I'm grateful when something does."

Nari grinned then his lips whispered over mine. "Thank you," he murmured. "That was a wonderful orgasm."

He kissed me, hot and open-mouthed, his tongue tangling with mine. Ricardo wound his arm around my waist and suddenly his mouth was there, too...his tongue, his lips, his teeth.

I sighed and let myself get lost in the wonderfully sensual three-way kiss.

Chapter Five

"Darling, people are already in a fluster about this one. I can't believe you didn't tell me until after the event." Naomi was sitting next to me at an exclusive West End club wearing a racy Vivian Westwood number. It was the official release day of *Il Piacere de Tre*, though of course the video had hit the Internet ahead of time and was already drumming up considerable controversy.

"I only found out about it myself an hour after I was supposed to be there," I said, sipping a deliciously chilled glass of Cristal.

She tutted. "How typical of you at the moment, and I have to say again…" She glanced at Ricardo and Nari, who were taking their seats at the next table along with several big wigs from the music industry, "You are one seriously lucky bitch. I'd writhe around with them any day. Whew, talk about drop dead gorgeous, those two could turn a nun to sin."

I studied them. It was the first time I'd seen *Ingresso Livello* since saying goodbye at The Savoy one month ago. Since then, I'd been proactive in trying to heal my broken heart. I'd been busy working in Paris and Milan, and had taken a trip to New York to visit my cousin and enjoy some retail therapy. I wasn't sure it was working, though. I still missed Dale every minute of every day. It was as though something vital in my soul had been removed and I had no idea how to replace it.

But *Ingresso Livello* were, as Naomi said, devastatingly gorgeous and every woman in the room was sneaking glances at them. Their finely tailored suits hung beautifully on their obscenely perfect bodies, their skin was flawless and tanned, and Ricardo had cut his hair a little shorter. It suited him.

Their manager took to the stage and tapped a microphone. The hum of conversation died.

"Thank you all for joining us this evening for the official releases of *Ingresso Livello's* latest sublime track, *Il Piacere de Tre*," he said with a self-important smile.

There was a ripple of applause and Nari and Ricardo nodded in acknowledgement.

I took a sip of champagne.

"Without further ado, please sit back enjoy the music and the show. There will be time afterwards for press to ask questions."

The lights dimmed and an enormous white screen glowed behind the stage.

I sat back, knotted my fingers in my lap and sucked in a deep breath. I hadn't had a chance to see the final result of our filming…I'd been too busy. Nerves, apprehension and curiosity suddenly flooded my system.

Through the silence of the packed room, the first tinkling sounds of a piano flowed through the air. The brightness of the screen slowly faded so that it showed the windows of the room we'd filmed in. They were blinding white against the pale carpet and walls, and in each stood a tall, broad silhouette—Nari and Ricardo. Standing only in jeans that appeared the palest shade of blue because of the way the shot was overexposed, they were perfectly still. The camera moved slowly from Ricardo to Nari, closed in on their beautiful backs and tight butts allowing the viewer to absorb every tiny indentation and sinewy taut muscle.

The tune picked up a fraction and the camera pulled back, suddenly my butt filled the screen, high and pert and fabulous in the striking scarlet lace thong. As I strutted towards the men, my feet were in perfect time with the notes playing out. The camera stayed still and my back and legs stretched into the shot and finally my swishing hair and bare feet.

Once level with Nari and Ricardo, I also became a silhouette. There I paused, then reached out and touched their shoulders.

The shot swung to Nari's face as he turned and studied me with an expression of red hot lust. His eyes were blacker than black and glistened shamelessly as he swiped his tongue over his bottom lip. He cupped my chin, drew me to face him. Our skin was pale and backlit by the sun, making our features all the starker.

The tune picked up to a racier pace, soaring through the air and the attention moved to our lips. The camera's focus hovered while we were a whisper apart, then as we kissed it zoomed in close so that it was just our mouths filling the enormous screen. It was highly erotic to see a kiss so huge and detailed and to observe Nari's mouth taking charge as it covered mine.

Ricardo's expression was next in the shot as the music dipped to a deep, masculine low. His longer hair, carefully messy, flopped forward slightly as he pressed his lips to my shoulder blades.

I squirmed on my chair. I could almost feel that soft kiss again.

"Fuck, those men look really hot for you," Naomi whispered into my ear. "Either they are Oscar-standard actors or they really did fancy a piece of your ass."

Draining my champagne to cover my discomfort, I gave a nonchalant little shrug.

The cinematography was awesome. Nancy had captured all of our expressions exquisitely. I glanced around the audience. Without exception, everyone stared up at the big screen, eyes wide, mouths slackened. The stunning music was sexy and haunting, and the images captivating and daring. I could hardly dare think of how she'd portrayed me when I'd climaxed.

Glancing up again, I saw Ricardo swirling the tip of his tongue over my navel. I flashed to a memory of a time when Dale had filled my navel up with ice cream. It had been cold and made me shiver, then he'd licked it out before licking me lower, making me shiver for an entirely different reason.

A waiter topped up my empty champagne as the scene moved to the bed. I was sprawled on the bleached sheets in my pretty lace underwear, legs and arms outstretched. I looked great, thin and long, and my expression one of relaxation and bliss.

"New range La Perla?" Naomi whispered.

I nodded.

Ricardo and Nari were kissing my feet, every lick and press of their lips caught by the camera, their dark hair a sexy contrast to the paleness of my flesh. Nancy then concentrated on their wonderfully elegant fingers as they smoothed up my legs then traced the outline of my hips and the material of my underwear. Four big, dark male hands exploring my body, leaving no section untouched. My spine was arching towards them, my flesh quivering under their fingertips, and my chest sighing beneath their palms. I hadn't even been aware that had all been happening. It certainly hadn't been acting on my part.

The music lifted, heading towards its big crescendo. My heart rate rocketed. I was sandwiched between Nari and Ricardo now, staring down at Nari's face. My expression was one of pure desire, eyes wide and mouth loose as if about to speak. I remembered only too well that had been the moment my clit had come into contact with his granite-hard shaft.

Sweeping down our squashed tight bodies, the shot showed how tiny I was between the two enormous men— my long limbs slender and delicate next to their big brawn. A textbook study of masculine and feminine, as opposite as night and day.

"You are one seriously lucky cow," Naomi muttered under her breath then knocked back her drink in one go.

Ricardo was moving his hips to the beat of the music, pushing me into Nari. My clit began to hum at the memory. There was nothing I could have done about the build to climax that day. It had been impossible to resist.

I glanced across the room at *Ingresso Livello*. As if sensing my eyes on him, Nari turned to me. He tilted one side of his mouth in a wickedly sexy smile as his gaze snared mine.

He knew my secret.

Looking up at the screen again, I was greeted with a mega-close-up of my face.

Oh shit!

Nancy had captured my orgasm in glorious detail and timed it to coincide with the crashing climax of *Il Piacere de Tre*. My eyes had widened so that all the white could be seen around my midnight blue irises, and my jaw was dropped low as if in a silent exclamation. Then with a sudden crinkle of my features, my jaw tensed and my teeth came together. My eyes rolled back in their sockets as my lids fluttered shut.

The shot rolled to Nari's face, his expression exquisite agony, then to Ricardo's back, moving and writhing and coated in a glistening sheen of sweat.

A flush of mortification ran through me as the music came to a lulling end and the screen flicked off.

"Fabulous acting, darling," Naomi said, nodding approvingly. "Simply fabulous."

"Er, thanks." I studied her face, looking for signs of sarcasm. There didn't appear to be any. She just looked impressed.

"Hopefully Rachel will be getting calls from Hollywood," she said, "after that performance." She lit a cigarette, despite the no smoking rule.

"Yes, that would be great." Applause rang through the club and I glanced at Nari and Ricardo, who were smiling and accepting compliments from all around the table. There seemed to be much handshaking and back-slapping going on.

Had I got away with it?

Naomi knew me better than anyone—well, except for Dale—and she'd thought I'd been acting. It seemed my sneaky orgasm would be a secret between Nari and me...and that was okay, because I knew a much bigger secret about them.

I suddenly felt hot and wanted a moment alone before I had to get involved in the excitement. Naomi's smoke was thick and I knew no one would dare ask her to put it out. Reaching for my bag, I pulled it over my shoulder as I stood.

"Back in a minute," I said to Naomi.

Spinning on my heels, I then strode to the exit, intent on finding the ladies' restroom and recovering my composure.

I stopped.

Froze.

My breath caught in my chest.

Standing in the doorway, his impossibly wide shoulders filling the space and his head nearly skimming the frame, was Dale. He wore his soft, black leather jacket and leather cycle trousers and held his motorbike helmet in his right hand.

What the hell was he doing here?

I stepped up to him, trying to ignore the fact that he was even more soul-achingly gorgeous than I'd remembered. He'd had his hair braided into corn rows and it suited him, highlighted his masculine features and his high cheekbones.

"Tiffany," he said, in a quiet murmuring voice that made my knees turn to jelly.

"Why are you here, Dale?"

"I needed to see you."

The dim lights in the room cast shadows on his coffee-coloured skin and I could see that he looked tired. "You haven't needed to see me in four months," I said, folding my arms. "Why today?"

He shook his head and his blacker than black eyes narrowed as he pulled his brows low. "Because I've finally realised what a fucking idiot I've been, Tiff. Without you I'm empty, hollow. There is no reason to get up in the morning, no damn reason to go to bed at night."

A bubble of hope grew in my belly. *Was he saying he missed me the way I missed him?* I beat down that teasing emotion, the possibility of letting it grow then having it burst was too scary...more than my bruised soul could cope with. I was getting on with my life, getting over Dale...

Wasn't I?

"Baby," he said, reaching out and cupping my jaw. "Can you ever forgive the idiotic way I've behaved?"

I shook my head, felt the sharp nip of tears behind my eyes.

He set down his helmet then placed his other hand on my opposite cheek. "You know I found it hard—you dashing off all the time, fancy cities and fancy people, leaving me at home waiting for you."

"You were working, too," I managed even though my throat was as dry as a desert.

His wide, full lips tipped into a grin. "Yeah, but not doing the sort of stuff you do." He nodded over my head at the screen. "Did you enjoy that assignment?"

I shrugged. "It was a job, it paid well." He didn't *ever* need to know exactly how I'd been paid for my troubles. That was none of his business. Not when we hadn't been together at the time.

"You look great even if it does pain me to see other men worshipping your body... I'm sure it will get you plenty of acting opportunities."

I swallowed tightly. "I hope so."

Dale lowered his head, his mouth a hair's breadth from mine. "I'm different now. I've had a chance to get my mind around the fact that *my* woman is always going to earn more money than me, is always going to have people adoring her body. It took time apart for me to sift through the emotions."

Placing my hands on the cool material of his jacket, I urged him to go on with a furrow of my brow.

He sighed. "I'll admit I was jealous of everyone who was getting a bit of you. I felt like battling away on the stocks to make a wage that was insignificant compared to what you earn made me less of a man. But then when I put all that out of my head —"

"Where have you been?"

"Over to LA to stay with my cousin. Quiet time, long walks on the beach missing you, early nights...missing you."

"You didn't call." I tried hard to keep the whine from my voice but I couldn't help a pout. "Not even to let me know you were okay."

He shook his head. "I'm sorry, I should have. I should have called to see if *you* were okay. You were pretty upset when I left."

He touched his lips to mine and that pesky bubble of hope grew to the size of a hot air balloon.

"Baby, take me back," he breathed against my mouth, "say you will forgive a jealous, confused fool and allow me to spend the rest of my life making up for the last four months. I love you, Tiffany O'Dell. You are devastatingly beautiful on the outside, but I also know how caring and considerate and flawlessly beautiful you are on the inside too."

He released my face and reached into his pocket, pulling out a pink heart-shaped piece of paper I recognised.

"I found this when I put on my jacket this morning." He held it up so I could read my neat, boxy handwriting — *I will always love you.*

He tugged at his bottom lip with his teeth. "I miss the notes you were always leaving me. Notes with words that would make my heart sing all day."

I took the slip of paper and ran my finger over the ink. It was true, I would always love Dale. He was the one for me. No one else had ever made every aspect of my life feel so rich and perfect.

Suddenly he dropped to his knees, cupped my small hands in his big, dark ones. "Tiffany O'Dell," he said, his eyes glued on mine. "Would you do me the very great honour of marrying me?"

His words took a moment to register. They swam and swarmed in my mind, struggling to settle into place, but when they did, a huge, dazzling light filled my soul and my heart soared.

Dale still loves me.

Dale wants to marry me.

After the agony of not being with him, the sudden wild elation seemed so much bigger, so much sweeter—a heady drug to feast on. "Yes, oh yes, you know I will. Dale, I love you so much, I always will."

I dropped to my knees and threw my arms around his neck, burying my face against the skin and scent I wanted to be close to for all of time. He hugged me tightly and possessively, and with every wonderful, desperate kiss we shared, I knew that true happiness had—finally—returned to my life.

THREE-PART HARMONY

Elizabeth Coldwell

Dedication

For Fi, my fellow Wistow Witch

Chapter One

Mark quit the band six days before we were due to embark on our comeback tour.

It was the timing that really upset me, more than the news itself. After all, I'd been expecting him to leave at almost any time over the last eleven years, ever since the day I'd told him Stefan and I were getting married. Instead, he'd stayed—channelling all his sense of loss, betrayal and stone-cold determination never to let another woman hurt him the way I had, into songs that catapulted us to a level of international success far beyond our wildest dreams. Even during the eighteen-month hiatus we'd effectively been on between finishing our last tour and starting work on our latest CD, Mark had given no indication he was unhappy with the state of affairs. Indeed, the flow of ideas, the creative understanding between the three of us who wrote the songs, was as strong as it ever had been. So why walk out now, when Older, No Wiser was top of the download charts and the concert promoters were adding extra dates to the tour after the original ones had sold out within hours?

At least he'd had the decency to announce the news to our faces before leaking it on his Twitter feed. When he'd walked into the rehearsal room, lugging his faithful Stratocaster in its battered leather case, I should have realised something was wrong. But somewhere down the years, the almost telepathic understanding we'd once enjoyed had faded, and now I simply assumed he was grumpy after a bad night's sleep in a strange hotel room.

"Oh, and about time, too!" Paul put his coffee mug down on top of the speaker stack with a theatrical flourish and went to sit behind his drum kit. As half of the rhythm section responsible for keeping time and pulling everything together tightly, he liked to extend that role into the rest of his life. Mark's lack of punctuality never failed to annoy him.

"Sorry, guys. I would have been here sooner, but—" Mark sighed, pushing a hand through his black hair. "Look, there's no easy way of saying this, so I'll just come right out with it. I talked to Jeannie for a couple of hours last night, and I just... I just don't feel my place is in the band anymore. I've got things in my life I need to sort out. Things I should have dealt with years ago. I'm going over to Bodega Bay to stay with Jeannie for a while. She's going to help me work through them."

"So what you're saying is you're walking out on us?" Stefan sounded strangely calm. I was anything but. I knew if I opened my mouth now it would be to emit a scream of pure rage. "A week before we're supposed to open the tour in Pittsburgh, and you've decided that's it? You're off?"

"I appreciate this might not be the greatest time to do it, but I just can't get up on stage night after night. Not with my head where it is right now."

When had Mark stopped talking like the born and bred North London boy he was and started justifying his actions with a stream of mid-Atlantic psycho-babble? Probably about the same time he'd met and married Jeannie Montacute. A New Age therapist who ran an exclusive rehab facility on the California coast, she had encouraged Mark to quit drinking, start eating a macrobiotic diet and perform yoga on a regular basis. Even though they'd split up within two years of the wedding, they were still close. Closer than the rest of us thought, apparently, if the fact he'd gone to her for advice was any proof.

"And it gives me a chance to spend time with the boys," Mark continued. "God knows I haven't seen enough of them over the last couple of years."

The boys were Mark's four-year-old twin sons, Gunnar and Sky. He carried photos of them everywhere, dog-eared from being pulled out of his wallet and looked at repeatedly, and their names were embroidered on his guitar strap. A combination of touring and the breakup with Jeannie meant he'd missed their first steps, their first words. Furious as I was with his decision, I couldn't fail to appreciate his need to watch them grow up.

For a long moment, the five of us exchanged awkward glances. The tension in the room enveloped us like a clammy blanket. Then Davey, always the most forgiving soul, stepped out from behind his bank of keyboards and enfolded Mark in a huge hug.

"All the best, mate. I really hope it works out for you." Davey pulled back, regarding Mark with a rueful look. "And remember, whatever else happens, we'll always have that night in Prague with the strippers and the Danish tour guide."

Stefan's farewell to Mark was curt, but given the history between the two men, it was hardly surprising. Paul, summoning up his trademark crooked grin, shook Mark's hand and told him, "Just fuck off and don't come back, you old bastard," in a tone conveying the exact opposite.

I almost couldn't bring myself to say goodbye to Mark. The announcement of his departure had hit me like a physical blow, and I was afraid if I started telling him how I felt, I'd never be able to stop. But he pulled me into his arms, once such a safe haven for me, and simply murmured over and over, "I'm sorry, Aimee. I'm sorry."

"So am I," I replied, certain he knew I wasn't just referring to the fact he was leaving. When we finally broke the embrace, we both had tears in our eyes.

With one last affectionate ruffle of my hair, Mark turned and left the room. His slamming of the door seemed to echo for an age after he'd gone.

It was typical of Paul to break the silence. "So that's us fucked, then." He glanced at his watch. "The Miller's Arms should be open, if anyone wants to join me for a pint. There are worse places we could have a wake for the band."

"Someone should speak to Martine," Davey pointed out. "The press are going to be all over this as soon as they find out. She can put out the official statement saying the tour's off."

Stefan shook his head. "No, she can put out a statement saying we wish Mark all the best in his future career and we're starting the audition process for a new guitarist as soon as possible."

Paul spoke for all of us. "Are you out of your mind? Do you seriously expect us to find someone to replace Mark before next week?"

"Of course. We might have to reschedule the first couple of dates on the tour, but I'm sure the fans would rather see us later than not at all." He pulled his bass lead out of the amp, a sign we would not be rehearsing today. "But Paul's right. We all need a drink. Come on, I'm buying."

As we followed him out of the rehearsal room, I couldn't help admiring Stefan's confidence in our overcoming this unforeseen setback. It was one of the things I loved best about him, along with his soft hazel eyes and his deliciously firm arse. But somehow I found it impossible to share that confidence. Mark had been such an integral part of Sweet Lies, I simply couldn't imagine life without him.

* * * *

I was still thinking about Mark's departure when I stepped into the shower that evening. Stefan, Paul, Davey and I had decamped to the pub for a couple of hours, though we'd spent more time reminiscing about our more outrageous adventures on the road than discussing a potential new guitarist. We'd managed to let Martine know the bad news before it popped up on the cyber-grapevine. A no-nonsense Geordie, she took it in her stride, as she always did everything. As the band's PR officer for over ten years, she'd grown very practiced at dealing with our various upheavals, whether musical or domestic. As the only girl in the band, I sometimes needed to get away from the boys' club atmosphere that could take over, particularly when we were on tour, and I'd come to regard Martine as my closest female friend. She'd been a shoulder to cry on when relations between Mark and I had become strained, and I'd shared secrets with her I didn't think even my husband knew about. But though I could discuss Mark's departure with Martine on a purely emotional level, I doubted she would really understand how the arrival of a newcomer—always assuming we managed to find one—would affect the dynamic within the band.

With the water beating down and the glass door of the shower cubicle steaming up, I wasn't aware of Stefan's presence till he pushed open the door.

"Room for one more?" he asked.

As he joined me, I drank in the sight of his gorgeous naked body. A couple of years shy of forty, he still had an enviably thick head of chestnut hair and the solid, muscular build that first attracted me to him. He'd been working hard in recent weeks to get in the best shape he could, in preparation for an extensive, gruelling tour, and the results were clearly visible.

Even though he spent most of the set lurking towards the back of the stage, laying down a simple, steady beat on his bass, Stefan still needed to be fit. We all did. We simply had different approaches to fitting the necessary exercise into our lives. I took weekly classes in jazz and contemporary dance at the Pineapple Dance Studios. Stefan went jogging in Hyde Park. Davey rode his horses, Butterscotch and Bonnie, in the countryside near his Rickmansworth home. Paul claimed he kept fit by chasing women.

"Need a backrub?" Stefan joined me beneath the almost tropical spray.

"Mmm," I replied. His fingertips might be calloused from years of pressing against the thick bass strings, but there was magic in their touch. Martine swore by her

Treble

aromatherapy massage sessions at her favourite day spa in Covent Garden, but as far as I was concerned there was no better masseur than my husband.

"Wow, these are serious knots in your shoulders," he commented, working his fingers in hard, circular motions. "You're tense, Aimee."

"Wouldn't you be, after the day we've had?" I relaxed into Stefan's caress, feeling his cock stiffening against the small of my back. "But you know what, the more I think about it, the more certain I am we're going to find a new guitarist."

"Really?" Now his hands moved round in front and gently squeezed my breasts, squishing citrus-scented bubbles between his fingers. "Why's that?"

"I just know someone's out there. Think about it...we have at least two tribute bands doing the rounds, pretending to be us every night. They must know our songs at least as well as we do."

"But how would you feel about someone taking Mark's place who didn't just sound like him, but looked like him, too? Wouldn't you find that a little weird?"

"Maybe." Until Stefan mentioned it, I hadn't considered that aspect. I turned around to face him, standing on tiptoes as he bent over me, so our faces were almost on a level. My fingers traced the tattoo on his right shoulder, the interlinked letters S and L that made up the band's logo. "But I could live with it. And anyway, there's a place in my heart that belongs to Mark. No one else could ever take it."

"Really?" Stefan quirked an eyebrow. "I thought I did a pretty good job of that."

Our lips met, softly at first, then with a passion all our years together had never managed to dim. Stefan's tongue traced the contours of my mouth, probing deeper, tasting me, possessing me intimately. When we finally pulled apart, I threw my head back, exposing my throat to him. He nipped at the skin there, while his thumbs brought my nipples to hard, tight peaks. My fingers twined in his wet hair, liquid heat building between my legs. It had been a while since we'd had sex in the shower, but it had been one of our favourite places when we'd first been together, trying to find places to be alone, away from Mark and all the drama of my failing relationship with him.

"You have all the rest of my heart, Stefan. Now and for always. You know that." I grasped his cock, pulling at it gently, soft skin sliding over the steely inner core. "But let's not talk about Mark or the band anymore. Let's just fuck."

"God, I love it when you talk dirty." Stefan pushed me up against the wall of the shower, his long cock jutting up, demanding entry to my pussy. "You look so innocent, Aimee, but you have the filthiest mouth…"

The coldness of the tiles on my back sent a sharp thrill through me. "Take me, lover," I murmured. "Show me how much you want me."

He lifted me up, using all his considerable strength to hold me in place while I reached down and helped to guide his cock between my wet, puffy lips. Gravity pulled me down on to his length, and I clung tight—arms round his neck, legs locked around the small of his back—as I welcomed him all the way inside me.

Water poured down on us as Stefan thrust into me, droplets falling from his hair and trailing down his broad chest. Nothing felt better than to be joined to my husband like this, our whole world reduced to the places where our bodies connected. Here, now, I was able to forget about all our troubles with the forthcoming tour and Mark's unexpected departure. I could lose myself in the feel of

Stefan's cock pumping in and out of my welcoming channel, the sound of his breathing, harsh and heavy in my ear, the subtle male smell of him that even the citrus shower gel couldn't mask entirely.

Palms flat against the shower wall, he sped up his strokes, pushing me hard against the tiles. Every time he thrust, the friction hit me in just the right place, taking me ever closer to the point where my orgasm was inevitable. I didn't often come without the aid of something touching my clit—fingers, Stefan's tongue or one of my favourite toys—but tonight was going to be one of those nights. My body was as taut as one of Stefan's bass strings, and the sweetest of pleasures was about to be plucked from it.

Stefan stiffened, arse cheeks clenching tight beneath my drumming heels, and with a mighty roar he came, flooding me with his seed.

"God, you're amazing, Aimee," he panted.

"Love you so much," was all I could reply as waves of bliss rippled through my belly, spreading out till even my scalp tingled. Stefan held me as I rode out my climax, then gently helped me to stand.

We shared gentle kisses for a moment, both slowly coming down from the peaks we'd just reached. Eventually, Stefan turned off the water.

He reached for the robe he'd left hanging by the side of the shower cubicle. "I don't know about you, but I could murder a bowl of cornflakes." They were his favourite post-sex snack, sprinkled with sugar and drenched with ice-cold milk.

"Sounds good," I replied. Sitting in our cosy kitchen, munching cereal with my husband, I could pretend everything wasn't about to change, that our whole future wouldn't depend on whether or not we could find a suitable replacement for Mark.

The two of us had come through so much together, within the band and outside of it. Whatever happened, nothing would change our bond, our love. We had to treat the audition process as an adventure, and trust in fate to bring the right person to us.

Chapter Two

When we arrived at the rehearsal studios two mornings later, a dozen potential new band members were waiting for us. As I'd suggested to Stefan, a couple of these would-be recruits played in Sweet Lies tribute bands, if their tufty black hair and neat goatees, so similar to Mark's, were any way of judging.

Paul and Davey had already set up their equipment. "So how does this work, then?" Paul asked, between bites of the bacon and egg baguette he'd brought in from the cafe across the road. "Who's the nice one who encourages them, who's the nasty one who tells them to give it up and get a job in plumbing and who's the smarmy one with his trouser waistband up round his armpits?"

I laughed, instantly recognising the popular reality show he referred to. Still, I could understand Paul's reasoning. We'd never had to audition anyone to join our line-up before. When Sweet Lies had formed, it had been a simple coming together of two existing bands. Stefan, Paul and

Davey had gigged on the London pub and club circuit as Local Heroes, gathering a small but devoted following. Mark and I had been trying to make it as a singer-songwriter double act on the folk scene. When we found ourselves on the same bill, Stefan realised what we could bring to his band. We'd been together ever since, building a camaraderie that had survived all our personal ups and downs. Who knew if it would be possible for any of the strangers who waited outside to fit smoothly into our little gang?

"Let's just crack on with it, shall we?" Stefan said, obviously impatient to have the process over with.

In turn, each auditionee was ushered into the rehearsal room. Almost all of the twelve were ushered out almost as swiftly. The majority of them were session musicians, who would play for anyone as long as the money was right. They had the notes down pat, but there was no real passion in their playing, no sense they were interested in being part of the band long term. We might as well take a digital recorder holding all Mark's guitar licks on stage with us for all they brought to the party.

More impressive were the two guys from the tribute acts. They cared about the music, and we knew they'd both be thrilled to be a part of the band, but Stefan's words about the weirdness of taking on a Mark Deans lookalike still rang in my head. I honestly didn't know whether I could spend so much time around someone who was almost Mark...but not quite. Still, given what we'd already heard, we were convinced one of the two would become our new guitarist.

Then the last man walked into the room, and my heart missed a beat. He couldn't have looked less like Mark, with dirty-blond hair that fell in shaggy waves to his shoulders and a deep cleft in the point of his stubbled chin. In his mid-twenties, he was by some distance the youngest person we'd auditioned today. And when he opened his mouth, his accent placed him from somewhere on the west coast of the United States. Yet the reaction I experienced on his arrival was every bit as powerful as the first time I'd seen Mark. I knew with absolute certainty that one day very soon, we'd end up in bed together.

I didn't know whether Stefan saw the flush rising to my cheeks as I watched the newcomer shrug out of a well-worn leather jacket that appeared to be older than he was. Beneath it, he wore a sleeveless black T-shirt revealing honey-tanned, muscular arms. An intricate piece of knotwork circled his left bicep. I wondered whether that was the only tattoo he had, or whether there was something else, in a more intimate place where no one but his lovers would ever see it...

Dragging my mind away from the thought, enticing as it was, I heard him say, "Jake Anderson."

"And are you playing for anyone at the moment?" Stefan asked.

Jake shook his head. "I was in a band till a couple of weeks ago, gigging most nights of the week. We were just on the verge of signing a pretty sweet deal, then the record company decided they only wanted our lead singer. So here I am, looking round for a break, and you guys announce you need a guitarist. I don't believe in fate, but seriously, the chance to play in Sweet Lies..."

His mention of fate echoed my own thoughts on the situation so closely, I managed to find my voice. "Why is it so important to you?"

"Because... God, you guys have been such a big part of my life. My dad bought Same Destination when I was thirteen, and the first time I heard it, it changed everything for me. I must have played that CD till it wore thin. Hell, I learned to play the guitar because of Mark Deans. I stood in front of my bedroom mirror, imagining I was on stage with you guys at Madison Square Garden. Oh, it sounds crazy now, but I always believed that one day I'd make it happen for real."

The fervour in Jake's voice was unmistakable. He had all the passion for the band the session musicians lacked, but did he have the same knowledge of our back catalogue as the tribute acts, or the facility to learn the songs from our latest album in time?Stefan invited him to plug his guitar into the amp. It didn't surprise me in the least to see Jake owned a vintage sunburst Stratocaster, just like Mark's.

We'd asked everyone to learn Guinevere's Garden as their audition piece. It was the first track Stefan and I ever collaborated on. He'd taken the simple, stately tune I'd picked out on my portable keyboard and built it in a steady crescendo, driven by his galloping bass line and Paul's tightly controlled drumming, to a monstrous finish that had crowds yelling along and beating the air with their fists when we played it live.

The acappella opening of the song showcased the tight, three-part harmonies that characterised our sound. Mark had a classic English rock tenor voice, almost heartbreaking in its purity, which blended perfectly with Stefan's soulful baritone and my soaring three-octave range. We loved to perform the song as our final encore of the night. When the lights came up for the last time – after we'd let the fans chant our names and demand more for a good couple of minutes – and we launched into the opening lines, the effect could be spine-chilling. Whoever took Mark's place not only had to be able to nail those harmonies every single time, he had to be a guitar virtuoso, too, ready to let loose as the bass and drums pushed the song to its climax.

"So walk with me through the garden,
We'll watch the wildflowers bloom,
The light that fades too soon,
Still serves to guide the way…"

Upon hearing Jake's smoky voice for the first time, weaving with mine and Stefan's in an exquisite tapestry of sound, my skin goosepimpled. Davey must have felt it, too, because he missed his cue. His keyboards failed to chime in with the melody, leaving the three of us staring in confusion at each other.

Stefan grinned like a maniac. "All right, Jake! Let's take it to the bridge…" His thumb strummed the strings, going into the heavy riff at the end of the song. Paul picked up the beat, foot hammering his bass pedal.

"Walk with me," I chanted, Stefan joining me with the low harmony. "Walk with me through the garden."

Jake hit a power chord, then charged into the solo. I'd heard it so many times over the years, but this was like the first time all over again. He wasn't just copying what Mark did, he was adding a little flourish here, a run of notes there that stamped his own, fresh mark on what had come before.

When the last notes died away, Stefan gave a subtle nod to the rest of us to bring the song to an end. There wasn't any question in my mind that we'd found our new member, and I was sure the others felt the same. Even Paul, who'd initially bristled at Jake's brash American tones, was beaming with delight. Still, there were things we needed to discuss before we came to our final decision.

"Jake, could you step outside for a moment, please?" Stefan said.

"Sure." Jake slung his jacket over his shoulder and left the room.

Once he'd gone, Stefan asked us, "So, what did everyone think?"

"Do you really need to ask?" Paul stepped out from behind his drum kit, linking his fingers together and stretching his arms till his knuckles cracked. "When was the last time we hit a groove like that?"

"Yeah, the kid's got it," Davey chipped in.

Stefan turned to me. "What about you, Aimee?"

I think he's perfect, I wanted to say. Instead, I phrased my words more carefully. "He could be really good for us. He's what, twenty-six? I know that's quite a bit younger than us, but it could help expand our fan base."

"Yeah." Paul sounded enthusiastic. "Just think of it, loads of hot twenty-something girls getting into the band. Some of whom will be looking for an older, experienced man to show them the ropes…"

"And the nipple clamps and the riding crop, knowing you," Davey commented.

Before the two could descend into one of their regular bouts of amiable bickering, Stefan silenced them by saying, "Okay, so if we're all agreed, I'll bring Jake back in here and let him know he's the new guitarist."

We nodded our general approval. A moment later, Jake was ushered back into the room, biting his lower lip in a nervous gesture.

"Well, thanks very much for coming today, Jake," Stefan said, his demeanour making me think of Paul's earlier reference to the TV talent show, where contestants were led to believe they'd be going home by the host, who strung out their agony before letting them know they'd made it to the next stage. "I have to let you know…you got the job!"

"Seriously?" It took a good thirty seconds for the news to sink in, then Jake was hugging each of us in turn, exclaiming, "Thanks, you guys, this is awesome!" over and again.

When he took me in his arms, it was as though I'd received a static shock. All the little hairs on my arms stood up, and the electric thrill was echoed by one deep between my legs. The look Jake gave me as we broke the embrace suggested he'd felt it, too.It was a warning sign, and one I needed to heed. A one-sided crush I could deal with. One that was reciprocated was something altogether more dangerous.

* * * *

Things moved quickly once Jake came on board. A meeting had to be arranged with our management team, so he could sign the contract that would outline his role within the band, the share of the money he would make from the tour we were about to undertake and what he could expect in terms of writing and recording royalties for future albums. We had to think about new publicity shots featuring Jake, and get our official website updated with his photo and bio. Martine was, as Paul put it, "running round like a blue-arsed fly" getting the story about our new band mate out to the music press, radio stations and newspaper gossip columns. It left barely any time for the all-important rehearsals before we flew out to Chicago for the new first date on the tour.

Even in the limited time we had together, though, it was obvious Jake was a perfect fit for the band, in terms of vocal style and musical ability. More importantly, we all seemed to get on. When you're spending months on the road, locked into a schedule that takes you from hotel room to arena to tour bus day after day, with very little time off, it can be very easy for people to get heartily sick of the sight of each other. Nothing in our initial contact with Jake suggested that might quickly become a possibility. He would never understand all the in-jokes that peppered Paul and Davey's conversation—half of them continued to go over my head, even after all the years I'd known the two of them—but he was funny, good company, and he could fight his corner in any argument.

I still didn't want to admit to myself quite how handsome I found him, or examine too closely the feeling that he was equally as attracted to me. After leaving Mark for Stefan, I'd sworn never to get involved with anyone else. I loved Stefan too much to cheat on him, and I still regretted treating Mark so badly. Jake had been moved to become a musician by the songs on Same Destination. He couldn't have known then how those songs had been based on all the intrigue of the tangled relationship between Mark, Stefan and myself, or that he would one day find himself in a rehearsal studio in West London, preparing to perform those songs in front of a sell-out crowd of eighteen thousand in less than a week's time.

He couldn't know, either, that I was already scribbling lyrics in the notebook I carried everywhere, inspired by my initial reaction to him.

"First sight is insight,

Telling me when something's right,

Won't sleep alone tonight…"

I'd always found that when my muse came out to play, as it had with a vengeance since Jake's arrival, I felt more horny than usual. Though I ached for Stefan to fuck me, we were working stupidly long hours in rehearsal, and when we got home, we were too exhausted to do anything more than flop on to the bed and fall asleep within minutes.

Working late into the night, we started kicking around ideas for the surprise cover version we always slotted into our encore. We always left this till right at the end of the rehearsal process, once we were happy we had a tight, professional set of tunes and could start to relax and have fun. Jake, noodling on his guitar, picked out the riff to the Don Nix classic, Goin' Down, and within moments the boys were playing around with it. I loved the song, but it was much better suited to Stefan's deeper vocal range than my own.

Spotting the opportunity to grab a relatively early night for once, I caught Stefan's eye and mouthed, "I'm off home, if you don't need me?"

He took his fingers from the frets of his bass long enough to blow me a little kiss. I slipped silently out of the room, leaving them to their jamming.

An unpleasant drizzle was falling as I emerged on to the deserted streets of Westbourne Grove. Fortune was smiling on me, as a black cab turned the corner, its yellow light shining to indicate it was available. Once I'd hailed it to the kerb, I gave the driver our address in Holland Park. At this time of night, I knew I'd be home in less than ten minutes.

The cabbie, middle-aged and bull-necked, glanced at me in his rear-view mirror. "'Ere, has anyone ever told you you look like the bird in that band? What do they call them...?" He racked his brain, searching for the name.

"Sweet Lies?" I smiled. "Yeah, I get that all the time."

When he dropped me off at the house, I was looking forward to making myself a warming mug of hot chocolate and curling up in front of the TV to wait for Stefan's return, even though I knew I'd be asleep when he finally made it home.

But while searching through my bedside drawer, looking for the soothing overnight foot treatment I liked to slather on when I'd been on my feet all day, my fingers instead curled round one of my favourite sex toys. Discreet yet powerful, it was shaped at the tip to resemble a dolphin. I'd picked it up on a tour to Japan back in the days when all you could find in London sex shops were vibrators made from six inches of boring beige plastic, and it was still going strong. Stefan might not be around to pleasure me tonight, but the daring dolphin would make a more than adequate substitute in his absence.

All thoughts of a hot drink and the late-night film forgotten, I climbed on to the bed. Where there was a vibrator, there was lube, and I doused the toy generously with the sticky stuff. Even before I switched it on, I knew the fantasy I would use to help me come.

In my mind, I was backstage in a club in New York's Alphabet City, a venue we'd played on our first American tour, when we were still trying to establish ourselves. The place had been a real dive, with carpets so sodden with beer your shoes stuck to them as you walked, and huge, scuttling cockroaches in the bathrooms. But something about its sleazy ambience made it perfect for the fantasy.

The green room had a rickety table where the bands' rider was left—in those days, the record company had splashed out on nothing more fancy than a crate of beer and a couple of plates of chicken wings—but in the fantasy, the room was deserted and the only thing on the table was me. A shirtless man came to join me, his bare chest gleaming with sweat.

He was no one I knew, just a face in the crowd. Someone I'd picked out for a brief, anonymous fuck that would be forgotten when I moved on to another city, another lover. He gazed at me. I gazed at him. There was no need for words. Lying there, sprawled on the table waiting for him, what else could I possibly want?

Closing my eyes, losing myself further in the fantasy, I let the straps of my black silk nightdress slither off my shoulders, freeing my breasts. In turn, I ran the vibrator over each nipple, feeling them crinkle into tight peaks as they responded to the insistent stimulation. Slowly, I moved the toy lower, slipping it under the hem of the nightdress and applying it to the insides of my thighs. Soon, I would need more, but for now I put off the moment when the vibrator would make contact with my clit.

In my mind's eye, my mystery man watched as I cupped my tits through my top, teasing myself for his benefit. He pulled his cock out of his fly, stroking it as he stared down at my brazen display of lust. It was long and veiny, so thick my fingers would struggle to close round its girth. I knew it would stretch my pussy like it had never been stretched before, but I was ready for him.

I was still dressed in the outfit I'd worn on stage, an oversized white T-shirt over denim shorts. My lover reached for the neck of the T-shirt, wrenching till it ripped in two. It had been too hot in the club to wear anything beneath it, and my full breasts were revealed to him as he stripped the ruined garment off me, my nipples poking up towards his greedy gaze. He yanked open the fly of my shorts, pulling them and my panties down in one swift movement, exposing me completely.

He straddled me, not bothering to remove his jeans the whole way. That seemed so much ruder than if he was naked, just the tops of his arse cheeks bare for me to touch. With a hard thrust, he lodged the fat crown of his cock between my soft, wet pussy lips, making me cry out as he filled me so completely. Eyes locked on mine, he started to fuck me, pushing me along the torn baize covering of the table with every thrust.

My fingernails raked down his back as my passion grew, my body writhing beneath his delicious onslaught. Grunting and gasping, he rammed into me without finesse, his rough, untutored technique just what I needed to push me to a squealing climax.

I couldn't stand it anymore. The vibrator circled over and around my clit, nectar trickling down my thighs to mingle with the lube already coating them. In the moments just before my delightfully dirty fantasy and the buzzing toy combined to bring me to my peak, I would always imagine that a figure stood in the green room doorway. Stefan, watching with a look of approval on his face and his rigid cock in his fist. As ever, the thought that at any moment he would stride over and put that gorgeous, big thing to my lips, making me suck it while another man continued to plunder the depths of my cunt, never failed to send me spiralling into orgasm. But tonight, I almost seemed compelled to look away from him and back to my lover, realising I was no longer being fucked by an imaginary stranger.

Instead, the man whose shaft was buried so deeply in me at the moment when I yelled out and came…was Jake.

Chapter Three

Whether or not fate had contrived, as Jake claimed, to bring him to the band, it certainly seemed to be doing its best to push the two of us closer together. Martine arranged a photo shoot the day before we left for the States, sending us to the Soho studio of Gregg Parker, one of the best respected photographers in the business and a man who'd snapped everyone from the Rolling Stones to Lady Gaga. His concept for the shoot saw the five of us arranged on a king-sized bed with rumpled white silk covers, Stefan lying on my right, Jake on my left.

Without too much persuasion from Gregg and the watching Martine, Jake removed his shirt for the final few shots. I couldn't help but think back to my fantasy of being fucked by a semi-clad hunk, and it was all I could do to stop myself from stroking his naked chest when the camera wasn't clicking away.

Afterwards, as I changed out of the exquisite floor-length black lace gown I'd worn for the shoot, Martine joined me.

"Well, that was an unexpected treat," she murmured, fluffing out her newly-dyed aubergine locks in front of the mirror. "Young Jake dresses very nicely. Or should that be undresses?"

"Martine Ashworth, you're a happily married woman," I reminded her.

"Doesn't mean I can't do a little window shopping." She helped me place the dress back on its hanger. "And don't tell me you didn't enjoy the view, too."

"Yeah, I'll admit he's cute, but I'm really not interested in anyone but Stefan."

Martine rummaged in her bag for her lip gloss. "Okay, well, when you've been cooped up with that gorgeous piece of Californian man-totty on the tour bus, come back to your Aunty Martine and tell her that's still the case. But I don't think she'll believe you."

* * * *

I was still mulling over our conversation when I walked into the cafe near the rehearsal studios to pick up coffee and croissants for Stefan and myself, craving carbs after a morning spent running through the finalised set list. My own voice soared out from the grease-spattered transistor radio on a shelf above the till.

"We're walking different roads

To get to the same destination…"

It was no surprise to hear the song—our first worldwide number one single, it was always playing on some oldies station or other—but the coincidence still freaked me out. I'd written that song in the first, heady flush of my affair with Stefan. Unlike the almost instantaneous attraction I'd felt for Mark, my desire for Stefan had been a slow burn. We'd known each other for almost three years, sharing an easy friendship, until the morning I'd awakened and realised the face I wanted to see on the pillow next to mine was his. All the songs I'd contributed to the Same Destination album had been about the thrill of new love, the mystery of how friendship could turn to something deeper and so much more passionate. Mark, meanwhile, had been writing songs that were heartbreakingly beautiful and bitter in equal measure. That complicated, compelling mixture — one reviewer had described us as "teetering on a see-saw of emotions" — had sent the album to the top of the charts, where it stayed for nearly a year.

"I'm walking away from what I knew,
But the long, hard road is leading me to you…"

I paid and dashed out of the cafe, knowing Stefan was waiting for his late breakfast. In a couple of days time, I'd be standing on stage in Chicago, making those lyrics sound fresh even though I'd sung them thousands of times before. Though part of me couldn't wait for that first gig, I was still thinking about Martine's words. Out on the road, travelling in a little isolated bubble, the rules of everyday life no longer applied. Though I told myself I was going to behave, that what I had with Stefan wasn't worth risking, if temptation was placed in my path, would I be able to resist?

* * * *

From the moment the plane touched down at O'Hare airport, it became obvious that this tour was going to be the craziest we'd ever embarked on, both in terms of the schedule and in the reaction of both press and fans. Jake, already wide-eyed at the novelty of turning to the left upon boarding and experiencing the luxury of travelling first class, was even more astonished to see the paparazzi out in force as we headed for passport control.

"Oh, man, is it always like this?" he asked as yet another camera was thrust under his nose, flashbulbs popping all around us.

"Get used to it," Davey told him. "For this week at least, you're big news. All you have to do is make sure you don't get caught sneaking groupies into your hotel room, and they'll leave you alone soon enough."

"And the best way to do that," Paul added, "is to sneak them into ours…"

Only once we'd all piled into the limo waiting to take us to our hotel did we feel as though we could start to relax. Tonight, we'd stay up late and try to get ourselves accustomed to the six-hour time difference between London and Chicago. Tomorrow, we'd take to the stage for the first date on the tour. That's when we would really know if Jake was the right choice for the band, and if the fans reacted to him as positively as we did.

* * * *

In the backstage gloom, Stefan held up a hand and curled his fingers into his palm, one by one, in a slow countdown. That was our signal to stroll back out on stage for the final encore of the night. The auditorium rang to impatient cries of, "More!" and a low, steady chant of, "Sweet Lies! Sweet Lies!" All bands teased their audiences this way, making them wait till they reappeared to play the songs the fans had been waiting for all evening.

Beside me, Jake clutched the neck of his precious Strat, wide-eyed as a kid at the wild clamour.

"You okay?" I asked.

He nodded. "It still kinda feels like a dream, though. You know, being here with you…"

Something in his words gave me the impression he was talking about me alone, rather than the band as a whole, but I didn't have time to analyse them. Paul was heading for his drum kit, the crowd whooping and yelling at his reappearance, and I knew I had to follow.

A deafening wall of noise met us as we took our places behind the mic stands. We waited for it to die down, then launched into Guinevere's Garden. It was hard to hold the harmonies steady when everyone let out a huge cheer of approval, but we managed it…three voices in perfect harmony.

When we'd first started playing the big stadiums, this song would be greeted with a sea of lighters held aloft. Now, thousands of mobile phones were raised, display screens blazing like artificial flames. The depth of emotion behind the gesture remained the same.

By the time Guinevere's Garden reached its hard-driving climax, I knew all my fears that Jake wouldn't be accepted by the fans were unfounded. Girls in the front row were begging for him to come close to them, and when he tossed his sweat-sticky T-shirt into the crowd as we took our last bows, they fought each other to claim it as a souvenir.

Stefan hugged me close, dropping a kiss on the top of my head. "They loved us."

"Fucking right they did!" Paul exclaimed as we left the stage and the house lights rose, signalling to the audience that the show was over. "Now, I think a celebratory drinkie is in order. Don't forget we've got a virgin with us tonight." When we looked at him quizzically, he clarified the point. "Jake. This was his first time with us, and we've got to mark the moment he lost his Sweet Lies cherry." He wrapped an arm round Jake's bare shoulders, steering him in the direction of the after-party. "Trust me, Jakey, a tour this size really is like sex. The more you do it, the better it gets…"

* * * *

A couple of weeks into the tour, it seemed Paul's words were being proved correct. Every night the music was tighter, the light show more smoothly coordinated, the crowd's reaction more ecstatic. I had a spell during the first encore, as the boys performed their rowdy version of Goin' Down, when I could join the friends, fans and hangers-on who watched from the wings and simply revel in the show. At first, it felt strange to look stage right and see Jake throwing shapes, hopping on and off Davey's keyboard riser before jogging over to jam with Stefan, the two men standing back to back and grinning like maniacs with the sheer joy of making good music. That had always been Mark's place, and I couldn't quite shake the feeling that one night I'd look up and see him standing there.

Stefan, though, seemed to be enjoying having Jake alongside him. The two had developed an easy camaraderie Stefan had never shared with Mark, even in the days before they became two sides of our very high-profile love triangle.

Some nights, I could swear the chemistry so evident between Stefan and Jake verged on the sexual, before telling myself I must be projecting my own lust for the two of them on to the scene in front of me.

Mark wouldn't have been so prominent in my thoughts if I hadn't had a phone call from him shortly before we'd gone on stage that first night in Chicago. "Break a leg,

Aimee," he said. "I hope it goes well for you all, I really do."

"How are you?" I asked.

"Getting there. I carried round a lot of baggage for a long time, and you can't let go of it that easily. But Jeannie's really helping, and I love spending time with the boys. They're in kindergarten now, you know."

He sounded a lot brighter than he'd done when we'd last spoken. Knowing things seemed to be working out for him made it easier for me to step back out on stage when the boys had taken their bow and sing Changing, the song I'd written as an overdue apology to Mark for the way I'd treated him.

"When everything around you's changing,
And you don't know where you stand,
Just look for me and I will be there,
You know I'll lend a hand
The way I always planned…"

With Davey's electric piano the only accompaniment to my voice, I'd always been able to reduce an auditorium to awed silence with the song. Somehow, it was easier to sing now Mark wasn't standing a few feet from me every night, but I could still summon up the raw emotions that flooded through me when I wrote it.

Except for the night in Cleveland when I looked over to see Jake casually stripping off his shirt at the side of the stage, exposing his rock-hard stomach, and very nearly swallowed my tongue.

Performing only took up a fraction of our time. Much of the rest was spent on the tour bus, travelling from one venue to the next. Johnny, our tour manager, had hired us a big beast of a bus, with a comfortable seating area boasting a state-of-the-art sound system, bunks that each had their own mini TV, a kitchenette and bathroom.

Boarding it, Jake had whistled in approval. "Wow, this is bigger than my apartment!"

"Get used to it, mate," Davey had said, "because you're going to be seeing a lot of it."

We all managed to find ways of killing time on the bus. Paul and Davey played video games for hours upon end, taking each other on at Call of Duty or Pro Evolution Soccer. I'd often walk back from making myself a snack in the kitchenette to see Paul's shaven head leaning close to Davey's blond one, both of them grumbling and cursing as their thumbs flickered over their games consoles and another computer-generated soldier expired in a hail of bullets. Jake was very quickly persuaded to join in, proving to be just as competitive and excitable as they were.

Stefan found it harder than I did to ignore the constant noise they made. He would lie on his bunk reading, having loaded up the e-reader I'd bought him for his last birthday with an extensive selection of crime and horror novels. Gradually, he was working his way through everything Stephen King had ever written, though I often told him if he really wanted to frighten himself silly, he should simply go into the tour bus bathroom after Paul had paid it a visit.

I liked to work on my embroidery. I took my frame and silks everywhere, always finding a quiet spot among the mayhem to sit and stitch. Currently, I was sewing a pattern of forget-me-nots on to a white linen tablecloth for Martine, after I'd caught her admiring something very similar in an interior design magazine.

When my eyes ached from squinting at my stitch-work, I retired to my own bunk, losing myself in fantasies that always began with Jake shrugging off his shirt to stand bare-chested in front of me. Unable to resist the come-on in his grey-green eyes, I would slither down his body, dropping to my knees so I could undo the fly of his jeans. His hard cock reared up, waiting for me to wrap my lips around it and begin to suck.

As the fantasy developed, it changed from a simple, highly-charged encounter between Jake and me into one where Stefan took an increasingly major role. Now my husband was the one who unleashed his cock and demanded to be orally serviced, and Jake joined me at his feet, the two of us taking it in turns to lick and suck Stefan's thick, imposing shaft and nuzzle at his heavy, low-hanging balls.

I had no idea where this new scenario came from. Until now, my ménage fantasies had always seen me at the heart of the action, with two men lavishing all their attention on me. So why did it turn me on to think of sharing Stefan with another man, both of us doing everything in our power to make him come? The confines of the tour bus weren't exactly the right place to cuddle up to Stefan and tell him, "Darling, I'm making myself really horny thinking about Jake sucking your cock," so I kept my naughty thoughts to myself until such time came as I could sit down and discuss them with him at length.

At least, that was the plan. Everything changed when we reached New York.

Due to play three nights at Madison Square Garden, we were booked into a hotel overlooking Central Park, a little bit of welcome luxury after the best part of a week sleeping on the bus. Our schedule meant we could take time out to explore the city if we wished. It was easy enough to dress down and hide behind dark glasses, and even if someone did recognise us, it would only be at the cost of signing a few autographs and earning a two-line mention on one of the celebrity-spotting blogs.

Until I woke in the morning with a migraine. In my teens and twenties, I'd suffered from blinding headaches every couple of months, but over the years their frequency had gradually diminished. This was nowhere as bad as some of the attacks I'd had, but I knew there was no way I could leave the hotel until the profound headache and waves of nausea subsided. From past experience, I knew the symptoms would clear if I could manage a couple of hours sleep, leaving only a residue that would fade over the next day.

Having swallowed a couple of strong migraine relief tablets with a glass of water, I pulled down my eye mask and retreated back under the covers. Stefan, naturally concerned about my well-being, offered to stay with me rather than go out with the boys, but I waved him away. It was a fine September morning, ideal for pounding the pavements of Manhattan rather than keeping an eye on me while I slept.

"Have a good time," I told him. "Bring me back something nice." Then I pulled the covers over my head and let the painkillers do their stuff.

When I awoke, it was early afternoon. Long rays of sunshine slanted through the gap in the partly-drawn curtains. The pain in my head had faded to be replaced by a gnawing hunger. There was a room service menu on the nightstand. I reached for it, deciding that a bowl of chicken soup would be the perfect pick-me-up.

"Of course, Miz Caine." The concierge who took my call couldn't have sounded more solicitous. "We'll have that straight up to you."

I wandered into the bathroom and splashed cold water on my face. Once I've eaten, I decided, seeing the row of premium bathing products arranged on the side of the tub, I'll take a nice, long bath. I had plenty of time. We didn't need to leave the hotel till five to get down to the venue for our sound check. When Stefan returned, I knew he'd be delighted to see I was almost back to my old self.

Hearing a sharp rap at the door, I called out, "Come in!"

Expecting a waiter to respond, I was stunned to see Jake bring the tray bearing my meal into the room.

"Hey, Jake, what are you doing here?"

He flashed me a soft smile, placing the tray down on a low, glass-topped coffee table. "I was just on the way back to my room, and I bumped into the waiter outside. I figured if he was bringing food you must be feeling okay, so I thought I'd check and see how you were. Don't worry, I tipped him. Gave him a little extra for letting me into the room, in fact."

I patted the bedcovers, encouraging him to sit down at the side of me. "Are the others with you?"

"No, they were gonna go up the Empire State Building, then maybe grab a beer, but I thought I'd come back and put my head down for a spell. I really want to be sharp for when we go on stage."

Remembering Jake's story about his childhood dream of playing Madison Square Garden, I said, "Tonight's really important to you, isn't it?"

"This is the pinnacle, Aimee. Going out there in front of all those people screaming for us, thinking about everyone who's played there before, that's when I'm gonna feel like I've made it."

I lifted the lid of the soup tureen. A rich, savoury aroma wafted out, causing my stomach to growl in anticipation. Aware of Jake's eyes on me as I took a spoonful of soup and lifted it to my lips, I asked, "Have you eaten?"

"Yeah, we found this great little deli just off Times Square that does the best pastrami on rye. You would have loved it."

The soup was every bit as tasty as it smelt, and I'd almost cleared the bowl before Jake spoke again.

"Aimee... Can I confess something to you?"

It was a strange question, but I reckoned I was prepared for anything Jake had to throw at me. We didn't have the wildest reputation as touring rock stars—indeed, we'd once been described in a magazine article as less likely to trash a hotel room than to tidy it up before we checked out—but we'd been around. If Jake had got up to something with a groupie, I wouldn't be shocked. Jealous, possibly, but he didn't need to know that.

"What is it?"

"Okay, this is a little hard for me." He twisted the edge of the plum satin comforter, as if debating whether to continue. "You know I said I've been a fan of the band since I was a kid? Well, it still feels kind of weird that every night I get up on stage alongside you all. I look around and I think, 'Wow! That's Aimee Caine at the side of me. And Paul Grover on the drums. This can't be real...' And I want to pinch myself. I keep thinking I'm going to wake up back in my shitty rented apartment in Camden, with damp crawling up the walls, wondering where the next gig and the next paycheque are coming from."

"Well, you seem to be coping with it all just fine. And the fans love you—especially the girls."

Jake blushed a little at that. "Yeah, that's kinda fun, seeing them all screaming and lifting their tops to flash their boobs at you and knowing you could have any of them, if you wanted. But..." He took a deep breath. "I don't want any of them. Aimee, please don't get freaked out by what I'm about to tell you, but when I was eighteen, I had a poster of you on the wall of my college dorm room. It was one of the publicity shots you did for the Low Tide album."

Even before he spoke, I knew exactly the shot he was referring to. I'd never marketed myself as any kind of sex symbol, not wanting to steal the focus from the rest of the band. However, we'd done that particular photographic shoot in the grounds of an English stately home. It had been a long day in high summer and a generous amount of champagne had been provided to help get us through it. Not only had Stefan and I managed to sneak away when we broke for lunch to enjoy a quickie fuck in the long grass, when I'd returned, glowing and satisfied, I'd been persuaded to pose for the raunchiest photo of my career.

"You're sitting on a tree stump," Jake continued. "Your legs are bare and you're wearing this clingy blue top. You've got one hand tangled in your hair, and the other one's pulling the top down between your legs, because it's so obvious that's all you've got on."

That wasn't the case. I'd actually been wearing a tiny pair of bikini-cut panties, but I had been concerned they'd show in the legs-apart pose I was encouraged to adopt. The result was ruder than actually revealing my underwear would have been.

"Yeah, I remember it well." Now I was the one blushing. I took a sip from my glass of iced water to cool myself down.

"God, you just looked so hot. Whenever my roommate was out, I used to lie on my bed, looking at that poster and dreaming of you. I used to imagine you were in the room, dressed just like in that shot, and that you'd pull the top up over your head. You'd sit there, naked, with your legs wide apart, letting me see everything, then you'd slide a hand down between your legs and start stroking yourself…"

He broke off, realising how quiet I'd gone.

"Oh, now I've gone and embarrassed you, haven't I? I'm so sorry. Sometimes my big mouth just runs away with me."

"I'm not embarrassed," I told him. Quite the opposite. Listening to Jake's fantasy had got me all hot and bothered. The idea of him, naked and playing with his cock as he dreamed of me, was a powerful turn-on. I couldn't help thinking how exciting it would be to bare myself for him, just as he'd described. It would be so easy, too. All I wore was my silk dressing gown, loosely belted around my waist. "If anything, I'm flattered. What I want to know is whether you still have those fantasies these days."

A wildness seemed to infect my blood, brought on by being so close to this gorgeous, sexy man. All the promises I'd made to myself to resist temptation when Jake was around melted away. It didn't matter that he was twelve years younger than me, or that I had a husband I loved so very much. This moment was about Jake and me, and a rising passion neither of us seemed able to deny.

I let my hand fall on his firm, denim-clad thigh, feeling the heat of his body even through the thick fabric. Another inch and I would be touching the solid bar of his cock. He didn't even try to pull away.

"Yes, I do," he said, his voice barely rising above a murmur. "I dreamed of fucking you every night when I was eighteen, and I still dream about it now. But I know it's never going to happen. I look at how happy you and Stefan are, and what a great couple you make. I wouldn't want to do anything to break you up."

"Don't worry, you wouldn't be."

Our faces were only inches apart, and now Jake grew bolder, realising I was giving him permission to act on all his fantasies. He ran his fingers through my dark brown curls, cupping the back of my head and pulling me even closer to him. Eyes half-closed, I surrendered to his kiss, feeling the smoothness of unfamiliar lips against my own. Almost forgetting to breathe, I let Jake explore my mouth with his tongue. I wanted to ask him if this was anything like he'd imagined, but I was enjoying the kiss too much to even attempt to speak.

Jake's hand slipped into my robe, to close round the fullness of my breast. I wriggled against the covers, feeling my pussy grow wet. That was the moment when we heard the unmistakable click of the key card in the door, and Stefan calling my name.

Chapter Four

Jake and I sprang apart. By the time Stefan stepped into the room, my robe was firmly in place once more, and Jake was busying himself with my meal tray. If I looked a little flustered, Stefan didn't appear to notice. He seemed more pleased to see that I was well enough to have rediscovered my appetite.

"I wasn't expecting you back so soon," I said, as he came over to the bed and planted a kiss on my cheek.

"Well, I thought I should come and see how my lovely wife was doing. Oh, and I wanted to give you this…"

From the folds of his long black overcoat, Stefan produced a snow globe with a tiny but exquisitely detailed model of the Empire State Building at its heart. When I shook it, scraps of glitter whirled about it like a miniature snowstorm.

"It's beautiful, darling. Thank you." Over the years, I'd collected dozens of snow globes as we'd travelled around the world, displaying my favourites in a cabinet at home.

They weren't quite as precious to me as the Grammy awards on the shelf above them, but it was so thoughtful of Stefan to track down one from New York, a city missing from my collection until now.

Shrugging off his coat, Stefan turned his attention to Jake. "Been looking after Aimee for me, have you?"

"Yes, sir." Jake's voice betrayed none of the passion that had flowed from him in the moments before Stefan interrupted us. "But if you don't mind, I'm going to go grab a nap."

"Sure. We'll see you in the lobby, just before five."

Once Jake left, I got up from the bed, intending to take a bath. Stefan caught me in an embrace. Even when I rose on tiptoe, my head barely reached his shoulder.

"It's nice to see Jake taking an interest in your welfare," he said. "I can't imagine Mark being that concerned...unless he thought you were going to miss the gig, of course."

"You're being a bit harsh on Mark. Whatever happened, we never really stopped caring about each other on some level. We were friends for so long, even before we were ever in the music business, and we were never going to throw all that away."

"But you seem a lot happier with Jake around."

I waited for Stefan to elaborate, wondering how much he'd seen when he came into the room, but he appeared to be simply stating a point rather than letting me know he'd caught us in the act.

"I think we're all happier having Jake around. He's really rejuvenated our sound and, more importantly, he's just a thoroughly nice guy." I broke away from Stefan, reckoning what he didn't know wouldn't hurt him. "Now, if you don't mind, I'm going to go and make use of that luscious-looking orange flower bath oil."

"Okay, just yell if you want me to come and wash your back."

I knew exactly what that might lead to, but my senses still tingled from Jake's tender kisses, and I was afraid if Stefan took over where he had left off, I might call out Jake's name at the wrong moment. Maybe I should put what had happened between us down to a temporary lapse in judgement, but as I stepped into the warm, fragrant water, I knew that wasn't the case. Jake wanted me just as much as I wanted him, and the current of desire flowing between us was so strong I wasn't at all sure how easily it could be turned off.

* * * *

The show that night was one of the best we'd ever played. Along with the other two nights at the Garden, it was being filmed for a DVD to be released at the end of the tour. Cameras mounted on tracks swooped low over the audience, and two cameramen moved around the five of us on stage, capturing the action at close quarters. I'd expected their presence to be intrusive, their lenses only a few inches from my face as I sang, but they proved surprisingly easy to ignore.

Paul, ever the showman, played up to the cameras, pulling faces, tossing his drumsticks in the air and encouraging the crowd to go wild. The atmosphere was electric, better than anything we'd experienced on the tour so far. When Jake came to share the microphone with me during the chorus of Same Destination, I asked, "Is this how you dreamed it would be?"

He shook his head. "It's even better. Whatever happens in my life from now on, it's going to be pretty hard to top this."

After a show as good as tonight's had been and all the partying backstage that followed, I was on such a high I knew it was going to prove hard to fall asleep. But it wasn't the buzz from the fans or the champagne that had me tossing and turning in my hotel bed while Stefan slumbered peacefully beside me. I'd honestly believed I would be able to keep my feelings for Jake a secret, but guilt gnawed at me. The urge to confess everything was powerful, but I didn't know how Stefan would react if I told him I had the hots for our cute young guitarist. Perhaps he wouldn't be surprised. After all, I'd first slept with him while Mark and I were still a couple. Maybe it was a pattern I was programmed to repeat, only this time I would manage to find some way of working through my feelings for my new lover without destroying the relationship I had with my old one.

Stefan woke in the grey of dawn to find me curled up in the wing-backed chair by the window, scrawling in my notebook. Words tumbled out on to the pages, more than enough for an album's worth of songs. Later, I would go back and refine them, but for now I simply wanted to get everything down on paper, channelling all my confused feelings into black and white.

"Hey, Aimee, come to bed." He smiled, patting the empty space beside him. Looking at his face—the first faint lines of age around his eyes somehow adding to his handsomeness, rather than diminishing from it—I knew I had to tell him everything.

Slipping beneath the sheets, I let Stefan put his arm round my shoulders, feeling strangely comforted by the warm, bare-chested bulk of him. "Stef, there's something I have to tell you."

My hesitant tone seemed to alert him to the fact this was serious. "Nothing bad, I hope."

"I don't know. I really don't know how you're going to react to this, but just be sure that whatever happens, I love you with all my heart." Gazing into his eyes, I plunged straight into my tale. "And once we got together, I never thought I'd be interested in anyone else. But that changed the first time I saw Jake."

"Oh, Aimee, it happens to all of us. All those pretty girls in the front row—I could fall in love every night of the week with no effort at all." He kissed the top of my head. "But it's all just a fantasy."

"This is a little bit more than that. This afternoon, Jake admitted he had a huge crush on me when he was in his teens."

"Why sound so surprised? Aimee, you're a gorgeous woman and you're the singer in a rock band. Of course horny teenagers are going to want to fuck you."

"Well, Jake's not a teenager any more, but he still wants to fuck me. And if you hadn't come back to the room when you did, he very probably would have. We kissed…and it was like kissing you for the first time all over again." I looked away, afraid to see how Stefan was taking the news.

"Let's get this straight. He wants to fuck you, and you want to fuck him. So what's the problem?"

I couldn't believe how blasé Stefan sounded. "The problem is that I don't want to do anything to risk our marriage. I mean, I had a pretty good thing going with Mark and I screwed all that up by—"

"By leaving him for something even better." Stefan grinned. "I mean, how do you think Mark would have taken it if you'd gone to him after that night in Madrid and told him what we'd been up to?"

Memories came flooding back. A hot night in Madrid…a sell-out gig…Stefan and I sharing most of a bottle of Rioja on the tour bus while Mark lay asleep in his bunk. Soft, exploratory kisses turning into something more passionate. Stefan stripping off my panties and going down on me on the soft couch, turning me to a writhing mess with his talented mouth. Biting the fleshy part of my thumb so I wouldn't wake anyone with my screams as I came...

"He'd have gone mad. He'd probably have had a knock-down fight with you and left the band on the spot."

"Right, because he couldn't handle the thought of you with someone else. But I can. My attitude to these things is a lot more open than his. And I have no objections to you sleeping with Jake, on two conditions."

"And what are those?"

"The first is that you don't do anything behind my back. When you fuck him, I want to be there."

This was starting to sound like all my filthiest fantasies. Stefan watching, biding his time while Jake's cock stroked in and out of me, then joining in, filling my mouth as completely as Jake filled my cunt. His next words took me into even kinkier territory.

"You see, you're not the only one who's been dreaming of bedding Jake."

It took a moment for the implications to sink in, and when they did, I gaped at him. "You? You want to fuck Jake?"

"Don't sound so shocked. It wouldn't be the first time I'd been with another man."

"Oh, now you're going to have to tell me more." Why, I wondered, was this something we'd never discussed before? I'd thought I knew Stefan inside-out, so to discover he not only had a bisexual side but had actively indulged it drew the breath from me.

"It was before you and I met, when Paul, Davey and I were still in Local Heroes. There were four of us in the band in those days. We had this really talented lead singer, Stu, and a couple of times he and I got drunk and fooled around together, like a lot of guys do. It was mostly stripping off, getting hard in front of each other, playing with each other's cocks…that kind of thing. But one night Stu sucked me off, and it was the most incredible feeling. He left the band not long after that, so I never found out what fucking him would have been like. I always regretted not having the opportunity."

I found myself looking at Stefan in a whole new light, picturing him naked and entwined with another man. It was a deeply appealing image—even more so when I imagined him with Jake. "So why haven't you tried it since then? There must have been occasions when it could have happened."

"Of course, but I've never met anyone I really wanted to do it with. Until Jake."

"Well, I'm okay with that. More than okay, in fact. But what's the other condition?"

"That you take the punishment I'm going to give you for being such a naughty girl as to try to fuck Jake behind my back."

"Punishment?" It sounded serious, but Stefan hadn't stopped smiling. "What kind of punishment?"

"The most appropriate one I can think of. A spanking on your bare bottom."

"Oh, please, not that. I'll be good, I promise, just as long as you don't spank me." My protests were half-hearted, designed to stoke my husband's lust to greater heights. I knew how much he loved to have me over his knee, skirt raised, waiting in a stew of nervous excitement for him to bring his hand down hard on my bum. It was a while since we'd played this particular game, and I felt an immediate thrill as Stefan hauled me on to his lap.

"Let's have this off so I can see that gorgeous arse of yours." He reached underneath me, fiddling with the belt of my robe. Once it was undone, it was easy for him to push the thin robe down over my shoulders before removing it entirely. "Oh, yes, very nice…"

I shivered at the feel of Stefan caressing my bottom. His touch was gentle now, but I knew that very soon he'd be spanking me quite hard, crimsoning my soft white flesh. It seemed he was determined to string this out more than usual, though, and the longer I waited before that first slap, the more the nervous butterflies fluttered in my belly. He let me wait till I was almost begging him to spank me, just get it over with, then his palm slammed solidly against my cheek.

"Naughty girl," he crooned. The spanks quickly fell into a rhythmic pattern, alternating from one cheek to the next. "Bad girl to have fantasies about Jake, to want him to fuck her, to dream of cheating…"

"I'm sorry." The words were almost wrenched from me as I wriggled on his lap, each hard slap more fuel to the fire by now raging in my pussy. "I just couldn't help myself."

"Just think what Jake would say if he were here now, watching you being spanked by your husband. Would you like him to watch this, see how red your beautiful bum is?" Stefan broke off to run an exploratory finger between my legs. "And how wet you are. So wet and ready to be taken…"

Beneath me, I could feel Stefan's cock, poking from the fly of his boxer shorts. Much as he tried to play the stern disciplinarian, I knew all he wanted to do was pull me on to that hard length and order me to ride him until we both came.

"God, I wish he was with us." I shifted position so my clit was directly on top of Stefan's shaft. When he spanked me again, I pressed against him, getting the friction exactly where I needed it. Each slap took me a little closer to the edge, but just before I tumbled into the welcoming embrace of orgasm, Stefan stopped. My squirming must have been having an effect on him, because he simply lifted me up as though I weighed nothing at all, guiding me on to his erection.

I sank down, lodging Stefan's cock snugly inside me. Holding still, I gazed into his eyes, reminding myself of just how lucky I was to have such a wonderful, understanding husband. Our mouths met in a souls-deep kiss, then need overtook us. Stefan took handfuls of my tender arse cheeks, pulling me a little harder on to him. Moving to a rhythm only I could hear, I rocked back and forth.

"Oh, Aimee..." Stefan's thick finger sought for my clit, strumming it as I gyrated faster, lost in a dream of having four hands to stroke me, two cocks to play with, two mouths locking greedily on to my nipples. Twice the fun, twice the pleasure.

My last thought before an unstoppable orgasm surged through me was that it didn't need to be a dream any longer. I had permission to make it happen. The only question remaining was how soon.

Chapter Five

The tour bus hit the centre of Boston at a little after four. Thanks to a ten-vehicle pile-up on the Massachusetts Turnpike, we were running late and would barely have time to check in to the hotel before leaving for the sound check. Davey, who always hated anything disrupting his pre-gig routine, looked anxiously out of the bus window.

"Is it much farther?" he asked, too twitchy to admire, as the rest of us were doing, the old colonial buildings and the spacious brownstone homes of the upmarket Back Bay area.

"Nearly there." Pat, our driver, took the next left turn. Within a hundred yards, he was pulling the bus to a halt before the hotel.

"And very nice it looks, too." Paul roused himself from his recumbent position on the couch to punch Davey lightly on the shoulder. "There you go, mate, you can stop fretting now."

As we climbed off the bus, it was obvious the Rockingham Retreat was a departure from the usual hotels we found ourselves booked into. Though luxurious enough, they were always big and a little soulless, with the same inoffensive decor and bland breakfast menus, pitched at the corporate traveller who never paid too much attention to their surroundings. The Rockingham had only five rooms and was more suited to a romantic getaway, as Stefan and I discovered when we walked into our suite to see a muslin-draped four-poster bed, claw-footed tub and antique love seat.

I peered out of the window to the garden deck below, its railing draped with trailing vines. "D'you think Martine had something to do with booking this place?"

Stefan wrapped his arms round me, pulling me close. "What makes you ask?"

"Well, it may have escaped your attention, but it is our wedding anniversary today. And here we are — champagne in the fridge, a hot tub on the roof. It almost makes me wish we didn't have to play the gig tonight."

"You know I'd never forget the day we married." Stefan's lips were soft against mine, reminding me of the moment when we'd sealed our vows with a kiss in front of the small congregation gathered on a Hawaiian beach. "The look on Davey's face when he thought he'd forgotten to bring the rings… Tell you what, we'll sneak away from the after-party as soon as we can, have a private little celebration of our own. How does that sound?"

If this was indeed Martine's doing, then I needed to thank her the next time we spoke. With all the stresses of the tour, time to chill out with my husband was always more than welcome, especially in such cosy surroundings. "It sounds wonderful, Mr Caine."

As we kissed again, a wicked little idea popped into my mind. Sharing the tub with Stefan was one thing, but if we could only persuade Jake to join us, this might really become a night to remember.

* * * *

The green room was crowded with people who worked for our record company, members of the music press, the winners of a 'meet and greet' competition organised by a local radio station and a handful of fans, mostly female, who'd managed to talk their way past backstage security. Making a slow circuit of the room in search of Jake, I spotted Paul in conversation with a blonde who couldn't have been any older than twenty. His eyes were fixed on her big breasts where they threatened to spill from her tight corset top, giving me the impression he might not be spending the night alone.

I risked interrupting them. The girl looked a little annoyed, no doubt thinking I was trying to muscle in on her attempts to hook up with Paul, until she recognised me. I flashed her a smile and she blushed. "Hi, have either of you seen Jake?"

"Yeah, I think he was over there, getting a beer." Paul gestured to the makeshift bar set up in one corner.

"Thanks, Paul." Leaning close, I whispered so only he could hear, "Enjoy yourself tonight. She's hot."

A harassed-looking man with a press pass dangling around his neck tried to stop me for a word, but I shook my head. "Sorry, I'm in the middle of something right now. Maybe later." Not that I had any intention of sticking around to speak to him or anyone else. When I'd shared my plan to seduce Jake with Stefan, he'd agreed without hesitation. It was just a question of getting Jake on his own, putting our proposal to him, then hoping he wouldn't back out on learning that not only did I want to sleep with him, but so did my husband.

Jake was where Paul had said he'd be, clutching an almost full plastic pint glass of beer and chatting to a middle-aged executive type dressed in ill-fitting jeans and a box-fresh Sweet Lies tour T-shirt. From the look Jake gave me, he seemed rather relieved when I whisked him away with a polite, "Excuse me, urgent band business," directed at his companion.

"Hi, Aimee." Jake took a swallow of his beer. "Can you give me any tips on how to look interested when people start talking about sales figures and merchandising strategy?"

"Just nod and smile. It always works for me." I put a hand on his forearm, thrilling at the contact of my cool fingers against his warm, bare skin. "Are you as bored as you look?"

"Yeah. I know these are important people and we have to be nice to them, but I'd rather be anywhere else but here right now."

"Well, Stefan and I are planning to sneak away any minute now, and we'd like you to come with us." Taking a deep breath, I launched into the speech I'd rehearsed in my head. "Jake, there's a connection between us. I know you feel it, and if Stefan hadn't come back to the hotel in New York when he did, we would both have acted on it."

"What happened? Did he find out? Is he mad? Does he want me to leave the band?"

He looked so alarmed at the possibility I wanted to take him in my arms, hug him and let him know everything was all right. "Yes, Stefan knows, but he's cool with it."

"Seriously?"

"Not only that. He's really into the idea of us getting together. But he's into more than that, and I'll understand if you say no to this part of it. Jake, he...we want a threesome. And not the kind where you and Stefan pleasure me at the same time. We both want you."

Jake digested the implications for a moment. "So," he said at length, "what you're saying is you want to fuck me. You both want to fuck me?"

I nodded, so sure he was going to turn me down flat I was unable to speak for fear of voicing my disappointment.

"That is just the downright dirtiest thing I've ever heard." He looked around for the nearest available flat surface to deposit his beer glass. "And hell, I'm game for it. I mean, I've never been with another guy before, but if I'm ever gonna try it, I can't think of anyone else I'd rather do it with."

I wanted to leap up and down and squeal with delight, but I knew that would draw too much attention to us, and from now on we had to be discreet if we wanted to get away without being noticed.

Stefan was lounging by the door, trying his best to disguise his anxiety. He'd made sure to speak to all the competition winners as soon as we'd come off stage, as had I. With that welcome obligation out of the way, we both felt able to leave without compunction. When he saw me coming towards him, Jake in tow, his face brightened.

"All sorted?"

I gave him a quick thumbs-up. "But how are we going to get out of here without people realising we've gone?"

"We'll be fine. Look round you. All anyone's really interested in is how much longer the booze is going to keep flowing. And the guy handling security's gone for a cigarette break, so now seems like as good a time as any to leave."

With that, he set off down the corridor towards a nearby side exit. If any fans were still hanging around, hoping to catch a glimpse of us or get autographs and photos, we knew they'd be waiting at the main doors backstage. This way, it was easy to avoid them.

As we stepped out into the night air, I had the giddy feeling of playing truant. Stefan's right. No one will really miss us, I told myself to stave off any guilt.

A couple of taxis were circling, hoping to pick up any late stragglers from the gig. Stefan flagged one down, and we piled into the backseat as he gave the driver the address of our hotel. After the journey we'd had earlier in the day, we were hoping for a smooth, fast ride. Instead, we found ourselves in heavy traffic once more.

Leaning forward into the gap between the front seats, I asked the driver, "Is it always like this in Boston?"

"It is when the Red Sox are playing. And it don't help none when they schedule a big concert the same night as a game." He gave a 'What can you do about it?' shrug.

"We'll be there soon enough," Stefan murmured in my ear, pulling me back firmly between himself and Jake. "Just enjoy the ride till then." With that, he let his hand rest on my leg, fingers tracing spidery patterns that inched ever closer to the apex of my thighs. Our lips met, and even though I knew the driver could see everything in his mirror, I didn't object as my husband's other hand squeezed my breast.

Not wanting to leave Jake out of the action, I reached down to touch the bulge in the crotch of his tight black jeans. He moaned, the sound taking on a strangled quality as I deftly pulled down his zip. I slipped my hand inside his fly, feeling the contours of his cock and balls cradled in soft cotton underwear.

Stefan's tongue battled with mine and his hand moved up under the hem of my skirt. My breathing was heavy, and my panties were soaking. I was so turned on, I would have happily let him finger me till I came, but the cab was pulling up in front of the Rockingham Retreat.

We almost tumbled out on to the pavement, Jake not even bothering to zip himself back up as Stefan paid the cabbie, giving him a generous tip on top of the fare.

"It's a good job he didn't have a clue who we were," I said, "otherwise we'd be all over the gossip columns tomorrow. I can see it now. Sweet Lies Stars in Taxi-Cab Orgy."

"Babe, if you think that was an orgy, I've got an awful lot to teach you." Stefan gave my bum a loving squeeze. "I'll go get the room key. Why don't you take Jake straight up to the roof? I don't know about you, but I really want to try out that hot tub. Just don't start anything without me..."

Hand in hand, Jake and I climbed the stairs to the roof deck, where steam rose from the surface of the sunken hot tub. As well as the tub, big enough to take four people with ease, the owners had fitted the deck with a low wooden table and a couple of matching chairs, and a small cabinet containing glasses, thick, fluffy towels, a portable CD player and a small selection of music to play on it. To my amazement, the CD on the top of the pile was a copy of our latest album, Older, No Wiser.

Sliding the disc into the player, I forwarded it to the eighth track, a slow, bluesy instrumental of Mark's called Painted Lady. As music floated out on the night air, I beckoned Jake to me. "Let's dance."

Slow-dancing with Stefan could be awkward, given he was so much bigger than me. Jake and I were an easier fit, and I rested my head on his shoulder as we swayed together. When Mark had first played us the rough demo of Painted Lady, I'd never dreamt I would find myself listening to it on a Boston rooftop, in the arms of a man who was about to become my lover and waiting for my husband to join us for our first ever ménage.

With my hands locked round Jake's neck, I didn't resist as he tugged at the buttons running down the front of my dress, undoing them one by one. Once the dress was off, he turned to my bra, flicking the catch open with ease.

"Now that's a sight to gladden the heart." Stefan stood on the edge of the deck, holding a bottle of champagne and one of the towelling bathrobes from our room. "My beautiful wife being stripped by her lover." After putting down the robes, he popped the champagne cork. Retrieving glasses from the cabinet, he said over his shoulder, "Well, carry on. Don't mind me."

I let Jake peel my panties down, glad to be free of the wet, clinging lace. Not waiting for the men to join me, I slipped into the hot tub. Pressing the control button, I set the water bubbling and relaxed back against the side of the tub,

Stefan handed me a glass of champagne. "Happy anniversary, darling."

"Make it happier. Come and get in with me. You, too, Jake."

Pulling my gaze away from the twinkling lights of the Boston skyline, I watched Stefan and Jake race to get naked. I knew Stefan's body so well that almost subconsciously I concentrated on Jake, getting my first view of his strong young cock, thick and curving to the left as it rose up from his groin.

When they came to join me in the tub, Stefan made sure Jake was sitting between the two of us. Three glasses clinked together, Stefan making the toast.

"To everything three people can do together."

The phrase dripped with possibilities. Still, I wasn't sure how to move the situation on. Stefan stepped in and took control.

"I know I interrupted a kiss when I walked in on you the other day. Why don't you show me what I'd have seen if I'd been just that few seconds earlier?"

Jake and I glanced at each other, then set our glasses down. Excitement bubbled in my pussy as Jake took the point of my chin in his slim guitarist's fingers and teased my lower lip with his tongue, encouraging me to open up and take him in.

His mouth tasted of champagne and the gum he liked to chew. I gave myself up to the kiss, fingers linked round the back of his neck as we feasted on each other. His hand dipped below the waterline, hunting between my spread thighs to find my clit.

"That's it," I heard Stefan mutter and realised he must have known from my little whimpers what Jake was doing to me.

By the time Jake and I broke apart, I was breathless but ready for much more. But now it was my turn to watch, as Stefan pressed his lips to Jake's. Ever since we'd started talking about the idea of a threesome, I'd been fantasising about the moment when the two men would kiss, but nothing had prepared me for the delicious reality. They looked so hot, I couldn't stop my hand slithering down to rub my pussy.

Jake's eyes widened and he gasped against Stefan's mouth. It took me a second or two to notice Stefan's subtle arm moment and realise he must be wanking Jake under the water. Now, that I really did want to witness uninterrupted.

Rising out of the tub, I reached for my robe. Immediately, Stefan stopped what he was doing.

"Aimee, are you okay with this?" The anxiety in his voice was evident, as though afraid he'd pushed me past my limits.

"Absolutely," I assured him. "I just thought maybe we could go down to our suite, so I can get a better view of the proceedings."

In moments, Stefan and Jake were joining me on the deck. Even though there was very little chance of our bumping into anyone, the booking for the Sweet Lies party having as good as given us the whole hotel to ourselves, they still wrapped towels around their wet hips before following me down the stairs.

We were barely through the door before they were kissing again. I adored the sight of them—hard, flat chests pressed tightly together, Stefan's hand curled around the base of Jake's cock. Now Jake seemed to have grown used to the feel of another man stroking him, he was keen to reciprocate. His fingers circled Stefan's thick shaft, and I bit the back of my hand so as not to shriek out loud, so strong was my response to the sight of the two men wanking each other.

Settling back against the generous pile of pillows, I sipped from my glass, toying with my clit as Stefan pushed Jake up against the wall and started to lick a slow trail down his neck and the upper slopes of his chest. Before joining us on the roof, he'd set candles burning in red and gold jars dotted around the room, their heady jasmine scent perfuming the air. Everything about this scene was so decadent, so uninhibited...just what I was sure people imagined when they talked about the excesses of the rock and roll lifestyle. A bed big enough for three, vintage champagne, two hot men she was crazy about — what more could a woman need?

A soft groan diverted me from my musings, and I realised Stefan was on his knees, Jake's cock in his mouth. Unable to remain a passive observer a moment longer, I went to join them. Stefan and I exchanged a look as I sank down beside him, and I knew he was enjoying this scene just as much as I was. He licked along Jake's shaft, before taking each of his tight balls into his mouth in turn. As used as I was to the feel of Stefan's hot lips and tongue stimulating me in all my most intimate places, I couldn't begin to imagine how it felt for Jake to be pleasured in the same way. From the way he writhed against the wall behind him, he seemed to be loving every moment of it. But I knew if one mouth was good, two would be better.

When my lips closed around the head of Jake's cock, he almost lost it on the spot.

"Oh, God, Aimee, that's too fantastic." Jake's voice was husky, wracked with passion. "I want to come in your mouth..."

"Slow down, babe," Stefan cautioned me. "We've got all night, remember? Why don't we all get comfortable on the bed and see where we go from there?"

Where we went was to a place where time seemed to lose all meaning as hands and mouths explored soft flesh, three bodies melding into one as we sampled all the permutations of our delightful arrangement. One moment, I would have a cock in each hand while Jake and Stefan lapped at my nipples, then we'd roll over and suddenly Stefan's hard length would be in Jake's mouth as my husband and I exchanged the hottest, sloppiest kisses. Fingers — Stefan's, Jake's, I couldn't tell whose and I wasn't sure I cared any more — dipped into the flowing well between my legs, smearing juice over the pucker of my arse so they could lightly tease me there.

"Want to be fucked. Need to be fucked." The words were wrung from my throat. My desire was like a wildfire, raging out of control and threatening to burn me to a cinder.

"What the lady wants, the lady gets." Stefan pulled my thighs widely apart. Kneeling, he fed his cock into my depths. Then, holding me steady, he rocked back and forth, spearing me with short, fast jabs that had me bouncing on the bed. In that position, Jake was able to attend to me, too — sucking my nipples and nibbling at my earlobes.

Every thrust sent powerful sensations through my whole body. I'd never felt so alive, so wanted...so loved. I tried to let Stefan know this, but my words came out as nonsense as the strength of my orgasm robbed me of the power to do anything but babble and gasp and finally lie limp against the bedsheets.

Stefan wasn't finished. Not by a long way, as he pulled his cock from me, shining with my cream. "Are you ready for me, Jakey boy?" he asked.

Jake glanced at Stefan's sizeable length, then gamely nodded. "I'm all yours."

Even with the lubrication from my pussy, Stefan would need more assistance to penetrate Jake's arse for the first time. The hotel owners had provided a little wicker basket filled with travel-size toiletries. Stefan hunted through it till he found a tube of aloe vera body lotion. Uncapping it, he rubbed a generous amount into and around Jake's back door. That alone was enough to have Jake groaning and humping his cock against the bedcovers.

Stefan chuckled, urging Jake on to all fours so he could get in place behind him. "Just as greedy as my wife, aren't you? Okay, here we go."

With that, he pushed at Jake's hole. Watching, I was convinced there was no way Stefan could possibly fit himself in such a tiny entrance, yet slowly, surely, he did just that. The play of expressions on Jake's face moved from apprehension to discomfort to wonder as Stefan entered him. Once Stefan was satisfied his lover was comfortable with being so full, he pumped back and forth, taking things at a much gentler pace than he had with me. It was obviously doing the trick for both men, as deep grunts of pleasure filled the room.

The discarded tube of body lotion lay on the bed close to me. I squeezed out another dollop, slicking my palm with it. Snaking my hand under Jake's body, I found his cock and wrapped my fingers round it. Now, with every thrust his cock was pushed into the tunnel I'd made to contain it. The extra friction that created was enough to have him spurting his cum within a few strokes, crying out so loudly I was glad we didn't have neighbours to alarm with the noise.

Barely had I released my grip on Jake's cock than Stefan was coming, caught in the tight vice of his lover's spasming arse. The two men collapsed together before Stefan thrust out a weary arm to pull me into the circle of their embrace.

We shared kisses and soft words of gratitude, all three of us slowly coming to terms with the reality of what had just happened. Glancing from Stefan's face to Jake's and back, I saw only good things and the promise of more to come.

"Thank you, darling," I murmured in Stefan's ear. "I didn't think you could make me love you any more than I did, but…" Letting the sentence trail away, I let my head rest on his sweat-sheened chest. "And you, Jake. You're the most wonderful lover any couple could hope for."

There was one more person I needed to thank, but he wasn't around to hear the words. When Mark had walked out on us, it had seemed like the end. But instead, if he only knew it, he'd brought about a delightful new beginning. I'd never dreamed when we recruited Jake that it would not only revitalise the band but take my marriage to a whole new level. But as we lay entwined on the bed, sleepy and satisfied and full of love for each other, I was excited about the future I knew Jake, Stefan and I were destined to have together.

Words drifted into my head, and for once I didn't immediately rush to write them down. There'd be time for that in the morning. I closed my eyes, mentally fitting a tune to the lyrics that summed up our new relationship to perfection.

"Three sides to every story,
Three players in this game,
No losers, only winners
For in our hearts I know we feel the same…"

SAVIN' ME

Wendi Zwaduk

Dedication

JB for nudging me to finish this
CM for the swift kick
SB for being awesome
JPZ for savin' me

Chapter One

"You scared?"

Juniper sat at his feet, silent. Jacoby gazed down at her as he petted her honey-coloured hair, comforted by the silky texture and the scent of her flowery shampoo. Clad in nothing more than the silver, rope necklace collar and black stilettos, her head bowed and her hands folded over her lap, Juniper made the perfect picture of a submissive. Her lack of response served to fulfil his unspoken demand. "You may answer, pet."

"Petrified."

The certainty and honesty in her reply resonated to his core. He'd married her. He loved her and yet, he'd always felt there was something—*someone*—missing. He would never leave her, had never wanted to. "Look at me, love."

Slowly she met his gaze. In her blue eyes, a million questions brewed. The collar glittered in the soft lamplight. He owned her heart. When they entered the bedroom, she willingly became his. Juniper should've been enough for him. Jacoby patted his lap. "Sit. I want to look at you while we talk."

Rising to her full height of five feet four inches, she stood before him. He ran the backs of his fingers over her taut nipples. When God created woman, he created perfection in the form of Juniper. She smoothed her hands over her hips, drawing his attention to the gentle swell. With curves in all the right places and an imagination nothing could snuff out, she suited him perfectly. She parted her lips and thrust her breasts towards him. The tight little buds beckoned to him, erect from desire, steel barbells glistening in the soft light. Nipple play factored into their lovemaking each time and he loved to hear her gasp and moan when he captured the dusky tips in his mouth or tugged them with the chain.

"You want to play, pet?"

She stared at him, unmoving.

"Although you are right to remain silent, I wanted an answer. Tell me, should I punish you?" The faint smile on her lips also lit up her azure eyes. He nodded. "A spanking. Four strokes should work—*after* we talk. Sit." He loved their play, loved her more than life, but it wasn't the same.

Juniper straddled his hips, cradling his denim-clad cock between her thighs. Jacoby wound his hand behind her neck, drawing her down for a kiss. The taste of her, a combination of her mint toothpaste and the salty musk of his cum on her tongue, intoxicated him. Even after three years together, she brought out his need to love and possess her. Only one other had ever brought him to the brink with little more than a kiss.

When she backed away, the spark of desire in Juniper's eyes dimmed. "Jacoby."

He should punish her for speaking out of turn and using his name. Should want to smother her with kisses until she begged for release. He couldn't do either. The sadness in her voice combined with his inner turmoil zapped his heart.

"You're thinking about him, aren't you?"

Jacoby bit down hard on his tongue. He could lie. Parkur Thompson walked away from him, from the both of them, more than a year prior. He'd wanted the band and the fame, not the sanctity of the music. He'd wanted just a wife, not a male lover and a wife. *I can't be with the both of you. It's not right.* Jacoby closed his eyes. The hurt, fresh even after the passage of time, gnawed at his soul.

Juniper cupped his cheek, bringing him out of his silent pity party, smoothing her thumb along his jaw. "What did the letter say?"

The letter. The damned impersonal correspondence from the record label. "You and I are to be in the Atrius Building downtown at seven p.m."

She tipped his chin to meet his gaze. "Think he really wants us?"

"Fuck if I know." Parkur's mood swings were legendary. One moment he'd wanted the threesome—needed them to be solid for the band, the music, for him. The next minute he needed a traditional wife and children.

Juniper snuggled against Jacoby, resting her head on his shoulder. "We made a good band. The people liked Razrs Edge when we were all together. Despite the sales for our album together, he's probably realised the new line-up isn't suited to our music."

"But why now? Because the fans hate Rhiannon and her screaming horse-shit songs?" To hide the frustration coursing through his veins, Jacoby wrapped her tight in his embrace. "We're not here for him to use us to make money. Been there, done that, over it. I like my life, and I love you. Fuck him."

Juniper sat silent for a pregnant moment. She'd been a founding member of Razrs Edge right along with Parkur. Hell, she'd been involved with Parkur until Jacoby came along. Instead of reacting with jealousy, she'd welcomed him into the musical relationship. As for the physical relationship, it had taken time and tenderness to get the three of them into a groove.

"I *want* to say it's because he truly needs us. Bone-deep, can't-live-without-us desire." Her hand stilled over his and her voice wavered. "But this is Parkur. He's the only one who knows what goes on in his mind."

Jacoby raked his fingers through his hair. "It won't be the same."

"Never is."

As if he'd flipped the switch deep within her, Juniper stiffened. Jacoby sensed her fear. The sheer veracity of the love between the three of them wasn't something that could last. Damned near came apart when they'd first began the tryst. Jacoby kissed the top of her head and rested his cheek against her forehead. "Ju, I feel the worry in your bones." His heart splintered when her tears wetted his chest. "I love you, flower girl. His being around won't change things for you and me."

"You still love him," she said in a husky voice he barely recognised. "He is your soul mate. I'm a placeholder. I've accepted it."

Jacoby shifted in the recliner and cupped her chin, forcing her gaze to his. "We were meant to be three. The music, the laughter, the fucking…it all equalled our magic number." Time to show her she meant the world to him. "Stand, pet."

Juniper complied and scurried off his lap. With her hands at her sides, she bowed her head. Jacoby unfolded himself from the chair and crossed the few steps to her position. "I won't leave you, Ju. You're mine. Always." As he kissed her, invading her mouth with his tongue, he nudged her against the wall. He pinched her nipple, eliciting a squeak from deep in her throat. The excited sound sent pinpricks of excitement coursing through his veins. Just one good fucking against the wall to show her he loved and cared for her.

Groaning, Juniper rocked her hips against his thigh. Cream from her pussy slicked his denim-covered crotch. Damn, she wanted him. Jacoby ground into her then reached down between them, rubbing her clit with the pad of his thumb. "Fuck, pet." Jacoby panted and stroked his cock against her lower belly. "Need you now."

"Take me." She wrapped her legs around his waist, granting him access as he lifted her from the floor. "Please fuck me, Sir."

Releasing her long enough to unzip and withdraw his erection, Jacoby gathered her back into his embrace and slid into her body. The walls of her pussy clenched around him, creating delicious friction. Damn, he'd never last. He built the rhythm in time with her writhing and drove into her slick channel. A melody played in his brain, the same one he heard whenever he made love to her. All he needed to make it perfect was Parkur's steady drumbeat, his soul with them…

Maybe one day.

"Jac!" Juniper clung to him, her body a mass of shudders.

Jacoby buried his face against her neck and came with one final surge, coating her womb with his seed. "Damn."

Lowering one leg to the floor, Juniper sagged in his arms. "I love you, Jac."

"Love you, flower girl."

* * * *

Bass music pumped into the recording studio, drowning out the casual conversation. Parkur clenched and unclenched his fists. Today he'd see them again. Today he'd get answers. Today he'd leave them faster than they'd fucked him over.

Juniper and Jacoby Binder. The people he cared for the most and the ones he hated with a vengeance. Every time he heard the *Shards* album, his heart ripped apart all over again. They'd written and created the music — their special triad. Fans loved the darker, romantic rock music. The soundtrack to their relationship. Each song found its way on to the playlist during the tour, reminding him of what had been and wouldn't be again. Hearing those same words on just his own lips with Rhiannon and the replacement backing band wasn't the same. It sucked ass. The fans knew it, he knew it. Too bad management hadn't received the memo.

Zero, his current backing singer and lead guitarist, plopped down next to Parkur. "They'll be here."

"Not worried about it." *Liar.* Parkur folded his arms to hide the nervous gesture. "Few people pass up the chance to make music with a top band. They're no different."

"Cold." Zero shook his head and crackled the plastic cup in his thick fingers. "You do realise that you've become a bastard since they left."

"Me? I'm the picture of happiness and upward mobility." Sort of. Parkur ground his teeth together. Happy was the last word he'd use to describe himself.

"Upward mobility?" Zero snorted. "That's a crock of shit."

"If I lie enough, it'll be true." God only knew, Parkur forgetting the two people who made his battered heart whole wasn't going to happen anytime soon. "I hear they got married and settled down." *Without me.*

"And it's burning your ass because you want to be with them."

"Fuck off." Zero's words hit way too close to home. He had no idea what had gone on. Hell, *Parkur* wasn't even sure when the train had come off the rails. Not totally.

Zero leant forwards and rested his elbows on his knees. "Look, I know things went to shit. I saw more of it firsthand than I wanted to. I didn't believe it then, and I don't buy it now." He sighed. "You know me, I'm not one to peddle advice, but this time I am. Rhiannon is a bitch. She hates the music you write, and with Hank's help has run RE into the ground. Instead of us recording more of her sad excuses for songs, why don't we work on the stuff you wrote on the road?"

"Hank said it sucked." Parkur groaned. Hank Clark hated almost everything Razrs Edge released – unless the song went multi-platinum, then the tune was his favourite. "It's too emotional and not edgy enough for RE."

"Where'd the emotion for the music come from? His ass? No, it came from your broken heart."

"Shout it to everyone."

"I will. They pulverised your heart and, because of it, you wrote some damned haunting music. My guess? Juniper and Jacoby will clamour to record it and beg to have you release it."

Parkur stared at Zero. "How are you so sure?"

"I'm not. I want you to be happy and they made you happy. You all have something special when you're together. It's how it should be—her singing, you drumming, him tearing up the bass line and the rest of us in the background. I'm dying to get back to business as usual."

The door slammed behind them, causing Parkur to jerk in his seat. "Are we done with the touchy-feely moment, girls?"

Parkur closed his eyes. One person grated on his nerves to the point of breaking them—Hank. The man could insult and compliment in the same sentence without blinking. Opening his eyes, Parkur folded his hands in front of his mouth to bite back a nasty response.

Zero stood and smashed the plastic cup in one hand. "It was a great day till the worm showed. Don't you have a contract to screw us with?"

"You wanted a businessman, you have me." Hank slapped Parkur with the back of his hand. "Why aren't you warming up? We record in an hour."

"I'll be ready when it's time." Parkur stood and nodded to the piano. "Don't disturb me unless Ju and Jac show up. I need the right people to round out the songs."

"The label wants the rough cuts by the end of tomorrow. You can't piss around." Hank snarled and pounded his fist into the back of the office chair. "You already stepped out of their collective shadow. You don't need those two. When will that fact get through the cement in your head?"

Ignoring the ramblings of his manager, Parkur crossed the threshold into the actual studio. Collective shadow his ass. *He'd* started Razrs Edge. Him and Juniper.

And Jacoby had made the band complete. He'd made the music complete.

Parkur toyed with the crumpled sheet music on the stand then plopped down before the piano. He'd written Jacoby's bass lines to mimic the deepest desires in his heart. With Juniper singing, the words would take on multiple levels of meaning. He found the notes and began a simple melody. He'd fucked up. He wasn't sure how or when he'd lost control, but he'd driven them away. Juniper had cared about Parkur and his music enough to encourage him to record it. Jacoby had understood the inner pain and could translate it into a form the masses understood.

And now? What did Parkur have to show for his pain?

A fat lot of loneliness in a crowded room.

Parkur palmed the braided silver at his throat. The collar. The fans believed it to be his symbol of resistance and rebellion. If they only knew it was his true link to Jacoby, his Sir. He hadn't given up on the man who made his heart thunder, nor the woman who'd made him smile when the rest of the world turned away. He should want revenge, want to make them hurt. He pressed his hands together in front of his lips. Rhiannon had been a mistake from the word go. She wanted Hank and the notoriety of fronting a band.

Ju and Jac soothed his wounded soul.

"Save me," he whispered.

Chapter Two

"It's ten till seven." Juniper wrapped her arms around Jacoby's biceps. "Ready?" Despite the unseasonal warmth of the April evening, a chill ran through her bones. She peered up at the Atrius Building, hulking in the fading purple light. She'd recorded some great songs after nine at night—always with Jacoby and Parkur.

Jacoby's jaw tensed. "This is shit."

She glanced at the sheaf of papers in Jacoby's hands. The songs Parkur had sent weren't up to par. Not even close to his talent level. Did he want to continue to record crap to sell records in the pop market? Before the split, Parkur swore he'd never write what wasn't in his heart. Songs about guns and destruction didn't fit Parkur's style at all. Something felt off about the meeting.

Jacoby's words brought her out of her musings. "Let's go so we can get out of here. This won't last."

The first floor echoed with their footsteps on the dull linoleum floors. Juniper sighed. In the eight months since the building had changed hands, the decorators had taken away every last bit of originality in the foyer. No more murals of musicians, no more folk art statues of instruments. Just bland beige walls and potted plastic palms. She wrinkled her nose. The faint scent of cigarette smoke lingered in the air.

"Looks like no one wants to record here since Clark took over." Jacoby pressed the buttons on the elevator pad. "He was an ass when Parkur insisted we hire him. I'll bet things haven't changed."

"Don't hold back," she murmured as the elevator ascended. "Tell me how you really feel."

"Like I'm walking into a fucking hornet's nest. I hate Hank and want nothing to do with Parkur." Jacoby's words came out in a growl, making her jerk in his embrace. He rubbed the back of his hand over his stubbly chin. "I'm sorry, babe."

The bell dinged for the eighth floor, but Juniper halted the car with the emergency stop. "I hate Hank, too, but I've been thinking about this. If we go in with a combative attitude, the whole thing will go to shit. What if Parkur does want to try again? What if he's had a light bulb go off and realises he needs us? I'd love to know why he kicked us out of the band, but we have to go about this with our heads on straight. Give him the rope to hang himself. If he's going to, he will. If not, then we see where things are going."

Jacoby stared at her with a blank expression in his blue eyes. As the seconds ticked by, Juniper's heart sank. She rarely talked out of turn—not out of fear, but out of respect. When she did speak up, he listened...she hoped.

"I should write a song for you, something simple, but ball-breaking. Every time I'm close to the edge, you step in and save me." He slapped at the button, engaging the car and kissed her hard on the lips. "How about *Savin' Me*? It's got your name all over it."

With another ping, the doors opened to the recording studio foyer. Juniper twined her fingers with Jacoby's and followed him into the room. Garish posters from the various Razrs Edge tours festooned the black walls. Gold record awards lined the reception desk. It felt odd to be in their former hangout, and a sensation of stepping into Neverland coursed through her veins.

Although no one sat behind the reception desk, conversation rumbled in the room. "Yeah, I'll do that. After a couple smokes." Trent 'Zero' Grazia ambled through the studio door. When his gaze locked with hers, the frown on his lips curled into a broad smile. His silver eyes gleamed. "Well, look what the cat dragged in. How the hell are you?"Crossing the room in three strides, Zero thrust out his hand. "I missed you. Ain't the same with the witch at the helm." He shook hands with Jacoby and gathered Juniper into a bear hug. "There's room for one woman in the band. You."

Juniper slapped his steely shoulder. "How much do I owe you for that compliment?"

"Free of charge." He nodded to the recording studio. "The bass awaits and the mics are set. You two ready to hit this hard? We need someone to really understand the music, not mangle it to make it poppy."

A trace of a smile tugged at the corner of Jacoby's mouth, quickly replaced by his trademark stony expression. Juniper glanced in the direction of his glare and shuddered. Hank.

"I thought you had to have that last cigarette?" Hank stopped mid-step and held open his arms. "There's my precious little musicians. You still in charge of her, Jacoby?"

"I'm not a slave." Juniper rubbed Jacoby's back, if only to calm her own frustration. "Do we need to sign contracts?"

"If he's in charge, then yes. If you want me to rep you, then it's all taken care of. Duane's in the conference room awaiting your answer, darling."

"I'm not your darling," she snapped.

"Where's Parkur?" Jacoby folded his arms, his body tense and his stance wide. The guy exuded power from his six-foot, muscled frame.

"I see where you both stand." Hank narrowed his black eyes. "Juniper, run along and make nice with P-dog while Jac and I work on the contract with Duane." Hank tipped his balding head towards the recording studio sound room. "We have lots to discuss."

P-dog? She cast another glance to Jacoby before taking a wide path around Hank. The less she had to touch their former manager, the better. She snuck one more peek at Jacoby before slipping through the open door. "*Love you,*" she mouthed. The slight dip of his head was the response.

When she entered the sound room, she noticed Parkur sitting alone at the piano. Barefoot and clad in nothing more than faded denim and a sloppy T-shirt, Parkur appeared to be a broken man. His sandy hair flopped over his brow as he hung his head. If he'd wanted sympathy, his plan worked. Her heart squeezed within her chest. The last time he'd looked so distraught was the day he told her he wanted a relationship with Jacoby.

Shoring up her courage, she knocked on the glass. Jerking upright in his seat, Parkur glanced around the room. When his gaze settled on the glass, a smile brightened his face. Like nothing had happened between them, he raced across the studio and flung open the door. "Ju!"

She squealed when he tugged her into the soundproof room and shut the door. He swung her around in a circle. "My muse has returned!" He placed her feet on the ground and rested his forehead against hers. "This means everything to me."

"I haven't done anything," she murmured. "You never needed me to be creative."

With one hand wound into her hair and the other cupping her cheek, Parkur rubbed his nose along hers. "You have no idea the hell I've lived through. I wasn't going to admit the truth—not yet, but I can't hold back, babe. Promise you aren't leaving."

What truth? The scent of his cologne twirled around her brain, fuzzying her thoughts. "I won't go until we do what we do best."

"Make love?"

"Make music." Although making love sounded delicious and damned if she wasn't turned on. "If it was so rough, why didn't you call before now?"

"Kiss me."

"That doesn't answer my question."

Taking her by surprise and pinning her to the keyboard of the piano, Parkur moulded his lips to hers. She sighed and melted in his arms. Unlike Jacoby, Parker took his time. His smooth chin bumped against hers. He nibbled her bottom lip, swiping his tongue over the tender flesh. His erection pulsed against her abdomen as he captured her tongue in a deeper connection. She forked her fingers into his hair. They had to stop. To keep the kiss from turning to something primal. Tell her libido that. When in the presence of Parkur Thompson, she felt like a damned groupie. Throw Jacoby into the mix and they could thaw the thickest iceberg in seconds. Her pussy wept, dampening her panties.

Panting, Parkur broke the kiss. Only a faint ring of jade showed around his ebony pupils. "You did miss me." The tinkling of notes from the piano flooded the room as Juniper shifted in his embrace. The rest of the world melted away around them.

"I want to spread your naked body across this piano and taste your sweet cunt." His hips rocked, simulating sex. "When I've had my fill and you're screaming my name, I want to feel that pussy clench around me."

Sure. Sounded like heaven...with one six-foot, raven-haired catch. "What about Jacoby?"

"I didn't forget him. He can watch and then fuck me into submission when you come."

She sighed and blinked back tears. The words alluded to Parkur wanting things back the way they'd been. The idea sounded wonderful but somehow jagged, like chunks were missing.

"What? Talk to me." He brushed the wetness from her cheeks. "Where'd I go wrong?"

Her chin quivered. Moments earlier, she'd been more than willing to lift her skirt and let him have his way. Hell yes, she wanted Jacoby to watch and instruct them. But not before they each had their say. She wrapped her fingers around the back of his neck...then stopped cold. She hadn't seen it moments before and might not have believed it had she not touched it, but there it was.

The collar. The match to the silver braid she wore about her throat.

"I made mistakes, but not that one," he murmured. "He owns my heart and soul, just as you do."

Didn't that *revelation change the playing field.* "We need to talk."

"I agree. Besides the music, I want to know what's going on." Parkur plopped down onto the piano bench, caging her between his knees. "I can't do the lead vocals on this group of songs, and I assumed you'd send me your thoughts." He folded his arms, the muscles bulging under the cotton T-shirt. "I want back on the drums. I hate being in front."

"Have Rhiannon sing."

"I like my eardrums." He slumped forwards, unfolding his arms and resting his elbows on his knees. "She's moving on with her own band."

"Oh."

Parkur tipped his head and cocked one brow. "I figured you knew, but then again, I'm shocked you showed."

"Yeah? Why?"

"You two left in a fucking hurry when she joined the band." The softness in his eyes garnered a harder edge. His jaw tensed. "I barely had time to say goodbye."

"There wasn't much choice."

"Oh? You could've chosen to be with him and me...or just me. No, she showed up so you bailed and took him with you. I ain't the brightest bulb, but it sure looked like I was just in the way."

"Jacoby claimed *us*—not you, not me. Us."

"Bullshit. The day I come to you with a whole album of music, ready to commit as a monogamous threesome, you both up and fucking leave. I wanted to marry you, Juniper."

He'd wanted to...marry her? "Then why in the name of God did you fuck her? You cheated on us."

"I've never slept with Rhiannon," Parkur bit out. "She means shit to me."

Juniper wobbled and sank down onto Parkur's lap. It sounded like all the things she and Jacoby had been told were false. Parkur could fake smiles or laughs, but never sincerity. She rubbed her temples and processed his words. "Wait, I missed something. Songs? Commitment? I thought… Wait. We need to bring Jac into this."

"Yeah, I'd like to know why he cock-teased me."

"Jac's hard as steel, but he's never been a cock tease. He cares about you as much as I do."

The door creaked behind her. When she looked in the direction of the sound, Hank leaned against the doorframe. "At least you look cosy. I didn't think you two would work it out."

"What do you want?" Parkur's words came out in a growl. He grasped her hand. "We were in the middle of a conversation."

"We heard, P-dog. The mics are on." A sneer curled Hank's thin lips. "You need to talk to Zero about the chorus on *Slipped*. He's next door murdering it."

"Right now?" Shaking his head, Parkur smoothed his fingers through his hair. "Tell him we're using B and to get his ass in here. And stop calling me that lame-ass name."

"I'm not your bitch. You work for me."

"Damn it." Easing her off his lap, Parkur popped up out of his seat and strode to the door. Before he left, he spoke over his shoulder. "We aren't done here."

Juniper grasped the bench for stability. "Agreed."

Parker trudged through the sound room and slapped the buttons to kill the mics. He wasn't sure what Hank was up to, but he knew Zero better than most. If his lead guitarist had an issue, he sure as hell didn't use Hank as a go-between. As he stepped into the foyer, his breath clogged in his throat. He'd know the silhouette against the bank of windows from anywhere. Spiky hair, thick steel hoops in both ears, and a body filled out with solid muscle.

Jacoby.

Parkur jammed his hands into his pockets. He wanted to talk to his former lover, to embrace him and admit he needed him. Jacoby thought Parkur had cheated on them. Wasn't possible. He stood rooted to the spot, hesitant to make his next move.

"You never could make up your mind." Jacoby's words ricocheted off the glass.

"Why are you out here and not rehearsing?"

"Wasn't asked in."

Jacoby was never a man of many words. Parkur sighed, unsure how to get through to his former lover. "I want you here. Always."

"Ask Hank."

"Fuck Hank. I'm asking you." Other words formed on his tongue. Hell, he wanted the whole damned story. He wanted his partners back. "Come in and record with me."

"At least you found your balls."

"What the fuck?" Anger wouldn't help mend the rift between them, but Parkur could only take so much. "If you hate me so much, why in the name of God did you come here?"

Jacoby turned from the windows. Lines crinkled around his azure eyes. From strain? From regret? Parkur wasn't sure. He yearned to smooth his fingers over the ravages of time and ease the pain. Jacoby placed his palm over Parkur's heart. The heat seeped straight through his chest and settled in his groin. "Do you still have the collar?"

Parkur blinked. Things made a bit more sense. Jacoby didn't deal in emotions well—he left that to Juniper and the music. In his left-of-centre fashion, Jacoby cared. The thought knocked down a row of walls around Parkur's heart. "I've always had a spine and my balls. It's different when I'm with you, but I'm no less of a man."

Jacoby's jaw tensed. Apparently the comment hit a bit too close to home.

"I have the collar. I refused to take it off, even when you ditched me. I won't take it off. I can't."

"Because it's your shtick?"

The overriding desire to slap Jacoby crossed Parkur's mind, but what would violence accomplish? He pinched the bridge of his nose. "It reminds me I belong with you."

Although he wasn't completely convinced, Parkur swore Jacoby's stony expression softened a bit. Maybe he'd made progress. Hope welled within his soul. If he could make them see they belonged together—for the band and for each other—things would turn out right.

"When the rest of the world seems like a joke and I feel like I'm worthless, you save me. You know when to reel me in and when to send me soaring. Call it cheesy, call it campy, but yeah, I never let go. We made a great team. Or we used to. Why'd we let it fall apart? Because you thought I fucked Rhiannon? Sorry, but no." Parkur folded his arms and sighed. "I don't expect an easy answer, but I want to sort this out. I need you and Ju for more than any music. You both complete my soul."

Behind him a door slammed. "That's it. I'm out." Parkur glanced over his shoulder as Juniper stormed to Jacoby's side. "I gave it my best shot thinking the studio could make it sound better. Sorry, I can't work with this shit."

Ice thickened in Parkur's chest. He knew the songs she'd been given. Hours and hours of pain and heartache had gone into the words. "What's wrong with the lyrics? The melodies need tweaks, sure, but that's where you two come in."

"Not this crap. I know your work. This ain't it." Juniper shoved a sheath of papers into Parkur's hands. "Razrs

Edge was never operatic, and I refuse to sing about a robot lover."

Confused, Parkur riffled through the pages. Besides not being in his handwriting, the melodies written didn't make sense—sharps and flats written in a mishmash and mixed with high and low notes only a singer with a wide range could hit—not at all their style. He furrowed his brows. "This isn't the music I sent with the courier. Where'd this come from?"

Jacoby wrapped his arm around Juniper's shoulders. "That's the notebook you sent us in the mail. We tried to work out what to play, but it's damned near impossible."

Parker shook his head. He clearly remembered handing the manila envelope to the courier two weeks prior. "You're right, Ju. This piano work is shit." He leafed through the pages, appalled by what he saw. "This doesn't even qualify as shit."

"What are you going to do about it?" Jacoby's baritone echoed in the small room. "We're here to play, not waste your time."

"This is my studio. We have all the time in the world because the record label wants an album of vintage RE. Fuck the time sheets. They'll get it when it's ready and not a moment earlier. What's in this notebook isn't what I wrote, and I'll be damned if we record it. Are you hungry? I need some air."

"There is a place where we can talk." Juniper squeezed Parkur's hand. "If you're in."

Parkur nodded and held his breath. Jacoby held the key. If Jacoby wanted nothing to do with Parkur, then no amount of words or begging would repair the relationship. After what seemed like ages, Jacoby growled the words Parkur had waited a year to hear. "Parkur, Juniper…do you wish to play?"

She squeezed Parkur's hand once more and they spoke in tandem. "Yes, Sir."

Chapter Three

Jacoby refused to get his hopes up. He knew Juniper's heart. She loved to play their games. Damn near burst his eardrums with her squeals when he'd asked her to marry him and take his last name. But Parkur? He remained a mystery. If Parkur's track record spoke for anything, it was that he wanted to play for the short term. Jacoby wouldn't stand by only to have his heart trampled again because of a whim. He needed trust and time. He nodded to the notebook. "If that's crap, then we play, talk, and write the album, agreed?"

"And after?" Parkur's Adam's apple bobbed. "What happens after?"

"We'll see."

"I'll send Zero a text." Parkur whipped his phone from his back pocket. "He needs a night off anyway." He glanced over his shoulder as Rhiannon and Hank slipped out of the elevator.

"Where are you going?" Rhiannon squeezed Parkur's shoulders. "Are they here as studio musicians?" She crinkled her nose. Venom shone in her dark eyes. "We work in three takes. If you can't handle the heat, we can't use you."

Hank chuckled. "These two can't play anything smoothly...except Parkur. They've got *his* tune down pat."

"Give me five minutes." Parkur forked his fingers through his hair as he stalked into the reception room. "I'm not putting up with this shit."

Casting his glare at Hank, Jacoby clenched his fist. "You seem to be doing well. The record made the Top One Hundred."

"The public knows decent music." Rhiannon stepped toe to toe with Jacoby. "It took me a moment, but now I remember. You're the harpies who think they know decent music. Let me give you a tip. He needs a woman in his life, not you."

"Bitch," Juniper snapped.

"You're nothing but another hole." Rhiannon's lip curled.

Parkur appeared behind Rhiannon, coat in hand and tennis shoes on his feet. "I'm ready." He leaned in close to Jacoby, brushing his lips over Jacoby's cheek. "Save me?"

"Save us." Jacoby led Juniper and Parkur to the stairwell. His heart sped. They needed to get out of the damn building. "The apartment is two blocks. We'll walk."

On the front steps of the building, Zero sat twiddling with his phone, a cigarette dangling from his lips. "Go get 'em, Tiger, and make us proud."

Parkur nodded and tucked himself into Jacoby's side. Blood rushed through Jacoby's system and settled in his cock. Memories of burying himself deep within Parkur's ass while Parkur fucked Juniper formed in his mind. Getting them both home and naked sounded wonderful. *Home.* The dream had been an apartment for the three of them. Always together.

Could the dream still come to fruition?

Seven-thirty on an April evening wasn't the best time to take a walk. The breeze whipped around them, causing Juniper and Parkur to clasp more tightly to him. Jacoby swallowed a groan. The nip in the air might chill them, but it did little to stifle the fever swirling through his body.

The downtown building seemed to go by in a blur as they hurried to the loft. When they reached the foyer, Jacoby released Parkur. Nodding, Parkur opened the door for them. Jacoby's heart pricked with a twinge of sadness. As much as he wanted to make love to Ju and Parkur, he didn't want the play to feel like true punishment. Everyone had made mistakes…himself included.

Juniper slipped through the open door. Bracing his hand on the frame, Jacoby nodded to Parkur. "Go."

Parkur pushed a windblown lock of hair from his eyes and flashed a grin before entering the foyer.

The bell for the elevator pinged and echoed off the walls. Juniper breezed into the elevator. Parkur paused for a moment before shuffling in beside her. Jacoby pressed the correct button, closing the doors. The car surged skyward, then Jacoby slammed his fist into the emergency stop.

Time for a little test.

Juniper's nostrils flared and her gaze vacillated between Jacoby and Parkur, who stood with his head bowed and his hands behind his back. Nice.

"Show me his collar then mark him, pet, wherever you please."

Rubbing her hands over Parkur's chest, Juniper nuzzled his cheek. She curled her fist in the folds of his T-shirt and planted kisses on his neck. She paused then nipped and sucked at his jugular, eliciting a low groan from Parkur.

Jacoby drew in a long breath then let it out slowly. Seeing his wife leave a purplish bruise on his former lover's neck heated his blood. Could the three of them get back to the love and music they once shared? He spread his fingers across the back of her neck to halt her action. Juniper eased away from Parkur and met Jacoby's gaze.

"Well done, pet." Jacoby pressed the button to restart the elevator and wrapped an arm around Juniper. She tipped her head back and grinned.

Jacoby hovered a whisper from her lips, testing her. Instead of meeting him for a kiss, she stood still. "Beautiful." Fusing his lips to hers, he licked the seam of her mouth. The taste of mint and the salt of Parkur's skin exploded on his tongue.

Before he could break the kiss, the elevator dinged, signalling their floor. He pulled back from her and gasped. "We're here. I'll ask once more, do you want to play?"

"Yes, Sir."

"Yes, Sir," Juniper replied, mirroring Parkur's response.

"Parkur, go to the bedroom and remove your clothes. Kneel on the bed until we arrive. You'll find it." He nodded. "On your way."

With a nod, Parkur strode through the elevator doors. Jacoby drew a ragged breath into his lungs and placed his hand on Juniper's shoulder. "Wait."

She crossed the threshold into the foyer then stopped and met his gaze.

Jacoby fumbled his hands together. In the bedroom, he dominated. With emotions… *Damn it.* "I need to know where you stand."

Juniper threaded her delicate fingers with his. "This is what we need—closure or a second chance. If it's really meant to implode, then this is a sweet farewell. It'll give us all the opportunity to heal. If it's meant to be a second or third act, then let's make it a doozy."

"I love you, flower girl."

"I love you, too." Her eyes flashed with desire and mischief. "Now spank my ass and make me come."

Thank God he had her. She knew the perfect things to say to break his tension. "Naughty." He loved her spark, her fire, her way with words...and her need for pain with her pleasure. "You want the punishment." He shook his head. "Instead of doling out red marks all over your sweet little ass, I think I'll make you watch."

She licked her bottom lip and the grin grew to a full smile. Even the 'punishment' wasn't true punishment.

"You, naked on the pillows. No touching yourself."

He followed her scampering form through the apartment to the bedroom. He stopped short in the doorway. Just as he'd commanded, Parkur knelt on the bed, deliciously nude. The sight of his muscled lover gave him reason to pause, but the writing on Parkur's back wrenched the breath from Jacoby's body.

Juniper broke the silence. "We're entwined..."

Chapter Four

Well, fuck her twice into next week. Juniper stole a glance at Jacoby. His lips parted and a glassy, shell-shocked look mirrored in his eyes. She shifted her attention back to Parkur. He'd had their names inked between his shoulder blades. A calligraphic J took up the most space along his spine and began both her name and Jacoby's. Running vertically, from the *A* in *Jacoby* down through the *U* of *Juniper*, was *Parkur*.

Linked. Forever.

Gonna be one helluva hurt to get it lasered off. Juniper balled her hand to keep from reaching out to trace the lettering. On stage, Parkur rarely wore a shirt. He preferred to show off his muscles and piercings. Paired with the things he'd said in the studio, she now wasn't sure what to believe. Didn't matter, really. Seeing Parkur and Jacoby together would be worth every moment, even if it ended up as spank-bank fodder. Call her foolish for loving to watch bisexual men showing love for each other, but she did.

Jacoby snapped his fingers, drawing her from her thoughts. "Pet?"

"Oh." She quickly wriggled out of her clothes then took her place on the bed. Now wasn't the time for a sensual striptease. Hell, they'd never pay attention to her even if she did. This moment was all about them and damned if she was going to miss it while trying to get free from her clothing.

Jacoby sank to one knee behind Parkur and tilted Parkur's head. Parkur parted his lips as Jacoby crushed his mouth down on Parkur's. Both men groaned. Juniper sighed and settled on the bed. Sizzles from the kiss she hadn't shared lingered low in her belly. Cream slicked between her thighs. The contrast of Parkur's baby-soft skin against Jacoby's hair-roughened jaw made a striking portrait. Oh, to be able to just come then enjoy the rest of the show.

Jacoby slapped Parkur's bare ass. "Mine." He fingered the collar about Parkur's throat. "You are mine."

"Always," Parkur replied.

"Remove my shirt. I want that mouth on my nipples."

Inch by agonising inch, Parkur unbuttoned the buttons down Jacoby's shirt and exposed more and more of his flesh. He scraped his nails down Jacoby's chest, leaving three red scratches on the pale skin. Jacoby thrust his hands into Parkur's hair and held him against his breast.

Juniper squeezed her legs together. Parkur hadn't even put his hands on Jacoby's dick yet and she already wanted to come. Hell, neither man had touched *her*. She licked her lips as Parkur sucked on Jacoby's mocha-coloured nipple. She loved to run her tongue over every last bit of Jacoby's body. She dug her fingers into the tops of her legs. Double damn it. No touching herself, either.

Jacoby groaned. "Fuck. Yes. Suck me."

Grinning, Parkur worked the mechanism on Jacoby's belt then unfastened the button of his jeans. He divested Jacoby of both the pesky denim and his boxer shorts in one downwards tug. Parkur stood and grasped both his cock and Jacoby's cock in his hand. Their twin piercings sparkled in the low light.

"I missed this," Parkur whispered.

"On your knees." Jacoby's voice came out ragged and slithered over her skin.

The words were a command, but the tone of Jacoby's voice amplified his need and his inner turmoil. Jacoby obviously loved being in control, but could he fall back in love with Parkur? Juniper wished both were possible. Even after the fights, the bitter words and the parting, she still loved both men.

Parkur sank back down to the floor and cupped his fingers around Jacoby's heavy sac. He curled his tongue to lave along the thick vein on the underside of Jacoby's engorged cock and hummed.

With stuttered breaths, Jacoby placed his hands on his hips. He might be in charge, but Parkur held the cadence of their lovemaking.

Juniper nestled into the pillows. Not coming was agony. Each lick, each suck reverberated in her system. She wanted to jump in next to Parkur and trade ministrations.

Jacoby cupped the back of Parkur's skull in one hand. "Take all of me."

Parkur angled his head and did as Jacoby commanded. Juniper whimpered.

"Do you see what you're doing to Juniper?" Jacoby stilled Parkur, his cock buried deep in Parkur's mouth. "She's wet and ready for your cock. Or mine?" He reached down to tweak Parkur's nipple. "Turn over and show me your pretty ass."

While Parkur scurried onto the bed, Jacoby rummaged through the nightstand. He produced a bottle of lube and a foil packet. "Juniper."

She stood next to the bed and held out her hand for the lube and condom. Jacoby gave her the items and stepped a foot from Parkur. Her heart thundered as she knelt before her husband and stole a taste of his dick. The minty taste of Parkur lingered on Jacoby's skin and the piercing clacked against her teeth.

"Bad girl." Jacoby's words came out scolding with a twinge of amusement. He squirted the lube onto his hand and coated his fingers. He winked at her and buried his middle finger in the depths of Parkur's ass.

"Shit." Parkur bowed his head.

"Tell me if it hurts." Jacoby slid his finger in and out of Parkur's rectum with slow strokes. "I refuse to fuck you up."

"Been a long time." Parkur moaned. "Still like it rough."

Juniper looked at Jacoby. His head cocked ever so slightly. Was he shocked? She was. She assumed Parkur had sown his wild oats the moment they walked out the door. Maybe he topped now. She bit the inside of her cheek. She wanted to see Jacoby bend Parkur in half and slam into his ass with zeal.

Adding another finger, Jacoby continued to finger-fuck Parkur. "Tight."

"Feels so fucking good," Parkur said. "Too damn good. Won't last."

Juniper bobbed her brows and ripped open the packet. She wrapped her fingers around Jacoby's cock and slid the latex down his length. Jacoby closed his eyes and sank into Parkur.

The sight of Jacoby's cock disappearing into Parkur's ass gnawed away at the last vestiges of Juniper's restraint.

She'd already played with fire by licking Jacoby. Damn. Both men know how to tease her. They knew what she needed.

"Do you want to come?" Jacoby said and stilled.

"Yes, Sir," came Parkur's strangled reply.

"Juniper." Jacoby nodded to the bed. "Give him the pussy he craves."

Holy shit. Her turn to participate. "Yes, Sir."

Juniper scampered into position, opening her legs before Parkur. He moaned. Having Jacoby's thick dick buried in his ass made him burn. He'd forgotten what it felt like to have the piercing at the tip of Jacoby's cock rubbing over his sensitive tissues. Dynamite. With Juniper on display beneath him, it took all of Parkur's fortitude not to blow his wad. Love bubbled in his heart for the both of them. Parkur braced his hands and dipped his head to taste her sweet cream. Her essence flowed over his tongue. With every lap, every thrust, he fell further into the old feelings.

Could it be I'm really in love? Forever love?

Hell, love sounded a lot better than sleeping alone and writing shit songs. As three, they'd made magic. He wanted the magic back.

"I want to hear her scream, Parkur." Jacoby's rumble vibrated straight down Parkur's spine.

"Yes, Sir. With pleasure."

Parkur lowered his head again and licked the delicate skin of her labia. Between each push from Jacoby, he nipped and tugged the piercing in her clitoral hood. Juniper writhed her hips, dancing to the rhythm of their brand of lovemaking. He speared his tongue into her wet depths and smiled to himself. This was how it should be. Three.

Juniper's pants increased and tremors ran the length of her legs as she bucked. At the same time, Jacoby pistoned harder into Parkur's ass. Jacoby reached around Parkur and pinched his nipples. Holy shit. Parkur fisted his hands in the sheets, focussing on Juniper and the rightness of their collective actions. Anything to keep his mind off coming.

"Yes, pet." Jacoby grunted and dug his fingers into Parkur's flesh. "Fuck."

Juniper threw her head back and grabbed Parkur's hands. "Oh!"

Cream filled Parkur's mouth. A little more and both Jacoby and Juniper would reach orgasm. Parkur pushed back into Jacoby's furious thrusts. Jacoby's balls slapped at Parkur's tight sac, sending delicious sizzles through Parkur's veins. Hell. He sucked at restraint.

"Oh my God." Juniper whimpered and crushed her folds against Parkur's face.

Behind Parkur, Jacoby growled another curse and then slumped against Parkur's back. "Fuck me, you grab hard." His hot breath tickled the nape of Parkur's neck. "Fuck Juniper. She needs to come." Jacoby withdrew from Parkur's pleasantly sore hole and flopped onto the bed beside him.

Parkur kissed Juniper's inner thigh. Her heavily lidded gaze met his. She smiled. "Lay down. I want to ride." The grin faded a bit. "Please?"

Jacoby nodded. "Anything for my flower girl." He tossed a fresh condom in Parkur's direction and slapped Parkur's ass.

Juniper plucked the foil packet from its resting place on the comforter before tearing the package open with her teeth. Parkur's cock hardened past the point of pain. He needed to be inside her. Now. He rolled onto his back and reached out for Jacoby.

With another smile, this one stronger, Juniper sheathed Parkur. She dipped her head to nuzzle his balls and stroke his cock. He panted, too caught up in the luscious sensations of her lips and hand on his body. "Please?"

"You both need to come, tease." Jacoby squeezed Parkur's hand. "Juniper."

She spread her legs over Parkur's and positioned him at the mouth of her pussy. He groaned as she sank down onto him. Two good thrusts and he'd be done for. Somehow, it didn't matter. He'd waited for over a year for this moment. He'd longed to be between them — fucking them, loving them. No one else mattered or moved him like Juniper and Jacoby.

He arched his hips and fucked her. Heaven help him, he wasn't about to stop. Juniper squealed and cupped her breasts. "Fuck me, Parkur. Fuck." Her head lolled on her shoulders. Her body quaked and her lips parted. Jacoby's grasp on his hand tightened. Parkur surged up into Juniper one more time. Stars exploded behind his eyes. Wetness slid over his hips and ass as Juniper came. A sense of calm surrounded him and a new tune played in his head — a rollicking drumbeat with a melody in the key of C throbbing over the top. God, he loved when sex brought out his creative streak.

Opening his arms, he snuggled Juniper against his chest. He turned to Jacoby. The bear of a man grinned and stroked Parkur's cheek. Parkur's heart swelled. All he had ever wanted now surrounded him. For the moment, they'd saved him.

Damn, it felt good to be saved from his shitty self. Parkur stared at Jacoby until his eyes grew heavy. The weight of Juniper's body became heavier in his arms. He should chuck the condom, but sleep sounded wonderful. He rolled the used latex down his shaft and aimed for the waste bin next to the bed. Unsure of whether he'd hit the target, Parkur closed his eyes. He'd found them, found his heart and found home.

Now to stay there.

Chapter Five

Warm breath fanned over Jacoby's chest. An arm squeezed across his stomach. He shifted and opened his eyes. The arm had a fine sprinkling of hair. A moment of confusion jolted him awake. *What the...?* Juniper curled against his side, her hair tickling his neck. On his left, Parkur lay flopped on his stomach.

Jacoby's heart pounded. He knew full well what they'd done. He stared at the ceiling. Tension throbbed behind his eyes. Part of him wanted to continue with Parkur and Juniper. Hell, he loved being with them. He loved her, and he'd once loved Parkur. Could he again?

Sighing, Juniper rolled over and yanked the blankets with her. Jacoby chuckled. The woman was perpetually cold.

With his hair mussed and sticking out in every direction, Parkur raised up on one elbow. His sleepy smile faded. "She's still chilly?"

"Go in the other room and talk." Juniper snuggled down tighter into the blankets. Only the top of her blonde head showed. "Fix it and go. Sleep has my name on it."

Jacoby snorted and shook his head. "Go."

Without looking in his direction, Parkur grabbed his jeans from the floor and exited the room.

Well, fuck. Yeah, he and Parkur needed to talk. He even appreciated Juniper's blunt suggestion to sort it out. But what the hell should he say? Grunting, Jacoby nabbed his boxer shorts from the floor then headed into the living room. Reversing their roles from the studio, Parkur now stood staring out of the window overlooking the city. Fingers of yellow sunshine caressed his taut body. Even the mussed look made Parkur look ruggedly handsome.

"Beautiful view."

"Ju picked the place. She wanted to see the water."

"Water?" Parkur snorted. "I don't see the lake."

"She says she can see it." Jacoby shrugged and bit the bullet. "Did you love her?"

"Juniper, yes. Rhiannon, never."

At least the man answered quickly. Still, the answer wasn't enough. Jacoby moved to block Parkur's view. He needed to see Parkur's eyes as he spoke. "Then why?" He fought to keep his emotions in check. The harder he bit his tongue, the harder it became to hold things in. If he didn't get things out in the open, they'd never make progress. "You said we weren't enough."

Parkur's shoulders slumped. "We all said a lot of things we didn't agree about."

"You don't want to admit that you pushed us away."

"I'll admit to the truth, but I swear I didn't push you anywhere." With his head lolling back on his shoulders, Parkur looked towards the ceiling. "I fucked up, but I never fucked her."

"Liar," Jacoby roared. He'd seen the evidence. The strewn bedclothes, the array of whisky bottles and a very nude Rhiannon sprawled across an equally bare Parkur.

"Boys," Juniper shuffled into the room. She rubbed her head and shoved an errant lock of hair from her eyes. "Just like old times. You two disagreeing and me having to keep you from throttling each other." She plopped Jacoby's phone into his hand. "Someone texted you."

Jacoby wound Juniper in his embrace and pressed the buttons to retrieve the text. Her nearness settled a little of his fury. As soon as the message appeared on the phone screen, he growled. Hank. The bastard.

I own Razrs Edge. Don't fuck with me. Record the fucking album.

Jacoby erased the text, silenced the phone then tossed the device onto the coffee table. The issues needed to be settled before he bothered to deal with Hank. "If you never fucked her, then tell me what the fuck happened to the three of us?"

Parkur folded his arms. "Let's start with the last day. Other than you thinking I'd cheated with Rhiannon, I can't figure out where the fuck we went wrong. No matter how many times I go over the timeline, there's a missing piece on May sixth."

"Let me think." Jacoby's patience frayed. "Aside from what I walked in on, you said we weren't enough. No questions. Just done. And then you send two letters. One says our band is through and the other saying you'd lied — you weren't bi-sexual and didn't love either of us."

"You never called to question me?"

"We tried." Juniper nodded. "No one would let us into the Atrius and every time we called you, it went to voicemail. I sat by your car one night waiting and ended up having to talk my way out of being arrested for vagrancy."

"That makes no sense." Parkur turned away from them and threaded his hands behind his head. "I'd planned to propose—to marry you, Ju, and have a commitment ceremony to Jac. I'm not meant to front a band. Never said I could or even wanted to."

"Why didn't you?" Jacoby replied.

"I don't know. Maybe because the day I came to you guys, that's the day you walked out." Parkur dropped his hands. "I need your music to complement my lyrics and your voice, Ju, to convey my feelings. Giving either of you up wasn't an option. We were always meant to be three."

Juniper curled tighter against Jacoby. "Is that why you inked our names on your back?"

"It was part of the surprise. We share the three collars— three interwoven chains—but I wanted a permanent reminder. The pain, the pleasure, the laughs and tears...all equal our three." He snorted. "Hank saw it and went fucking ballistic."

"Then why sleep with Rhiannon?" Juniper whispered.

"I didn't!" Parkur slapped his thighs and turned around. "God! I got drunk to forget our fight at that club in Detroit. Numb the pain and all that shit. I drank so damned much I puked all over myself. She was there when I woke up. The scene apparently worked to her advantage. You left and she got the helm."

Jacoby released Juniper and propelled himself into the kitchen. He grabbed a bottle of water from the refrigerator to buy time to think. Things began to make sense—more than it ever had. He grabbed two more bottles and headed back into the living room. "Where's your heart now?"

"With the both of you."

The words came out sure, not a wobble or catch. Jacoby toyed with his wedding band as he faced his lovers. "You didn't happen to grab the lyrics you wanted to show us?"

"In my coat." Parkur's brows knotted and crimson infused his cheeks. "Why? We argue and now suddenly you want to work? I never did understand you."

"There comes a time in a man's life when he has to surrender." Jacoby grabbed his guitar. Time to just let go of the past and do what came naturally.

The fury drained from Parkur's face. He cocked his head the slightest bit. "You should record that."

Jacoby's heart sped and the blood rushed through his veins. "Then put it to music." His fingers flicked the bass strings. "Ju will follow. Sing it."

Little by little, they worked through the notebook full of words, turning them into full-bodied, haunting tunes. The colour returned to Juniper's face and happiness glittered in her eyes. Her voice got stronger with each line.

The smile broadened on Parkur's lips. His drum riffs became more intense the longer they worked. "God, I forgot how much this fucking rocks."

Jacoby packed his enthusiasm behind a wall of uncertainty. Things were working out way too well. Time for the other shoe to drop.

* * * *

"We have fifteen good songs for an album, but my guess is it'll run long." Parkur tapped the notebook with both pencils, punctuating his words. "But with what we've got, long is a good thing."

"What about an EP? Or a bonus album? Bands do that all the time." Juniper sat on her hands and leant forwards on the piano bench. Her heart thundered. Making music soothed her soul and completed her. Better than a stiff drink and more important than the air she breathed. Now how to get the music out to the ones who mattered most—the fans. "We could do an extended version that has bonus features, like three acoustic songs—old favourites or something. How about as a present to the fans for sticking with us?"

"Good thinking." Jacoby resumed tuning his bass. "We could release something on the site as a member-only track."

"Good thing I have you two around. I hated making these decisions on my own. Rhiannon was no help at all."

Juniper shifted in her seat. Again with Rhiannon. The woman was the bane of her existence. She shot Jacoby a look, hoping he'd smile or nod...*something* to bolster her confidence. As per usual, he hid behind a stony expression. Damn it.

"Why'd you hook up with Rhiannon?" There. She'd asked the question. Did she truly want the answer? Not really. Where was the rewind button when she needed it?

"Blunt." Parkur leaned towards her and placed a kiss on her lips. "I love you blunt."

"Always," Jacoby added. "How about you answer? She's waiting."

Why didn't Jacoby's addition settle the unease in the pit of Juniper's stomach? Because she'd been replaced by him, originally. Parkur had started Razrs Edge to make the music in his soul. She'd come along for the ride. When Jacoby had at first auditioned for lead guitar and then taken his place on the bass guitar... Yes, things found a balance, but only after a tense period. She'd hated being the one left out when they made love. Sure, she got used to watching and playing the voyeur. She loved her role once she found her groove. But what if they did it again?

What if they wanted her to warm the bench while they ran the bases?

"Juniper?"

She grabbed a can of soda and downed a large draw. "I'm paying attention."

"You're over-thinking." Jacoby tugged her tight against his side.

"You've always been the smart one. Not me." Parkur grimaced and continued. "It boils down to this. Rhiannon is Hank's protégé. He's grooming her for stardom because he didn't feel he got enough of a cut of RE's revenue. I thought she'd sing some backup and move on. I had no idea he'd put her in front of the band. Next thing I know, the contracts were rewritten to give her top billing."

"Razrs Edge never had a dedicated front man." Juniper sat up a little straighter. "Always equal."

"Honey, there's only so much room in RE." Parkur rubbed his thumb over her bottom lip. "She was never a true part of the equation."

Juniper chewed the inside of her cheek. If the contracts had been changed without their knowledge…

Who could they call for proper legal representation? A thought came to mind. "Jac? Why don't we call your cousin down in Crestline?"

"Nate? He's in estate planning."

Parkur's eyes lit and he nodded. "It's still legal shit."

"Maybe he could help us out." Juniper met Jacoby's confused stare. "We need someone in our corner who really gets all that fine print."

Parkur clasped both Juniper's and Jacoby's hands in his. "Worth a shot."

Jacoby scratched the patch of hairs on his chin with his free hand. "I haven't talked to Nate in…God, five, maybe six months."

"He'd help." Parkur scooted to the edge of his seat. "He's your family and as I recall, he never liked Hank."

Juniper squeezed Jacoby's thigh. "Whatever it takes, Jac. I want—I want things the way they were." Her heart clenched. If she had her way, she'd rewind time to the day before things fell apart and start there fresh.

"I'll call him." His whole body moved as Jacoby nodded and grabbed his phone from the side table. "Right now."

Parkur slapped his thighs. "Ya know, after a recording session, the next best thing is making love. I think once Jacoby gets done yakking with Nate, it's time for a little bow-chicka-wow-wow."

Chapter Six

Parkur sank down a bit in his chair and held his breath. Had he taken things too far? He loved saying exactly what he thought.

Until it came back and bit him in the ass.

Jacoby leaned into Juniper and whispered something into her ear. Her gaze flicked to Parkur as she nodded. A faint smile curled the corner of her mouth. The more Jacoby whispered, the more the grin widened. Tearing her attention from Parkur, Juniper squeezed Jacoby's arm as she slipped off his lap. Giggling, she strode from the room.

"What was that all about?" Parkur rubbed his clammy hands on his pant legs. "Want to clue me in?"

Jacoby placed his hands on his hips. "Shower."

"With me? I'd be honoured." Parkur batted his lashes. Never let it be said he didn't at least try to work his assets. "What about Miss Juniper?"

"She got hold of Nate and he's going to be here later today. Don't worry about her. Right now is about you and me." Jacoby twiddled his thick finger. "Strip."

The commanding tone sent shocks through Parkur's system. Oh yeah. Time to play. He nodded once and yanked the T-shirt up over his head. Jacoby crossed the short distance to him and splayed his palms across Parkur's bare chest, toying with the piercings in Parkur's nipples. Damn. Parkur stifled a groan. Tingles from his nipples soared to his cock.

"Like that?"

Unzipping his jeans, Parkur bit out a reply. "Yeah." He worked the constricting denim over his erection and let the fabric drop to pool at his feet. His dick bobbed between his legs. Blood rushed from his head to his groin.

"Nice." Jacoby slid his hands down along Parkur's stomach to the thatch of curls at the base of his penis. He gave Parkur a squeeze and his balls tightened.

If he pleaded, maybe Jacoby would give him relief. Maybe.

"It's ready," Juniper called from somewhere behind Parkur. He swallowed hard. Would she be involved? He wanted her, sandwiched between him and Jacoby.

"Shower." Again, Jacoby wriggled his finger.

Bowing his head, Parkur made his way to the bathroom. Steam billowed in the surprisingly cavernous room. Whatever they paid in rent was worth it, if for nothing more than the bathroom. Wall to wall granite tile, the blue grey shades of a winter Cleveland sky. Glass blocks separated the shower stall from the rest of the room. A claw foot tub, perfect for at least two people, lined the far wall.

"Here's where she sees the water."

Parkur jerked as Jacoby eased up behind him. Jacoby's thick cock nestled between Parkur's ass cheeks. "It's gorgeous."

"She fell in love with the bathroom." Jacoby slapped Parkur's ass and the crack bounced off the tiles. "Forward."

With a soft moan, Parkur stepped into the shower stall. Jets of water fell like rain from the ceiling. He tipped his head back to sluice the water over his body. Another moan escaped his throat. "Heaven."

"I haven't done anything—yet." Jacoby reached around and pinched Parkur's nipples. His breath tickled Parkur's earlobe. "I want to talk, then fuck."

Speechless, Parkur stared over his shoulder at Jacoby. The moment had come. The moment Jacoby planned to let him have it. He inched towards the chilly tiles and clasped his hands behind his back to keep from reaching for Jacoby.

"She's scared." Jacoby grabbed a washcloth and added some creamy pink soap before working it into a lather. He pressed the cloth against Parkur's chest and smoothed the suds along his skin. Just like things had been before the split.

"But what? I know there's a 'but' in there." Parkur's throat clogged with more than tears. He didn't want the relationship to end. God. After the crap they'd been through... He couldn't blame Jacoby or Juniper for wanting closure. First he needed to shut down the negative thoughts. Think positive. And hope like hell.

Slapping Parkur's ass once again, Jacoby grinned. "There's the butt. Nice and firm." When Parkur didn't grin in return, Jacoby commenced washing him. His expression faded to blankness. "She hasn't come right out and said anything, but she's scared you're gonna bail."

Moving at Jacoby's command, Parkur turned his back on his lover. "I'm lost."

"Parkur." Jacoby's voice sounded tired, even above the splash of the water. "Look at me."

Parkur faced Jacoby. Something stung his eyes. Soap? Tears? Fuck. He hated to cry. Hated himself for the past.

Bracing one hand on the tile behind Parkur's head, Jacoby leant forwards. He sighed and shook his head. "There are some serious trust issues here. Neither one of us is sure when the other shoe's gonna go, taking you with it." With his free hand, Jacoby rubbed his thumb over Parkur's chin. "I'm hoping that the third time's the charm. Yeah, she married me. We lean on each other more than most people think. But it's not the same. The only time she makes music is when she does guest spots. I haven't picked up the bass in I don't know how long. We can't go on in this limbo. Either stay or go. Don't drag it out."

Thoughts swarmed through Parkur's brain. At least they'd suffered. Not that the knowledge helped much. They'd all hurt bad. All because things had got out of hand. No wonder Juniper felt abandoned. He'd done it not once, but fucking twice. What an asshole. Rubbing his hands over his eyes to wipe away the water, Parkur forced himself to look Jacoby in the eye.

Jacoby stood upright and resumed soaping Parkur's body. He took his time, massaging every ripple and swell on Parkur's body. Heat surged through Parkur's veins. He swayed on his feet as Jacoby caressed his cock. His balls constricted. Too much more action on his junk and he'd come like a teenager.

"Rinse."

Parkur snapped his eyes open and stepped under the spray. His breath caught fast in his chest. Jacoby stroked Parkur's cock, bringing him close to orgasm once more.

He peered up at Jacoby. Sexual torture? Kinky, but he rather liked it. Jacoby bridged the gap between them and gave Parkur's dick a squeeze. Tingles shot from Parkur's toes up to his brain then to his cock. He shuddered as Jacoby brought his mouth down hard onto Parkur's mouth. His tongue pierced between Parkur's lips and twined with his.

Almost as fast as the duel began, Jacoby retreated. He stood nose to nose with Parkur. "This has been a fun little trip down memory lane, but if that's it—a jaunt through the past and nothing more—then just fucking go. Her heart can't stand shattering again. I'll pick up the pieces with her, but I won't guarantee she'll ever stand to see you again. And I won't. Ever."

Nodding, Parkur backed Jacoby against the wall. Time to take charge and show them exactly who he wanted. "I want our three. I want the magic on stage, in bed, in love. This is the charm." Parkur pointed to his collar. "This is our link. The constant." He sucked Jacoby's bottom lip between his teeth. "I want your pain, your torture, but I want your pleasure. You and her. Forever."

"Good." Jacoby turned the water off. He gave Parkur's cock another stroke. "Do you want to play?"

"Yes, Sir." Parkur stood still as Jacoby rubbed the downy soft towel over his body. Every nerve ending came to life. He couldn't gulp enough air into his lungs.

Jacoby offered his hand. Entwining their fingers, Parkur followed Jacoby into the bedroom. The sight before him wrenched the breath from his body.

Juniper lay on her side, one leg bent, with what had to be an eight-inch—if he had to guess—strap-on jutting from her body. She wrapped her fingers around the flesh-coloured sex toy. "Ever been fucked by a girl?"

"There was this one…" His mouth watered and his cock hardened to the point of pain. He dug his fingernails into his hips to keep from coming at the sight of her.

"On your back." Jacoby swatted Parkur, nudging him forwards.

With his gaze locked on Juniper, Parkur crawled onto the bed. "You look gorgeous." He ran the pads of his fingers down her cheek then neck to the swell of her breast. "Always." He'd come this far—no way he'd just assume the position without sampling her. The blue of her eyes disappeared in the black pools of her pupils. Dipping down, he sampled her lips and groaned. She tasted of cherry lip gloss and minty toothpaste. When the hell had she brushed her teeth? And why did he care?

Juniper broke the kiss. "Lay down," she murmured.

Nodding, Parkur eased down the bed and spread out on his back. A rush of cool air licked his body. His nipples beaded. What did they have planned?

Jacoby stood over him, blocking the light. "I like a clean toy when I play." He yanked Parkur to the edge of the bed. "Spread 'em."

Parkur bent his knees and grasped his ankles. A shiver darted up his spine as Jacoby knelt between his legs. His tongue swirled around the tight bud of nerves. Parkur gasped. He loved a good rim job. The feel of Jacoby's mouth on him turned his brain to mush. His eyelids fluttered shut.

Another sensation added to the mix. "Holy fuck." Parkur wriggled as Juniper took his cock in her mouth. She smiled at him around his dick. He wasn't going to last. With each pull, each draw, she sucked him towards orgasm. His muscles went taut as Jacoby eased his middle finger into Parkur's ass.

"Nice and tight," Jacoby rumbled.

"I'm—I'm…" The rest of his words faded as his balls constricted. He thrust into Juniper's mouth, emptying his seed down her throat. Fuck. The room span a little as he slipped back onto the bed. Closing his eyes, he sucked air. His limbs felt like Jell-O. Just a few moments and he'd be ready to go…just needed to snooze a moment.

"Flip over."

The words registered somewhere in his consciousness, but Parkur didn't react. He couldn't. Was it possible to die from an orgasm?

"No sleepy time. Sorry, pal." Juniper bit down on his nipple. She sat straddling his hips, and the dildo flopped onto his stomach. "Wakey, wakey."

"I'm alive." Parkur opened his eyes. "Give me a moment. I swear I'm on the edge of dying. Everything's numb."

Juniper shrugged. "Part of our evil plan. You'll get used to it." She groaned and inched forwards. Her breasts jiggled and bounced in his face. "Oh!"

Words of encouragement. He liked that, but he loved the feel of the dildo rubbing and sliding against his erection. Parkur moaned and wrapped his fingers around both cocks. For a man who'd sworn only moments earlier he'd died of pleasure, his desire renewed. Jacoby fucking Juniper while he lay beneath them sparked his libido. Parkur darted his tongue out to tease the tender buds in time with Jacoby's thrusts.

"Oh my God." Juniper wriggled. Her hair tickled Parkur's chest in time with Jacoby's pushes. Her arms quaked and her eyelids drooped.

As quickly as they'd started, Jacoby stilled. Juniper's eyes widened as she met Parkur's gaze. Jacoby backed away from their tangled bodies and he folded his arms.

"Flip over."

Juniper stood in front of Jacoby and grabbed a bottle from the nightstand. She stroked the dildo, coating it in lube. The flesh-coloured sex toy glistened in the low light.

Hell, yeah. Parkur couldn't get his body to move fast enough. Once on his knees, Parkur waved his bottom in the air. The taunt would get him punishment...but what kind? Didn't really matter. He'd embrace whatever Jacoby could dish out.

"Spank him," Jacoby rumbled.

"Please?" Shit. Parkur sounded needy even to his own ears. He glanced over his shoulder. Juniper winked.

The crack split the air as she spanked his ass. Hard. The immediate imprint of her hand combined with the sting shot straight to his cock.

"More," Parkur groaned. He needed this. Needed to know they cared enough to punish him. Desired their love above all else. Yearned for their music.

Their three.

Instead of rewarding him with another slap, the blunt head of the dildo pressed against his rectum. Parkur shivered. His eyes rolled back into his head. He couldn't get enough air into his lungs. As she pressed the toy into his tight body, he moaned. Rough. Right and rough. Just the way he liked it. He backed into her, sending the unyielding behemoth farther into his ass.

Juniper's nails bit into his shoulders. Her tiny whimpers vibrated down his spine. He peeked over his shoulder again as Jacoby moved closer behind her.

"Fuck yourself on her dick," Jacoby murmured. His hands spread across Parkur's hips. Arching his back, Parkur rode the sex toy while he fisted his hands in the comforter to keep from stroking himself. His balls drew tight beneath him. So close to the edge.

"Oh my God," Juniper gasped. The force of Jacoby moving within her propelled her into Parkur like one well-lubed fucking machine.

"Ohfuckohfuckohfuck." Jacoby's thrusts grew more erratic and the curses slurred together.

"Need. To. Come," Parkur bit out. Every nerve ending within his being sizzled. So God damned close.

"Now."

As if Jacoby held a magic key to their combined orgasm, Parkur came. Semen coated his stomach and the comforter. Juniper slumped against his back, moulding herself to his body. Jacoby's growl ripped through the room. He, too, slumped forwards, bracing himself on his forearms.

In a mass of tangled limbs, Jacoby coaxed them both onto the bed.

"Best sex ever," Parkur puffed. "I know I'm dead."

"Yeah," came Juniper's sleepy reply. "I can't crash with the harness, but I'm…tired."

"Sleep," Jacoby whispered.

Jacoby's footsteps padded on the carpet. The sound of buckles and rustling sheets filled Parkur's consciousness. A moment later, the bed dipped. Parkur grabbed Jacoby's hand, sandwiching Juniper between them. Parkur rolled onto his side to stare at Jacoby over Juniper's head. Her soft breaths feathered over his chest. Parkur stroked the sprinkling of hairs on Jacoby's arm, memorising the feel of his lover's skin. For a moment, everything felt right.

"I love you," Parkur murmured. "I love you both."

Jacoby stared at him with a hint of a smile on his lips. "Now convince her."

Well, shit.

Chapter Seven

Parkur folded his hands and rested his elbows on his knees. No wonder he hated legal jargon. None of it made sense to him. All the words looked Greek or something. Juniper sat on the arm of Jacoby's chair and picked at the cuff of her sweater. He hadn't seen her smile since three nights prior. Fuck if he knew what had changed. Jacoby sat hunched over the papers, nodding at things Nate Waterford said. Sure, Nate was a great guy and decent lawyer. But damn, the tension in the room suffocated Parkur.

"I've looked at what you have." Nate leant back in his seat and tossed the pen onto the teak coffee table. "If you haven't signed anything new, then these are outdated. All Hank did was paste in what he wanted changed. The dates are all different from the dates with the signatures. Write up what you want included and excluded. Leave off the individuals you don't want involved in the record.

Hell, I'd start my own label if I were you. You'd be in charge of all the rights and a lot happier."

"Where's this leave Hank?"

"He owns the rights to the older material, yes, because he was your counsel at the time." Nate placed the papers in front of Jacoby and Parkur. "Let's word this sucker so we can stick it to Hank."

"I'll be right back." Juniper jumped from her perch and left the room.

Jacoby's shoulders slumped. The crinkles around his eyes deepened. "Give us a minute." He stood and padded out of his living room.

So much for meeting in their apartment. For a long moment, Parkur stared at the hallway. He should go after them. Should find out what the hell was going on. He turned his attention back to Nate, who tapped his paperwork into a tidy stack.

"So…" Nate shook his head. "You're back."

"I am." Parkur sat up straighter in his chair.

"You fucked them up," Nate said quietly.

"I know."

"Can't say I'm thrilled to see you back. She cried her eyes out and I swear he destroyed at least three walls by putting his fist through them."

"Yeah." The knowledge that they'd suffered so much felt like a kick to the gut. So many mistakes. Parkur gritted his teeth. And now he had the chance for true redemption. Damn it, he'd take the chance. "Can you look into something for me? You said something about owning our own label. I think it's doable already."

"How so?" Nate shuffled papers again and didn't look up. "You've got a recording studio in your back pocket?"

"Sort of. I own the Atrius Building on Ninth Street here in town. I never signed anything over to Hank when I bought it. Did the deal with the realtor on the down-low because I didn't trust Hank. Hank, being Hank, is sneaky."

Slowing his movements, Nate stared at Parkur. "No shit?"

"It's mine. Lock, stock and barrel. If Hank doesn't have his hand in it somehow that I don't know about, I want to change the deed."

"My respect for you has grown." Nate whipped out his touch phone and scribbled notes. "I looked at your bank accounts. There's some money being moved and not replenished. I can look at the deed and the documents of the sale. What do you want to do?"

"Can you put it in our names?" Parkur cracked his knuckles. The rock formerly between his shoulder blades disappeared. His spirits soared. "Yes, I want to change the deed."

"Updating the deed is a quick fix. You'll need their signatures, but it's easy."

"Cool." Parkur nodded and tapped Nate's ring finger. "When did you jump off the market?"

"Didn't think you'd noticed."

"I notice hot men. I just don't act on every whim."

"Right. I remember when you made a pass at me after the showdown in the Flats in '08. And yes, I still appreciate you noticing my hot ass." He tapped the phone screen and glanced down at the papers once again. "I married Courteney about six months ago in a little ceremony in Crestline." He paused and grinned. "Ju sang 'Love Song' after we exchanged vows. Made damned near everyone cry. I think you'd like her. She's got every one of the RE albums."

"Ya know, I think organising a party is in order when those two come back in here. I'm thinking a big party to launch the record and the label. Plus, I'd love to meet your bride."

"I see." Nate crooked a brow. "Usually I'm giving Arran advice. Helping Jacoby never crossed my mind. I'm glad you all called me.

"I think it's a great way to thank our new permanent counsel." Parkur stood and offered his hand. "What do you think?"

Chuckling, Nate grasped Parkur's hand. "Money would work, too."

"Absolutely."

Juniper stared out of the windows overlooking downtown Cleveland. She rubbed her face with both hands to erase the proof she'd been crying. The sounds of conversation softened to a lull, blotted out by footsteps behind her. "Jacoby."

"You've never called me by my name in almost the entire time I've known you." Jacoby wrapped his thick arms around her shoulders. He rested his forehead on the crown of her head. "What's wrong?"

"Nothing."

"Juniper. Don't put me on," he murmured. His semi-hard cock nestled between her ass cheeks. "I know you better than you know yourself. Meeting here in our apartment isn't sitting well with you, is it?"

"I'm fine." Kind of. Sort of. Not really. "Go work on the contracts with Parkur."

"You don't just leave the damned room." Jacoby turned her around in his embrace. His brows knotted together and his eyes flickered with intensity. "Talk. Or I'll get the handcuffs and whip it out of you."

Her throat clogged with tears and not from the impending punishment. God, this was irrational. The signs weren't exactly crystal clear between the three of them. Still, she couldn't hold back the onslaught of emotion. "Am I—Will we make it?"

"What are you talking about?" He brushed the tears away with the pad of his thumb. His jaw tightened. "Explain, please?"

"Think about it." She wriggled away from him and threaded her fingers together behind her head. "In the beginning, it was me and him. Then you came along. Things got bumpy and I got the shaft."

"We worked through it," he said softly.

She dropped her arms and stared him straight in the eye. "What if three isn't us? Sure, we work well on stage and in the studio, but I can see it plain as day. He loves you. Down to his emo, rebellious core, he loves you. Me? I'm not sure where I stand."

"Ju, you're inked onto his back. I gave you my last name. What else do you want?"

"I've been on the outside looking in and it sucked." Her voice cracked and tears slid down her cheeks faster than she could wipe them away. "I don't want to be there anymore."

"You can't be replaced—by him or me." Jacoby scooped her into his arms then sat on the bed with her straddling his lap. "You said it yourself—this is either a time for closure and healing or a time to start fresh. Either way, I'm in this with you. What's that cheesy country song you listen to when you think I don't know…? You can't get rid of me?"

She giggled. "Lose. You can't lose me."

Behind Jacoby, the door creaked.

"Me neither." Parkur inched into the room and shoved his hands into his back pockets. "Is this a party anyone can join?"

"Up to you, flower girl." Jacoby smoothed her hair from her eyes. "My badass image has been tarnished."

"You're a tough guy to me. Always." She kissed him hard on the lips and whispered, "Thanks." She glanced over her shoulder. "Come on in."

"I'm not interrupting?" Toying with the hem of his T-shirt, Parkur leaned on the doorframe.

"No." Juniper sat side-saddle on Jacoby's lap. "Come here."

"I knew this wouldn't be easy—us getting things sorted out." Parkur plopped down at the foot of the bed beside them. "I know you're both afraid. Hell, my track record sucks…" He shook his head and jerked from his seat. "I made more than my share of mistakes, but you both mean too much to me to give up. Jac, I love you. Never stopped. You make me tick."

Parkur's shoulders slumped and he bowed his head. "Ju, I know what you're thinking. You're scared the past is gonna smack us all in the head." He lifted his gaze to hers. "I let you go twice now. Never again. I can't. You're a part of me. The best part of me." He hooked his fingers under her chin. "Without you, the music doesn't work. Without you, Jacoby and I can't function."

"Absolutely." Jacoby grasped her hair and fused his lips to hers. The kiss turned harder as Parkur nipped her jaw. The feel of both men worshipping her body resonated down to the core of her soul.

Whimpering, she arched into the both of them.

"Time to show her how much we care about her?" Parkur wriggled his brows. He shimmied out of his pants and yanked the wrinkled T-shirt up over his head. His hair stuck out in odd angles, framing his face in wild, wheat-coloured tangles. A smile broadened across his lips as he plopped back onto the bed and opened his arms.

Juniper hesitated. Sure, she longed to just jump into Parkur's arms. What girl wouldn't want to fuck the rock star of her dreams?

"Stand." Jacoby urged her into standing. His broad hands moved over her body, divesting her of the sloppy button-down shirt and jeans. She shivered in her bra and panties. From behind, Jacoby reached around and tweaked her nipples.

"You want to make love to him," Jacoby whispered. The timbre of his voice sent fresh shivers along her nerve endings. "You want to feel his cock deep in your cunt." One hand stayed on her breast while the other travelled down her stomach to the thatch of curls above her pussy. "And while he's blowing your mind, I'm taking your sweet little ass." One finger dipped between the slippery folds and speared into her vagina. "You belong to us."

"Ours." Parkur tugged the dampened cotton down her legs then flicked the catch on her bra, baring her body to them.

As if her body wasn't her own, Juniper moved forwards and straddled Parkur's hips. She shifted, rubbing the blunt head of his cock against her clit. Fisting her hands in the bedcovers, she moaned. Damn. How long had she been on the edge?

"That's right, love. Get yourself off on me." Parkur drummed his dick against the bundle of nerves. "Pour your cream all over me. Feels so good."

She framed his face between her hands. "Fuck me."

Nodding, Parkur prodded then thrust up into her body. The sheer force of his action stole her breath. Memories of the first time they'd made love blurred into the present. Flutters started low in her stomach. Each vein, each ridge on his cock caressed her inner walls.

"Harder," she gasped. "Please?"

"Yes, babe." Parkur's fingers bit into her skin, not that she cared. Sweat glistened on his brow as he drove into her body.

"Not yet." Jacoby punctuated his words with a swift slap against her ass. "You're ours."

Another slap spread heat over her flesh. In the same moment, Jacoby pressed chilled fingers against her sphincter. Oh hell yes. Both men at the same time. She whimpered again—not from pain, but pleasure as Jacoby worked his middle finger in and out of her ass. He added a second digit into the tight space. Fireworks licked her skin from within. The urge to come sat within reach, but the moment she thought she'd succumb, both men changed pace.

"Our music," Parkur murmured.

"Always three." Jacoby removed his fingers and pressed his penis against the tender tissues. "Our three."

Juniper swallowed a yelp. The fit...so tight. So good. Her breath caught fast within her chest as Parkur and Jacoby alternated their actions, creating a rhythm all their own. Her limbs trembled.

"Come for us." Parkur rubbed the back of her neck, drawing her down for a kiss. "I can't hold back."

At her back, Jacoby shuddered. His thrusts became more frantic and his hips slammed against her legs. "Fuck." Almost at once, hot seed coated her womb and deep within her ass.

The coil wound tight in her belly finally uncoiled. The weight of the breakup evaporated. Juniper locked gazes with Parkur. His sated smile, lazy and oh-so-sexy, combined with Jacoby's warm kisses between her shoulder blades, shattered her reserve. The tidal wave of pleasure tugged her under. She slumped against Parkur and went with the weightless feeling. With both men still nestled within her body, things felt complete.

"Fuck." Jacoby's hands spread out on either side of Parkur's head. Slowly he pulled out and crawled off her. "Either that was the fuck of a lifetime or I'm getting too old for this shit."

"Romantic." Parkur chuckled. "Nice."

Water ran somewhere in the distance. Juniper rested her head on Parkur's chest, lulled by the rampant beat of his heart. "Can't move."

The bed dipped beside her as Jacoby plopped down. "Super Bowl of romance. That's me. Roll over, Ju. Let me clean you off."

Her eyes opened and the fuzzy visage of Jacoby hovered over her. Warmth seeped down into her bones.

Parkur yanked a cover over their bodies. He patted the empty spot on the bed. "Hey, Jac, I've been thinking."

Juniper snuggled down between her men. Go figure he'd want to talk. "Hence the green smoke?"

"Har." Parkur rose up on his elbow and spread his hand out over her stomach, lacing his fingers with Jacoby's. "We've been holed up here for almost a week. Don't you think Zero would like to know what he's supposed to play? I can't text him the songs."

"And have him find us all in the nude?" Jacoby snorted. "Remember that ninety-six-hour party in Vegas? He saw more of Juniper than I liked."

"That was one hell of a weekend." Parkur drew circles on the top of her hand. "Almost forgot about that."

"I don't remember it." Juniper opened her eyes. "What are you talking about?"

Jacoby cupped her face in both hands. "We ate, drank and fucked until we dropped and then Zero strolled in looking for us."

"Now I remember. That's why Parkur bashed me with the pillow."

"It was an accident." Parkur's cheeks flooded with colour. "I wanted to save your innocence."

"Sure you did." She patted his hip. "A pillow to the backside isn't saving anything."

"But Zero's good people. He knows he's the best lead guitar in the Midwest and won't argue if we ask him to play on the record. I say we knock out the rest of these foundation tracks and fuck like rabbits."

"Sex won't cure everything." Jacoby muttered.

"Maybe not," Juniper replied, "but it's a pretty good reason to be together."

"Well, what about this? Nate's hunting down ole Hank. He's going to get the contracts fixed." The smile on Parkur's lips glittered in his eyes. "As soon as I get the text, the studio will be free and clear."

"Call Zero, Mason and Gareth." Juniper wrapped her arms around both Parkur and Jacoby. "It's time to record the new Razrs Edge album."

Chapter Eight

The next afternoon, Jacoby conceded to Parkur and Juniper's requests. He stood in the recording studio at the Atrius and simply breathed in the aura. Creativity and excitement crackled in the air. Nate's drive and determination set the wheels rolling to get the contracts changed. In the back of his mind, a tiny voice cheered. Things weren't completely fixed, but damn if it didn't feel right to be back. The sight of Juniper at the piano and Parkur inspecting his massive drum set warmed Jacoby's heart.

"It's a lot better in here without the tension." Juniper's fingers glided over the shiny keys as she practiced scales. "Just like the good old days."

Parkur tossed his drumsticks in the air and caught them both in one hand. "If I remember, the good old days included fucking on the piano." He nodded to Jacoby. "How 'bout a quickie before we play?"

"Later." Jacoby wrapped an arm around Parkur, snuggling his lover close. Juniper tickled the ivories with a tune Jacoby had never heard before. Her eyes closed and she leaned towards the keyboard.

Caught up in the music, Jacoby also closed his eyes. He breathed in the scent of Parkur's aftershave. Words formed in his mind.

I remember the taste of your skin, the touch of your hand.
I can't take our being apart.
I won't make it without your love.
You both have my heart.

"What the hell is this?"

The sweet music stopped in a slur of contrasting notes. Jacoby opened his eyes and stared at the control room. Rhiannon glared from her position behind the glass. Her dark hair looked green in the diffused light.

"Is it just me, or does she look like Medusa?" Parkur snorted. "Nah, Medusa was probably cuter."

Juniper smothered giggles behind both hands.

"This is my band," Rhiannon growled. She pounded both fists on the glass and shouted into the mic. "Why are you here?"

Parkur stood and folded his arms. "We're recording music for the new album. I believe this is called warming up." He nodded his head. "You can dick with your techno pop shit next door."

"So the buzz is true. You're cutting me."

Shrugging, Parkur sat back down. "You've been doing your own thing for two months now."

Jacoby let go of Parkur. His stomach clenched. Something in the poison in Rhiannon's words shook him deep into his core. The hairs on the back of his neck stood on end. He inched towards Juniper.

Rhiannon stomped into the studio room. Her eyes narrowed to slits. "You want to be with him and her, huh? Not me."

"Looks like," Parkur snapped.

"If I knew you liked being slapped around and told what to do, I'd have been more persuasive."

"Just a fucking minute." Jacoby stepped towards Rhiannon. "Don't pass judgement on what you don't understand."

Parkur put his hand in the air. "She's right. She would've been more persuasive, and I'd have run away."

"Oh please." Rhiannon rolled her eyes and tapped her booted foot. "You're a pussy with five o'clock shadow."

"The problem is, Rhiannon, you only think about number one. Anyone else doesn't mean shit." Parkur stood toe to toe with his former band mate. "There isn't room in RE for divas."

"Really? Don't go there, Parkur." She circled around Jacoby and poked her finger into his chest. "I've seen what you do to your sweet little diva, Jacoby Binder. Beat the life out of him while the bitch watches. That's fucking twisted." Spittle flew from her lips. "Any idiot can beat someone, but it sure as shit doesn't make your music better. It's still wimpy, whiny shit."

Jacoby wrapped his fingers around her bony wrist, stopping her actions. "Uh-huh. And you're here interrupting the session…why?"

Wrenching her hand from Jacoby's grasp, she turned her attention back to Parkur. "You're supposed to be in a relationship with me. Kick these assholes to the kerb once and for all."

"While Hank fucks you senseless? No way, babe. When you signed on to sing backing, you knew I wasn't interested. This whole changing of the guard crap he's plugging is a joke. The fans aren't here for me or my music. They want your stuff. Tits, ass...and your lyrics about sex with your vampire lover."

"How? He said..." She sank down onto a stool. "I'm a joke?" Rhiannon shook her head. "I mean, yeah, I've seen the ticket sales and the loot at the merchandise counter. I know the crowds, but...I won an award. I'm legit."

"You need direction other than Hank's hand stuffed in your pussy." Juniper shrugged. "Someone had to say it."

"She's right." Parkur began to pace. "Razrs Edge was never meant to be your launching pad. Get a couple of your pretty boy cronies, write songs about what you're passionate about, and go out on your own. You've got the following."

"You sound like a Hallmark card." Rhiannon giggled. "With piercings and tats."

"It's my emo side hitting the forefront. Sue me." Parkur put his hands in the air. "No, don't. I can't afford it right now."

"Look, you have to pay your dues a little and learn the craft." Jacoby widened his stance. "Don't expect Hank to hand it to you—awards or not."

"He'll shit a brick."

"Why?" Parkur stepped shoulder to shoulder with Jacoby. "He'll still have his money-maker."

"You're all being nice to me. I don't deserve it." Her shoulder hitched in a small shrug. "Hank set this all up so we'd hate each other. I wish he hadn't. I might be popular, but you three are off the charts. I'm—I'm sorry I've been a bitch." She raked her blood red nails through her inky hair. "I'm going to take your advice. I've got a couple of good friends who would make a fantastic backing band." A wide smile lit her face. "It's time to give Lazer a call."

"Lazer Reinhold?" Parkur clicked his tongue. "Good choice. You'll have him eating out of your hand."

"Then I've got my plan." Rhiannon put one finger in the air. "Speaking of plans... Why don't you three just record your comeback album and get it over with? Everyone wants the next Razrs Edge album...me included." She snapped her fingers. "Get to work!" She span on her heel and strolled out of the studio.

"I didn't see that coming." Parkur turned. "Did you?"

"Spooky." Juniper closed the lid on the piano keys. "Looks like it's just the three of us again."

"She's warped, but she's also right. We are off the charts. Together." Parkur hoisted himself up onto the closed piano lid and grasped Jacoby's hand. "I said it before and I'll say it again. My life, the music, all of it wasn't the same without you two." He cupped Juniper's jaw with his other hand. "It's not run of the mill to be three, but it is our magic number." He stared at the floor. "That's why we're here. I knew if I could convince you to record with me, then there'd be a chance you would save me."

"Just for the music?" Jacoby turned away from Parkur. Blood pounded in his temples. Fear slithered through his veins.

"The music and the three of us — it's one and the same." Parkur spread his hand across Jacoby's back. "Even if we only recorded for our own pleasure, I couldn't do it without the people in my soul. I only wish you'd married me, Ju. But I understand and I'm glad you hooked up with him. I acted like an ass before I left."

"We've saved each other." Juniper tugged on Jacoby's hand. "It's time to heal and start again."

Jacoby shook his head. Time to heal, time to move on... He rubbed his hand over his lips. The smile on his lips was real. Damn it felt good. He grabbed a handful of Parkur's shirt and met him for a kiss. "Love you."

"Oh, isn't this the fucking after school special moment of the year." Hank sneered from his side of the glass. "You fuckers found a way to get back together. Well, fuck me."

Parkur slipped down from his perch on the piano. "Hank."

"Queer bastards." Hank clenched the mic in a white-knuckled hand. "You want to be a cute little threesome?"

"Don't do this, Hank." Jacoby clenched his hand. "Don't trash it like this."

"I gave you the best years of my life and you go and replace me with some tight ass lawyer?" He tapped a semi-automatic Glock against the glass. "I don't lose." He narrowed his eyes and aimed the gun in Juniper's direction. "Bitch gets it first."

"Down," Jacoby shouted and dove in front of Juniper. As he went down, he grabbed the back of Parkur's shirt, pulling him to the ground and the tenuous safety behind the piano.

"Mother fucker." The rest of Parkur's words were blotted out by the thunder of gunfire.

Juniper curled into Jacoby's arms. Her hands fisted in his shirt and her body trembled. "I'll keep you safe, flower girl," Jacoby murmured. "I won't let anyone ever hurt you."

"Bastard. I just had that fixed." Parkur punched buttons on his phone. "Always ruining shit."

Adrenaline flowed through Jacoby's body. His brain couldn't process the scene fast enough. His heart pounded as he scoped out the room. No windows. No extra doors. Fuck. Nothing to hide behind besides the damned piano. "He's got us fucking cornered. What the hell do we do?"

"Cops are on the way." Parkur scrubbed the back of his hand across his mouth. "I had bulletproof glass put in after we shattered the windows during one of Zero's brawls with Gareth. If we stay put, we should be safer than someone being a hero."

Fear shimmered in Juniper's eyes. With each breath, she curled tighter against Jacoby. Parkur gave Jacoby a nod and scooted next to Juniper. He wrapped both arms around them, resting his head on Juniper's shoulder. In the midst of the chaos, peace settled around Jacoby. They'd found the chance to heal and embraced it with open arms. They might not have forever together, but they had now.

"I love you, babe," he murmured. Jacoby squeezed Parkur's arm. "I love you, too."

Something akin to astonishment shone in Parkur's eyes. The tiniest smile curled the corners of his mouth.

"You all right?" a voice called out.

The smile on Parkur's lips broadened. "Zero."

"Parkur? Jac?" The door rattled and footsteps thunked across the floor. "Juniper?" Zero's voice cracked and rose an octave. "There you are. Thank God." He knelt next to Parkur. "I didn't hear anything and... Y'all scared me. You okay?"

"Yeah." Jacoby nodded. "What the fuck happened?"

"It's heavy, man." Zero shook his head and sank to his knees, the colour still missing from his face. "Hank offed himself in our studio."

Parkur disengaged from Jacoby and Juniper. He clapped Zero on the back. "Cops should be here any moment." Drawing a long breath and letting it out slowly, Parkur strode towards the control room. Blood and glass littered the floor. The acrid scent of gunpowder hung thick in the air. He crinkled his nose and peered around the doorway. A pair of legs lay sprawled on the tile.

Bile and the hamburger he'd had for lunch reversed course in Parkur's stomach. Where Hank's face had once been was nothing more than a disorganised mass of smeared blood and shattered bone. Parkur covered his mouth with his hands and turned away.

"It's bad?" Jacoby asked. "He's gone?"

Parkur shook his head once. "Dead."

More footsteps pounded on the floor. The scratch of radios and the hum of voices split the silence. "Police." A man in a navy suit coat strode towards the doorway. "I'm Detective Brennen. We'll need to speak with all of the witnesses."

"Sure," Parkur mumbled.

With Juniper in his arms, Jacoby crossed the room and nodded to Parkur. "I'll talk to the cops. Hold her. She's scared to death."

"Can't say as I blame her." Parkur gathered Juniper into an embrace and sat on the righted piano bench. "Sweet girl. No one will hurt us now." He petted her hair. "No one will separate us."

"It's really over?"

Her voice came out ragged and mascara smeared down her pale cheeks. For one of the few times he remembered, she looked more like the girl he'd fallen in love with over fifteen years prior than the road-weary vixen who stood beside him on stage. Jacoby, strong and in control, reminded him of the man who'd stolen his heart nine years before. He'd thought he'd loved them then. But that didn't begin to compare to how much he loved and adored them now.

"Yup. My studio's a mess, but it can be fixed." He wiped the tears from her face and kissed her forehead. "We're

352

together and nothing less than an act of God or nature will tear us apart. Got me?"

Juniper offered him a wobbly smile. "Did he destroy the recordings?"

Parkur threw his head back and laughed. "Of all the things to worry about." He kissed her temple. "I'm glad you care. Hell, I'm fucking in love."

On the other side of the room, Jacoby shook hands with the detective and stole a look at Parkur. He cocked his head.

"I heard what you said when you thought we were all done for."

Parkur winked. "I love you, man. Yeah, I said it out loud and I'll do it as many times as it takes, in front of anyone who'll listen."

"I see." Jacoby nodded to the departing officer and started across the room. "It looks like we owe you more than just affection. Your bright idea saved our asses."

"What?" Parkur frowned. Jacoby's words weren't exactly the declaration of requited love he'd expected.

"Your glass idea. The first bullet ricocheted. According to the officers, the bastard didn't feel a thing. The other bullets were reflex actions." Jacoby knelt down and wrapped his arms around the both of them. "But we're safe."

Juniper sat up and kissed Jacoby on the lips. "Thanks for grabbing me." She patted Parkur's cheek and kissed him as well. "Thanks for ducking. I wouldn't have forgiven you for dying. We have an album to make and a life to start together. Us three."

"We'll have to find a place to record." Jacoby grinned. "I see you have a studio. Might need a little TLC, but Ju and I know our way around tools and paint. We'll work in exchange for recording time."

"Hell no." Parkur slithered out from under Juniper and stood. "You will not fucking work for me." He forked both hands into his hair. "I make a declaration, pour my God damned heart out and you all think you'll work for me?" He snorted and knelt down before them. "The Atrius is ours."

"Ours?" Juniper and Jacoby asked in unison.

"Ours." Parkur took Juniper's hand. "Having the studio wasn't some fucking indulgence. I bought it right before we split. Thought, you know, we could live here, fuck here, make music together—all under one roof." He shrugged. "When you all were having the emo discussion the other day, I talked to Nate. He got the deed changed. All you have to do is sign. I planned to volley the idea at break time. Tell me you'll at least think about it."

Jacoby's eyes widened. A broad grin twitched on his lips. "What do you think, Ju? Is he worth it?"

Juniper wiped her cheeks once more. She bobbed her head. "I don't know. He's been fickle in the past. But..." She blew out a breath, fluttering the lock of hair drooping over her forehead. "Juniper and Jacoby in the morning was good, but Jacoby-Parkur-Juniper all the time sounds perfect."

Jacoby squeezed Parkur's hand. "We're a magic number."

"Yes," Parkur replied. "We are."

RHAPSODY

Imari Jade

Dedication

This story is dedicated to all the women in the world who have ever wondered what it would be like to be with two men sexually, and to those brave enough to do it without worrying what society may think of them. And lastly to all the musical groups that have inspired me all my life and who continue to keep me focused while I write.

Chapter One

"You have to choose," Axil Simmons told her.

Why should I? Bryanna Trosclair thought. *It's their problem, not mine.*

"She's not going to choose," Collin Ripley, the falsetto-voiced lead singer of Simmer replied angrily.

He's right. How could she choose between him and the twenty-five-year-old golden-haired Axil, who'd been her best friend and confidant since they were ten? "I'll tell you what. The two of you fight it out and the winner gets me," Bryanna said, hopping from the stage and heading up the aisle.

"Come back here, Bryanna," their tenor and lead guitarist Axil shouted into the microphone for everyone in the auditorium to hear. "You can't just leave like this."

Of course she could. She, being a liberated female, could do anything she wanted to...except break up a friendship and one of the hottest bands in America.

"Okay, don't decide," he told her.

Bryanna stopped in her tracks.

"What are you saying, dude?" Collin replied from his side of the stage. "Of course she needs to decide."

"No, she doesn't." Axil's tone was defeated. "Put yourself in her shoes. Could you make this choice?"

Bryanna turned to face them and waited for Collin's answer.

"No!" He stomped away from his keyboard and went backstage to sulk.

"You're killing us, Bry," Axil said. He strummed his guitar and began playing a haunting tune. He used music to cope with his problems. He'd been this way even as a child, disappearing into his attic studio whenever things got tough. During those times his music had lulled her to sleep at night as the sound spilled over to her house next door.

Bryanna sat down in one of the seats to listen to the sweet sounds of the strings as the music permeated everything around them. Axil was unreachable when he was like this, turned on and tuned out to the rest of the world. He could make a guitar sing when he put his mind to it. He'd wanted to be a rocker for as long as she could remember. Now he was the hottest guitarist in Northern America. How could she decide between him and the dark-haired, dark-spirited Collin, who with just one look had stolen her breath away?

Collin returned from his sulk and took his position behind the keyboard again. He tickled the ivories and began playing along with Axil.

Bryanna gazed up at them. Where Axil represented everything bright and sunny, Collin represented the darkness — twinkling stars, moonlit nights and secrets. His jet black bangs bounced against his forehead as he played. Bryanna shivered. Such sorrow and despair. Had she caused this? They continued to fill the air with their deep, soulful song. Bryanna shook her head. Maybe she should just leave and put both of them out of their misery.

The doors opened and the rest of the band members filed in. Axil and Collin kept playing, each refusing to give up.

Kurt Vanderbrom, their drummer, sat down and placed his hand on top of hers. "I could hear them battling all the way from the parking lot, Bry. You know this is wrong."

Bryanna turned and faced him. "What would you do if you were me?"

"Screw them both," Kurt replied seriously.

Bryanna blushed. Those were the last words she expected to come out of his mouth. "How did you get so smart?"

Kurt chuckled. "Years of practice watching the three of you do some pretty dumb things."

"Thanks, but what you're suggesting is not only improbable, but I'm pretty sure it's immoral too."

"Maybe so," Kurt replied. "But the three of you are a trio—two sides and middle…a treble. Without one, the other two cease to exist."

Bryanna leaned her head against his shoulder. "Maybe I should just choose you."

Kurt chuckled. "Please don't do me any favours, Bry. You're too high maintenance."

The music battle finally ended and she glanced up to find both men staring down at her resting her head on Kurt's shoulder. The look in their eyes told her Kurt would be in serious trouble if she didn't cease and desist. Yes, it would have been so easy to just choose Kurt as a lover. She sighed. But unfortunately he was into boys. *What a waste.*

"Let's get this rehearsal started," Axil growled.

"I think he means us," Kurt reasoned since Jimmy Jones and Damon Brown were already in place on stage.

"Probably." Bryanna rose and stretched out the kinks in her neck and shoulder blades. Collin watched her every move from where he stood.

"I've pissed both of them off already."

Kurt rose and took her hand then led her to the stage stairs...and then relinquished her to the wolves. Both Collin's and Axil's eyes closed in on her as she took the mic and began swaying to the music. She chose to ignore them but the testosterone in the air seared the back of her head. If they wanted to continue to make music together, the two of them had better learn to share.

The first lyrics came out of Collin's mouth soft and kind of sexy. He had the sweetest voice she'd ever heard, reminding her of a member of an all-boys choir she'd heard as a child. He made it through the first verse and the rest of the guys joined in to help with the chorus. And then it happened. Collin hit the high note, shattering a glass in the auditorium and causing the maintenance people and the security to run into the hall to find out what had happened.

"Sorry," Collin apologised. "I got carried away."

Bryanna approached the stage. "Maybe you'd better bring it down a notch when you practice. But you can let go for the concert since you're going to be entertaining outside, away from glass."

He nodded, not taking that deep blue gaze from her face.

Just that look make her wet between the legs.

Axil cleared his throat. "I think we need to get back to work."

Party pooper. His words had spoiled the moment.

Bryanna moved her eyes in his direction, catching that cherubic smirk. He knew how she felt about Collin — about both of them — and he went out of his way to make her miserable every chance he got. One of these days she was going to show him. She wasn't a young girl anymore and she needed a little human contact. Bryanna went back to her seat just as the last maintenance guy walked to the back with his broom and a dustpan full of broken glass.

* * * *

Bryanna didn't normally join the band out on the town, but tonight she was in a festive mood and felt like unwinding. The tavern where they met served great food, featured a house band and served the best mixed drinks in Cambridge. They always ended up there whenever they came to Massachusetts because of the atmosphere and the friendly people, and they didn't have to worry too much about fans stalking the band.

Combel's catered to a more collegiate bunch, mainly students from the local universities, young professors and people who appreciated rhythm, blues, jazz and soul music.

"I'm really looking forward to tomorrow night's concert," Kurt said to her.

He stood six foot one, with sandy blond hair and deep chocolate eyes. He needed a haircut. His hair hung down in his face, around his muscular shoulders and ran down his back. But there was no way he could be mistaken for a chick. There was just too much of him.

Bryanna took out her laptop. "Kurt needs a haircut," she read aloud as she typed.

Kurt snarled at her.

"You don't frighten me," she told him. "The stylist can fit you in at nine."

"My hair is my thing."

"No, drumming is your thing. The ends need trimming and it would be nice to see your face every once in a while."

Kurt continued to frown. "What's in it for me?"

Bryanna winked at him. "I'll make sure Jonathan spells your name correctly on your paycheque."

"Money is not the answer to everything."

"I'll bake you some brownies…"

Kurt stopped frowning. "The kind with pecans?"

Bryanna nodded. She spoilt them rotten.

"Okay, just a trim."

"That's all I'm asking." Bryanna pressed a button and finalised the appointment with the stylist. "The rest of you could use a sprucing-up, too," she informed the other band members as she made appointments for them. "Axil's bangs are longer than mine, and…" She paused, gazing over at Collin, trying and failing to find an imperfection. "You can just go to show moral support."

Collin sneered at her.

Jimmy Jones, the group's percussionist, elbowed bass guitarist Damon Brown in the side. "Told you she liked Collin better." Damon and Jimmy were best friends, recruited in Harlem. Jimmy wore his hair in short twists, while his friend sported long dreadlocks.

Bryanna rolled her eyes at the African-American pair. "It's not a matter of liking him better. I've never seen him with a hair out of place."

Collin continued to stare at her, aloof.

Bryanna tore her eyes away before she blushed and made a fool of herself.

Axil nudged her thigh beneath the table. "Would you care for another beer?"

"No, I'm straight." Bryanna put her laptop away. "One beer is my limit." More than one sent her running for the ladies' room. "I need some room for dinner."

The waitress had already taken their orders and had been gone about fifteen minutes. Combel's only served one type of food—fattening. Most of them had ordered the same thing—Buffalo wings and fries—except for Collin, who had ordered a grilled chicken salad because he was a bit of a health nut. He nursed a glass of beer and watched the house band as they performed a medley of songs from the seventies and eighties.

The barstools were packed with people watching a college basketball game, and every now and then they cheered whenever one of the teams scored. The rest of the place was taken up with people around their age who had just stopped in to eat and to listen to the music. There were even a couple of brave souls on the dance floor, rocking it out to an ancient Chicago tune.

The food arrived and the waitress flirted shamelessly with the guys, stroking their already large egos and giggling as they responded to her. Bryanna watched it all with mock interest. Neither Axil nor Collin seemed comfortable with the situation. In her haste, the waitress accidently gave her Collin's meal, which Bryanna quickly swapped before Collin could complain.

Bryanna lifted a fry and bit off an end. The heat seared her tongue. She blew on the fry to cool it and then bit into it again. She sighed blissfully.

Out of the corner of her eye, she noticed Axil trying to sneak a fry from her plate. She reached out and slapped his hand.

"Ouch, what did you do that for?" he asked as he popped the fry into his mouth.

"Because you have your own."

"But I'm a growing boy."

Bryanna rolled her eyes. He and Collin were both six feet tall. "I already feel like a shrimp around you guys."

He reached over and pinched her cheek. "But you're a cute shrimp."

Kurt agreed, "The cutest. If I had a baby sister, I'd want her to be cute like you."

Bryanna wrinkled up her nose at them. Cute was nice but she'd prefer to be considered sexy. She ignored them and went back to her meal. Bryanna bit into a wing. "Oh my God, this is so delicious."

"And messy," Axil added as he reached over to wipe sauce from her face with a napkin. That's just the type of person he was...helpful and brotherly to a fault.

"You missed a spot," Collin replied, leaning over and licking the sauce from her cheek.

Bryanna trembled at the touch. That's the kind of person *he* was...dangerous and wicked. He went back to his meal as if nothing had happened.

The other guys attacked their food after they stopped watching them. Out of the blue, Collin reached over to brush a lock of her hair away from her face and tuck it behind her ear with no explanation. He then turned his attention back to his meal, leaving her to wonder what was up with him this evening. Sometimes he barely acknowledged her existence, and tonight he was being his version of charming. She sighed. Men were such oddities.

* * * *

The basketball game ended. Most of those people left and a new crop entered. Collin knew a few of the band members on stage, and they persuaded him to join them for couple of numbers, leaving her to entertain the overprotective blond at her left.

"Let's dance," Axil said, pulling her to her feet without giving her a chance to answer. Axil wrapped his arms around her shoulders and her arms automatically went around his waist. She didn't miss the way Collin stared at them as Axil slow-danced her around the floor.

"Collin is positively steaming," Axil whispered to her, as one slow song blended into another one and he still hadn't released his arms from around her neck.

"Why?" Bryanna asked.

"Because I'm dancing with you."

"Yeah, right." Bryanna closed her eyes and let Collin's rich, sexy voice entertain her ears.

Axil's cock hardened and pushed against her stomach. She had danced with him before and hadn't caused this type of reaction in him. Why now? The song ended and Axil led her back to the table. He excused himself and walked towards the men's room.

Collin left the bandstand to a healthy round of applause and headed in the same direction.

"Maybe I should go check on those two," Kurt suggested.

"Don't you dare," Jimmy told him. "Let them settle it."

"Settle what?" Bryanna asked.

"It's a man thing," Kurt said picking up his beer. "You, being a girl, wouldn't understand. It has something to do with breaking a guy rule."

"A guy rule?" Bryanna asked, looking back towards the restroom.

Damon nodded, sending his hair in front of his eyes. "It's like friends never let friends drive drunk or the proverbial bros before hos."

"Huh?" Bryanna asked. Men were so complicated.

* * * *

Bryanna should have been flattered that two drop-dead gorgeous men were vying for the chance to drive her home from the bar, but both of them were drunk and there was no way she was getting into a car with either of them…plus they had arrived by limousine. "Come on, guys," she said to Kurt and the other two, who were less inebriated than Axil and Collin. "Help me get these two into the limo."

"I'm not drunk," Axil said as he leaned over her.

If he threw up on her, she was going to kill him.

"You certainly are drunk," Collin said. He, too, hovered over her. Of the two, he surprised her the most because she'd never seen him drink more than one or two beers since she'd known him.

"Move off of me. You two are horrible."

Axil and Collin got into the limo. Axil pulled her inside and put her next to him while Collin sat across from them. Kurt, Damon and Jimmy entered next. The car moved from the kerb, entered the traffic and headed towards their hotel.

"Why do you put up with us?" Axil asked her after several minutes of silence.

"Because I'm your friend," Bryanna told him. "Who else would put up with you?"

Axil reached over and ruffled her hair. "Is that the only reason?"

Bryanna nodded. "Yes, big boy. And because someone needs to look after you. What were the two of you thinking by drinking so much? You do have a concert to perform tomorrow night."

"We'll be sober by then," Axil assured her. "We were just celebrating being back in Massachusetts."

"Well, you're going to feel like hell in the morning," she reminded him. She looked over at Collin who had his head back like he was asleep. "Look at him," she said to Axil, pointing at Collin. "That's just disgraceful for someone who hardly ever drinks."

"Bite me," Collin told her.

"I would if I weren't afraid you'd bite me back. What's your problem?"

Collin sat up and glared at her. "You," he said bluntly without explaining any further.

What had she done except dance with Axil? She would have danced with him had he asked.

Axil was now snoring peacefully at her side.

"What do you see in him?" Collin asked. "It's not natural for a man and a woman to be best friends."

She wondered how long this had been on Collin's mind. "Why are you so curious about us? Axil and I have been friends since elementary school. And what's wrong with it? We look out for each other."

"He's a big boy. He doesn't need anyone to look after him. You, on the other hand, need to be out dating."

Bryanna chuckled. Collin had picked a fine time to become talkative. "Dating is so overrated. I have to put on makeup and pretend to be interested. Then I get all disgusted when they get clingy or never call again."

"You could go out with me," Jimmy teased.

Collin rolled his eyes at the young man. "I'm not talking about her dating you. She needs to go out and meet other people. When was the last time you went out on a date?"

Bryanna thought about it. It had been a long time. "I can't remember. Anyway it doesn't matter. I'm very busy with making sure you guys show up for concerts. I'll have plenty of time for dating when we retire."

Collin shook his head. "You need to get a life," he said, lying back against the seat again. "Think about yourself sometimes. We'll survive if you decide to have a little fun."

Bryanna pouted and looked towards the other three for help. Kurt shrugged, obviously not wanting to get involved. The three of them were closer to Collin than she was, and if they had no idea what his problem was, she sure didn't have a clue. Collin didn't say another word the rest of the way to the hotel, which totally pissed her off.

Axil had sobered up some by the time they reached the hotel, and he got out of the limo without assistance. His stubbornness kept him from embarrassing himself in front of hotel employees and possible fans. All six of them walked into the hotel and boarded the elevator.

Kurt said goodbye and got off the elevator on his floor. Then Jimmy and Damon got off on their floor, leaving her with the twin behemoths. They stared angrily at each other for some reason unknown to her. Unfortunately, she had the honour of occupying the room between theirs. Collin entered his room first without saying goodnight, leaving her alone with Axil.

"Asshole," Axil muttered.

"What's wrong with the two of you?" Bryanna asked as she stood outside her door.

"We need to talk," he told her, hovering over her like an expectant prom date. He toyed with her hair.

"After you've sobered up some," she said, swiping his hand away.

"I might not have the courage then," he replied. "Or remember." He pulled her away from her door towards his.

"Why can't we talk in my room?" Bryanna asked as Axil slid the card into the lock and opened his door.

"This is just in case I pass out. You're going to catch hell trying to get me out of your room."

His statement made a lot of sense. The last thing she wanted to have was a six foot blond drunk and snoring loudly in her room. "Okay, only for a little while. We have a busy day tomorrow."

He took her hand to escort her inside his room.

Axil pointed to a chair. "Sit. I need to use the john and freshen up a bit. I'll be back."

Bryanna sat down and reached for the remote. She turned on the television to block out the sound of him urinating then the sound of the shower. Moments later, the water turned off and Axil stepped out of the bathroom with a towel wrapped around his waist and another around his head.

Bryanna ran her gaze over his chest and down to the towel. He sat down on the bed and began to dry his hair.

"What is so important it can't wait until tomorrow?"

"I'm in love with you," he said as he continued to rub the towel over his damp hair.

Bryanna opened her mouth to say something but she couldn't form the words, especially since she already knew how he felt about her.

"I know I dropped this on you suddenly, but I just thought you should know."

He didn't seem a bit embarrassed to confess his feelings to her wearing just a towel. "Why are you bringing this up now?"

"Because of Collin."

"What about Collin?" she asked, avoiding his eyes.

"Because he told me he's thinking about asking you out, and I know how you feel about him."

She had no choice but to look at him. "Now it all makes sense. You're just afraid Collin will beat you at this game. Why are men so competitive?"

Axil rose and pulled her to him. Bryanna felt the towel slip from around his waist and drop to the floor at their feet.

"No, it's true." He wrapped his arms around her and lifted her from the floor. "Now I think I have to make love to you."

Bryanna gulped. *Now what am I going to do?* "You're still drunk." *And thick and hard.* She moved away.

"No, I'm not," Axil assured her. He reached for her, but Bryanna escaped his grasp.

"We can't do this, "she told him. "It will mess up what we have."

"What do we have, Bryanna?"

"A very long friendship that has withstood a lot of shit."

Axil sighed then reached down for the towel and covered himself.

"When it happens between us, I don't want it to be because you're competing with Collin. I don't want to be a pawn between you guys." She headed towards the door. "Good night." She opened the door and left.

"You are so stupid," she said to herself as she walked to her hotel room. It was the first time she'd seen him nude. She shook her head as she entered her room. *Thou shalt not screw your best friend.*

Chapter Two

The sounds filtering in through her dressing room door made Bryanna jittery. They had sold out in Massachusetts a couple of days ago, and now they had also sold out the Los Angeles arena. Their manager, Jonathan Meyers, had popped his head in earlier to congratulate her. Apparently now they had sold out every venue he had booked them at for the next month or so. She sighed. Tonight, Simmer planned to introduce new songs and Jonathan planned to record a live music video during the concert. Sometimes it all seemed too much — like a dream.

The bad thing? Neither Collin nor Axil had spoken to her since before they'd left Massachusetts. Axil wouldn't even look at her. Men could be such babies at times, especially when it came to such things as love and sex.

The lead-in group, Eruption, sounded like they had the crowd on their feet. The stomping on the stadium arena floor shook the walls.

Someone knocked at her door. "Ten minutes to show time, Ms Trosclair."

"I'll be ready," she shouted at the door.

The man went off without another word.

Bryanna slid out of her seat and paced the floor. She didn't normally get stage-fright, but she was running high on adrenaline, worried something might happen during the concert. She stopped pacing long enough to check out her costume in the mirror. The wardrobe girl had put her in a short little black dress and helped her slip her feet into stilettos. Her shoulder-length auburn hair had been combed to the top of her head and styled in a French twist to keep it out of her eyes while she performed. "Passable," she judged before heading towards the door.

The other band had left the stage to a loud round of applause, and now it was Simmer's time to shine.

Kurt caught her by the arm as she walked down the hall past the men's dressing rooms. "Your dress is too short," he told her.

Bryanna scowled at him. "I don't design these costumes. I just wear them."

Someone coughed behind them. Bryanna turned her head enough to confirm it was Axil.

"Try not to trip," Kurt teased. "But I think he's checking you out."

"I won't," Bryanna said, trying to keep her backside from bouncing as she walked. She was pretty sure Axil was still pissed off at her for turning him down. And there was really nothing she could do about her butt bouncing all over the place. Blame it on nature and genetics.

Kurt helped her up the stairs. Damon and Jimmy entered from the other side and positioned themselves behind their instruments. Axil arrived from her side of the stage while Kurt walked to his drums. Normally Axil gave them a pep talk or gave her shoulders a comforting squeeze before performances...but not today. Mr Sunshine acted cold and distant.

Collin arrived last. He, too, marched past her without so much as a nod. Distance she could tolerate, but Collin's took arrogance to another level. If they thought they could get to her by using the silent treatment, they were mistaken. She had ignoring people down to a science.

"Ladies and gentlemen," the MC announced. "Simmer!"

The curtains raised and the crowd went wild. The stage lights blinded her ability to pick faces out in the crowd. The music began to play...one of their older familiar songs. The crowd recognised it and began clapping louder.

Bryanna sang the first verse then Axil added his deep tenor voice to her sultry alto. Their harmony and pitch went together like bread and butter.

She left her mark and travelled across the stage with her mobile mic, taking command of the audience's attention. An overhead spotlight followed her as she danced expertly atop her heels. The audience roared as she made it over to Collin, anticipating the next part of the song. Collin's soft, sweet treble made her knees quiver like it did the first time she heard him sing. *Amazing*, she thought as he reached inside himself and hit the highest note on the male soprano range. She braced herself waiting for the glass in the windows to rattle. If it did, she couldn't make it out over the screaming crowd.

The audience continued to scream at the top of their lungs. Jonathan was probably loving all of it and getting some great video for their DVD.

Bryanna danced her way back over to her mark and the song ended. She bowed and then they began one of their new songs. Axil had the vocal lead on this hot soul number. The strings of his guitar echoed through the mic and filtered out through the huge stadium.

Damn, he could play.

Bryanna fanned herself with her hand. *Damn him.* Axil could really get down and dirty when he had to.

Kurt, Jimmy and Damon harmonised the chorus with him then she and Collin joined him for the next verse. Their three voices blended beautifully and got a big round of applause from the audience.

Collin left his keyboard for the next song—a rocking little number only his sweet voice could master. He tore the house down when he danced, slim hips moving erotically to the beat. Young women tried to storm the stage and get to him. The security guards kept them back and they just stood there mesmerised by one hundred and sixty pounds of hip-wiggling dynamite. If he wiggled any more, she'd orgasm on the spot. Collin threw her a heated look then danced back over to his keyboard as they ended the song.

The curtain lowered for intermission, much to the audience's evident dismay, and the band left the stage to change costumes.

"Baby, you were great," Jonathan told her as she made her way to the dressing room amidst a sea of people. "Your butt is rocking the dress." Jonathan always said whatever was on his mind—good, bad or inappropriate.

"If it was any shorter, she would have flashed the entire audience," Axil said gruffly as he walked past them headed to his dressing room.

"Don't pay him any mind," Jonathan told her. "The audience loved it." He kissed her on the forehead and followed the rest of the guys.

Bryanna was just about to enter her dressing room when Collin appeared, damp and sweating from his erotic performance on stage. He roughly shoved her inside then followed her in.

"Hey…" Bryanna whined, nearly falling from her heels. "What is your problem?"

He pulled her towards him, lowered his head and smothered her lips with his.

Damn, she thought as he pulled her tighter, squeezing her breasts against his muscular chest. Bryanna gasped for air as he pulled back, pushed her into a chair and headed towards the door. "I don't ever want to see you in that costume again, you God damn little tease," he spat out. He walked out, leaving her confused, dumbfounded and angry.

"Red lipstick does not suit you," Kurt told Collin when he walked into the dressing room.

Curious eyes turned in his direction. "Go to hell," Collin said before he wiped the lipstick from his lips then began stripping out of his costume.

"I'm already there," Kurt said as he started changing out of his.

"What did you do?" Axil asked him. "I could hear you all the way down the hall."

"Nothing," Collin lied. Bryanna deserved everything he did to her and more.

Axil came after him, but Damon and Jimmy stopped him. "If you laid one finger on her I'll…"

"You'll do what, blond boy?" Collin asked. He wasn't afraid of Axil and they could take it to the mat any time he was ready. "She's lucky kissing her is all I did."

Axil stormed out of the dressing room.

"You're walking on thin ice," Jonathan warned him.

"I don't need a lecture from you," Collin told him. "The costumes you design for her are inappropriate. Bryanna is not a piece of meat."

"It got a reaction out of you, didn't it?" Jonathan said. "I've never seen you dance that way on stage before and the audience loved the interaction between the two of you."

"So it's your plan to continue dressing her in skimpy outfits to keep me motivated?" He didn't need any help.

"No—to keep you lusty and passionate. I bet you gave every female in the audience damp panties."

"You are such a perv."

"Call me what you want, but my quirks have put Simmer at the top of the charts."

Collin frowned. Jonathan was such an arrogant bastard...and one of the best managers in the business. Still, he didn't have to stoop to showing off Bryanna's body to the world. The young woman could sing and perform like the best of them.

He wiped his lips again. *And kiss.*

Axil re-entered the dressing room, breathing fire and scowling at him, no doubt wanting to kick his ass for kissing his precious Bry. Collin stopped dressing and faced him. They were the same height and build. In a battle, he didn't know if he would win but he'd try his best to knock Axil on his behind if it came to blows.

"Is Bryanna okay?" Kurt asked.

"She'll survive." Axil stared daggers at Collin. "No thanks to him. She's a bit shocked but she'll finish the concert."

Axil was such a big drama queen when it came to Bryanna. He made it sound as if Collin had stolen her virginity.

"I didn't hear her complain," Collin replied. "Apparently she enjoys a man stealing a kiss from her and not the weak affections of a little boy."

Axil went after him again. This time Kurt stopped him.

"You two are acting like a pair of kids. Can't you put all this aside until after the concert?"

Axil pulled away from Kurt and began shrugging out of his costume. "Kurt's right, Ripley. We'll finish this later."

"Any time or place, blondie," Collin argued.

A stage man stuck his head in the door. "Five minutes to curtain."

The men quickly finished changing.

Collin silently agreed to a truce as he pulled up the zipper on his black trousers, pulled on a grey shirt and put on a black blazer. But this would end tonight.

As Collin made his way back towards the stage, Bryanna walked before him in a stunning black formal gown that exposed her bare shoulders and back to him. The waistline of the gown came just above her spectacular behind. His trousers tightened in the crotch. She looked like a princess as she moved before him. He hurried to catch up to her.

Bryanna looked over, appearing surprised to see him at her side.

"I'm sorry," he apologised quickly. "For the rough treatment, but not about the kiss. You mean the world to me and I would never do anything to harm you."

"You're right," she replied angrily, turning away. "You are sorry."

Collin cringed. He deserved that. He'd never done anything so stupid in his life, but Bryanna drove him crazy. "Let me make it up to you. Let me take you out to dinner after the show."

Bryanna looked his way again. "We have an after-concert party to attend, remember? Photographers will be there to take our pictures and journalists will be there to interview us."

"Afterwards," he amended. "I know it will be late, but this may be the only chance I get to have a few minutes alone with you."

Bryanna began her ascent up the stairs. "Okay," she said finally.

Collin couldn't help looking up at Bryanna's behind. He bit his bottom lip. The sight literally took his breath away and made him want to do seriously foolish things. He also climbed the stairs and walked over to the piano. If he couldn't win Bryanna's heart with action, he planned to use his voice to serenade it with his songs.

* * * *

"Why do guys have to drink so much?" Bryanna asked, watching Axil and the rest of the guys slurping down champagne as though it was water at the after-concert party. All except Collin, that was, who stuck to bottled water. He stood apart from them, talking to reporters and giving interviews. Every now and then, he'd look across the room at her and smile. *Arrogant asshole*, she thought. Damn, he just oozed sex. It affected her in ways too embarrassing to speak of. And Axil coming to her rescue made it worse. Maybe agreeing to go out to dinner with Collin later might not have been a good idea.

"Come dance with me, darling," Axil invited, suddenly being nice to her after treating her like a pariah for the last couple of days. He had changed out of his costume and now wore a black tuxedo.

"Sure." She accepted his hand and allowed him to lead her to the dance floor.

The disk jockey for the event span a mixture of hip-hop and soul music. She and Axil were fortunate enough to have him begin a slow number for their dance. Her three-inched heels brought her up to Axil's chest as he wrapped his arms around her shoulders, pulling her close to him. He smelt faintly of lemon drop mints, champagne and sensual male. And his cologne was so nice. She inhaled as he moved her slowly around the floor.

Axil tightened his grip on her and pressed his body to hers. Her nipples hardened on contact. Bryanna sighed. What was she supposed to do? He was her best friend. When exactly had their relationship changed from playmates to potential lovers?

"I could dance with you like this all night," he told her as he rocked his hips from side to side. Axil, like Collin, was a very good dancer.

Their parents had always thought they'd grow up and marry each other. *Hmm*, Bryanna thought. Maybe they were right. She and Axil were perfect for each other and had a lot in common. She glanced over at Collin, still near the press people. But where Axil had her heart, Collin had every other part of her mind, body and soul.

"Let me take you out of here. I'm dying to see Los Angeles."

"Sorry," Bryanna said regretfully as the dance ended and they walked over to where their group had assembled. "I have a date later."

Axil looked at her as though she'd slapped him. "With whom?"

"Don't get mad," she cautioned before she spoke the other man's name. "Collin."

Axil's body tensed beside her. "Why? After what he did to you earlier?"

"Don't make a scene. He's taking me to dinner as his way of apologising. He said he's sorry." She smiled for a picture.

"And you believe him?"

"Can we get a picture of the two of you together?" a female photographer asked.

Axil put his arm around her shoulders and drew her near. They smiled and a flash went off in their faces.

"Yes," Bryanna answered. "I do. Anyway, I promised and I don't break promises."

"What if he tries something with you?"

"We're going to a restaurant. I'm sure I'll be safe."

"Collin? Can we get a picture of you and Bryanna?" the same female photographer asked.

The anger radiated from Axil, making the huge hall feel stuffy.

"Sure," Collin said taking her hand and pulling her away from Axil.

Bryanna grimaced. She felt like a yo-yo.

"Smile." The photographer snapped their picture. "Now one with all three of you together."

The three of them moved together for the picture.

"Smile," the photographer coached.

Bryanna sighed. She knew then that only she could fix their cracked triangle.

* * * *

Collin took her to a cosy little Italian restaurant. Instead of hopping into the limousine with the rest of the band, he'd hailed a taxi and escorted her into it, much to the obvious chagrin of Jonathan and the other guys in the band, who weren't used to Collin being so gallant.

Axil hadn't even looked in their direction. She felt like she'd betrayed him, stabbed him in the back. But she couldn't show favouritism just because she'd known him longer than Collin. She promised herself she would give him plenty of face time tomorrow on their date to see Los Angeles.

A waitress gave them menus after seating them in a private booth decorated with a red tablecloth and red tapered candles. All in all, it was a very romantic setting.

Everything looked so delicious and tantalising, including the man across the table from her, who impressed her to no end by ordering for them in fluent Italian. His private life was almost as mysterious as his past.

They'd met three years ago when Jonathan had held auditions for a lead singer for Simmer to offset her and Axil's deeper voices. He'd stuck out even then, with his jet black hair and piercing blue eyes and just a hint of five o'clock shadow.

"If you keep staring at me, everyone around us will assume you like me."

Bryanna looked around. A few people stared but she bet it had nothing to do with her. Collin Ripley drew attention everywhere he went. "Maybe it's true," she replied. "You are sort of cute."

He smirked. "Sort of?"

Bryanna nodded. "You have your moments."

"Is this one of those moments?" He rewarded her with one of those rare smiles.

"Yeah, you're pretty cute at the moment."

"So you've forgiven me?"

"I wouldn't be here if I hadn't. The next time something I wear offends you, just tell me."

He eyed her sheepishly. "I didn't say the outfit offended me, just...distracted me. It's hard to remember words to songs when you..." He paused.

"When you what?"

"When your eyes are focussed on your band mate's behind."

Bryanna chuckled. "I'll remember to keep my butt out of your eye range on stage."

He smiled at her again and the weight of his gaze reached all the way over to her and down her body to her crotch.

The waitress arrived with their food and she drew her eyes away from Collin.

The young woman popped the cork on the white wine and filled both their glasses and then she left them.

Collin lifted his glass in a toast. "To making decisions."

Bryanna lifted her glass but did not comment. If his plan was to get her drunk to make her choose between him and Axil, he should give up now.

"I've always wanted to spend time with you like this but the opportunity never presented itself."

"We've eaten dinner together thousands of times," Bryanna told him as she cut into her veal Parmesan.

"Yes, with the rest of the band…but never alone."

The food looked good but not better than the man seated across from her humbling himself.

"How's the veal?" he asked.

"Delicious and very tender." Bryanna put another piece in her mouth and chewed then washed it down with some wine.

As they ate, they continued to make small talk, skirting around their romantic situation. When they were finished, they left the restaurant and walked, talked and held hands like teenagers. After a while, Collin hailed a taxi to take them back to the hotel. They got out about fifteen minutes later, and he had to use his key card to gain entry into the hotel because of the late hour.

Collin pushed the elevator button and they climbed inside. Truthfully, she expected to find Axil waiting for them, but there wasn't a soul around except for the hotel night crew.

"This has been fun," Bryanna broke the silence, standing outside her hotel room.

"It doesn't have to end." Collin leaned over her.

Somehow she'd known the night was going to end something like this. Making a decision, Bryanna ran her key card through the lock then opened the door. She caught Collin's hand just as he started to walk away. "No, it doesn't." She tugged him inside and closed the door.

Chapter Three

His lips were on hers before she could lock the door and seal it with the burglar bar. She did so blindly, reaching behind her in an awkward position, listening for the clicks.

Collin picked her up and carried her into the bedroom. They fell onto the bed with a thud hard enough to break the bed or disturb the neighbours in the room below them. In her haste to take him to her bed, she'd nearly forgotten that Axil had the room next to hers. Thank God they didn't have adjoining rooms. *Fuck it*, she thought. She was going to have this night with Collin.

Collin planted kisses all over her face and the crook of her neck while opening the buttons of her blouse at the same time. "Pretty bra," he said as he kissed a path from her chin down to her breasts. "Victoria's Secret, front-locking, underwire." He ran a finger down her sternum and then used two fingers to unlock the bra, exposing her breasts. "C cup," he mumbled just before burying his face between the twin orbs.

Soft lips encircled one of her nipples. Bryanna arched her back, giving him better access.

Collin's hands manoeuvred their way upwards to cup each breast.

Bryanna moaned loudly.

Collin ran a tongue against one of the nipples. Bryanna shuddered as his warm breath heated every inch of her body.

He helped her out of her blouse and the opened bra then went back to sucking her nipples until they budded and hardened.

Bryanna ran her fingers through his dark hair as he kissed his way down her stomach. Each touch added to the excitement.

"I want to see the rest of you," Collin said hoarsely as he lifted his head. He peeled the skirt, hose and panties away from her body and looked down at her. "You are positively beautiful."

The look of desire in his eyes made Bryanna shiver. Collin was so freaking hot.

Collin ran a finger slowly from her navel down to her hairline. The fingers dipped lower, teasing her but not exactly giving her what she desired.

"Don't tease me, Collin," she begged.

Collin looked deep into her eyes as his finger ran along the folds of her labia and then finally along the clitoris.

Bryanna trembled. The fingers entered her moist hole and Bryanna shuddered with need. Her stomach clenched as he delved deeper. Bryanna reached for his arm trying to control the movement but Collin had everything under control.

"You're so wet," he told her, his voice suddenly dropping an octave. He withdrew his fingers and moved to the end of the bed. He raised his shirt over his head and removed it from his body with one quick tug then turned and began crawling back up to her.

Bryanna slowly parted her thighs.

"Damn," he replied. "The view from down here is breathtaking."

Bryanna giggled.

"Oh, darling," he said. "That sounds so sweet." He lowered his head and ran his tongue along the same path his fingers had travelled.

Bryanna's body lifted slightly off the mattress as he nibbled the clitoris. The muscles in her butt clenched when his tongue finally reached its destination. She gasped as he slowly began to wiggle his tongue into her moist folds.

Collin gripped both sides of her hips and pulled her closer. He was relentless, not giving her a chance to catch her breath.

"Oh, my God, Collin," she moaned as the orgasm powered over her. Bryanna closed her eyes and enjoyed the sensation until it ended.

Collin had already joined her at the top of the bed and watched her, appearing fascinated as she recovered. His lips were still wet with her juices. He leaned over and kissed her passionately.

Bryanna clung to him, not yet ready to give up the warmth from his touch.

"I'm not going anywhere, sweet darling," he told her tenderly. He slipped out of her grasp. "Just making a costume change."

Bryanna's gaze moved from the beautiful sculptured face, down his bare chest and came to rest at the crotch of his trousers. His erection strained against the seam. Her lashes lowered and she ran her tongue across her bottom lip, as he slowly unzipped his trousers then eased them down his narrow hips. He kicked out of them and stood before her in just his briefs.

Bryanna moved to the edge of the bed and beckoned for him with her finger. When Collin moved closer, Bryanna took control, fingering the waistband of the tiny briefs and then dipping her entire hand brazenly in and cupping him in her palm.

Collin moaned and leant forward.

"Impressive," she said as she looked up at him. His eyelids had lowered with just a hint of blue shining through.

Bryanna stopped groping him long enough to slide the briefs down his hips. Collin assisted her by lifting his feet and stepping out of them.

Bryanna was upon him before she had time to think, gripping his cock in her hand and slowly masturbating him until his knees trembled.

"Oh my," he said as she gave attention to not only the staff but also the balls. She pulled him closer to her and lowered her mouth around the head. He tasted unbelievably clean, sweet and manly. She made slurping sounds when she released him.

Collin moaned with delight.

Bryanna went back down on him, truly enjoying his taste and the way he felt in her mouth. She came up for air and then kissed her way back up until she reached his lips.

Collin quickly reached for his trousers, pulled out a condom and slipped it on. He wrapped his arms around her and drew her on top of him. His manhood jolted between her legs. He lifted her, parted her and then slid into her.

Bryanna pushed herself upwards into a seated position.

Collin grabbed her hips with both hands and helped to move her up and down rhythmically. He thrust deep inside of her. With one hand, he reached up and played with her nipples in turn.

Bryanna's head went back, and her hair spilled down her back and caressed her skin.

"You are one phenomenal young lady—beautiful, talented and sensual."

He didn't need to flatter her. She intended to give him her all...heart, soul and body. All he had to do was keep loving her and never stop.

Collin positioned them until she lay against the mattress and he was on top of her, parting her thighs and thrusting inside her. She didn't even mind giving up control to him. Sometimes a girl had to step back and let a man lead. And how Collin did lead, thrusting in and out of her until her stomach clenched again.

Bryanna bit her bottom lip and tried not to scream out in pleasure. She raked his back with her nails to try to prevent it but the orgasm tore her up as it erupted deep within her. "Oh, oh, oh!" she screamed as she came.

Collin roared as he pumped his hips and maximised her pleasure. His entire body shuddered above her. "I don't think I can hold back any longer," he muttered as his body shook. He slowed his pace and began teasing her sore, wet opening with little thrusts. The movements became more calculated, precise. His back arched, and then he came, gripping her hips tightly and moving her body up and down.

Bryanna came again with him as his cock rubbed against her sensitive clitoris.

Collin slipped down upon her and kept thrusting deeply until their orgasm ended and then he just lay there exhausted, breathing hard on top of her. A few minutes later, he rolled off her, gathered her into his arms, kissed her on the side of the head and then drifted off to sleep.

Chapter Four

Axil furiously paced the carpeted floor in his hotel room, angry at himself for not voicing his opinion when Bryanna informed him she had a dinner date with Collin, and also angry for believing she would choose him over Collin. To make matters worse, Bryanna had brought Collin to her room and screwed him, knowing Axil's room was right next to hers. What had that girly-voiced crooner done or said to persuade her over to his side?

The clock on the nightstand beside the dishevelled king-sized bed read eight a.m. — time for Jonathan's breakfast meeting. Axil stopped pacing, sat down on the bed and put his face into his hands. He had to get his mind together and get his emotions in check. Tears welled in his eyes but he refused to let them fall. He shuddered. He loved Bryanna and had from the moment she'd moved into the house next door to his and come over to introduce herself.

Axil got off the bed. He'd show them. He'd march right on down to the restaurant in the hotel lobby for breakfast and pretend like he hadn't heard a thing. He grabbed his jeans jacket, pushed his wallet into his pocket and left the room.

He spotted first Jimmy and then Kurt. Kurt waved him over. Jonathan and a few of the roadies were already seated, and he spotted Damon coming out of the men's restroom and heading towards the long row of tables.

Collin and Bryanna were noticeably missing.

Kurt made the point known when Axil arrived at the table.

"Where are the other two parts of your trio?"

Axil shrugged. "Haven't seen them since last night."

"They're probably still asleep," Jimmy replied. "I think they got in real late last night."

How did Jimmy know, unless he was waiting up for them to return? Had he seen the two of them when they came in? He couldn't ask Jimmy without seeming jealous.

"I ran into Collin around five this morning when I came down for a newspaper," Damon replied. "He came down to the lobby to get some juice from the bar. He looked pretty drained."

Axil sighed.

Collin entered the restaurant a few minutes later, looking bright-eyed and bushy-tailed for someone who was surviving on just a couple of hours of sleep. Brown corduroy jeans, a tan and brown checked short-sleeved shirt and dark brown boots completed his ensemble. And dark sunglasses.

"Now the only one missing is Bryanna," Damon replied.

"She'll be down," Jonathan replied. "I've never known her to miss breakfast or a meeting."

Axil frowned. Apparently none of them knew Bryanna as well as they thought.

The doors to the restaurant swung open and Bryanna entered wearing dark sunglasses, with her hair tied back in a ponytail. She had thrown on a pair of jeans and a T-shirt and wore a pair of thong sandals, looking less like a pop princess than usual.

"Good morning, everyone," she said, flopping down in the seat next to Axil.

"Good morning," everyone replied except for him. He didn't trust his voice.

Bryanna elbowed him. "What's up with you this morning?"

"Nothing," he grumbled.

"Sounds like you got up on the wrong side of the bed," she teased.

"I didn't get much sleep last night. The people in the room next to me were very noisy."

She shrugged but didn't comment.

The waitress arrived before he could goad her into confessing.

"What would you like, miss?"

Bryanna opened the menu without removing her sunglasses. "Everything looks so good." She looked over the breakfast menu before selecting. "I'll have oatmeal, fresh fruit, and a couple of strips of bacon, scrambled eggs, toast and coffee."

"Wow," Kurt said on her left. "Usually you have a bagel and coffee."

"Not this morning," Bryanna said with a yawn. "I'm starving and tired. I need something to energise me."

"You should try going to bed at a decent hour," Axil replied.

Bryanna lowered her glasses, revealing bloodshot eyes. "What?"

"You got in pretty late last night."

"Not especially," she said. "I was in bed by three."

Axil strummed his fingers nervously on the table.

The waitress made it to him. "What will you have, sir?"

"Just wheat toast, fresh fruit and coffee."

"Are you dieting?" Bryanna asked.

"Not really, "Axil replied. "I don't really have much of an appetite."

Bryanna lowered her glasses and looked at him. "Have I done something to insult you?"

"Don't flatter yourself."

Collin was the last one to order. "And you, sir?"

"A breakfast steak, hash brown potatoes, scrambled eggs, a biscuit and black coffee. I'm feeling kind of hungry and tired too."

The waitress left to fill their orders.

Collin slid his glasses down the bridge of his nose and stared over at Bryanna, who was staring right back at him.

Collin blew her a kiss.

Axil's blood pressure shot up but he refused to let Collin's actions get to him.

* * * *

So he knew. *Big deal*. It wasn't as though he didn't know they'd been out on a date or how she felt about Collin. What happened last night didn't change anything, and she still hadn't made a decision.

Bryanna walked out of her hotel room and took the elevator down to the lobby. No Axil. She waited a couple of minutes past their scheduled rendezvous time, but he still didn't show. *His loss,* she thought as she donned her dark glasses and headed out of the door. She hailed a taxi.

"Where to, miss?" the driver asked as he opened the door for her.

"The Los Angeles County Museum of Art," she replied. She'd always wanted to see the popular tourist spot. The driver was just about to shut the door when a big, booted foot came through the open door, followed by a leg and then the rest of a tall male body...*Axil.*

"Women are sure impatient," he said as he slid the rest of his body into the seat.

The driver closed the door.

"You said one o'clock," Bryanna replied as though she wasn't surprised and glad to see him. "And it's..."

"Five after one," Axil said, showing her his watch.

He knew how she felt about punctuality. There had been many mornings she'd had to go to his house and drag him out of bed so he wouldn't be late for school or rehearsal.

The driver drove away from the kerb.

"I'm glad you decided to join me," she said, getting comfortable in the seat.

"I wouldn't have missed this for the world." He reached over and squeezed her hand tightly. "We've wanted to see Los Angeles since we were kids."

He remembered. For now, everything between them was back to normal.

Collin watched the cab pull away from the kerb while he waited for Damon to finish his cigarette.

"Nothing is going to break up their friendship," Damon replied, putting out his cigarette and rising.

Collin waved the offending second-hand smoke away from his face. "Yeah, I know, and it isn't like I haven't tried." Let Bryanna have her little fantasy date with her childhood friend. Tonight she would once again be his.

"Jimmy and I are thinking about going on a tour," Kurt said as he approached. "Do you guys want to join us?"

"Sure," Collin said, suddenly feeling the need to get some fresh air. Seeing the town didn't sound like a bad idea. "Where's Jonathan?" he asked.

"In his hotel room," Kurt answered. "He won't be joining us. He's checking plans and schedules for Seattle." It was their next leg of the tour. "He said have fun and stay out of trouble."

Collin smirked. He intended to be the poster boy for niceness today. "Let's get one of these cabs." He walked away and the other three band members followed.

* * * *

The Los Angeles County Museum of Art was everything the tour book said it was and more, Axil discovered as he watched Bryanna's face light up as they moved from one exhibit to another.

"Look at this," she said, pointing to an ancient sculpture. "It's over three thousand years old."

Axil looked down at the relic. It was hard to believe civilisation had been so advanced and skilled back then.

Bryanna loved visiting museums and everything else pertaining to ancient history. If she hadn't become a singer, she would probably be a museum curator or an archaeologist, no doubt.

An hour later, they held hands as they walked to hear an outdoor concert...something he'd always wanted to do. They'd always shared each other's interests, camped out in each other's yards under moonlit skies and been there for each other through the good times and the bad.

Evening came too soon, Axil noted sombrely as they rode back together in a cab. They pulled to the kerb of the hotel and Axil paid the driver, then he and Bryanna walked up to the door. He stopped her before she could enter. "Let's not end it just yet."

Bryanna paused.

"Let's just have a beer and talk."

Bryanna nodded. "Okay." She followed him to the hotel lounge. It was still early and the place swarmed with other hotel guests.

"Maybe this is not such a good place," Axil said. "Let's try the pavilion out back."

Bryanna nodded and followed him out of the side door to the little garden area near the back of the hotel away from the smoking area. They sat on a bench amidst the freshly cut grass and the newly planted flower beds.

"Why?" he asked her before she had a chance to get comfortable.

Bryanna just shrugged. "It just sort of happened."

Axil pulled her closer to him. "Do you love him?"

"I don't know," she said with a sigh. "I'm so confused."

"I can't say I'm not jealous or envious. I'm just trying to say, don't sell me off yet."

Bryanna leaned over and kissed him on the cheek. "That's what I love about you. You always know the right thing to say. Too bad you can't make this decision for me."

"I would if you want me to," Axil replied.

Bryanna chuckled. "We wouldn't be Simmer without Collin."

Axil sighed. "I know, and he knows it too. Even if we could find a replacement for him, it still wouldn't change the way you feel about him. I just wish you felt the same way about me."

"I care for both of you. You both bring something special into my life." She sighed. "I can't explain it. And if I could, I'd marry both of you guys."

"But since that's illegal, you decided just to date both of us."

Bryanna nodded. "I know you're hurt, but it's all I have. It's either date both of you or let both of you go. And since neither one of you is ready to just kick me to the kerb, I'm stuck here in the middle."

Axil kissed her on the head. "I understand." He paused. "Would you have slept with me the other night in Massachusetts if I hadn't been drunk?"

Bryanna chuckled. "In a hot minute. But I want our time together to be memorable, not clouded by alcohol."

Axil hugged her tighter. "I'll never touch beer or alcohol again."

"And for the record, sex and love is not the same thing."

"But we will have sex one of these days?" he asked.

"Yes," Bryanna answered. "I promise."

Chapter Five

The events in Los Angeles were long forgotten by the time they reached Seattle. Everyone felt drained from multi-state touring. Jonathan, on the other hand, was the exception — in his glory basking in the glow of the band's sold out performances and the great video footage.

It was raining and gloomy when they arrived in Washington. They spent their first day there practising inside the Dome, glad they didn't have to perform in the rain, but a little concerned that Collin could blow out the windows or shatter them if he hit a high note again.

"I just won't attempt it," Collin suggested. "Or maybe we can just remove the song all together."

Bryanna shook her head. "Fans are expecting for us to perform it, and they're expecting you to give them your best performance. So a toned-down version might work if we let you sing your new song."

"That might work," Axil said. "We could do *Baby be Mine.*" Collin had written the song before they left Atlanta.

"Okay," Collin said. "Let's check the acoustics."

Bryanna smirked. The two of them had been getting along surprisingly well since they'd left Los Angeles.

The boys cranked up their instruments and started the rehearsal, adding Collin's new song. Midway through the song, he left his mark, travelled over to her and invited her to dance with him.

"What the hell?" She finally gave in to him, acting silly. She displayed some fancy footwork...something she'd seen on one of those teen dance shows. The band members really seemed to get a kick out of it. Sometime during the number, he danced her back over to her mark then returned to his without missing a beat. The song ended and a single round of applause sounded through the Dome...Jonathan.

"Great," he said walking to the front edge of the stage. "The fans are going to love it."

"We were just having some fun," Bryanna said. "It's not a part of the act."

"It is now," Jonathan replied. "I love the interaction between you and Collin. And what a spectacular movie video this is going to be."

"What movie video?" Axil asked.

"The one Wayne just shot." Wayne was their head video person.

"Where is he?" Kurt asked looking out into the audience. It was hard to see under the stage lights.

Jonathan pointed up to the balcony. Wayne waved to them.

"Shit," Bryanna said.

"Bryanna, honey, you were wonderful and spontaneous," Jonathan argued.

"And acting a fool," she said. "Remember no air time without my approval."

"Who is running this show, honey?" Jonathan asked arrogantly.

"Don't forget I know where all your skeletons are hidden," she told him.

Jonathan paled and turned to Wayne, making a cutting gesture across his neck. Jonathan hurried backstage.

"Bryanna, darling," Axil said, "one of these days you are going to tell us what you have on Jonathan."

"No way," she replied.

"I hope you don't talk in your sleep," he teased.

"No, she doesn't," Collin replied, hanging up his mic and walking off the stage.

* * * *

Rain did not stop the fans from coming out in droves to the Dome the next night. It wasn't a hard rain, just the type to piss you off after you'd washed and waxed your car.

Axil leaned against a wall in Bryanna's dressing room, taking up a lot of space while the makeup artist and hairstylist did their thing to her. He was quite obviously making sure she didn't get any pushy, unwelcomed visitors like she had the last time.

"You're going to have to leave so she can change into her costume," Della, their wardrobe manager, told him. Della had been with them from the beginning and had no problem speaking her mind with Axil and the rest of the band.

Axil stood a foot taller than Della and outweighed her by many pounds. "Says who?"

"Says me," Della threw back at him. "A lady needs privacy."

Bryanna listened to the conversation while the hairstylist put a hot curling iron to her hair.

"Bryanna and I don't have any secrets," Axil told Della.

"Are you sleeping with her?" Della asked.

"Well...no," Axil answered.

"Then she still has a secret." Della pushed Axil towards the dressing room door.

"I'll be waiting right outside, darling," Axil said to Bryanna.

Bryanna smirked. Maybe he thought Colin would walk in and invite her to dinner again. She sighed. Axil had already made plans for her to join him for dinner after the post-concert party.

Collin, not to be outdone when he'd found out, had invited her to join him tomorrow for a tour of Seattle. One thing for sure — at this rate, she'd never make a decision.

The makeup artist and hairstylist left. Bryanna heard both of them giggle as they stepped out of the dressing room and found Axil still standing there like a big blond sentry.

"I like this costume better than the one you wore in Massachusetts," Della said. "Sometimes I don't know what Mr Jonathan is thinking. Pretty girls don't need to advertise the goods. They need to leave something to the imagination."

Bryanna looked at her black one-shouldered jumpsuit in the mirror. It did cover her legs, but it moulded to her body like a second skin. She also wore a pair of black boots that made her appear nearly six feet tall. Bryanna frowned. Maybe it was time for her to start designing her own costumes.

"You'll have those two young men fighting over you for sure," Della replied.

"Huh?" Bryanna asked.

Della nodded towards the door. "The drop-dead gorgeous blond I just ran out of here and the blue-eyed demon who is always watching you when he thinks you're not looking. You know, the one with the sexy girly voice."

Bryanna smirked. Were there no secrets in their camp? Did everyone know about her and her two Romeos? "I don't know about this costume either," Bryanna said, trying to stretch the material down over her hips and butt. "Don't you think it's a little too much?"

Della shrugged. "What I think does not matter. Mr Jonathan insisted you wear this on stage for the first half of the show." Della said goodbye and left Bryanna to ponder what would happen once the fellows saw her.

A stagehand came to her door. Bryanna answered. The young man gawked, blushed and couldn't look her in the face. "Five minutes to curtain call, Ms Trosclair."

"Thank you," Bryanna told the youth. God, he couldn't be any older than eighteen, and Jonathan no doubt had sent him to get the kid's reaction to her new outfit. The young man continued to blush as he walked away.

Bryanna peered down the hallway towards the men's dressing room. She smirked. Axil had apparently given up and left his post. If she left now, maybe she could make it to the stage without any sarcastic comments.

Bryanna slipped out of the door and began walking down the hall. She had just about made it to the stairs when she heard a whistle. Bryanna span around. *Kurt*. He caught up with her.

"Are you trying to start a world war?"

Bryanna shook her head. "Another one of Jonathan's brilliant creations."

"I think I'd better get you on stage before Axil and Collin see you."

"They are going to see me eventually."

Kurt nodded. "But they won't get the full effect of seeing you from behind like I just did. Girl, you have parts moving I didn't even know you owned." He growled.

Bryanna gently elbowed him in the stomach. "Are you sure you're playing for the other team?"

Kurt nodded. "Sure, but that doesn't mean I can't enjoy the scenery in someone else's garden every now and then."

Bryanna allowed Kurt to help her up the stairs. For some reason this had become his regular duty. She didn't mind because she liked being in his company. He headed over to his drums just as Damon and Jimmy entered from the other side. Both men gave her more than just a friendly glance. She ignored them, concentrating on the sound of the crowd just outside the drawn curtains.

Collin entered from the left and Axil from the right. The lights were quickly doused and then the MC announced them. The curtain rose and the music began to play. The din from the audience sounded through the hall, but she blocked it out and waited for her cue. She began to sing and the spotlight beamed down on her. Any problems she had disappeared as she got into the song...a solo Collin had written for her. Her deep alto voice filtered out through the mobile mic as she sang. Axil and Collin sang the backup chorus. Bryanna glanced over at them. They were dressed in black like her, but they had room to breathe.

Bryanna moved away from her mark and the spotlight followed as she continued the sultry song. She had to strut across from one side of the stage to the other so she could give some attention to both sides of the audience. Her image appeared on big screens so the people in the upper balcony could catch every part of the act. She caught the look on Axil's face when he finally got a look at what she wore. His gaze ran from her face to her feet and then back to her eyes again, locking with hers. His pupils dilated and his nostrils flared. Her insides vibrated. Axil looked primal, hungry and not a bit friendly.

Bryanna gulped and walked over to her mark only to catch the blue eyes of the keyboardist. Collin did not appear angry this time, just overly interested.

The song ended and Collin began his newest song.

Oh my God. She had to dance with him like she did yesterday in her form-fitting cat suit. Her band mates began playing the song with their eyes trained on them instead of the audience.

Collin did not miss the opportunity to garner the audience's attention and participation. He got them clapping and stomping to the lively tune as he did his wicked little hip wiggling. His hips undulated and gyrated to the saucy beat. He left his mark and danced his way over to her. Bryanna accepted his hand and before she knew it she was deep into the number, acting silly right along with Collin and the crowd was loving it.

Collin moved behind her to hug her from the back, swaying seductively with her, pressing against her as they moved. Then the little tease released her. The crowd roared with delight. Collin danced her back over to her mark then moved back to his just as the song ended.

Bryanna's heart continued to beat rapidly in her chest from the exertion of the dance. Before she had a chance to catch her breath, Axil began serenading her with his guitar from across the stage. A spotlight beamed down on him. His deep tenor voice filled the air as their third number began. She added her voice to his and the audience clapped when they recognised the tune. Fans shouted their names as their voices mixed and harmonised.

Bryanna began the next chorus, belting out the soulful song, and a third spotlight beamed down on Collin as his soft voice mixed with hers. Bryanna left her mark and joined Collin and Axil at centre stage to entertain the audience with their signature hit. Both Collin and Axil went out of their way to sing only to her.

By the end of the number, all three were sweating from the bright lights and from the heat rolling off their bodies. The curtains were drawn for intermission and a costume change. The guys left the stage as Jonathan stepped up and detained her to rave about her costume and the crowd's reaction to it.

"It's too much," Bryanna told him. "I'll be choosing my own wardrobe after this tour."

Jonathan's smile disappeared. "Why?"

"You know why. These costumes are too provocative. Do you know what it's like to have men ogling you? I look like a slut."

"No you don't," he argued. "You have a sensational body and the entire world should see it."

"Thanks, but no thanks. They're too distracting to the other band members."

"It sets you apart from the guys."

"We are a group. It's not the Bryanna show. Either you tone it down or I will." She walked away from him, hoping he wasn't watching her butt, and stormed back to her dressing room oblivious to the people around her. Bryanna opened the door and paused in the threshold. Axil was waiting inside. He breathed a deep sigh like a wounded animal and pulled her into his arms and squeezed her tight.

"What's wrong with you?" she asked, wiggling out of his grasp.

"Your costume…" he began. "It's just too much."

"Are you here to lecture me like Collin?"

"No, just the opposite," Axil replied.

Bryanna looked him over. Great, the big lummox had a king-sized erection. She could just strangle Jonathan. If she didn't know better, she'd swear he was only doing this to antagonise Collin and Axil.

"Where's Collin?" she asked as he swooped her into his arms again.

"In the dressing room. Kurt's keeping an eye on him."

"Why?" Bryanna asked.

He answered her by placing his lips on hers.

Bryanna succumbed to the sudden onslaught, wrapping her legs around his waist. His cock dug against her cleft.

"How much time do we have?' Axil asked as he buried his face into the crook of her neck and kissed her throat.

"Not enough," she answered as her body responded to his.

"Oh," he groaned as he released her slowly. "I don't think I'm going to make it through the second act without…"

"A cold shower," she finished for him.

"Don't joke at a time like this. I want you so desperately."

"It's the costume," Bryanna told him. "It drives men insane." She walked away from him, her legs wobbling nervously.

"Why did you ask me where Collin is?"

"I kind of figured he'd beat you in here."

Axil grimaced and headed towards the door. "You haven't forgotten about going out with me tonight, have you?"

"No," Bryanna replied with a smile. "It's a date."

Axil smiled at her. "I better get out of here before someone comes in."

"If it's worth anything, I think you can take Della."

* * * *

Bryanna didn't know how he'd done it, but Axil had made it a date to remember. It began with a chauffeured limousine ride to the restaurant, followed by a carriage ride through the streets of Seattle—around the financial district, residential areas and the panoramic waterfront. Even the weather had turned out to be perfect. Then they went out dancing until the wee hours of the morning. And the best part of all, Axil kept his promise...no drinking, except for water.

And she kept her promise, too. The date ended in his hotel room at three in the morning.

Morally, she had issues with what she was about to do. How could she be with Collin and now also be with Axil? She tried to just dismiss her conscience for the evening, especially once they started slow dancing in the bedroom to the music spewing from the radio, with Axil looking at her as only he could. Even if fifty men came and went through her bedroom, Axil would always be number one and own the key to her heart.

His kiss was gentle and unassuming. For all extents and purposes, he was still the Axil she'd known since childhood—shy and soft spoken and caring—wrapped up in a grown-up package. And if anything was going to happen between them, she would have to initiate it because, quite frankly, she believed he feared he would break her.

Bryanna reached up and began loosening his tie then helped him out of his jacket. She unbuttoned his shirt and he removed it and tossed it in a heap on the floor with the jacket and tie. She smirked. Practical Axil still wore Tshirts beneath his clothes like his mother always told him to as a child. He removed it as well, displaying his naked torso.

Bryanna ran a hand over his bare chest and Axil trembled. *So cute.* Could it be possible he'd never been with a woman before? *No…preposterous.* Axil had had a lot of girlfriends during high school. But seriously, except for groupies hanging around him, when did she ever recall him dating anyone since they had grown into young adults? Most of his time was taken up with Simmer. As their leader, he always had his hand in something in order to enable their rise to the top then continue their success. The thought that he could be untouched intrigued her.

"Would you unzip me?" Bryanna asked, turning her back to him and raising her hair out of the way so he could see the back of her dress.

Axil's big, long fingers trembled and fumbled until he unhooked it and then he ran the zipper down the track.

Bryanna slipped her arms out of the sleeves and let the dress land in a puddle at her feet. She kicked it aside and stood before him in sizzling black underwear she had purchased in Los Angeles. She raised her fingers and unsnapped the front locking bra then added it to the growing pile on the floor.

Axil stared and gulped. "You're so beautiful."

She reached for his hand and guided it to one of her breasts. "It won't break."

Axil's touch was very tender as he stroked the nipple. It hardened and budded between his fingers. He was like a kid in a candy shop…wide-eyed and looking like he wanted to sample everything in the display case but wasn't quite sure where to start.

Bryanna helped him out a bit by pushing her breasts out to him. Axil's head automatically lowered and he captured one of the nipples with his lips and began to suckle. Bryanna moaned as the heat from his breath made her feel all warm and toasty inside. She ran her fingers through his thick blond hair. It felt like silk. While he nursed at her breasts, Bryanna got busy lowering his zipper and sticking one of her hands inside his briefs. Axil gasped as she wrapped her hand around his length.

"Don't fight me, Axil," she told him as she stroked him slowly.

"I won't fight you," he said lowering the trousers so she could have better access.

Bryanna's eyes widened. He was much longer than she'd imaged. No problem. She was going to enjoy this. Bryanna stopped fondling him long enough for him to get out of his trousers, briefs and shoes, then she pushed him down on the bed into a seated position. She walked away from him, turned up the music and began to dance.

Axil stared as she transformed into a bad girl, slowly undulating her hips and teasing him with her stripper routine.

"Where did you learn to do that?" he asked, staring— fascinated.

"Cable television." She slipped her fingers into the waistband of the panties then slid them down her hips to draw his attention lower. She was out of them by the time the song ended. Bryanna walked over to him, clad in only her high heels, and mounted his lap.

A blush rose on Axil's delightfully innocent face.

"Are you embarrassed?" She rocked to the music and put her arms around his neck.

"I think there's something I need to tell you, darling," he said, burying his head into her breasts again.

"No time for words," she said as she threw her head back and let him have at her breasts. She ground her pelvis into his crotch. "Do you have a condom?" she asked as she planted kisses along his face and chin.

His head bobbed slowly. "In my wallet."

Bryanna slid from his lap and reached down for the trousers, giving him a good look at her backside. He rewarded her with a very sexy sigh.

Axil dug into his pocket and quickly retrieved a silver, round packet from his wallet.

Extra large. Bryanna smirked. She liked this so much. Axil rose and slipped on the condom. She moved her eyes quickly as he sat back down on the bed so she wouldn't make him more nervous. She approached him cautiously, straddled his lap and wrapped her arms around his neck and kissed him.

Axil was a quick learner, kissing her back deeply and running his big hands up and down her back and bottom. He pulled her closer to him.

"You are so soft and warm," he told her. "And you smell so sweet."

Bryanna chuckled. "It's the cologne you gave me for my birthday. You have excellent tastes in cologne."

He kissed her more deeply this time, allowing his tongue to dip inside her mouth. Bryanna moved her tongue around and teased the insides of his jaw and allowed her tongue to dance with his. She didn't know how long he could last, so she again took the lead, dipping her hand between them and touching his cock. It jumped in her hands and he leant forward and moaned.

"I've never wanted anyone as much as I wanted you."

Truer words were never spoken. He had saved himself for her. The thought pleased her. Why couldn't she decide? She wanted so much to choose him, but Collin meant a lot to her too... Bryanna lifted her body, inserted the tip of his cock at her opening then sat down on it. They gasped simultaneously as the head pushed inside of her.

Bryanna's hips rotated slowly, taking him in deeper. Axil put both his hands on her hips, raised her body a little and then lowered her down upon his swollen member. He filled her completely, stroking her inside walls and making her tremble with ecstasy.

Bryanna rode him until she got comfortable with his width. Her channel moistened.

Axil captured her lips again and Bryanna blocked out any uneasiness. It was just her and him...just as nature wanted them to be.

They changed positions. Axil took her missionary style — spreading her wide, securing her legs around his waist then driving home until he had her moaning and trembling beneath him.

The radio station seemed to play only for them as Hall and Oates' *One on One* set the scene with mood music.

Her body shook as Bryanna raised her hips and came passionately and deeply from Axil's powerful thrusts.

"Oh, baby, that feels so wonderful," Axil said as he slowed the movements of his hips to experience the orgasm with her.

Bryanna kissed his sweaty chest. She licked his nipple and Axil shuddered. "Ooh, Hall and Oates, double play," Bryanna replied as *Out of Touch* came through the speakers.

Axil rolled over and put her on top.

Bryanna literally danced on his cock, displaying her acrobatic skills and great muscle control.

Axil chuckled at her silliness but did not lose his powerful erection.

"Oh, I like this song," Bryanna said when the song changed.

"What is it?" Axil asked.

"*Proud*. It's by a Korean group."

"When did you start listening to Asian music?" he asked, concentrating on the mission at hand.

"Since I discovered YouTube. Listen."

Axil rolled her over on to her back again and took control. She didn't know if he was actually listening or not, but he was performing wonderful manoeuvres inside of her.

"I want to walk down the aisle to this song if I ever get married," Bryanna confessed. "It is so beautiful and sensual."

Axil paused a moment and then slowly ground into her.

Bryanna gasped, scratching his back with her nails. By the time the song made it to the second chorus, Bryanna climaxed again.

"I like the song," he finally admitted as his hips moved faster.

Bryanna raised her hips as Axil's body quivered above her. He raised her right leg, spread her wider and buried himself inside her as the orgasm passed through his body. He moaned loudly, straining and arching his back as he ejaculated.

Bryanna gazed up at him. Axil's face didn't contort but remained serene and gorgeous...his eyes misting with tears. He was truly sentimental and beautiful and hers.

"I love you, Bryanna," he announced as he sank against her.

"And I love you, too," she said once he'd rolled his weight off her and she could breathe.

"I want the name of that group," he told her as he pulled her against him.

"Why?"

"Because I want to make your dreams come true."

Chapter Six

Axil didn't even frown the next morning after breakfast when she crawled into a taxi accompanied by Collin.

Collin, being Collin, could not wait until the taxi left the parking lot before he pulled her closer to him and kissed her on the head. "How was your date with the blond jerk?"

"I wish you wouldn't call him names. Axil's not such a bad guy."

"I know," he replied, surprising her. "But we're rivals."

Bryanna put her head on his shoulder. He smelt sensational and he looked great in black. She was tired and she didn't feel like arguing. "Since when are you two rivals?"

"Since you refuse to choose," Collin told her, not bothering to spare her feelings.

So far she didn't see the point in choosing. She was selfishly enjoying both their company and not hurting anyone. "Seattle is a beautiful town," she said, changing the subject.

Collin chuckled. "Very subtle, Bry."

They spent a delightful day together visiting museums, sampling food at street-side vendors and walking along the water's edge. Collin truly opened up to her during their time alone together. He was like a completely different person, not a bit stuffy and overbearing. They returned to the hotel just before dusk. Collin kissed her goodbye at the door and didn't try to enter.

Bryanna gave him mad props for realising she needed to rest between lovers. Even she knew this couldn't go on forever between them. One day she would have to choose.

* * * *

Bryanna had barely adjusted to Seattle when they were off again. She stared out of the window as they reached a stretch of highway with nothing but trees. Their tour bus was comfortable and air-conditioned, but after a couple of days of eating fast food and seeing nothing but greenery and mountains, Bryanna wanted to scream.

"We'll be in New York tomorrow," Axil told her, sensing her aggravation as he tuned the strings of his guitar. The rest of the band played cards while Collin busied himself composing songs and Jonathan napped in one of the front seats.

"Not soon enough," Bryanna replied. "I think I'm going stir crazy."

Axil strummed the chord to the Commodores, *Sail On'* and he began to serenade her. He knew she loved her some Lionel Ritchie, and before long, she and the others joined Axil in their rendition.

"I like the way that sounds," Jonathan said, awakening and coming towards them. He flopped down in a seat and stretched. "I think you guys should use it."

Anything to make a buck, Bryanna said to herself.

"I'll speak to Mr Ritchie's people about obtaining the rights to record it."

"I'm starving," Kurt said a few minutes later.

"Me too," Jimmy agreed with him. "When are we going to take a break?" he asked Jonathan.

"Next city," Jonathan assured him. "We have a lot of ground to cover if we expect to make it to New York tomorrow."

"I want to see Broadway," Bryanna announced. "And eat at famous restaurants."

The band had been to New York before but never as a headliner. They'd open for another group when their career was just getting started, and after they'd performed, Jonathan just loaded them up on a bus and took them on to their next destination. Bryanna sighed. Sometimes she felt like she had spent most of her life on the road and she was just twenty-five.

"I don't know," Jonathan disagreed. "You guys are pretty popular now. You can't just be going off on your own like you did in Seattle and Los Angeles."

Bryanna wasn't a fool and neither were the guys. They always took every precaution not to get themselves into situations where they could get mobbed.

"We can go as a group," Kurt suggested.

Jonathan chuckled. "You guys always come back drunk."

"Not anymore," Axil replied. "I've given up alcohol."

Jonathan looked surprised. "Oh, why?"

"No particular reason," he said. "But apparently I'm at my best when I'm sober."

"Meaning?" Collin asked, suddenly interested in the conversation. Normally he just sat there, ignoring Jonathan and doing whatever he wanted.

"Let's just say I'm cuter and easier to love when I'm sober." He winked at Bryanna.

"Yuck," Collin gagged. "Forgive me for asking."

Axil chuckled, knowing Collin knew exactly what he meant.

Bryanna chose to ignore both of them.

"Then it's settled. We'll all go out on the town tomorrow and not get bloody drunk and return at a decent hour," Kurt replied.

"Boy Scout," Damon teased.

"Bite me," Kurt told him.

Damon shook his head. "My mouth isn't touching anything on you. Dream on."

Kurt blew him a kiss, and Collin just stared at the two of them like they'd lost their minds.

Kurt preferring guys wasn't a secret to anyone. He'd come out of the closet as a teen, and every now and then one of the members would playfully tease him about his sexuality. They didn't mess with him as much now, devoting most of their energy to the saga of Bryanna, Collin and Axil.

"Bryanna will be the only female accompanying you guys, I suppose," Jonathan replied.

"We've barely made it to New York," Jimmy said. "Unless you know something we don't, where are we supposed to pick up women that fast?"

Jonathan shrugged. "I'm just saying don't go out there and get into any trouble. Use protection if you have to go there, and never give them your real names."

Everyone groaned. It had been a long time since he'd given them the sex talk.

"Right," Jimmy agreed. "Wear a raincoat."

Collin surprised everyone by laughing out loud. "You guys are a bunch of morons."

"And you're an arrogant little song bird," Jonathan shot back. "You'll remember my warnings when you get some pretty little thing knocked up and she tries to sue your ass for child support and half your earnings. Babies are an eighteen-year expense."

Apparently this was a pretty touchy subject with Jonathan, which surprised her since he too preferred the company of men.

"Okay, okay," Collin said. "Don't get our knickers in a knot. If I score tomorrow night, I'll use protection."

Yes, he is so going to use it. Collin rocked her world but at the moment none of them were parent material...always on the road, sleeping on tour buses and only home for a few weeks out of the year. And now, with her having multiple partners, there was no way she wanted to transport an STD or be the recipient of one, either. She did consider herself a responsible young woman even if she was presently doing the nasty with two men.

Yes, it did sound slutty, even to her when she thought about it. But for the moment the three of them weren't hurting anyone.

"You guys better keep an eye on Bryanna tomorrow night," Jonathan warned. "And bring her back to the hotel in one piece."

Axil looked her way. "Make sure you don't cause us any grief, woman. No getting drunk and table dancing."

Bryanna saluted him. "I'll keep it down to a mild trawling the docks for sailors."

Jonathan shook his head. "Everything is a joke to you guys. If you let anything happen to her, I'll personally kick your asses."

Bryanna grimaced. *What's eating him?* And when did she get to be his favourite?

"We won't let anything happen to her," Collin finally said. "You have my word."

"Thank you for volunteering," Jonathan replied. "Should anything happen to her I'll kick your ass first...and then Axil's."

Axil looked at her and she shrugged. Everyone knew Jonathan was gay and had no romantic interest in her, so she must be of some monetary importance to him.

"If I keep her happy and safe then you guys will stay in line," Jonathan explained without anyone asking. "I've known for a long time how you all feel about her."

All the guys feigned innocence, which made her feel all warm inside. "I love you guys, too."

"But not as much as you love Axil and Collin," Kurt teased.

Bryanna smirked at him. "Not true. Drop your boyfriend and I'll be all over you like white on rice."

Kurt, for the first time ever, was at a loss for words.

* * * *

"Did you think we'd ever be standing here?" Axil asked Bryanna as they walked down Broadway holding hands.

Bryanna nodded. "I knew it from the first moment you announced you wanted to be a musician and form a rock and roll band."

Axil lifted her and sat her on the edge of the fountain near a hotel. "And you had faith in me, even back then?"

"Apparently, since we're one of the hottest groups in the United States."

Collin watched the two of them as he leaned against a tree nearby. He'd been trying to get Bryanna alone all evening, but Axil had been monopolising her time since they'd arrived in New York.

Axil used a finger to move a wave of auburn curls away from Bryanna's eyes. "I couldn't have done it without you and the rest of the guys, but especially you. You believed in me when no one else did."

Collin blew out an exasperated breath. Axil could be such a big baby at times.

"One of these days we'll play Carnegie Hall," Kurt said. "We'll all be dressed in tuxedos, including Bryanna, and an orchestra will play right along with us. Man, I can just see it. We're going to be big."

Damon gave him a high-five. "I'm thinking bigger…the Kennedy Honors and Rock and Roll Hall of Fame inductees."

These guys are too much. None of it made any difference to him without Bryanna to share it with him. More than once he'd dreamt of growing old with her, and Axil not being anywhere in the picture. He kept hoping Bryanna would come to her senses and realise she had to cut the friendship apron strings and send Blondie on his way. But looking at them together right now, he didn't see that happening. A sane man would just walk away and find some other good woman to love…but he'd never professed to be sane. It would be interesting to see how the night would end. Would Bryanna be with him or with Axil or just go back to the hotel room and go to bed alone?

Chapter Seven

"We might have to make the decision for her," Axil said to Collin as they sat in the lounge of the hotel late the next night, after the paparazzi had gone home and the rest of their band mates were up in their rooms, hopefully sleeping after their sold-out concert.

"I know," Collin said with a sigh. Neither of them was drinking anything stronger than water. "We can't continue like this." Last night Bryanna had just gone back to her room, leaving both men hanging.

"But can you be man enough to just walk away, yet continue to be around her everyday as a member of Simmer?"

"I don't know," Collin replied. "I never thought about it. What about you?"

Axil shrugged. "Bryanna and I have been together so long. I don't know what I'd do without her in my life."

"We're not talking about disappearing out of her life. As long as we're a member of Simmer, we'll always be together. I'm speaking romantically. Can you let her go?" Collin asked.

Axil shook his head. "This is not just a physical thing I feel for Bryanna." He rapped softly against his forehead with a finger. "It's emotional. We share the same thoughts, anticipate each other's needs and finish each other's sentences sometimes." What Collin was proposing was preposterous. He didn't even want to think about it. He wanted to marry Bryanna and for her to be the mother of his children. "What about you?"

Collin shook his head. "I wake up every morning with her on my mind. I think about her my every waking minute, and her image is the last face I see in my mind before I go to bed."

"Sounds more like an obsession," Axil replied. He raised a bottle of designer water and saluted Collin.

"Then we haven't accomplished anything with this discussion. We're still in the same place...a fork in the road." He sighed. "We should force Bryanna to make a decision."

Axil leant forward. "How?"

"Bryanna thinks she can continue to have a relationship with both of us, and so far it's been working for her...but making us miserable. Why not call her bluff?"

"You mean both of us walk away and find someone else?" Axil asked incredulously.

"No. I mean see if she can really handle both of us romancing her twenty-four seven."

Axil brow wrinkled. "You mean all three of us?"

Collin nodded. "It's bound to come to a head. She'll discover that it's foolish to try to date both of us." He paused. "I don't know about you but I want to get married one day and have a couple of kids. It might be quite awkward having Mother, Father and Uncle Axil living under the same roof and in the same bed."

Axil scratched his head. Collin didn't seem the paternal type. "I still don't know. I don't think I can tolerate you for twenty-four seven."

"Same here," Collin said. "But we'll test it tomorrow at breakfast."

Axil nodded. "I hope you're right about this."

"What's the worst that can happen?" Collin asked.

"She could leave both of us and hook up with Kurt. You know she thinks he's hot."

Collin raised a dark eyebrow in disbelief. "That would be a bad case scenario, but not the worst."

"What could be worse?"

"She could leave both of us and hook up with Jonathan?"

Axil reached for his water and took a big sip. "You're right. That would be simply disastrous."

* * * *

Bryanna's phone rang around eight the next morning. It was Axil. "Hello."

"Good morning, darling. It's time to rise and shine."

Bryanna scanned her mind for whether she had to be somewhere this morning. For the life of her, she couldn't remember an appointment. "Am I late for a meeting?"

"No, not a meeting."

"Then why the hell are you disturbing my beauty sleep?"

Axil chuckled. "You're always beautiful. Come have breakfast with me. I'm lonely."

Bryanna sighed. She could strangle him. Axil knew she wasn't a morning person, especially the morning after a concert. "Can't you have breakfast with one of the guys?"

"Probably, but I prefer to spend our last day in New York with you."

Bryanna sat up in the bed. "Everyone else is still recovering from a hangover, aren't they?"

"Probably. Kurt met someone last night, so I don't think I can entice him out of bed unless I offer him Collin."

Bryanna laughed. "You are so bad." But it was so true. When Kurt met Collin he took one look at the svelte, blue-eyed singer and fell in love. Collin having a soft girly voice only added to the infatuation. Unfortunately, Collin did not return his feelings. Kurt had said he understood, but every now and then she'd catch him sneaking a doe-eyed glance at Collin. "I doubt Collin will be switching teams any time soon, no matter how cute Kurt is." She yawned and stretched. "Give me about thirty minutes. I'll meet you downstairs in the restaurant."

"I'll be waiting," Axil replied. "See you then." He hung up.

Bryanna pushed the covers from her body, rose and walked into the bathroom to shower. After dressing, she put on her dark shades and stepped out of her hotel room.

"Good morning, gorgeous."

Bryanna looked up startled. "Collin?"

"What? You don't recognise me?"

He did look especially delicious in a brown sweater and tan slacks. "What are you doing up and about so early?" Like her, Collin wasn't a morning person.

"I thought I'd come over and invite my favourite girl to breakfast."

Bryanna eyed him curiously. Collin was acting unbelievably chipper, and he had shaved and put on cologne. "I was just about to meet Axil for breakfast in the restaurant."

"Great," he said, locking arms with her. "The more the merrier."

Bryanna sniffed him playfully. "Are you drunk?" She didn't smell alcohol or tobacco, just sexy, dark, brooding male.

"No, I'm perfectly sober." He led her towards the elevator. "Why do I have to be drunk to invite you to breakfast?"

"It's not the inviting me part. It's the not making a face when I mentioned Axil's name."

"I've decided to take your advice and try to get along with him. It's not like Axil has ever done anything to me, and he *is* our fearless leader."

If he fed her any more bull, she wouldn't have room for breakfast. But it would be good if the two of them could get along.

They entered the restaurant. Axil had already appropriated a table.

"I hope you don't mind me barging in on your breakfast with Bryanna," Collin said to him.

"No," Axil said. "And since for some reason Bryanna likes you, I guess I need to get used to eating with you, too."

Collin chuckled and agreed.

Okay, this was too spooky for her. Had something happened last night between them after she went up to her room? *Or am I still dreaming*? Bryanna pinched herself. *Ouch. No.*

Axil sat at her right and Collin made himself comfortable to her left. A bit too close for comfort and both of them smelt great, which in some aspect made her very giddy.

A waitress appeared and took their order. More people entered the restaurant, including Kurt and a dark-haired man who resembled Collin.

"Do you have a younger brother?" Axil asked Collin.

"Funny. Yes, and he's an adorable blond like you."

In three years since they'd met, this was the first bit of information he had shared about his family.

They gave the waitress their order and she left.

"How old is he?" Bryanna asked Collin.

"Who?" Collin asked.

"Your younger brother?"

"Nineteen," Collin answered. "He's a sophomore at Boston University."

"So you're from Massachusetts?"

Collin smirked. "Yes. What's with the fifty questions?"

"Well, you've been with us for three years and we know absolutely nothing about you." She paused. "Why didn't you go home for a visit when we were there?"

"Because we don't have any family there anymore. We were orphaned at a young age."

"Oh," Bryanna said. "Sorry for prying."

"No, you're right. There should be no secrets between us. You can ask me anything."

He was being too generous.

"I have nothing to hide," Collin replied. "Ask away."

"What are you and Axil up to?"

Axil chuckled. "Of all the questions you could have asked him, that's the one you come up with?"

"Humour me," Bryanna said. "You two have been at each other's throats since forever. Now this morning, you're able to sit down and eat breakfast together without fighting. What gives?"

"Okay, you busted us. We decided to call a truce for your sake," Collin replied. "We realised that it was wrong to ask you to choose. So since you obviously want to date both of us, we've decided to share you."

Bryanna looked at him and then at Axil, whom she directed her next question to. "Define share?"

"Exactly what it sounds like. The three of us do everything together from now on — eat, sleep and..." He didn't finish the sentence.

"Date?"

Axil nodded. "Do you think you can handle it?"

"That depends on what your definition of date is," Bryanna replied.

"Everything Bryanna. Do you think you could take both of us to your bed at the same time?"

Bryanna reached for her grape juice and sipped some through the straw. "Sure," she replied. *Oh my God, what have I got myself into*?

Collin cleared his throat, reached for his coffee and sipped. "Then it's settled," he said.

"Seems so," Axil replied. "The family that plays together stays together."

* * * *

Bryanna couldn't remember what she had eaten. Take both Axil and Collin to her bed at the same time? *Ridiculous. Or is it*?

Bryanna rolled over onto her back on her bed and tried to conjure up a scene in her head...one taking her from the front while the other taking her from behind. She giggled and blushed shamelessly. No way. Not even in her biggest fantasy. They were still trying to trick her into choosing because they knew she would never agree to this. Maybe she should call their bluff and see which one backed down first. She reached for her phone and first dialled Axil's number and invited him out to dinner with her, and then she called Collin. Both men agreed. *I'll show them not to mess with me.*

* * * *

Most of the group was drunk by the time they returned to the hotel, but Collin and Axil were stone-cold sober as they said goodnight to the rest of the gang in the elevator and rode up with her to their floor. Both of them escorted her to the door and looked lustfully at her as she opened the door. Collin was certain she would panic.

"Come on in, fellows," she replied bravely. "Let's get this party started."

You could have knocked both of them over with a feather, especially Axil—the look on his face almost comical when he realised their plan had backfired.

Bryanna kicked out of her heels, turned on the music and began a seductive little stripper's dance, much to Collin's delight. He'd plopped down in the room's only chair to enjoy the show as she wiggled out of her little red slinky dress.

Axil sat down on the bed.

Bryanna walked over to Axil, stooped down and kissed him while standing in nothing but her underwear.

Axil slid his arms around her and kissed her back.

Bryanna broke away from him then slid over to Collin, sat on his lap and kissed him, too. Collin pushed his tongue into her mouth and French-kissed her. Bryanna's nipples budded beneath the lacy red bra. He slid his hands down her back, making her arch and moan. He gently helped her descend to the floor and rose to get out of his shirt, well aware that Axil watched his every move.

Collin helped her back off the floor and unsnapped her bra. Her breasts fell free, and then he turned her to face Axil.

Axil rose from the bed to join them in the middle of the room. He removed his shirt and then reached for her breasts. He cupped them in his hands and gently teased the nipples while Collin sidled up behind her, swept her hair aside and planted kisses on her neck and down her back.

Bryanna's mind fought against what was morally right. The pleasure they were bestowing on her made the decision for her.

Axil moved lower, kissing her stomach.

Bryanna gasped as his warm breath tickled her skin. He slipped his fingers into the waistband of her panties then slid them down to her ankles. Bryanna lifted her feet to step out and Axil tossed them aside.

Collin moved towards the bed, taking her with him. He sat down, positioned her on his lap facing Axil and spread her thighs.

Axil's eyelids lowered at the sight and Collin's generous invitation. He dropped to his knees, crawled over and buried his face between her creamy folds.

Bryanna moaned from pleasure and surprise. Who was this man between her legs giving her pleasure with his fingers and mouth, and where was her boyishly shy Axil?

Collin's erection strained against her bottom through his jeans. While Axil took his time savouring every inch of her from below, Collin massaged her breasts and kissed her senseless. He whispered into her ear. "Only for you, Bryanna."

Axil pushed two fingers deep inside her and moved them around. Collin continued to French-kiss her. Axil touched her clitoris with his tongue and she whimpered with delight.

Collin's tongue played inside her mouth while his fingers pressed and squeezed her breasts. Their tongues plunged into her mouth and cunt simultaneously, sending her over the edge. She came, feeling the ripples of ecstasy from her breasts down to the pit of her stomach.

Axil moaned below her as she drenched his face with her juices. He raised his head, gasping for air and then licking his lips. "She tastes like honey," he said to Collin.

"I told you," Collin replied.

She slid from Collin's lap to kneel before Axil and kissed his lips. She came up for air long enough to turn to Collin. "Strip," she demanded.

Collin obeyed, rising and wiggling out of his trousers, briefs and shoes while she gave Axil a little face time.

"You surprise me, darling," she told Axil.

"Collin said you'd like for me to do that to you."

"Thank you," she told him. "But I only want you to do what you feel comfortable doing."

"Don't worry." Axil stroked her face. "I have no complaints."

Bryanna giggled. "Let me see your gorgeous body while I thank Collin for his kind suggestion."

While Axil rustled out of his clothes, Collin waited patiently.

Bryanna turned to him on her knees and cupped his balls while he sat on the bed. She signalled for the completely nude Axil to join them. He hesitated a moment then sat down next to Collin.

Bryanna smirked. *This is no time for Axil to be shy.* Collin might be a more experienced lover, but Axil was packing a bigger gun.

Two hands, two desirable men and two erections…what should a poor girl do? Bryanna ran her tongue over her lips as she stuck her hands between both their legs and began masturbating them. Twin moans, one deep and one high-pitched, filled the air as her fingers and hands went to work on them.

Bryanna moved a little closer to Collin and lowered her head between his legs while continuing to masturbate Axil, allowing him to watch her perform fellatio on Collin so he could get comfortable with the act.

"Your lips are lethal," Collin said.

Axil moaned, knowing what was in store for him.

Bryanna kept both hands moving, knowing she couldn't show favouritism. She slowed down with Axil, because he seemed so close to the edge. She removed her mouth from Collin's cock then moved between Axil's legs. While she serviced him, she grasped Collin's erection and with her hand, pumped him into submission.

Axil shuddered and began pumping his hips, sending his cock down her throat.

Bryanna moved her head up and down as she sucked on his shaft. Axil shook, gasped and sent a stream of warm semen down her throat, sinking back on the bed once she released him.

Satisfied with Axil's reaction, Bryanna went back between Collin's legs and sucked him until she made him come. Both men lay side by side, spent and recovering, while she thought up her next move.

Control of the situation was taken out of her hands when Axil sat up, reached for his trousers and pulled out a condom. *Damn, he has great recovery time.*

"I don't know how this is supposed to work, but I think I need to be inside you now," he told her.

"You kids go at it," Collin told them. "I think I need more time to recover."

Axil lifted her from the floor and put her on top of him. He raised her hips, spread her open and slipped his hard length inside her. Bryanna moaned softly as Axil claimed her. She wrapped her arms around his neck and looked deeply into his eyes. Axil put his hands on both sides of her hips, leant forward and kissed her. His tongue plunged between her lips as he moved her back and forth on his cock. Bryanna gasped for breath when he stopped kissing her, overcome by the emotions of making love with her best friend and the need building deep inside her. She continued to ride until the orgasm claimed her. Axil shuddered and came right along with her as she climaxed for a second time.

Collin had recovered by that point, suited up in a condom, and he took control once Axil rolled over and went to sleep.

"Come to daddy," he told her. Collin put her on her knees and entered her from behind.

"Oh shit," Bryanna gasped as Collin filled her tender pussy. She ignored the pain and concentrated on the pleasure. He screwed her with powerful thrusts, not giving her a chance to do anything but kneel and submit to him. He found her G-spot and she exploded again. "Don't give out on me yet," he said as he pumped steadily into her. "Ah!" he moaned melodically in his high-pitched voice, loud enough to wake everyone in the hotel. He pushed into her, sending his cock deep until his body jerked and climaxed.

"Oh my." Bryanna slid down onto her stomach, exhausted.

Collin groaned, rolled off her and landed on his back next to her.

* * * *

Bryanna awoke the next morning trapped by arms and hairy legs. "Still want me to choose?" she asked after the two men awakened. Bryanna untangled herself and climbed over Axil as Collin tried to pinch her butt. She slapped his hand away and hurried into the bathroom to the shower without another word.

* * * *

A couple of hours later they climbed aboard their tour bus headed for home…Atlanta.

Both Axil and Collin snoozed at her sides as they left town.

"What's wrong with them?" Kurt asked. "Did the three of you go down to the bar for drinks after we parted last night?"

"No," Bryanna replied. "They must still be tired from dancing."

"Or from too much Bryanna," Kurt replied sarcastically and then he winked at her.

"Where's David?" she asked, getting all into his business like he was getting into hers.

"He's meeting me in Atlanta in a couple of days. He's coming down for a vacation."

Bryanna smirked. "He's cute and could be a keeper."

"Hey, I can't let you guys have all the fun."

Collin stirred and turned his head to face her in his sleep. Bryanna kissed him gently so she wouldn't disturb him.

"You decided yet?" Kurt said, reaching down to stroke Collin's hair.

Bryanna smiled, knowing Collin would just die if he woke up and found the big blond stroking him tenderly.

"No, they did," she replied.

Axil moved in his seat and she bent over and kissed him, too.

"Let me guess, they just decided to live for the moment?"

Bryanna nodded. "Sometimes it's just best to take life one day at a time and enjoy every bit of it."

"Great," he said. "I'm looking forward to more emotionally spurned love songs from these two. Jonathan is right. You do bring out their passion and creativity…a perfect triangle." He waved and went back to his seat.

Bryanna closed her eyes and drifted off into a contented sleep between the two men who loved her.

About the Authors

Desiree Holt

I always wanted adventure and change in my life, and I certainly got it. I grew up in Maine, a beautiful place to live, then lived in the Midwest and Florida. Now I make my home in the Hill Country of Texas, truly God's chosen place on earth. My husband, David, is a sixth generation Texan, tracing his roots here back to the time when Texas was a Republic, so retiring here was a dream we finally fulfilled.

I've had a lot of firsts in my life – first female sports report on The Michigan Daily at the University of Michigan; first woman to own a rock and roll agency in Detroit, the home of Motown; first woman president of the Pasco (Florida) Economic Development Council.

I graduated from the University of Michigan with a double major in English and History, and a minor in economics, and went on to have at least four careers. When my children were small, I satisfied my need for writing by working for weekly newspapers. I had a wild and wacky time managing rock and roll bands. I joined the insanity of retail with a string of shoe stores. I worked in fundraising, public affairs and community relations. But writing fiction was always my dream. I had a lot of stops and starts, but it wasn't until we retired that I could devote myself to it full time.

My wonderful husband, David, encourages me and supports me in my dream. Our children are all grown and on their own, and are my biggest fans.

When I'm not writing I'm an avid reader – anything and everything – and watching football, especially my beloved Michigan Wolverines. David and I golf and target shoot., and of course enjoy life in the gorgeous Texas Hill Country, where most of my stories are based. I am a member of Romance Writers of America, and San Antonio Romance Authors, Diamond State Romance Authors, and Passionate Ink chapter of RWA.

Lisabet Sarai

I became addicted to words at an early age. I began reading when I was four. I wrote my first story at five years old and my first poem at seven. Since then, I've written plays, tutorials, marketing brochures, software specifications, self-help books, press releases, a five-hundred page dissertation, and of course, erotica. I'm the author of four erotic novels and two short story collections.

My lifelong interests in sex and the written word became serendipitously entwined about a decade ago when I read my first Black Lace book by Portia da Costa. Her work inspired me to take my fantasies out of the closet (and the private email files) and expose them to the world. The rest, as they say, is history (although granted, no more than a minor footnote!)

I've always loved traveling; my husband seduced me in a Burmese restaurant by telling me tales of his foreign adventures. Since then I have visited every continent except Australia, although I still have a long travel wish list. Currently I live with him and our two exceptional felines in Southeast Asia, where I pursue an alternative career that is completely unrelated to my creative writing.

Lily Harlem

Lily Harlem lives in the UK with a workaholic hunk and a crazy cat. With a desk overlooking rolling hills her overactive imagination has been allowed to run wild and free and she revels in using the written word as an outlet for her creativity.

Lily's stories are made up of colourful characters exploring their sexuality and sensuality in a safe, consensual way. With the bedroom door left wide open the reader can hang on for the ride and Lily hopes by reading sensual romance people will be brave enough to try something new themselves—after all, life's too short to be anything other than fully satisfied.

Elizabeth Coldwell

Elizabeth Coldwell is the author of numerous short stories and two full-length novels, 'Calendar Girl' and 'Playing the Field'. Her stories have appeared in the best-selling 'Best Women's Erotica' series and Black Lace's popular 'Wicked Words' collections. Formerly the editor of the UK edition of Forum magazine, she now contributes a spicy monthly column, 'The Cougar Chronicles', to its pages. When she is not busy writing, she is an avid supporter of Rotherham United Football Club and can be regularly found on the terraces at weekends, cheering her boys to victory (hopefully!).

Wendi Zwaduk

I always dreamed of writing the stories in my head. Tall, dark, and handsome heroes are my favourites, as long as he has an independent woman keeping him in line.

I earned a BA in education at Kent State University and currently hold a Masters in Education with Nova Southeastern University.

I love NASCAR, romance, books in general, Ohio farmland, dirt racing, and my menagerie of animals. You can also find me at my blog.

Imari Jade

Imari Jade was born and raised in New Orleans, Louisiana. She is the mother of three grown sons and six grandchildren. Imari has been writing over twenty years. When the kids were younger she wrote and sold humorous articles on child-rearing and later turned to penning short stories, particularly horror. Then one day she decided to try romance. Her first erotic novel *A Christmas to Remember* was published by Star Dust Press and Imari never looked back. Currently, Imari writes for several publishers including Midnight Showcase Fiction, Sugar and Spice Press, Eternal Press and Carnal Desires Publishing and has just signed on with Moongypsy Press. She is also looking forward to a good writing relationship with Total-E-bound and getting to know the readers and fans.

Imari is an avid romance reader. Her favourite genre is paranormal romance and she has a thing for vampires and werewolves. She is a Buffy the Vampire Slayer fanatic and was totally depressed when the series ended. When she's not reading or writing, Imari spends her time watching Japanese anime. The romantic ones are her favourites and she also has a pretty extensive collection she hopes to pass down to her grandchildren.

All of the above authors love to hear from readers. You can find their contact information, website details and author profile pages at http://www.total-e-bound.com.

Total-E-Bound Publishing

www.total-e-bound.com

Take a look at our exciting range of literagasmic™
erotic romance titles and discover pure quality
at Total-E-Bound.

www.ingramcontent.com/pod-product-compliance
Lightning Source LLC
Chambersburg PA
CBHW030347030726
47497CB00002B/227